These Two Wrongs

J. Wolf

To those who kept going.

Playlist

"Water Fountain" Alec Benjamin
 "To Love Someone Else" Avery Lynch
 "Lies" Marina
 "Numb" Marshmello, Khalid
 "Delilah" Florence + the Machine
 "Teenage Dream" Stephen Dawes
 "Worst in Me" Julia Michaels
 "Pretending" Anthony Amorim
 "Interlude" Paramore
 "Twin Size Mattress" The Front Bottoms
 "Hey There Delilah" The Plain White T's
 "No Light, No Light" Florence + the Machine
 "Tribulation" Matt Maeson
 "I'll Be Good" Jaymes Young
 "Delilah" The Cranberries
 "Never Let You Go" People on People
 "Broken" lovelytheband
 "Brown eyed boy" Peyton Cardoza
 "Something in the Orange" Zach Bryan
 "Perfume" mehro
 "Angels Like You" Miley Cyrus
 https://open.spotify.com/playlist/1z03ENO9zNKH8GiYL2td
Gi?si=ea04411661ba443f

Author's Note

DEAR LOVELY READER,

This book delves into topics which might be upsetting to some readers. While these topics are handled with care, I would hate for anyone to go into this book without being forewarned.

Some of the sensitive topics represented in this book are:

-Physical assault

-Past child abuse

-Body image trauma

-Bullying

Please be kind when deciding whether or not to read this book.

Yours,

Julia

CHAPTER ONE
Delilah

MY ARM BRUSHED HIS, warm and solid. He didn't move away, so I let it linger there. My stomach fizzed and popped from the prolonged contact. One second, then ten, until finally, he shifted to turn the page in his textbook, and I was able to breathe again.

It was absolutely daft how such small touches affected me. A slip of a fingertip here, a knock of his knee against mine there, and I was practically panting. This wasn't me. I didn't lose my mind over boys. For me, crushes exploded and waned as easily as water slipping through my fingers. This one was persistent, though.

If there was anyone to blame, it was him. Tall and tattooed, he stuck out in the sea of sameness that was Savage Academy, catching my attention the moment he strode into English literature like he owned it.

The confidence captured me, but his voice, silky smooth and baritone, like the boom of a cannon on a cloudless night, had locked me in and thrown away the key.

He didn't speak often or for long, and it was better that way since his lilting Russian accent caused my heart to sit like a ball of yarn in my throat, scratchy and suffocating.

He tapped a long finger on a passage in the textbook we were both supposed to be reading since we were ostensibly studying together.

"This will be on the test."

I turned to him, finding his face tilted my way. He raised one dark brow, lazy and sure. His tie hung loose around his neck. The buttons of his crisp white uniform shirt were undone enough to reveal some of the tattoos on his chest.

Every day when he arrived at the library, he tore at his tie and unbuttoned his shirt, like he couldn't stand it another second. That *V* of exposed skin might have been only inches, but it distracted me as if it were miles.

"How do you know?" I asked.

The corner of his mouth tipped. "Look at this." It took me a moment to understand he was pointing to the textbook. "See the indents from pencils?"

I nodded. "Other students took notes on this page."

"Yes. We'll take notes too."

"It can't hurt."

"No. It will not hurt."

Ivan Sokolov and I had bonded over Jane Austen. Our mutual dislike of her books, that was. He wasn't into flowery romance, and I found her stories boring, but we both loved science fiction. We'd suffered through an Austen group project together, and our friendship had bloomed from there.

He took his grades seriously, as did I. Since we shared several classes, doing our work together had happened naturally. Most days, we met in the library after school to study and do our homework. He always chose to sit beside me at the oak table meant for six students, his long leg resting against mine, speaking lowly into my ear. When I wasn't able to join him, he expressed his disappointment.

And all those things made me wonder if these feelings weren't so one-sided. This wasn't a position I'd ever been in, but I didn't care for it very much. I preferred my slippery feelings that faded before they crash-landed.

Tucking those thoughts away for another time, I scribbled notes on the passage I read. Ivan glanced at me, and I nodded. He turned the page.

That was how we worked. Few words needed. We read, took notes, turned the page. He was easy to be with. I wouldn't say I was comfortable with him since I was hyperaware of every small movement he made, but there was an effortlessness to our partnership that wasn't something I had found with many people.

Ivan put down his pencil and stretched his fingers. I stopped midsentence, turning to him once again. He swiveled in his chair, his knees grazing the side of my thigh.

"Did you listen to the playlist I sent you?" Ivan tried to keep his voice down, but he was terrible at it.

We were in the very center of the library amid rows of identical, heavy oak tables that had to be as old as the academy itself. The students occupying the ones surrounding ours glanced our way at the crack of thunder interrupting the silence.

I tapped my finger on my lips and tugged on his sleeve, tipping my head toward the stacks. As much as I loved listening to him speak, I wouldn't subject everyone else to his inability to temper his volume.

He piled up his books and slid them into his backpack. I bit back disappointment that he was ending our study session. I wasn't quite ready for this to be over.

I led him to one of the rows in the back of the library where people rarely ventured. Satisfied we were alone, I spun around to face him. He'd been right behind me, so my breasts almost hit his chest.

Ivan draped one arm along the thick wooden shelves, tucking his opposite hand in his pocket. Casual, while my throat had gone desert dry.

"Did you listen?" he asked again.

My nose crinkled involuntarily. "I did."

He chuckled, a sonic boom in the silent library. "We like the same books but not the same music."

"It isn't that I don't like it. Actually, I've heard a lot of those artists through my sister."

With the playlist Ivan shared with me, I'd uncovered his first flaw: terrible taste in music, a trait he shared with my twin, Evelyn. EDM—electronic dance music—had no soul, as far as I was concerned. But Ev kept it streaming through her headphones all day, and apparently, it was what Ivan listened to in his spare time.

I didn't hate it, but I far from loved it.

"Hmmm...have you?"

"Yes." I shoved his chest lightly. "Did you listen to *my* playlist?"

His upper lip pulled into a snarl. "I did, and I did not like it. It's terrible."

I gasped. "Untrue!"

"It is true. So much whining, I could not take it."

I folded my arms across my chest, leaning closer to him. "I'm questioning everything I know about you. I can't believe you're calling Florence + The Machine and Dermot Kennedy whining. At least they write lyrics."

He shrugged. "There is no need for lyrics. The music should speak for itself."

"You're incredibly wrong." I narrowed my eyes at him. "I'm not sure I even like you anymore."

"You do." He tugged on the end of my hair. "We'll agree to disagree. Isn't that what the Americans say?"

"I've heard them say that before."

Born Greek and raised all over Europe, I'd only been in America—specifically California—since my junior year, when Ev and I transferred to SA from our Spanish boarding school. American idioms had slowly crept into my speech the more time I spent here. My roommates had been plotting to neutralize my accent since day one.

He slid his fingers along my hair. I raised a brow, and he grinned, nearly knocking me off my feet. Ivan's smile had that sort of power, at least for me.

"It's soft," he said.

"Conditioner," I told him.

"Hmmm." His brow pinched as he studied my lock of hair. "It's too bad you don't appreciate EDM. You were very nearly perfect."

"I—" I didn't quite know how to respond. I had been flirted with, admired, and even loved. But Ivan Sokolov turned me into a novice. A sputtering, inexperienced schoolgirl—and that wasn't who I was in the least. Not that I was some sultry femme fatale, but on a normal basis, I was fairly confident and went for what I wanted.

"I could say the same to you." Uncrossing my arms, I braced myself on the shelf near him, my fingers brushing his. "Perfection is overrated. Isn't that another American saying?"

He chuckled. "I have heard it said before, usually as an excuse for failure."

"Are you implying I'm a failure?"

He tipped his face down toward mine. "Only in your music preferences."

"Very rude, Ivan."

We were so close. And all alone. He dipped his head, bringing his face near mine. Perhaps he was waiting for a signal from me. Internally, I was waving him in, but on the outside, I remained calm. Cool. The type of girl Ivan probably liked.

"I would never be rude to you, Delilah. Then I would have to return to studying alone. I much prefer spending my afternoons with you."

I smiled at him, my fingers sliding over his, and took one step forward. Ivan smelled good. He always did. Slightly sweet and a lot spicy, like mulled wine.

"I like our afternoons too. Very much." This was it. I couldn't bear to let this moment pass us by. I licked my lips and pressed into him. "Do you ever think we could be—"

He slid his fingers from beneath mine and backed up a step, gripping the strap of his backpack. "I like being your friend, Delilah. We are good friends, yes?"

I yanked my abandoned hand down to my side and stared at him with wide eyes. He'd been so sure of his answer he hadn't even let me ask the question. And he'd managed to lower his voice, gentling it with kindness, which felt more like a sting than if he'd been booming.

It took me only a second to school my reaction, but it was too late. Ivan had read my dejection like a book and took another step away from me.

"I will see you later," he said. "Be good, Delilah."

He hesitated, giving me a long once-over before he nodded to himself. Then he swiveled around and strode out of the aisle, leaving me alone.

Thank god.

The burning humiliation of being rejected before I could even tell him my feelings was bad enough. If there'd been witnesses, it would have been a thousand times worse.

Closing my eyes, I covered my face with my hands and leaned against the shelves, exhaling a deep breath. Fortunately, I wasn't anywhere near tears. But my stomach had curdled, and embarrassment heated every inch of my skin. I'd have to leave this aisle eventually, though. It didn't seem I'd be able to turn back time so this had never happened.

A book slamming closed startled me.

"That was incredibly embarrassing."

Oh no. I recognized that voice. *Please let me be wrong. Please don't let it be him.*

Dropping my hands, I opened my eyes and turned my head. My stomach bottomed out.

One hand tucked in his trouser pocket, the other swinging his ubiquitous pocket watch by its chain, Rhys Astor stood a few feet away. And from the bemused expression on his freckled face, he'd seen and heard everything.

CHAPTER TWO
Rhys

IF I HADN'T BEEN avoiding the sounds of Charles Bloomberg's sweaty balls slapping against the ripe ass of his latest victim—pardon, *hookup*—I wouldn't have been in the library.

But someone in the housing department had seen fit to room me with the biggest hoser in school with no sense of common decency. Charles cared not if his roommates were in the shared suite. He banged indiscriminately, most of the time with the door to his bedroom wide open.

That was how I knew firsthand what his slapping balls sounded like. And though I would never be accused of being a prude, I drew the line at these particular testicles. I did not want to see them—not swinging or in repose. Sadly, Charles had no shame. Not a single ounce. And he managed to find naive girls who went along with what he said because of his last name and status at school.

It worked for them, so who was I to judge?

But I'd grown weary of the sounds. The scents. The entire show.

So, I wandered around campus instead. Today, my feet had taken me to the library. Up and down the aisles, I strolled, reading spines and taking deep whiffs of the old paper. I'd taken an interest in poetry lately. Sorting out the meaning behind the nonsense prose held my attention longer than most things.

When I came upon the couple in the last row, I nearly backed away and left them to it. But I had always been a curious cat and something about them had struck me as intriguing.

Ivan was doing his Ivan thing, which drove girls wild. Leaning in his signature I-don't-give-a-fuck style, tie undone, eye contact intense.

The girl's back was to me, but I recognized her thick thighs and plump ass, though her name escaped me. I should have known it since her bestie Luciana, and my boy Beckett were in the throes of true love, but I only had the desire to learn so many names, and I was full up.

It started with an *E*. No, a *D*. Dolores?

That didn't sound right.

I'd watched Ivan and Deborah's interaction, the slide of her hand over his, his subtle withdrawal, and winced so fucking hard when she was friend-zoned.

Big time.

My intention had been to leave well enough alone. Donatella was no doubt smarting, and I wasn't much of a shoulder to cry on. But I was somewhat fascinated to see her reaction.

Would she cry?

Rage?

Make tiny Ivan dolls and burn them in effigy?

When her round, olive cheeks flushed bright pink, I closed the book I was holding and sighed. *Embarrassed*. That was what she was.

"That was incredibly embarrassing."

Diana whipped in my direction, her balled hands flying to her chest. "What did you say?"

I nodded in the direction Ivan had disappeared as I sauntered toward her. "That was embarrassing, Danielle."

Her eyes narrowed. "That isn't my name."

"Isn't it?"

"No, it's not." She raised her chin, which was almost pointed, like the bottom of a heart.

"Hmmm. I know it starts with a *D*, and you sort of look like a Davina."

I sensed I was almost hitting the nail on the head. There were only so many D names.

"Is there a reason you're speaking to me?" she uttered.

I stopped in front of her. She was awfully short, though she held herself like she was taller. Squared shoulders and elongated spine, her eye contact was challenging.

"Why did you do it?" I asked.

"Do what?"

I nodded to where Ivan had been standing. "Go for it with him. Did you think he reciprocated?"

Her dusky-pink lips flattened until they were nearly white. "I have to ask again, why are you speaking to me?"

Dorit had an accent, which was a dime a dozen around Savage Academy. I stood out with my flat, nonregional dialect. I couldn't place hers, but that wasn't unusual here. Many of our classmates were from Europe. Being French, Swiss, or Dutch but raised in British boarding schools, or vice versa, distinct accents were pummeled out of them.

"I had no idea I wasn't allowed to speak to you. Should I have made an appointment?" I blinked at her as though I wasn't keenly aware of what she was really asking.

Her cheeks grew a more furious shade of red, which I hadn't thought possible.

I snapped my fingers. "I remember now. It's Dahlia."

"No."

"Hmmm. Are you certain?"

She shook her head and bent down to gather her messenger bag. The worn leather looked creamy and soft. I'd been scouting for a bag just like it. I almost asked where she'd gotten it, but we weren't friends, and I couldn't imagine she'd tell me. Maybe when I figured out her name.

"This conversation has been a nice cap to a lovely day, but I have to get going." She slung her bag over her shoulder. "Goodbye, Rhys."

I fell into step beside her as soon as she started walking. "You never answered my question, Dylan."

"Not my name. Isn't that a boy's name?"

"It's unisex now. Times have evolved."

The glare she threw at me was biting. "Thank you for that information. That doesn't change the fact that my name isn't Dylan."

"Fine. Tell me what it is."

"I'm certain I have before. If I tell you now, will you remember when I'm no longer in your presence?"

I chuckled, amused by her accurate assessment of me. "You have me there, Dara."

The growling sound she made was almost elegant, and it made me laugh even more.

"Are you an infant? No sense of object permanence?" she chided.

"No, I'm aware you continue existing when you're out of my sight. I simply stop caring."

She drew to a stop outside the library entrance and whirled around to face me. Her cheeks remained pink, humiliation replaced with indignation.

"We should speed up that phenomenon and part ways now. Lucky for you, you'll forget this conversation ever happened. Goodbye, Rhys."

Her fingers curled around the strap of her bag so tight they seemed in danger of losing circulation.

"You said that already, Delilah."

Her brown eyes—which were already almost too big—rounded before she wiped all expression from her face.

I leaned in. "Did I get it right that time? Delilah?"

She gnashed her teeth, which was an answer in itself. I grinned at her, pleased I'd guessed correctly.

It wasn't really a guess, though. I'd heard her name dozens of times, and now that it was bouncing around in my head, it was familiar. Some distant part of me had known it. I'd just been too lazy to dig it out of the recesses of my mind.

"Are we done now?" she asked.

"Sure. I'm headed over to the gym. Come with?"

Her mouth fell open, and on anyone else, it would have looked stupid. On her, it didn't.

"Are you making a joke?" she spit out. "I knew you were out of your mind, but I hadn't thought you were cruel."

I clicked my tongue. "That isn't very kind. I'm asking you to join me for a workout. You'll like it. Run some of that anger out. A nice sweat always clarifies things for me. I'll even let you explain why you made a move on Ivan when he clearly isn't interested."

Her lips went from an *O* to a tight *X*, puckered and leached of color. Without a single word, she swiveled in the other direction and stormed off.

I let her go. Angry women weren't really my thing.

With a whistle and pep in my step, I made my way to the gym.

· · · · ● · ● · · · ·

When it was founded a little over a hundred years ago, Savage Academy had been built to resemble a New England–style boarding school. Imposing brick buildings set in rolling, green hills crisscrossed by wide walking paths, the campus made an impressive picture at first glance. The insides had all been modernized and upgraded—nothing but the best for the neglected children of the elite.

That included the state-of-the-art gym. SA had two full gyms, but I used the one closest to the athlete's dorm most often. Felix and Beckett were hitting it hard on the treadmills when I arrived. I hopped on the one between them, pressing the buttons to get my machine started. It wasn't often I got the chance to run with them both since Beckett had all but abandoned our routine to run on the track with his girlfriend.

Not that I was salty.

Any other girl and I might have been. Luciana was more than tolerable, and Beck was content in a way he'd never been. I couldn't be too bitter about that, even if I tried.

Felix turned his head, raising a brow. "You're late."

"I spent some QT in the library. I was waylaid by a lovely conversation with Delilah. Do you know her?"

Felix scoffed. "Are you off your rocker? She's in our class. Of course I know her. How do you not?"

Felix Santos was the third roommate in our suite. My pairing with him had been less horrifying. We were what I thought of as friends-in-law. He was on the soccer team with Beckett, as well as his friend. Since Beckett was the only friend I cared about keeping, I put up with the people he added to our circle.

I felt Beckett looking at me, his feet pounding against the treadmill. "Why were you talking to Delilah?" Suspicion laced his question.

"I think she spoke to me first." I knocked on the side of my head. "No, wait. That was me. Why? Am I not allowed to speak to Luciana's friends?"

"You don't, so I want to know why you decided today was the day to start."

I lifted a shoulder. "A convergence of events led us to be in the same place at the same time, and we spoke. I'm under the impression she doesn't care for me."

Felix huffed a laugh. "Imagine that."

I peered at him through narrowed eyes. "I'm aware you're thinking her dislike is due to something you see as a personality flaw in me, but you're wrong. It's because I witnessed her being rejected by Ivan Sokolov."

Beckett groaned. "You were obviously a gentleman and pretended not to have heard anything."

That made me laugh. "Why would I do that?"

Felix threw out his arms. "Dude, come on. No one wants their humiliation to be fodder for jokes."

Beckett's eyes bored into the side of my head, so hard gray matter would soon be seeping out of the hole he was trying to make. "Did you make fun of her? Tell me you didn't."

It wasn't that he cared about my behavior. Or the girl. At least, I didn't think so. Beckett *did* care about Luciana, and if I was mean to one of her little friends, she wouldn't be happy. Beckett's least favorite thing was Luciana unhappy.

"I asked questions, that's all. I enjoyed our conversation." Now that I'd said it, I found it to be true. Even set back by rejection, Delilah had been feisty. Her face moved and reshaped depending on her emotions, capturing my interest, which had a habit of wandering. If the opportunity arose, I'd talk to her again. Or fight with her. I was game for whichever.

"Don't talk to her," Beckett groused.

Now that I didn't appreciate.

"Are you her dad? If the answer is no—and we both know it is—I don't see how you have any say in who I speak to. Really, Beck?"

Beckett slammed his hand down on the lit-up controls, bringing his treadmill to a stop. "Give it a rest. I know you're not actually interested in her, so drop it."

I scoffed. "Never once did I say I was interested in her for more than a conversation. How about you get the giant tentacle dildo out of your asshole?"

Felix barked a laugh. "Tentacle dildo?"

Beckett shook his head, a hint of a smile curling the corners of his mouth. "Don't get him started. You can't even imagine the kinds of books he reads."

I tipped my head toward Felix. "You can borrow them anytime you want, Santos. Just don't get them sticky."

Fortunately, the conversation moved on from Delilah. Not that I didn't enjoy a good argument here and there, but being at odds with Beckett gave me the skin crawls.

On the way back to our dorm, Beckett elbowed me. "Are you packed?"

"Christ." I shoved my fingers through my damp hair. "I was hoping if I ignored it, it wouldn't happen."

"Come on, man." Felix swung around, walking backward so he could face us. "Senior retreat is supposed to be the shit. A mountain resort with minimal adult supervision? I thought you'd be all over it."

Beckett slung his arm around my shoulders in sympathy. "It's the timing, Santos."

He cocked his head. "Timing?"

I rubbed my pocket watch with my thumb. "Your soccer season is over, but fencing is just beginning. There's no reason to waste time bonding with people I'll never see again in a few months—present company excluded, of course—when I should be training."

"Right, right, right. Fencing." Felix rubbed the back of his neck. "I'm gonna make it to one of your fights this year. I need to see you jabbing people with your little stick."

Beckett cleared his throat. "Rhys uses a sabre. Probably don't call it a stick again in his presence."

I raised a brow. "It's like me saying you kick around a rock, only more offensive."

He spun to walk beside me again. "That's truly my bad. I'll read up before your first fight."

Beckett cleared his throat again. "Match."

I sighed. "It's fine that my roommate and friend don't know anything about my sport. It's not like I've sat in the stands many, *many* times to watch you kick a little ball into a giant net."

Felix burst out laughing. "I get it. I suck. But I'm serious about studying. Once we get back from the retreat, my world is going to be fencing."

I cringed. If there were a way out of going to this retreat, I would have found it. Denial was no longer an option since it hadn't worked thus far.

It was a *fait accompli*. Time to pack.

CHAPTER THREE
Delilah

EVELYN TOOK THE WINDOW seat. She always did, and I never argued, although sometimes I would have liked to sit next to the window.

This was one of those times.

Not for the view, since our coach bus hadn't left Savage Academy yet.

Sitting on the aisle, I was much too exposed. I couldn't flip my hood over my head, press my face to the glass, and pretend no one else existed like my sister was doing.

A bubble of resentment percolated in my stomach as Ivan made his way down the aisle. Our eyes clashed, and I forced myself to return his smile. But I was a little bit mad I had to be in this position at all.

If I'd asked Ev to swap seats, she would have. It would have been difficult since this trip was already ramping up her anxiety, but she would have sucked it up for me.

I'd never ask, though.

It wasn't her fault I chose to put her comfort over mine. She had never asked me to, and she would probably be devastated if she realized I was doing it, so I had no right to feel any sort of resentment toward my sister, my twin, my other half. But the bubble was there, and it wasn't popping. Ivan was coming closer, and I couldn't curl up against the window and feign sleep like I so desperately wished.

When he was two seats ahead of me, I tipped my head back and mouthed, "Good morning."

He waited until he was within reach to pat the top of my head, then leaned down to speak as quietly as he was capable. "Hello, Delilah. Are you good?"

I let my head fall against the headrest, but his hand followed, palming my crown. "I'm always good, Ivan. And you?"

"I'm gonna go nap in the back of the bus." He jerked his chin at Ev. "Evelyn has a very smart idea."

"Sleep tight," I chimed with as much enthusiasm as I could muster.

"See you in the mountains." He gave my head another friendly pat, hammering the point straight into my brain. *Just friends. Good buddies. Best pals.*

Ivan was very, very tall. He towered over most of the guys in school and, therefore, had been blocking the line of people behind him from my sight.

As soon as he stepped past me, he revealed a bored, slightly rumpled Rhys Astor. A strand of his wavy, deep-auburn hair swooped across his forehead, and golden stubble dappled his strongly defined jaw. His forest green T-shirt was partially untucked from his cargo trousers, the hem of one sleeve flipped up. When he alighted on me, he visibly perked up.

"That had to have stung, Delilah."

I didn't know of many of Rhys's positive attributes, but I learned right then one was his ability to whisper. He could have taught Ivan a few lessons. No one seemed to glance our way when he spoke to me. Given the nature of our school—everyone knew *everyone's* business—that was a relief.

"You remembered my name," I deflected.

"I heard Sokolov say it." The corner of his mouth hitched. "Maybe I would have remembered on my own. You did make an impression on me yesterday."

"Not the one I intended since you're still speaking to me."

Rhys opened his mouth to respond, but Felix Santos shoved him forward before he could get a word out.

"Move it, Astor," Felix said without a hint of malice. "You heard what Beckett said."

Rhys whirled around, shooting daggers at Felix through narrowed eyes. "Don't fucking push me, Santos. That was wholly unnecessary."

Felix raised his hands. "Apologies. You just looked like you needed a reminder."

"Neither you nor Beckett is my keeper, and I don't take kindly to you pretending to be." Rhys didn't look at me again before he walked away. Felix offered me a smile so loaded with sympathy I was certain Rhys had told him about what had happened in the library.

I wanted to die. Rhys knowing was bad enough. Felix, and most likely Beckett, was tantamount to torture.

Felix dipped down and whispered, "Don't worry. I'm no gossip. My lips are sealed."

Folding my arms across my chest, I forced myself to unclench my jaw and put on a grateful little smile.

"Thank you so much. See you later."

He gave my shoulder a squeeze. "Enjoy the ride, D."

· · · • · • · • · · ·

Evelyn sat up when we were on the road, sliding her headphones back so they hung around her neck. She stretched her arms in front of her then tucked her legs in her seat so she could turn toward me.

"Was it awful?" she asked.

"I knew you weren't really asleep. You heard."

"I can pretend I didn't if you want me to. Is that easier for you?"

I huffed, wishing I could. "No. Of course not."

She cocked her head, her eyes sweeping over my face. When we were babies and toddlers, our parents thought we might have been identical since our features were exactly alike. They considered getting a DNA test to prove whether we were, but as we grew, it became clear our genes were different. We still shared the same face, but Evelyn was delicate and fine-boned, naturally thin like our mother.

My thick thighs, round, bouncy butt, padded hips, and full tits came from our father's side.

When we looked at each other up close like this, all I saw were our similarities. Her deep-brown eyes, surrounded by fluttery, black lashes, were a mirror of mine. We both had thick eyebrows and straight, high-bridged noses. My cheeks were fuller than hers, but the shapes of our faces were otherwise the same.

Since we'd been sent to boarding school as small children, Evelyn and I had become our own little pod. We understood each other like no one else ever would and didn't bother making other friends for years. We played quiet games, just her and me, and had our own secret words no one else knew. And during those years when we only had ourselves, we'd spent hours staring at each other, studying one another's expressions and the subtle differences between us. I knew her face better than my own.

We opened up our little world to others as we got older, but we would always be the core. Ev hadn't stopped studying my face, and I let her.

"Why do you think Rhys keeps speaking to you?" she asked.

"It's not often you get to witness a girl being rejected, is it? He's probably amused. I'm certain he'll get over it soon." I groaned softly. "I wish I'd ignored those feelings. We were such nice friends, and I had to go blow it up."

"You said the same thing last night."

My sister, always the blunt one.

"I know." I dragged a hand over my face. "I'm repeating myself because I'm wallowing. I can't think straight."

"This must be what Cristiano felt when you rejected him many times."

My hand dropped. "What? That isn't true."

Cristiano was a boy Luciana knew from her old school. In my head, I'd assumed he was a flirt and had never taken him seriously, but now that I was considering his actions, I realized he'd never flirted with anyone else when I was around him. I had always been his sole focus.

"Oh? Sometimes I get these things wrong, to be sure, but when we last saw him in town, he said you kept getting more beautiful with each passing day, and you laughed at him."

I bit down on my bottom lip. I remembered that. Ev and I had been in Savage River, at the bookshop, and Cris had wandered in. He'd been pretty delighted to see me, and yes, I'd laughed. Now, Ev was making me question our interaction.

"I don't think he meant it. That's just how he is."

She lifted her shoulder. "That might be true. But he didn't tell me I was beautiful, and we both know how alike we look, so I don't think his comment was only an observation. He said something sweet to you because he likes you, and you laughed."

My stomach swooped in an unpleasant way. "Is this supposed to make me feel better about what happened with Ivan?"

She rolled the string from her hoodie around her index finger. "No. The expression on your face reminded me of Cristiano, so the connection clicked in my mind. You rejected Cris, then Ivan rejected you. Same expression."

I leveled her with an unamused gaze. "You've succeeded in making me feel slightly worse, which I hadn't known was possible."

"I didn't mean to do that." Her mouth twisted, and she let the string unravel from her finger. "You know I despise when you're sad more than anything in the world."

"I don't know if I'm sad, really."

"A little?"

I huffed a laugh. "Okay, a little. Foolish is the ruling emotion right now, though." I waved a hand, dismissing my feelings. "Anyway, it's fortunate we're going away. A change of scenery and routine will be good for me."

She rolled her hoodie string around her finger again. "Ah, I was doing so well not thinking about that."

I tugged on the opposite string. "Oh, I get it now. Focusing on my issues was your way of avoiding the fact that we're going somewhere new, huh?"

Her lips curved into a sly little grin. "I'm a big proponent of using my resources."

"Me? I'm your resource?"

Her grin widened. "And my beloved sister, who is gorgeous and wise beyond her years."

That made me snort a laugh. "Shut up. You've used me, and I'm offended."

"You aren't."

"No, you're right. I'm not."

It would take a lot for Evelyn to offend me, and even then, I'd forgive her pretty instantly. She could shove me off a cliff, and instead of being angry, I'd try to understand what had made her do it. That wasn't because she was on the spectrum and sometimes her mind was mysterious to me. It was because she was my constant—the only person I would ever fully trust and let my guard down with. If she hurt my feelings, she always made it better in the next breath because that was who she was.

With a sigh, she bent down and picked up her tote bag from the floor. "I'm going to knit now...unless you need more support?"

"You've given me quite enough support," I told her.

Her eyes narrowed. "You *should* feel better. I've never rejected anyone, and you do it all the time."

Evelyn had rejected plenty of guys. She just wasn't aware since she basically ignored the entire male population.

"Wait, is this part of your support?"

"Yes. I'm reminding you of how hot you are. One singular boy wasn't interested. He's a drop in the ocean of your admirers."

"Ignoring catcalls doesn't count as rejecting men."

I didn't get a response, but I hadn't expected one. Once her knitting came out and her fingers sank into her yarn, she was lost to me.

Chapter Four
Delilah

I DIDN'T KNOW WHAT I'd been expecting the location of the retreat to be like, but this wasn't it. Nestled in the mountains, the resort was set near a lake. Small, fairy-tale-esque cabins bordered a cobbled courtyard, and in the center was a firepit surrounded by rustic, natural wood chairs.

Luciana, Bella, Evelyn, and I were sharing a cabin. Our chaperones had tried to shake up our pairings since we also roomed together, but no one cooperated, so they gave up and let us choose our cabinmates.

Bella spun in a tight circle, her blonde ringlets bouncing. "Okay, y'all, this is cute."

"Right?" Luciana tilted her head back to look at the exposed wood beams crossing the vaulted ceiling. "I was expecting a horror movie summer camp based on what I heard from seniors last year."

"I love it." Evelyn wandered into one of the two minuscule bedrooms and quietly shut the door behind her. Our friends didn't even blink at her disappearing, which was why they were our friends.

"Don't you think it's sort of a fun prank seniors play?" I asked. "They scare the class below them into thinking they have torture awaiting them?"

Bella yanked open the sliding glass door at the back of the cabin. "I think you're right. They were probably laughin' at how clever they are. Assholes."

Luc bumped my shoulder with hers. "We're totally doing that too, aren't we?"

I grinned. "Of course. It's tradition."

Bella poked her head in. "Come out here, y'all. We have a view."

Luc and I joined her on the tiny back porch, and my breath caught. We really did have a view. Our cabin was in the perfect position, unblocked by the other cabins, so we could see straight out to the lake and the mountains behind them.

"Doesn't look like Texas, huh?" Luciana quipped.

Bella shook her head. "And my parents wonder why I'm not comin' back when I graduate."

I turned to her. "Have you made up your mind about college?"

"Nope. I'll take classes in a dumpster as long as I don't have to go back home." She braced her elbows on the railing. "What about you?"

I shrugged. "It's expected we'll go back to Greece. Europe, at the very least."

"You don't want to," Luc stated. She didn't have to ask. She already knew the answer.

"No, I don't, but it's not often that what I want and what I'm allowed to do align. Besides, where I go, Evelyn will go too. We have to make the decision together."

"What's Ev say?" Bella asked.

I wrinkled my nose. "We're both avoiding the conversation."

We'd applied to schools in Europe *and* California. Once we found out where we were accepted, we'd have to truly address the situation. The idea of leaving this area filled me with dread. That I knew for sure. But I wasn't positive Evelyn was keen on staying. And our parents...well, they wanted us closer, but not too close.

It was a shit show for future me to worry about.

Bella straightened, stretching her arms over her head. "How long do you think we have until they try to force us to do *activities*?"

I checked my watch. "Half past very fucking soon."

Luc snorted. "Well, whatever. We might have to do lame trust exercises or arts and crafts, but we're not at school, and that counts for a lot in my book."

"Agreed. I'm ready to coast through the rest of the year now that field hockey's over."

"It's November," I reminded Bella.

"Too soon for coasting?" She stuck her bottom lip out in a pout.

I almost patted her head, but that reminded me far too much of Ivan, so I stuffed my hand in my pocket.

They didn't know what happened yesterday. I trusted them, but telling Ev had been enough. I'd wallowed for twenty-four hours. It was time to move on. Luc and Bella would support me, but I didn't need it, and I would rather choke than receive their pity. I'd tell them eventually. When I was fully over it.

For now, I'd folded my crush on Ivan into a nice, tidy box and stuffed it away in a deep, dark corner. It was still there, but hopefully, with time, I'd forget it ever existed.

······•·•····

The rest of the day included a brief orientation of the resort, yoga by the lake, dinner, and finally, freedom. My girls and I had congregated around the firepit with a handful of our classmates. Music was playing, there were s'mores, and more than a few people had brought flasks filled with spirits.

It was unspoken that our chaperones would turn the other way and let us do our thing so long as we didn't make a spectacle of ourselves. That was the way at Savage Academy in general. Most of us had been going to boarding schools since we were children, so by the time we were seniors, we were pretty self-sufficient.

Though, as Charles Bloomberg held his bare hand over the open flames, I questioned how he'd made it this far with all his limbs intact.

"Who dares me to lower my hand?" he called. "Come on."

"Do it," Rhys drawled without bothering to look up. "You want to be truly badass? I dare you to sit down in the center of the firepit and not get up until you're a pile of ash. That would be epic."

Charles flipped him off. "In your dreams, Astor."

I almost held back my snicker, yet Rhys seemed to hear anyway. His eyes locked with mine, and his head tilted, the barest hint of a smile playing on his deviant mouth.

I was the first to break eye contact, turning my head to where Luciana was perched on Beckett Savage's lap.

Luciana and Beckett were adorable. Perfect. He treated her like the precious gem she was, and she adored him. Nice. Very nice.

Except where Beckett went, his friends often followed. Rhys was bad enough, but Charles Bloomberg was atrocious. He was a caricature of a prep school football player, complete with a flipped collar, rape-y vibes, and all the fat jokes he could dream up.

Bella held out her pink, crystal-bedazzled flask. "Want?"

"Mmm...yes, please." I took it from her, rubbing my fingers over the crystals. Scooting down in my seat, I blinked up at the stars while I sipped. "This is nice."

"I'm pumped for the ropes course tomorrow," Bella said.

"I don't think that will be my thing," I replied. "I'm going to do the hike."

"*Boring*," she chided. "If there's no chance of death, what's the point?"

I giggled. "Isn't there always a chance of death? More so in the forest. What if I encounter a hungry mountain lion?"

"Never run from a mountain lion." Evelyn perched on the arm of my chair, coming out of nowhere. "They attack from behind."

Bella snorted so hard she dissolved into a fit of belly laughs. "Oh god, now I'm going to be worried about you tomorrow."

"Mountain lion attacks are pretty uncommon," Evelyn told her. "You shouldn't worry."

I reached up and squeezed her hand. "Thank you for setting us straight. What activity did you want to do tomorrow?"

"I was thinking I might do the lake walk with a forest ranger. It sounds the most interesting. You don't have to do it with me, though. I'll be fine." Ev folded her arms. "Let me guess: Bella is doing the ropes course with Luc."

Bella bobbed her head. "Hell yeah, baby girl. You want to come with us, just let me know. I'll get your ass up on the ropes."

"No, thank you," Ev replied. "My ass is fine near the ground."

She hopped up from my chair. "I'm going to see if there's any chocolate left. I would really love some."

She wandered off again, as she had a habit of doing, and I settled back, watching the stars.

· · ● ● · ● · · ·

The next time I looked up, it was due to Charles's braying laughter interrupting the mellow, low din of conversation. I cracked an eye, searching him out. He was easy to find. I simply followed his jackass laughs to the table holding the s'mores ingredients.

And there he stood, right beside Evelyn, who was nibbling on the corner of a chocolate bar.

"Why is Charles speaking to my sister?"

Bella moved in slow motion, her head turning in their direction. "Hmmm. He's probably showing off his new skill: walking upright. He's very proud, just look at him."

I squinted through the dark, attempting to decipher Ev's body language and expression. Through the fog of fire, smoke and lack of light, it was difficult to tell if she was uncomfortable. Charles wasn't touching or crowding her, but him just being near her sent chills down my spine.

"I don't like it."

"Should we go put a stop to it?" Bella shoved her fist into her hand, looking as menacing as a baby bunny.

"No, you stay. I'm going to check in with Ev."

While my sister could take care of herself, sometimes she found herself in social situations she didn't know how to extract herself from without making a scene. And the last thing Evelyn would ever want was to make a scene.

Neither of them noticed me until I was beside the table. Charles's voice was low, too quiet for me to hear what he was saying, and Ev was nodding along.

"Evelyn."

Shoulders jumping, her head whipped in my direction. "Oh! I didn't notice you were here."

"Looking for s'mores?" Charles suggested. "I'll make you one if you want."

"No, actually." I shuddered to think of his hands touching anything going into my mouth. Despite that, his offer surprised me. Charles normally only gave me the time of day to insult me. His politeness set me on edge, making me want to get Evelyn away from him even more than I would have if he'd been rude. "I'm here for my sister."

"Why?" He leaned closer to Ev, curling his muscular, athletic shoulders forward as if trying to make himself smaller, less of a threat. "She's good here."

"I'm sure she is. However, our friends were wondering where she was." I hooked my arm through Ev's. "Did you get lost finding chocolate?"

She held up the bar she was slowly eating. "My sense of direction is terrible except when it comes to chocolate."

"She's fine with me," Charles stated. "We were having a chat."

"Charles was telling me about his football skills." Evelyn blinked at me, which meant she was being sarcastic. Rapid blinking was her only tell. "He's very, very talented. Did you know that?"

I snorted a laugh. "I've heard him say that before." Then I tugged on her arm. "Come sit with us. You can bring your chocolate with you."

"You don't have to go, Evelyn," Charles argued. "Hang out with me."

Evelyn waved at him. "Maybe tomorrow. Good night."

We skirted around the fire on the way back to our friends. I tipped my head to whisper to her. "What was happening back there?"

"I don't know. He came up to me and started talking. I didn't mind it," she answered.

"He's the worst."

"I know. But sometimes it's interesting to speak to people who are terrible."

As alike as we were, Evelyn and I didn't look at people the same way. If I found someone abhorrent, like Charles, I did my best to stay away. Evelyn watched people and, given the chance, asked questions. Lots of questions. She didn't accept abhorrence at face value. Which probably made her the better person and made me even more protective of her.

At least I didn't have to worry about him going after her tomorrow. There was no way someone like Charles would pass up the chance to show off his athleticism on the ropes course, which Evelyn wouldn't touch with a ten-foot pole.

CHAPTER FIVE
Rhys

NATURE WAS FINE. I even enjoyed it from time to time.

Forced togetherness with my classmates in a nature setting I didn't choose? That I would never enjoy.

I had no need to bond with any of these people. I should have been in the gym, training for my fencing season. These few days away from SA were setting me back and annoying the shit out of me.

Naturally, the administration had waited until football and soccer season were over to schedule this retreat. God forbid anyone give consideration to the other sports.

Assholes.

I was kicked back on the small porch in front of our cabin when Charles came stumbling out. We'd shared a room last night, which had been a fucking nightmare. He had no right to look as tired as he did. Dude snored like a freight train, so I knew, for a fact, he'd slept all night. He didn't even wake up when I threw my pillow, a paperback, and a pair of shoes at him.

"Headed for breakfast?" he mumbled.

I let my feet fall to the ground. "Yeah, sure. I could use a cup of coffee. Are Ryan and Felix up?"

"They're still getting dressed." He jerked his head to the side. "I told them I'm not waiting. My stomach is about to start gnawing on itself. Come on."

With a sigh, I got up. Knowing Beckett, he'd most likely risen early and already made it to the dining hall so he could see Luciana. At least, I hoped. If I had to sit alone with Charles, I'd riot.

I needn't have worried, though. Beckett was already there, along with Luc and her friends. We grabbed food and joined them. Charles broke away from me to take the empty chair beside Delilah's twin.

I couldn't deny my amusement when I spotted Delilah's reaction to this. Her soft jaw went iron hard, and her thick brows angled into lightning bolts. She didn't appreciate Charles's proximity.

Not that I blamed her.

When he came near me, I didn't appreciate his proximity either.

"You wear your feelings all over your face," I said.

She jerked her eyes to me. "I've been told that before."

Laughing, I cocked my head. "Rough night?"

"My night was fine."

"Not mine." I scooped up some eggs on my fork. "Charles snores."

Hearing his name, Charles straightened. "What's that?"

"I said you snore. I threw my shoes at your head, and you slept right through it."

"Untrue." He balled up his napkin and tossed it at me. "Keep that shit to yourself. I know you don't want me spilling facts about you for everyone to hear."

I tossed his napkin back at him. He caught it one-handed before it could bounce off his head. A lot could've been said about Charles's lack of character, but no one could question his athletic prowess.

"I'll talk to Mathilde about your asshole. It seems to be inflamed lately." I turned back to Delilah. "That's my aesthetician."

"Fascinating," she intoned.

I waved my fork at her. "I don't think you mean that."

"I really don't." She ripped her piece of toast in half. "This can't become a habit, you know. I don't want to be your friend."

I sputtered. "Did you think I wanted to be yours? I'm full up, chick. No room at the inn."

This would teach me not to stick my neck out. Try to be friendly to a brokenhearted girl one time, and this was what it got me. Well, no more. Diane or Dana, or whatever her name was, was on her own.

She pushed her chair out and grabbed her tray. "Are you ready to go, Ev? I want to check out the lake."

Her sister got up while Charles was in the middle of saying something to her, gave him an absent wave, and disappeared with Delilah.

Charles watched them go with a scowl like his favorite toy had been stolen.

All I could do was laugh and eat my eggs.

· · · • · · • · · · ·

Charles came running up to me after breakfast when everyone was heading to their *activities*. Throwing his arm around me, he steered me away from the crowd.

"I need a favor," he said.

"Do you?" I stared at him for a long moment. "Oh, you need a favor from me?"

He folded his arms over his chest. "That's right. I noticed you and the ugly twin have a rapport going."

"Ugly twin?"

He flicked his hand. "Ugly, fat, whatever. Evelyn's sister."

Something told me I wasn't going to like where this was going. Actually, I'd known that before hearing anything he had to say. This was Charles, after all.

"Rapport would be stretching it. We've exchanged a few sentences.".

He leaned on the tree behind him and kicked up a foot like he was planning on staying a while. "All right. My point is you have some sort of connection. The thing is, she's a fucking cockblocker, and I need her out of the way."

My brows popped. Wherever I'd thought this was going, it wasn't there.

"You're into the twin?"

"Yeah. Evelyn. She's hot as hell and kinda weird. In my experience, that combination is wicked in bed. Girls like that will try *anything* out of curiosity."

I scrunched my eyes closed with disgust. Seeing Charles in action was more than enough to turn my stomach. Hearing him talk about his desires had me seconds from projectile vomiting.

"Clue me in on what this has to do with me, man," I pleaded.

"Simple." He shook his head like he couldn't believe he had to explain it to me. "You distract the ugly twin so I can be free to make my move on the hot one."

This was...not happening. He'd lost his mind if he thought I'd do anything to help facilitate his banging needs.

I held up a finger. "One, there's no ugly twin. Those girls have the same fucking face." Another finger. "Two, I have no say over where Delilah goes or what she does." I waved three fingers in front of his face. "Third, and most importantly, fuck off, Bloomberg. I'm not your lapdog."

He chuckled. "You know, I thought you'd say that. That's why I come to you with an offer."

"If it's anything short of you vaporizing and being blown away by a strong gust of wind, I'm not interested."

He grinned at me like everything was going his way. "You're not a nice guy, Astor."

"So it's been said. It doesn't affect me because I don't care." I glanced behind us, at our classmates joining up with the leaders of their groups. As much as I had no desire to participate, I'd rather do that than stand here another minute.

"Don't you want to hear my offer?" Charles pushed off from the tree to circle around me. "It's a good one."

"No thanks. You and your cock are on your own." I took two steps before he called out, bringing me to a halt.

"Three *Gs*."

I turned back, brow lowered. "You're offering me three grand?"

He nodded, pleased as punch with himself. "That's right."

"And what do I have to do to earn this money?"

I shouldn't have been entertaining this, but Charles knew things about me no one else did. I'd made the mistake of getting blackout drunk with him last year, and when I'd come to, he'd held a secret I'd been waiting for him to cash in on ever since.

He bounced on his toes with glee. "That's the trick. You don't have to do much. I just need my path to scoring with Evelyn to be clear. Your job is to distract the twin while I work my many charms."

My stomach soured at this whole idea.

"You're pimping me out, then."

He shook his head. "No, dude. I'm not saying you have to get with her. I'd be paying you more if I expected that. Just...I don't know, entertain her. Argue with her. You're good at that. Let me have the opportunity to shoot my shot with Ev, and you'll get your three *G*s when we get back to school."

When I didn't answer right away, he pressed a little harder.

"Come on, Astor. We both know you'd make good use of the money."

One of the things I'd revealed to him was how tightly my stepfather held his purse strings. Every cent I spent was accounted for. That wasn't to say he was stingy. If I wanted to buy twenty bespoke suits, he'd allow it so long as I presented him with receipts. But there were some things I didn't want him to know I spent money on. Three thousand free-and-clear dollars would be really fucking nice.

"All right. I'll do it. But if your girl turns you down, I expect to still get paid."

Charles raised his hands. "Of course. You know I'm good for it. And anyway, I don't expect she'll turn me down. I'll have to work for it, but I love a good challenge. It's been too easy lately."

"You'll spare me the details. Just make sure anything that happens is fully consensual."

"I like her. I'm not out to hurt her." He tipped his head to the side. "Now, I'm about to give up the ropes course to go walk around the lake and hold my dick. I'm gonna need you to find the ugly twin and make sure she doesn't see me joining Evelyn's group. Otherwise, I'll be SOL, and so will you."

Clicking my heels together, I saluted him. "Aye, aye, captain. Lieutenant Astor reporting for duty."

He rolled his eyes. "Not even a little convincing. We both know you'd be dishonorably discharged for insubordination before you even made rank."

My hand went from saluting to flipping him off. "Go on your little hike. I'm going to earn my keep."

I suspected Delilah was going to make me work for every fucking penny, whether she knew it or not.

Chapter Six
Delilah

THE SMALLEST GROUP WENT on the hike. There were ten or fifteen of us following a local guide through the woods. None of my friends except Ivan.

Since I'd moved on from what had happened in the library, I was happy to have his company.

Definitely not mortified in the least.

He walked beside me at times. Other times, he pulled ahead. But his legs were twice the length of mine, so it was probably difficult for him to keep pace with me.

When I rounded a bend, he was waiting for me, perched on a boulder, grinning as I approached. "Come sit beside me."

Because he was watching me, I measured my breaths so he didn't hear me panting. We were going straight up the mountain. Being out of breath was a natural consequence, but I didn't want Ivan to know I was human.

I sat down beside him and brought my water bottle to my lips, using it to hide my rapid breathing.

"How are you doing, Delilah?" His voice boomed off the granite. If there'd been snow, he would have caused an avalanche.

"I'm looking forward to making it to the peak." Turning my head, I swiped at my sweaty forehead. "I'm surprised you didn't do the ropes course."

He easily dismissed the suggestion. "I have no need to do that sort of thing."

"You find your thrills elsewhere?"

One brow winged. "Mmm. Do you need thrills to be happy?"

"I'm—" I closed my mouth, thinking over my answer. "No, I suppose I don't."

He lifted his water bottle to his lips, his eyes crinkling at the corners. "Neither do I."

Before I could respond, a rock sailed by, narrowly missing me. Jerking my gaze from Ivan, I spotted Rhys uphill, crouched down, checking his laces. Was he throwing rocks at me? Surely, he couldn't be that malicious.

"Ivan!"

From the direction opposite Rhys, Clarice Chin scampered up to our boulder with Veronica Shipley. They weren't nice girls or even bright girls, but they were pretty. Very, very pretty. Clarice was thin but curvy, with thick, black hair she wore in waves down her back. Veronica was equally thin, with long, long legs and a full head of auburn hair.

Neither of them were out of breath or the least bit sweaty. It was annoying.

More annoying was the way Ivan greeted them. Warmly, with a smile. He casually chatted with them while Clarice petted his arm and Veronica angled herself to block me out of their new little group.

"Oh my god, that playlist was so good," Clarice gushed, her enthusiasm landing on me like an ice-cold glass of water on a winter's day. I fucking froze.

Playlist?

"Right?" Veronica's head bobbed in agreement. "I felt like I was at a rave. Boom-ch, boom-ch, boom-ch."

The playlist Ivan claimed to have made for me?

"You listened?" Ivan moved his arm from beneath Clarice's roving touch and leaned back on his hands, at ease with all this attention. Who wouldn't love having three girls vying for their time? God, I am a right idiot for thinking there was something between us.

"Listened? I am obsessed." Clarice hummed one of the songs from the playlist Ivan had shared with me. "Last night, I was dancing in my underwear and—oops, I guess I shouldn't have told you that."

Veronica nudged me with her elbow as she shoved her tits in Ivan's face. I'd had quite enough of this little show. Since I would never compete for anyone's attention, I hopped off the boulder, gave Ivan a little wave—one I sincerely doubted he noticed—and started up the incline.

I had to pass Rhys on my way. I braced myself for his snark, but to my surprise, he kept quiet. Not even a sad little shake of his head, though I didn't doubt he'd seen everything that had just happened. Why wouldn't he have? The universe had made sure he was present for some of my low points. No doubt my being brushed aside by Ivan's fan club had amused him greatly.

His footsteps fell close behind mine. When it became clear he had no intention of saying anything, I heaved a sigh of relief and managed to put everyone out of my mind, concentrating on where I was and what I was doing. I'd come on this hike to enjoy it, not to worry about boys. That wasn't the type of girl I was. I liked boys. Crushes were fun and made life a little more interesting, but I could easily get by on my own. I hadn't had a boyfriend since we'd left Spain last year, and I wasn't in a rush for another one. I'd never bend over backward to win a guy's affection.

A guy who was worth it wouldn't want me to.

The sun peeking through the trees warmed my chilled skin. Twigs snapped and leaves crunched under my feet. A delicate yellow flower growing in one of the beams of light made me pause. I bent down to sniff it and snapped a picture with my phone. It was so small I'd almost missed it, but I was happy I hadn't.

Carrying on, I took a few more pictures. A bird perched on a low branch, midsong. The biggest leaf I'd ever seen. A squirrel scurrying away with an acorn. Nothing special, but I wanted to capture the little moments to show Ev. She was the only one I'd show these pictures to. She would appreciate them as much as I did.

We made it to the top, and the guide told us the history of the area and stories about wildlife he'd encountered.

I listened. Most of the group took selfies while he spoke. That wasn't to say I hadn't snapped a few, but for the most part, I sat on a rock, my elbows on my knees, blissed out in the sun. It was perfect after a shitty start to the day.

The way down was faster. I waited for Ivan to head down before I started on my way. He hadn't done anything wrong, and I desperately wished I was the cool girl who could get over the shot to my ego quickly, but I wasn't.

My feelings still stung, especially seeing how easily he tolerated Clarice and Veronica hanging all over him.

Once they disappeared on the trail, I followed, with Rhys's footsteps dogging mine. I ignored him since he wasn't bothering me. We were just two classmates on the same hike. He had every right to be on this mountain.

We were nearing the base when he caught up to me.

I turned to him. "Hey."

He jerked his chin. "How is your day going?"

"Really well. Yours?"

So formal. But I didn't know this guy, nor how to speak to him when we weren't fighting, so formal would have to do.

"I don't want to be here," he stated.

"No? Why not? Isn't anything better than school?"

"On a normal basis, yes. But I'm in the middle of training. I don't have time for leisurely hikes."

"It's a three-day trip, Rhys. Your muscles won't atrophy if you skip the gym for three days."

He raised a brow. "Are you suddenly a fitness trainer?"

Despite myself, my cheeks flushed. I didn't care what Rhys thought of me, and normally, I'd let a dig like that slide off my back, but I was just tender enough for those words to land a solid blow to my already fragile ego.

I clamped my mouth shut and stared straight ahead, picking up my pace. Rhys stayed with me, and though I refused to look, I knew he was staring at me.

"Why aren't you speaking?" he asked after a minute or two.

"I'm sorry. I thought your question was rhetorical." I glanced at him. "No, I'm not a fitness trainer, just someone with common sense."

"Hmmm." He leaned in, so his face was far too close to mine. "Did you think I was insulting you?"

I gave my head a shake, even though, yes, that was exactly what I'd thought.

"Okay. But if you were thinking that, knock it off. My humor is far too elevated for that sort of joke."

A huff of a laugh escaped before I could stop it.

When I didn't say anything, he leaned into me again. "What?"

"Nothing." I stole a glance at him, finding him staring. "Are you really miserable here?"

"This very second? No, I'm not."

"I mean, on this mountain. It's too beautiful to be in a bad mood. Even if you have a lot waiting for you back at school, this is where you are now. Look around you."

He clicked his tongue. "I get you. You're a glass-half-full kind of girl. You see the bright side in everything."

"I wouldn't say that. I can be a pessimist." My shoulder bumped his arm. Or, rather, his arm bumped my shoulder since he was the one who kept veering into my space. "Let me guess, you're a glass-half-empty kind of guy."

"More of a glass-splintered-into-a-thousand-pieces, liquid-spilling-everywhere kind of person."

My mouth curved in amusement. "So dark. You should consider wearing eyeliner and brushing your hair over your forehead."

"Did you just call me emo, Delilah?"

I lifted a shoulder. "If the scuffed-up, steel-toed boot fits."

He chuckled. "You'll find me dead before you find me wearing scuffed shoes."

The trailhead was just ahead of us, and congregating there was Ivan and his fan club. He was nodding along to what they were saying, his hands tucked in his pockets like he was in no hurry to part from them.

My breath was stuck in my throat. I kept asking myself how I'd gotten the signals so wrong. I supposed it had just been wishful thinking.

The same way I'd gotten caught up in the fantasy of him back at school, I got caught up in watching him instead of the trail, and my toe hooked on a big root instead of stepping over it, sending me tipping forward.

Time slowed, and I prepared myself to crash-land on my face. Because why wouldn't I fall on my face in front of Ivan? It seemed I was developing a habit of just that.

At the last moment, two powerful hands gripped my biceps and hauled me upright, jerking me so hard we collided. My soft chest pressed into Rhys's solid wall of muscles, and one of his arms banded around my waist, steadying me.

My heart skittered in my chest as I tilted my head back to gaze at him, blinking my daze away.

"Whoa," I rushed out.

"Are you all right?" He studied me, sweeping his gaze over me like he was checking for injuries.

"I think so. I was prepared to not be all right, so I'm a little off right now."

"Come on, Delilah," he murmured. "Do you really think I'd let you fall?"

"I don't—"

"Delilah!"

Ivan rushed up to us, concern etching lines on his face. "Are you okay?"

"She's fine," Rhys announced. "I've got her covered."

Ignoring him, Ivan took my hand and pulled me away from Rhys. He cupped my face and then my shoulders, examining me the same way Rhys had.

I shook my head. "Really, you didn't have to rush away from your friends. I—"

"They are not my friends." His mouth pulled into a frown. "I thought you were going to be hurt."

"It was a close one." I smiled and took a step back from him. He slowly dropped his hold on me, scowling. "Thankfully, Rhys was here."

I turned to where he'd been standing, but he wasn't there. I supposed he'd passed me on to Ivan as soon as he'd had the opportunity.

"What were you doing with him?" Ivan asked gently. "Was he bothering you?"

"We were walking together, that's all." My heart rate still wasn't back to normal, but I couldn't deal with another second of Ivan's concern. "I'm good now. Thank you for caring."

"Of course I care."

Right. Of course he did. The same way he cared about Veronica and Clarice. It would serve me well to never mistake it for anything more than it was.

Chapter Seven
Rhys

Charles nudged me with his beefy arm. "Get her out of here."

I swung my narrow-eyed gaze at him. I really didn't appreciate being manhandled while standing in line for my nightly slop.

Given how much money my stepfather spent on my schooling, if he found out about the poor excuse for food they were serving us in this hellscape, he would have gone to an early grave.

Come to think of it, he was due a phone call...

Charles nudged me again when I didn't hop to it fast enough. That would not stand.

"No. You're not going to put your hands on me. I might be your temporary employee, but I am not your indentured servant."

He chuffed, removing himself from my space. I was already regretting agreeing to this. Not because it was difficult but because it forced me to interact with Charles more than any person should ever have to.

"I need you to remove Delilah from the area. I made good headway with Evelyn on the fucking lake walk, but she requires finesse. I can't exactly do that with her warden hanging around."

I knew Charles. He didn't know the definition of finesse. Yet, he managed to bag almost every girl he went after, so maybe I was missing something. The bastard must've had some hidden charm he only turned on in the face of pussy.

"I can't remove her since she isn't an object." I folded my arms over my chest. "But I'll see if I can get her to join me in another location. May I eat my dinner first, please, sir?"

He rolled his eyes like I was the silly one. "Whatever, Astor. Just make it quick. I have a lot of work ahead of me."

I looked over my shoulder to the table where Delilah and her sister were huddled together with their group of girlfriends. I hadn't noticed the sister showing any interest in Charles, so I was pretty sure he was delusional, but whatever. Three Gs was three Gs. If he wanted to waste his money, he was welcome to waste it on me.

· · · · · • · • · · · ·

I didn't find an opening during dinner, but afterward, while people scattered around the resort, many congregating by the fire, I spotted Delilah. The sister was nowhere in sight, Beckett and Luciana were staring deeply into each other's eyes, or whatever they did, and Bella and Felix were in the midst of flirt fighting. That left Delilah alone and ripe for removal.

I wandered over to where she was sitting near the fire, sipping something out of a sparkly pink flask.

"Hey, Dorothy," I cooed.

She tipped her head back, almost smiling. "That isn't charming, you know."

"Who says I want to charm you?"

"I don't know what you want with me." She shook her head. "Thanks for saving me from smashing my face this afternoon. You disappeared before I could say that."

Bracing my hands on the arm of her chair, I bent over her. "That's right, you didn't. Well, you're welcome. I would have stuck around, but it seemed like your man took offense to you being in my arms."

"Not my man, as you know, and so very untrue. He probably thought you were trying to cop a feel."

"Who says I wasn't?" I hadn't been, but I'd inadvertently copped one anyway. There was something to be said for a body like hers. Soft tits pressing into my hard chest. The solidness of her in my arms, plastered against me. It hadn't been bad at all.

She sighed. "Don't be annoying."

"You should make up for being rude by keeping me company while I smoke."

Her eyes flared. "Being rude? What?"

"When you didn't thank me earlier. That was pretty rude."

She hesitated. At the very least, I'd piqued her interest. "Only keeping you company? Does that mean you're not going to share?" She lifted one of her eyebrows, eyes boring into me in challenge.

"You come with me, Daphne, and I'll let you have as much as you want."

She made a funny little grunt. "Never mind. You're probably going to push me in the lake. I'm not interested."

"Not much of a swimmer?"

"I'm an excellent swimmer."

I held my hand out to her. "Come on, Delilah. I won't push you in, and I'll share the spot I found. There's that nature stuff you like."

"Nature you say?" She slipped her warm hand in mine, and I helped her up. "Lead the way, Astor. But if you push me in the lake, I'm taking you with me."

When we'd gotten back from the hike, I'd explored a little since there'd been nothing better to do and had found the boathouse. The doors were locked, but we slipped in via the docks. For some reason, Delilah trusted me to lead her. I had her hand in mine still, pulling her along to the cabin cruiser I'd checked out earlier.

We climbed into it, and I found a few lights so we weren't stuck in the pitch dark. Delilah spun in a circle, then walked the perimeter of the stern, running her fingers along the polished wood and padded leather benches.

I took the time to observe her. It was fucking trite to say she wasn't like other girls, but I was getting that impression. Or maybe she wasn't like the girls I'd been paying attention to. She had this easy way about her. Casually confident. Hell, the fact that she'd chosen to go on the hike despite her friends doing other activities said a lot about her.

It made me wonder why she was choosing to spend any time with me. Surely, she had better options. Not Ivan, obviously, but other non-idiots.

Although, I couldn't think of any who attended school with us besides Beckett, and he was out of the running.

"This is nice," she remarked. "Are we going to be arrested for being in here?"

"I doubt it. You weren't planning on defacing property, were you?"

Her nose scrunched. "Not planning on it, but you never know."

Flinging myself down on a bench, I stretched my legs out then patted the space beside me. "Come here, Darla. Let's have a chat."

She grumbled and shot me a death glare but came anyway, stretching out beside me. We were shoulder to shoulder, but her legs were half the length of mine. I decided not to comment on it. I was already toeing the line with the *D* names. If I went too far, I'd fail at my job and not earn the money I'd already spent in my mind.

I sparked a *J*, and we passed it back and forth, everything quiet except for the sounds of the water lapping against the docks and the distant din of our classmates.

"I can't believe you don't like this," she said.

"Like what?"

She waved her arm in the general direction of the outside. "This. I know you didn't want to come, but how can you look around and not be pleased to be here? I don't get it."

"I don't give a shit about much, but I do care about fencing. I can't enjoy being here because I need to be elsewhere."

"I suppose that makes sense." Her eyes flitted over me. "I'm surprised you're serious about anything."

I tapped the end of her nose. "I'm serious about a lot."

"Hmmm."

That was all she said, and since I had no need to keep the conversation going, I let the subject drop. We smoked, drank a little out of her flask, and stared up at the roof. The boat gently rocked, and

I found myself relaxed not just from the weed but the atmosphere and company too.

This was going to be the easiest three thousand dollars I'd ever made. If I cared about being fair, I'd tell Charles to keep his money, but I wasn't that altruistic.

"Where's your sister? I thought you two were permanently attached."

She let her head loll toward me. "Ev likes her alone time even more than I do. When I left her, she was knitting in our room."

I almost laughed. Good fucking luck to Charles. He was going to have a hell of a time laying on the charm when the girl was locked away for the night. I was almost glad for it. No one could possibly deserve Charles's attention.

"Knitting?" I asked.

"It's her thing." She plucked at her sweater. "She made this."

Delilah's off-white sweater was loosely knit, the neck wide enough it slipped off one shoulder. Now that I was looking, I noticed I could see through the knots or whatever they were called, and it was her skin and black lace peeking through from the other side.

"It's sexy," I told her.

She snorted a laugh. "Are you for real? You can't even see my tits. How is this sweater sexy?"

Reaching across her, I trailed my finger down the line of her neck and shoulder. "This part. It's all soft and creamy. I'm used to you being in a uniform, so you're practically naked."

She swatted me away. "What are you doing?"

"Admiring your sweater." I'd lost all subtlety with the weed I'd smoked, so when I surreptitiously adjusted my hard dick, Delilah noticed.

And laughed.

"Oh my god, do you have an erection?" She curled onto her side in a fit of giggles, which might have been a boner killer, except she ended up on my chest, and my nose caught the rose scent of her hair, sending another rush of blood below my waist.

"Did you really call it an erection, like we're in middle school sex ed?"

She giggled even harder. "What shall I call it, then?"

I draped my arm around her, chuckling softly. "Do you have to refer to it at all? It would be polite to ignore it. I'm not calling out your wet panties."

She shoved at my chest. "They're not wet, Rhys. There's no reason for them to be. You're the one feeling up my creamy shoulders."

"Please." I chuffed at her denial. "Let's not play games, Delilah. We both know you're getting hot for me."

"We know that, do we?" She lifted her head, grinning down at me. "I'm not going to be tricked into proving you wrong, so cut that out."

"Fine. It isn't like I wanted to see your granny panties anyway."

Her eyes flared, and she smacked my shoulder. "You bastard. I've never worn granny panties in my life. And I'm still not going to prove you wrong."

I tucked her hair behind her ear, trailing the backs of my fingers along her jaw. It was amazing how something so soft could make me so damn hard.

"Let me see your tits," I murmured, shooting my shot. What did I have to lose?

Her pink lips pursed, and I braced myself to be told off. But that wasn't what came out of her mouth.

"Let me see yours first."

I didn't need convincing. It took me no time to yank my shirt up. She might've been joking, but she feasted on me nonetheless. Her lips parted as her eyes slid over me, giving me a thorough look.

"Like what you see?" I asked.

She arched a brow, attempting to look imperious, but her flushed cheeks gave her away. "I suppose your effort in the gym has paid off."

I laughed. "Honestly, the flattery is a little over the top. It's getting embarrassing."

"Shut up, Rhys." There was absolutely no heat behind her words.

She took another minute to study me and even slid her finger along the divot in the center of my abdomen. My breath caught as she paused at the waistband of my pants. Proper Delilah was a forward little thing.

Then she sighed and fell onto her back, her fingers gripping the hem of her sweater. "Fine. A deal is a deal."

I never, not in a million fucking years, would have imagined myself here. Not in this position, with this girl. Staring at the biggest, most perfect tits I'd ever seen, barely encased in delicate black lace. Her nipples strained against the sheer material, and all I wanted to do was put my mouth on them to find out if they tasted as juicy and sweet as they looked.

"Delilah."

She lifted her chin. "Yes, Rhys?"

"If you don't want me to touch you, cover yourself up right now. I only have so much gentleman left in me."

She blinked at me, arched her back, and yanked her sweater completely off.

"Control is boring," she rasped.

"You know, Delilah"—I took her tit in my palm and almost came on the spot from how good she felt—"you are really fucking smart. Do people say that a lot?"

She grasped my nape. "Do we have to talk?"

I met her heated gaze. "I need to be clear on what's happening right now."

"I thought it was obvious. Isn't this why you brought me here?"

I cocked my head. "You thought I brought you here to fuck you?"

She nodded. There was nothing in her demeanor that told me she was offended by that notion. Which, frankly, shocked me.

"Which means you agreed to come because you wanted to fuck?"

She nodded again. "Am I wrong?"

I peeled the lace off her tit, exposing the whole ripe thing, making my mouth water. I wanted to bite it, suck it, bury my face in the valley between them until I suffocated. I'd seen my fair share of tits, but none like these. They were luxurious and plush. Almost too rich for my blood, but I'd always strived to obtain the best of the best.

I lifted my gaze to meet hers. "That wasn't my intention, but no, you're not wrong. But if we're not talking anymore, then I need you to say it."

She squirmed under me as I rolled her nipple between my fingers. "I want to have sex with you. Is that clear enough?"

Dipping my head, I licked her pebbled nipple. "Crystal clear."

There were a lot of reasons I should have put a stop to this. Namely, the money, Beckett's warning, and the fact that I wasn't even certain Delilah and I liked each other. But then her mouth was on my throat, her hand was on my dick, and my morals evaporated.

This was happening. Consequences be damned.

CHAPTER EIGHT
Delilah

"Ouch!"

Rhys stilled inside me. "What? Am I hurting you?"

"You're on my hair." I tugged at his wrist. "Can you move?"

He shifted his hand, yanking out a few strands in the process. "Better?"

"Sure."

With that assurance, he proceeded to power into me. Over and over, he advanced and retreated, one hand gripping the back cushion of the bench, the other braced beside my head.

His eyes were glazed, focused somewhere in the distance. Since he wasn't looking at me, I watched him.

I'd sobered up since I'd asked him to have sex with me. And yes, it had been my idea. I'd initiated it. But he'd been right. My panties had been wet, and maybe I'd been eager for a distraction. With Rhys's big talk, I'd assumed we'd have fun and I'd get off.

But, dear lord, this was the most awkward experience of my life. I was just waiting for it to end.

For his part, it seemed Rhys was racing toward the finish line too.

It was a shame, really. His body was beautiful, and he was well endowed. So much so that when he shoved into me in one fast motion, he took my breath away. That might've also been because he'd barely fingered me to warm me up before rolling on a condom and getting to the main event.

After the dismal foreplay, I'd still held out hope, but he'd quickly dashed it.

We hadn't kissed. He wouldn't look at me. His rhythm had been hard and fast from the very start. I hadn't expected magic, but was an orgasm too much to ask for?

I reached between us to help myself along since he wasn't going to take care of me. His movements stuttered, and he bent his head to watch me.

"I'm close," he said through clenched teeth.

"Don't come yet," I told him. "I want to get there too."

His brow crinkled, but he didn't look away. His eyes were fixed on my arm, moving as I rubbed between my thighs. Sweat beaded on his forehead, and his shoulders stiffened.

"Fuck," he grunted.

That was when I knew it was over. His hips slammed into me with breathtaking force, knocking my hand away. I squeezed my eyes closed, waiting for it to be over.

It didn't take long. A few more rapid pumps and he fell over me, groaning beside my ear. Panting breaths heated my skin. At least he'd enjoyed himself.

I liked the weight of him on top of me. He smelled good too. And for a moment, in the beginning, when he'd been kissing my breasts and licking my neck, I'd liked that too. But the rest of it had been bad. So, so bad.

It wasn't like I was a sexpert, but dear god, a virgin would have known that wasn't good sex. Rhys had to know, didn't he?

I didn't know what was wrong with me lately. Why did I keep making these decisions with guys? It wasn't like I was desperate, but something had to be off. This wasn't me.

Eventually, Rhys rolled off me, and I yanked my sweater over my head. When I looked back at him, he'd gotten rid of the condom, pulled his pants up, and sparked up another joint.

Once I was dressed, I snagged it from him. We settled back in our seats like the bad sex had never happened. He didn't mention it, and neither did I.

Which was for the best.

A while later, Rhys walked me back to my cabin. He opened his mouth like he had something to say, but since I didn't want to hear it, I quickly waved and bounded up the steps.

"G'night, Rhys."

He bowed his head. "'Night, Dominique."

......•..•..

Once I was in my pajamas, I crawled into bed with Evelyn. Like she'd done since we were small, she scooted over and blinked at me in the dark.

"You smell different," she whispered.

"I had sex with Rhys."

"Hmmm. This is what Rhys plus sex smells like?"

"I guess. Is it bad?"

She leaned in and sniffed my hair. "No. Just different."

"I'm not ready to talk about it."

Her hand found mine under the covers, and she twined our fingers together. "That's okay. Do you want to sleep here?"

"Yes, please."

"Of course. Don't breathe on me, though."

"I would never."

She squeezed my hand before letting go. "I'm sleepy."

"Go to sleep, then."

"Okay."

....•.•...

I stuck close to my friends the rest of the retreat. Avoiding two boys wasn't easy, but neither seemed inclined to invade a group of girls. Only when we arrived back at our dorms did I breathe a sigh of relief.

Tossing my bag on my bedroom floor, I collapsed on my bed. Within minutes, Bella sauntered in.

"You're bein' strange." She plopped down on my bed. "You haven't begun unpacking yet. Are you gettin' sick? This is very unlike you."

"I know. And no, I'm not sick." I pushed myself to a seated position in time for Luciana to stick her head in the door.

"What's going on?" Luc pushed Bella aside so she could squeeze in beside me on the bed.

Deciding to get this part over with quickly, I blurted out, "I accidentally had sex with Rhys Astor."

Her mouth puckered as she eased into the room. "But...why?"

"I don't know." I slapped my forehead. "It was a really dumb decision."

"Don't hit yourself!" Bella grabbed my hand and lowered it to my leg, keeping hers on top. "Well, do you want to tell us about it? Did you like it?"

I shook my head. "It was bad, B. I don't know if we just don't mesh or all Rhys cared about was getting off, but it wasn't worth the five minutes."

That made Luc cringe. "Five minutes?"

"Please don't tell Beckett. I'd like to forget it ever happened."

Luc made an *X* over her heart. "I promise I won't. Beckett is protective over you, you know. He'd probably murder Rhys for messing around with you."

I blew out a heavy gust of breath. "I was the one who initiated it. If anything, he should murder me for messing around with his best friend."

She held her hands up. "And this is why I won't say a single word. No one's getting murdered."

Bella shook her head. "I'm still tryin' to understand how you ended up with Rhys."

Evelyn walked in and sat at my desk. She was knitting an octopus, her newest project. "Are we talking about the Rhys sex now?"

"Yes. But only for a moment, then I'm moving on with my life."

Bella swatted my knee. "I'm honestly surprised it was bad. I kinda thought Astor had game."

"Why was it bad?" Ev asked.

I covered my eyes. I'd hoped they wouldn't want to know the details, but that had only been wishful thinking. If any of them had slept with Rhys, I'd want the gory details.

"There was this buildup, kind of a spark between us, so I thought we'd get on. But once the clothes came off, it all became very clinical. What I imagine old married couples do when they're trying to make a baby or something. Insert tab *A* to slot *B* and repeat with vigor."

Luc pulled my hands away from my face. "Have you considered that your expectations are slightly skewed since you've only had sex when you were in love?"

"I knew it would be different than it was with Roman, but not terrible different."

Roman had been my boyfriend for over two years. Before that, I'd crushed on him from afar for years. As my older brother's best friend, he should have been off-limits, but Michael wasn't exactly protective. He didn't care if his friends went after his sisters, even though all of them were quite a bit older than us.

Roman had been my first and only, but I wasn't a nun. As heartbroken as I'd been when we'd ended, I'd gotten over him a while ago. I'd kissed boys since we'd broken up. One or two, I'd more than kissed.

Luc pressed her hand to mine. "I guess you can chalk it up to experience and move on."

"That's what I want to do. I'm not having sex with another guy unless we've properly made out first. If he's not a good kisser, then chuck it." I sucked in a deep breath and smiled. "I feel better having gotten that off my chest."

Bella flopped back on the mattress, her legs hanging over the side. "If we're getting things off our chests, Felix and I hooked up. Twice."

Luc and I exchanged a glance. This was no surprise. The two of them had been dancing around each other since forever.

"Oh wow, I can't believe it." I wasn't even pretending to be sincere.

Bella turned her head. "Is that sarcasm I'm hearing?"

From across the room, Ev answered, "She's being sarcastic because everyone knows you and Felix are into each other. The only surprise is it took this long for something to happen. Why *did* it take so long?"

Bella sat up, glaring at Luc and me, even though we weren't the ones who'd spoken. It was no use glaring at Ev anyway. She was too busy knitting to be bothered.

"Everyone knew?" Bella screeched. "*I* didn't know."

Luc shrugged. "It was pretty obvious." Then she threw herself at Bella. "I'm happy for you, girlie. I mean, if this is a good thing. If it's a Rhys and Delilah thing—"

"It is *not* a Rhys and Delilah thing," Bella declared. Then she mouthed, "Sorry," but I didn't blame her for not wanting to be anything like us. "We didn't go as far as them, but what we did was really nice. Really goddamn nice."

"Is he your boyfriend now?" Ev asked.

"No. We're just talkin', feelin' each other out." Bella's cheeks went pink. "But I'm all kinds of giddy to see him. Is it strange I'm gettin' butterflies over Felix Santos when I never did before?"

"I think you may have been just ignoring them, babe," I said gently.

She folded her arms across her chest. "Honestly, guys, you could've mentioned all this to me. It's real convenient you're actin' so smug after the fact, but where were you months ago when I was tellin' Felix to go drown himself in the Pacific Ocean?"

Luc's mouth stretched into a wide grin. I couldn't hold back the giggles.

Ev was the one who finally explained it. "We were waiting for you to wake up. Also, while we're on the topic, I made out with Charles Bloomberg yesterday."

My giggles immediately fell away, and I reared back. "Why on earth would you do that?"

Bella made a gagging sound. "Oh, gross. No offense."

Ev shrugged. "There was no real reason. He was hanging around me and asked to kiss me. I said yes because I couldn't think of a reason to say no. It was fairly pleasant. He doesn't have a slug tongue, and he didn't grope me or anything. I would do it again if the opportunity presented itself."

"But it's *Charles*." Luciana's gaze darted from me to Bella, seeing if we were all on board with her disgust. We were. No question.

I was going to beat him to a bloody pulp if he tried anything more on her. That kid was nowhere near good enough for my sister. The fact that he'd touched her, consensually or not, made me homicidal.

"I know he's abhorrent, but he's a good kisser." Ev went on knitting as if she hadn't dropped a bomb. The truth of the matter was, sometimes, things were as simple as that for her. If she became curious about something, she tried it. I suppose Charles had struck her curiosity in just the right way.

Lucky him.

"Okay, well, there's an upside to all this." Bella grabbed one of my pillows and tossed it at me.

I caught it and squeezed it in my lap. "What's that?"

She grinned at me. "Evelyn managed to make your questionable choice of partners seem not as bad by half."

Laughing, I threw the pillow back at her. "Shut it."

But she had a point. The Kastanos sisters were being really messy.

Now, though, we were back at Savage Academy. It was time to put our uniforms back on and get back to our regularly scheduled program.

That did *not* include Rhys Astor.

I hoped against hope for all our sakes it didn't include Charles Bloomberg either.

Chapter Nine
Rhys

I SWUNG MY POCKET watch around my finger. Once, twice, three times. That was all I allowed myself before slipping it back in my pocket. I knew the time anyway. Class would begin in a few minutes. A small group of us were delaying the inevitable in the hall outside the door. Students streamed by, some in a hurry, some meandering like they had nowhere to be.

I was watching out for one in particular. Bracing myself, really.

Felix knocked into my shoulder, drawing my attention away from the moving sea of bodies. "Are you glad to be back in your jacket and tie, Astor?"

I smoothed a hand over my uniform. "Like being back in my skin after being flayed."

"Dramatic, as always," Beckett drawled. "I know, for a fact, you weren't born in trousers and a button-down."

I raised a brow. "That's only because I wasn't aware it was an option."

I'd lost him. His gaze was laser-focused over my head. There was only one person who had that effect on him. My spine stiffened. If Luciana was coming, that usually meant Delilah was too.

Slowly spinning around, I confirmed what I already knew. Luc and Delilah were making their way down the hall. Luc was grinning at Beckett like they'd been apart weeks instead of a couple hours. For his part, he was equally goofy and googly-eyed. It was disconcerting.

Again, I wasn't salty. I just didn't know what to do with him now that he'd gone all soft.

As Luciana and Delilah closed in on us, I prepared myself for what was to come. I'd have to let Delilah down easy since Beckett was in hearing distance. He wouldn't take kindly to me freezing her out, which was my first instinct.

It was the most effective technique when girls thought hooking up meant more than it did. They simply ceased to exist for me. Of course, by my sophomore year, I'd wised up and stopped dipping in the SA pond. Delilah was the first exception I'd made in a long time. And that was all on her. I'd have been content to get high and maybe peek at her tits. She'd been the one to instigate. So, if her feelings were hurt now that we were back at school and I had no intention of playing house with her, that was on her too.

Luciana threw herself into Beckett's arms. I waited, my hands moving up to catch Delilah when she threw herself at me in the same way.

I'd push her away as discreetly as I could.

She looked good this morning. Her jacket downplayed her curves, and that was a shame, but the entire package was so nicely put together I couldn't stop myself from looking her over. Her ebony hair spilled down her back in thick waves that I knew felt like silk, and her face was made up with skill and precision. Sharp eyeliner, long lashes, full, glossed lips. She'd very obviously taken her time getting ready this morning, and despite myself, I let the knowledge stroke my ego. That had been for me.

My assessment took less than three seconds before I reverted to cool and detached, lest she get the idea

I had any interest. Kicking back, I rested my shoulders on the wall, one ankle crossed over the other.

And Delilah...waved goodbye to Luciana and Beck and kept on walking.

Not even a glance my way. Surely, she'd spotted me. There was no way she hadn't. I'd been standing right beside Beckett.

I watched her disappear down the hall, her pleated skirt bouncing with each step, waiting for her to turn back and coo, "JK." She didn't do anything of the sort. Delilah Kastanos faded from sight while I waited with my dick in my hand.

"What the hell was that?" I muttered.

Maybe she *hadn't* seen me. That was the only logical explanation. Otherwise, she would have said something. Or, at the very least, tried to make eye contact.

Felix frowned. "Talking to yourself, Astor?"

I scowled at him, confusion muddling my mind too much to come up with a clever quip.

"Fuck off, Santos."

Breaking away from the group, I tromped my ass into class and slammed into my seat. My fingers drummed on my desk as I took a few deep breaths, calming myself enough to consider the situation.

This was a good thing.

I didn't *want* Delilah interested in me.

But I couldn't get past wondering why she wasn't.

If this was some kind of game, she wasn't going to win. I wouldn't be chasing her. She could get over herself right now.

Not happening.

I didn't chase anyone, much less a girl I didn't even like. I huffed, tapping my thumbs in a steady beat.

Yeah, she had to be playing me. Trying to get my attention by ignoring me. Or she legitimately hadn't seen me, in which case, I was going to suggest she needed her eyes checked. Not that we'd be talking anymore. Someone should tell her, though.

Just not me.

Now that I'd figured out what had happened, I slid down in my seat. Relaxed.

All was right again.

· · · · • · • · · · ·

Except nothing was right. A few days passed, and the same exact thing happened again and again. Delilah and I had been an arm's length apart multiple times, and she'd breezed by without even glancing my way.

One of my least favorite feelings was when I was missing the joke everyone else was laughing about. Delilah snubbing me was akin to that. I did not get it, and that dug its way under my skin.

I jabbed at the food on my plate with no desire to actually eat it. The confusion this girl had caused had me all out of sorts.

Sure, we'd been little more than strangers before. I hadn't even remembered her name until recently. But I'd been *inside* this girl, and we hadn't had so much as a conversation afterward. I refused to believe this wasn't some sort of scheme.

Girls were emotional. In my experience, they required "the talk," even if the answer wasn't what they'd been hoping for.

It was exactly why I avoided going there with girls at SA. I had no capacity for little talks.

Charles slammed his tray down on the table beside me, startling me out of my thoughts. That gorilla motherfucker had managed to sneak up on me. He wasn't exactly a lithe little ballerina, which went to show how out of it I was.

"I need you again, Astor."

"All right. It makes me uncomfortable, but if you say you need me…" I opened my arms. "Come here, big fella."

He scooted his chair back so fast it screeched against the dining hall floor. A few heads turned, not that he noticed. "What the fuck are you doing?"

I spread my arms wider. "I'm waiting for you to come here, you big lug."

"Why would I do that?"

With a sigh, I dropped my arms. "I assumed you needed a cuddle. Is that not what you meant?"

"Christ." Grimacing, he shoved his fingers through his hair. "You really are a lunatic. If I need a hug, I'll call my granny."

I shrugged. "Your loss."

From the corner of my eye, I caught sight of Delilah and Evelyn winding their way through the tables, trays in their hands. Their resemblance really was uncanny. They were even the exact same height.

Short. Miniature, really.

As always, Delilah's focus was on Evelyn, who had her arm hooked with her sister's. Their heads were together as they spoke to each other on their way to an empty table tucked in the back.

"*That* is why I need you." Charles tapped his fork on the table. "The ugly twin is always glued to Evelyn's side. I made headway at the retreat, but now that we're back, I can't get to her."

I turned back to him. He was looking at Evelyn like a kicked puppy dog. I swore to all that was holy I'd never witnessed Charles Bloomberg so absolutely sprung for a girl.

"You like her."

He nodded. "She's strange and sexy. I want in there."

Okay, not so warm and fuzzy, but for Charles, even admitting he liked a girl as a human being was a big step.

"I hate to tell you, but I have no influence over Evelyn. I'm not sure we've ever exchanged words." I picked up my sandwich and tossed it back on my plate just as quickly.

"I don't want you talking to Evelyn. In fact, do *not* talk to her." His mouth pinched like he was sour over the very idea. "I need you back on the sister. Get her away from my girl."

"Not happening."

Even if I wanted to help Charles—which I did not—it would be awfully hard to get Delilah anywhere when I was clearly invisible to her now. If I had been a caveman like Charles, I could have shoved her in a closet—

Actually, getting Delilah in a closet didn't sound like such a terrible idea. Trapped in a confined space with me, she'd be forced to explain her recent behavior.

"Don't worry. I'll pay you for your efforts. I wouldn't expect you to do the job for free." Charles grew intense, his shoulders bunching as he leaned in closer to me. I hoped no one around us was watching and thinking I had invited this intimacy. The last thing I wanted was to be close to him. "There's another three grand in it for you if you keep her as busy as you can for the next couple weeks."

I sat back in my chair, arms crossed. What he was describing was an impossibility at this juncture, but he didn't need to know that. "Hmmm. I don't know if that's enough for two weeks' worth of labor."

It was unfortunate since I could use the money. The three thousand he'd already given me had been put to good use, but there was always a need for more.

He scowled until his gaze traveled to the corner of the room, presumably landing on Evelyn. Then he went soft all over, resting his chin on his hand like a besotted schoolgirl.

Very fucking disconcerting.

"You're staring," I said.

His scowl came back as he tore his eyes off his target. "I can do five. Just get the ugly twin away from Evelyn."

"You know"—I tossed my napkin onto my plate—"I'm not saying I'm right, but I feel like if you truly want to be with Evelyn, perhaps you ought to cease referring to her sister as 'the ugly twin.' It's just a thought."

He nodded like he agreed, though his frown remained plastered on. "No doubt you have a point. I'll try to remember. If I slip up in front of Evelyn, I'll never get her to spread her legs."

"You actually think you have a chance anyway?"

"I do. She's interested, I can tell. I haven't had a good girl like that, and I just"—his hands balled into tight fists, and the muscles in his shoulders vibrated like he was restraining himself—"need the path cleared, all right? I'll do the rest on my own. Are you in, Astor?"

Even though I loathed to agree to anything this asshole wanted, I knew my answer. The money would pay for...a lot. But beyond that, I had to admit I wasn't going to rest until I got to the bottom of Delilah's nonsense. Which meant I'd have to chase her down and get her alone, clearing the godforsaken path Charles was intent on trampling.

With a sigh, I stuck out my hand. "Fine. You have a deal."

Chapter Ten
Delilah

MR. CHEVALIER, MY SOCIOLOGY teacher, approached me at the end of class, asking me to stay behind. Since this was the first time this had ever happened, I was apprehensive. I racked my mind for a mistake I'd made or something I'd done that could have been misconstrued.

He quickly put my nerves to rest, though, and I kicked myself for jumping to the worst conclusion.

"As you might be aware, I'm the fencing team's coach," he began, and I shook my head. I hadn't known that. "Well, now you know. Our season is about to begin, and we're still missing a team manager. I heard through the grapevine that you managed the field hockey team. Coach Thompkins had nothing but praise for the job you did."

He paused, and I felt compelled to respond. "Thank you. I really enjoyed being the manager. It delighted my little organizer heart."

His smile was placating. "That's good to hear and brings me to my reason for asking you to stay behind. Would you be willing to be the fencing team manager?"

"This is a surprise. If I'm honest, I know nothing about fencing. Can you tell me about the season and what I should expect?"

Mr. Chevalier launched into an explanation of what the fencing season looked like and the time commitment it would be for me. My initial instinct was to turn it down, but I truly didn't have a strong reason to say no other than Rhys Astor being on the team.

And he wasn't a great reason. Returning from the retreat a week ago, things had gone back to normal. We were like two stars, existing in the same space while being light-years apart.

Exactly what I wanted.

Rhys hadn't made our hookup weird in any way, but I still wasn't keen on spending an extended period of time with him. And if I learned anything from my time as the field hockey manager, it was that I wouldn't be able to avoid him.

"Can I think about it?" I asked.

Mr. Chevalier blinked back his evident disappointment. "I—uh. Yes. Of course. This was a lot to spring on you. The thing is, we need someone soon. I can give you a day, then I'll have to try to find someone else."

"A day is fine." I needed that time limit. Otherwise, I might have found myself swinging back and forth forever. "I will let you know my decision tomorrow."

"Thank you, Delilah."

Grabbing my bag, I swept out of class, hurrying so I wasn't late for the next one. In my haste, I missed the lurker outside the door and almost collided with him.

His scent registered before his face.

Fresh rain mixed with cut grass. It shouldn't have been as enticing as it was.

Rhys caught my elbows as I stumbled back a step. The warmth of his hands seeped through the material of my shirt.

"In a rush?" he murmured, too close to me.

"Yes, I am, actually."

Neither of us moved. He cocked his head as if waiting for me to say something. I couldn't really say why my feet weren't carrying me away.

"Where are you going?" he asked.

"Computer lab."

He tipped his head in that direction. "Let's go. I'll walk with you."

"Don't you have class yourself?"

It wasn't much of a protest, and I didn't try to stop him when he fell into step beside me. This interaction would be a test. If we could get from sociology to the computer lab without fighting, I'd strongly consider taking the manager position. I really had enjoyed my time as the field hockey team's manager. I wasn't an athlete, not like Ev and the rest of my friends, but I was more competitive than I cared to admit. Being part of their team had been fun. Watching them kick ass from the sidelines had set my bloodthirsty soul alight and fulfilled my need to take care of people. I missed that, and I was sorely tempted to take Chevalier's offer to regain those feelings.

Rhys lifted a shoulder. "I don't let something as arbitrary as a bell ringing dictate my schedule."

I huffed. "I think it's the school that does that."

"My teachers don't expect me to be on time. If I were to show up before the bell, it would throw them off their game."

"So your tardiness is altruistic."

He bumped my shoulder. "You understand me, Dotty."

I wagged my finger at him. "That is a bridge way, way too far. I doubt you even understand yourself."

He hmphed and slipped his pocket watch from his trousers, rubbing his thumb over the intricate design on the metal.

"One year of AP psych and you're already evaluating me?"

Turning my head, I swept him with my gaze. "You remember we took AP psych together, but you can't remember my name?"

"That's right. I'm not a complete imbecile. I recognize who's in class with me. Remembering names is another step I don't often take because it doesn't matter to me. Though I do remember your name *now*."

"I guess I'm supposed to be honored or something."

He tucked his watch away and raised his empty hand. "You aren't supposed to be anything other than what you are."

That...was unexpected. I found I couldn't think of any way to reply as all the times I'd been told one thing or another was wrong with me and I'd have to change it to be lovable filled my mind. Even though I knew Rhys's comment was offhanded, it struck me deep. It wasn't something I'd been told before. Quite the opposite.

We were three doors from my classroom when Rhys's fingers closed around my wrist, and he tugged me to a stop.

"Are you taking the job?"

My brow crinkled. "What job?"

"As team manager."

Of course he knew I'd been offered it. He was the captain, after all.

"Oh. Well, I haven't decided."

"What will help you make your decision?" he pressed.

There was a freckle above his lip, slightly darker than the rest of them. I stared at it for a moment before meeting his intent gaze.

"I don't know. It was unexpected, so I asked for a day to think about it. It's a big-time commitment."

"It is." He rocked back on his heels but kept his hold on my wrist locked tight. "You should do it. Chevalier will go easy on your grades from here on out if you do."

"That's a pretty enticing incentive." Mr. Chevalier was well known for being a hard-ass when it came to grades. "I'll consider it."

He sighed. "Come on, Delilah. Do it. You know you want to."

I jerked my hand free of his hold and backed away two steps, my lips curving. "Peer pressure doesn't work on me. I said I'll think about it, and I will."

His lips rolled inward as he raked his warm-brown eyes over me. Often, Rhys came across as bored, but right now, there was a mischievous light behind his gaze that made my stomach twist.

"You should come to the gym with me after class," he drawled lowly.

There it was. The reason my guts were in knots. I had known it was coming by his expression, but it still landed like an acid bath.

"Your hints are more like Shakespearean soliloquies. I get it. I do. But the answer is no."

His mouth fell open. "What—?"

I spun on my toe, waving over my shoulder. "Goodbye, Astor."

It shouldn't have stung, but it had. This boy had seen me naked and was telling me to go to the gym. How could I not take that personally?

At least he'd made my decision easy. There wasn't any way I'd manage the fencing team while he was on it. I might not have loved myself every second of every day, but I respected myself too much to deal with Rhys any more than I had to.

· · • • · • • · ·

Ivan tapped on the textbook. "This is good."

"It is. I've written it down."

"Good."

I'd forced myself to continue studying with him as normal, though the truth was, I could have used a break to gather my self-esteem and wits. It wasn't that I'd wanted to end our friendship or study partnership. It was just...I needed some space to recover from his swift yet gentle rejection.

Saying that to him would have required speaking about said rejection, and that wasn't going to happen, so I sucked it up and fell into our routine.

Except it really wasn't the same. Both of us were stilted now, and Ivan was careful not to let any part of his body so much as graze mine.

It saddened me that I'd possibly ruined a friendship by thinking it could have been more. I should've seen the value in having Ivan as a friend. Now that I did, it was looking like it was too late even for that.

Ivan reached over, ruffling my hair, and I jerked away from him before I could stop myself. He shot me a crooked grin, and my stomach twisted.

The happenstance of Rhys walking by our table at that exact moment only made my stomach twist harder. He didn't pause or say a word, but from his winged eyebrow and our fleeting eye contact, he'd seen the whole thing.

Then he was gone, and it was just Ivan and me again, who was staring with his head tilted to one side.

"You don't like when I do that, yet you've never told me."

I pursed my lips. "If you knew I didn't like it, why continue?"

"You haven't always disliked it."

"I must have hidden it better before." I smoothed my hand over my hair. "I'm not a dog, you know."

"I know that." He shook his hand out. "If you were, I'd be bleeding."

"Ha. Very funny."

He studied me in the intense way he did most things, with no care for social norms or any self-consciousness at all. After many thudding heartbeats, his eyes met mine, serious yet kind. "Cheer up, Delilah. Nothing is that bad, is it?"

"You know women love nothing more than to be told to cheer up."

The intensity broke when he chuckled and leaned back in his chair, his hands braced behind his head, legs stretched under the table.

"I will not pet you anymore, and you will stop being sad," he stated as though it were fact.

"I'm not sad." That was the truth. Embarrassed and regretful, but not sad. It wasn't as if I had been in love with him. And now that my feelings had been somewhat exposed, I was well on my way to being over them. But things between us weren't the same, and I wished like hell we could get back to that place of ease.

I sucked in a breath and decided to be honest. "I do have a lot on my mind, though, and I might need some space."

"No." He smiled. "You can talk to me. I'm an excellent listener."

"What if you're the topic I want to talk about?"

His smile dimmed, and the corners of his eyes pinched. "I understand. Then we will not talk. We will study and take notes, as always." He pushed back from the table and rose to his feet. "I need another book. I will be back. Don't move, Delilah."

I patted the table. "I'm not going anywhere."

While he was gone, I was finally able to actually read the passage I'd been staring at for many, many minutes and jotted down a few notes.

Then I jotted down more. Soon, I'd taken notes on both pages, and Ivan hadn't returned. I didn't want to turn the page and move on without him. I scanned the tables surrounding us and the rows of shelves.

I finally spotted him off to the side, perched on the edge of a table. He had a book in his hand, but it seemed forgotten as he nodded to something Veronica was saying to him. Her body swayed forward until she was standing between his knees, and Ivan seemed in no hurry to break away from her.

I'd had enough. He was free to do as he wished, but there was no reason for me to sit around waiting for him while he flirted. I searched myself and realized the burning in my chest wasn't jealousy. It was indignation at being so easily disregarded.

Quietly stacking up my things, I slipped them into my bag and grabbed my phone. Just as I was slinging it over my shoulder, Ivan appeared in front of me again.

"I'm sorry, Delilah. I was held up." He glanced over his shoulder then returned his frowning gaze to me. "That girl somehow found my Spotify and keeps asking me about my playlists."

"Okay." I tugged on the strap of my bag, refusing to tell him it was all right when it wasn't. "I finished taking notes, so I'm going to go. I'll see you around."

He wrapped his fingers around my strap, keeping me in place. "We aren't done. Stay. No more interruptions."

I shook my head. "I told you, while you were gone, I finished. The book is there. You can do the rest on your own like I did."

He let go of my bag and shoveled his fingers through his hair. "I apologize." He really did seem remorseful, but I was too caught up in my own emotions to cater to his at the moment.

"I heard you." I patted his arm to show him there were no hard feelings. And there weren't, not really. "See you."

I made sure not to rush. My head stayed up and my spine was straight all the way out the door. Only then did I let the breath I'd been holding release and allow my shoulders to curl forward.

That wasn't fun. In fact, it sucked.

I had to admit to myself our studying partnership would have to go on hiatus. At least until I could get a handle on my feelings.

"Destiny!"

Oh no. I stopped in my tracks, even though it was the last thing I should have done and turned on my toes, watching Rhys rush toward me. Seeing his auburn hair falling across his forehead and the faint flush in his cheeks brightening his freckles did something to the knot in my stomach. It unfurled enough for me to take a deep breath and regain my composure.

"Destiny waits for no man," I quipped.

He came to a skidding stop a foot away, and the grin stretching his mouth wide made me almost forget the boat experience.

"And yet, there you stand."

I cupped my mouth and leaned closer as if telling him a secret. "My name isn't Destiny, so..."

He snapped his fingers. "Damn. I thought I had it for sure."

My mouth moved without thought, curving into a smile. "Was there something you needed?"

"There was. First, I'm headed to the gym and wanted to double-check you have no interest in going with me."

"You haven't gone yet? I thought you were going after class." Which had ended over an hour ago.

"I was waiting to see if you'd changed your mind. You might have noticed me in the library."

I tapped my chin. "Were you? No, I didn't see you. There was an annoying rodent that kept scurrying by, though."

"Rude, Demetra. So rude."

I made a buzzing sound. "Wrong again."

His smile widened until it was almost just him baring teeth like a wild animal. "Did you change your mind yet?"

"No." My fingers toyed with the buttons on my shirt, and Rhys's gaze homed in on them. "I'm not dressed for the gym. I'm headed back to my room."

In the beat of silence that followed, I realized Rhys wasn't looking at my fingers but what was behind them—my tits. I cleared my throat, and his eyes slowly lifted to mine without a single ounce of shame.

"Fine. I'll accept that answer today. What about the fencing team? Are you going to tell Chevalier yes?"

Just as I prepared to give him my answer, voices came from the direction of the library, and we both pivoted to watch Ivan and Veronica leave together. To be fair, his strides were long and fast, and she had to jog to keep up with him, so it didn't appear he welcomed her company, but the twisting in my gut returned anyway.

Rhys hissed. "Wow. It's got to sting watching him with her." His gaze flicked to mine, and to my surprise, there wasn't even a hint of glee. If my discomfort was entertaining to him, he didn't show it.

"Practices are after class?"

It took him a beat to catch up with my swift change of subject. "Yes. Starting tomorrow. Practice then gym time. Matches on the weekends."

I nodded sharply. "I'll talk to Chevalier."

His eyes swept over me. "You're making the right decision, Delilah." Then he finger gunned me. "Got it right that time, didn't I?"

He wandered off as I shook my head.

What was I getting myself into?

CHAPTER ELEVEN
Delilah

I SPENT THE EVENING studying fencing. When I was finished, I asked Bella into my room to quiz me on the facts.

She looked up from my note cards. "Three types?"

"Sabre, foil, and épée," I answered.

"How many players are on a team?"

"Nine."

"How many bouts in a match?"

"Twenty-seven." I squeezed my eyes shut to remember what I'd read. "Fourteen bout victories constitute a team victory."

"How many touches for foil and épée?"

"Six...no five. It's five."

She tossed the cards down beside her on my bed. "Girl, you've got it. Did you do this kind of prep for field hockey too?"

"Of course I did. I don't want to show up to the matches without any idea what's going on."

What I didn't say was studying fencing had stopped me from questioning whether this was a terrible decision. I knew myself well. If I hadn't given my mind a task, I would have been consumed with indecision.

My phone chimed with a text. Grabbing it from my nightstand, I slid my thumb across the screen.

Michael: *I'm flying into Cali in two weeks. Mom and Dad have asked me to visit you and Evelyn. We'll spend Thanksgiving together.*

I must've made some type of sound because Bella leaned in to read the text.

"Your brother?"

I nodded.

"You don't sound excited."

"We're not close." I tossed my phone aside and fell back against my headboard. I'd worry about his visit another day. I had enough to think about now. "He's the golden child and has always been treated as such. Ev and I were the mistakes, which he's never failed to remind us of."

Her nose scrunched. "Bastard. Why's he even botherin' to show up here?"

I flicked my hand. "My parents asked him to, and he does what they want. It's not out of caring for Ev and me."

"Do you even celebrate Thanksgiving?"

"Not really. Michael doesn't either, so I'm not sure what he's on about."

Her cheeks blazed with heat, and her curls bounced with anger. "You should just leave then. You and Ev can come to Texas with me, and Michael can go screw himself."

"As much as I want to say yes, I can't. That would cause more problems than I want to deal with." I sighed. "It's fine. Michael really is a bastard, but I'm used to him."

"All right. Well, the offer stands." She picked up the stack of notecards. "Let's get back to fencing."

• • • • • • • • • •

With a clipboard on my lap, I recorded times and victories during my first team practice. Along with the reading, I'd watched enough videos on YouTube to have a fair idea of what was happening.

I could also say with assurance Rhys was the star of the team. His specialty was the sabre, which was the fastest event.

It was absolutely breathtaking to watch him. Where he was often in a world of his own, during a bout, his focus was laser sharp. He slashed and jabbed, shuffling forward, scuttling back, so light on his feet it was almost like floating. I felt sorry for his opponent, who really didn't stand a chance against him. At the same time, I felt bad that Rhys didn't seem to be challenged by his teammates.

I found it difficult to watch the others, but it was my job, so I had to.

Someone screamed, making me jump for the hundredth time since practice had begun.

None of the videos had prepared me for the screaming and yelling. At first, I'd thought someone was injured but had quickly learned fencers yelled when their weapon touched their opponent.

In a room where multiple practice bouts were taking place, someone was screaming or shouting at least once a minute, and I jumped every time.

At the end of practice, I walked around the room, checking equipment, then gave Chevalier my notes. Everyone else had gone to shower, but Rhys waited by the door, his helmet tucked under his arm, his hair plastered to the sides of his head.

"How did I do, Darla?"

I rolled my eyes. One of these days, he would surely run out of *D* names and be required to use mine.

"You were fine," I answered.

"Fine?" He sputtered a laugh. "We both know I was more than fine."

"Do we?"

His brow pinched. "Yes, we do."

I bent down to grab my bag and slung it over my shoulder. "I suppose you're good at *one* thing."

His mouth opened then slammed closed. His jaw ticced as he studied me. Rather than standing in awkward silence, I tried to leave, but Rhys blocked the exit, and I truly didn't want to brush by his sweaty body.

"Is there some hidden meaning behind that statement?" he asked tightly.

"I don't know. Do you think there is?"

He exhaled through his nose and leaned into me. "What is it about you...?"

"I have no idea what you mean." I pressed my hand to his chest. "Move it, Astor. I'm done for the day, and you really should consider showering."

With a grumble under his breath, he stepped aside. Slowly. While glowering at me.

I was a few feet down the hall when he called after me. "You really have no interest in me, do you?"

I spun around to find him still in the doorway, considering me. I shrugged. "Is there a reason why I should?"

He stalked toward me, his free hand flexing at his side. I thought about trying to escape, but it was pointless since he was in front of me in seconds.

"The boat," he stated.

My brows popped in surprise. "Yes...?"

"You act like it didn't happen." His frown was so deep he was probably in danger of it becoming permanent.

"I'm not sure how I should be acting. I'm only being myself." My fingers wrapped around my bag's strap. "If there's nothing else, I'll see you tomorrow."

Without waiting for a response, I spun on my toes and strode away.

· · · • · • • • · ·

I'd walked in on a nightmare. Charles Bloomberg in my tiny living area, his arm draped over Evelyn's shoulders. And she...was leaning into him as though she enjoyed his company.

Ugh.

My sister was wonderful on many, many levels, but it couldn't be denied she had awful taste in men. She liked them rude, big, and annoying. I always thought it was because she was able to read people with those types of personalities more easily, but I'd never asked, and I wasn't certain even she knew what drew her to them.

Her taste wouldn't have bothered me, but she had a tendency to let herself be run over, and that, I wouldn't stand by and watch. Not again.

"Hello."

Charles lifted his head from nuzzling Evelyn's hair. For a split second, pure disdain dripped from his every pore, but he masked it quickly, smiling at me like he was happy to see me.

"Hey there, Delilah," he sang to the tune of the iconic song that had haunted me since my first breath.

I forced myself not to roll my eyes while Ev took care of things for me.

"Delilah has heard that thousands of times. She doesn't find it amusing."

Charles chuckled, and the look he gave her was nothing but sweet. It made me consider whether I was wrong about him, at least partially.

"I bet. People like to call me Charlie Brown or Charles Manson, so I get it." He shot me a wide grin. "That won't happen again."

"Thanks." I brought my bag to my room but didn't stay in there like I normally would. Charles might have been turning on the charm, but I wasn't convinced. I sat down in the armchair diagonal from them and pressed my hands to my thighs. "What are you up to?"

Another look of disdain flashed behind Charles's friendly expression, there and gone so fast, I could have almost convinced myself I'd imagined it. "Shouldn't you be at fencing practice?"

"It's finished."

Evelyn straightened, wiggling her shoulders with enough force that Charles had to take the hint and remove his arm or wind up looking like the utter asshole he was.

"Tell me everything." She leaned forward, her elbows on her knees, chin on her fists. "Was there very much blood?"

"Oodles of it," I told her.

"Oh, someone must have hit an artery. Did they make you mop it up in the end?" she asked in all seriousness.

"Yes, and they only gave me one small washcloth, so it took ages."

Charles's head whipped back and forth between us. "What do you mean? There's no blood in fencing."

Poor Charles had never been subject to my and Ev's games. When we got going, there was no stopping us.

Charles had never looked so confused, and I was in no hurry to relieve him. "Have you been to a match lately? If the real thing is anything like practice, there's blood spraying everywhere. I had to change my blouse; it was soaked with gore. I'm not certain I'll ever be able to get it clean again."

He rubbed his oversized face. "Are you joking? I can't tell if you're joking." He peered at Ev. "You're being funny, right?"

She blinked at him, her eyes wide. "Do you believe it's fair that Delilah was made to clean up oodles of blood with only a washcloth? I do not."

He huffed and, like a flash flood, went from calm confusion to angry indignation in the blink of an eye.

"You're fucking with me, and I'm not amused." He shot to his feet. "I don't find it fucking funny being made to be the butt of the joke. I expected better from you, Evelyn."

The sneer he directed at me said he'd expected nothing less from me.

He stormed out of our suite, slamming the door so hard a picture frame almost fell off the wall. Evelyn's hands flew to her ears, and her eyes slammed shut. Sudden, loud noises were her kryptonite, and I hated that she was with a guy who'd failed to notice or simply didn't care.

At least he was gone.

CHAPTER TWELVE
Rhys

MY BEDROOM DOOR WAS practically torn off the hinges. Charles loomed in the doorway like an angry gorilla.

"You're not doing your job," he seethed.

I glanced up from my laptop. His face was mottled red. Sweat dotted his brow. Chest heaving, veins standing out in stark relief on his temples and neck, he appeared seconds away from stroking out.

I raised a brow. "What's that now?"

Of course, I knew what he meant. There was only one *job* I'd done for him, and it killed me to do so. But I wasn't a trained monkey who would respond to his every tantrum, even with him holding five Gs over my head.

He stalked into my room, kicking the door shut behind him. I set my laptop aside and rose from my bed. If he was going to come at me, I wasn't going to make it easy.

"The ugly bitch is always around. You're supposed to be keeping her busy, Astor."

"We've done this before, but let's try it again in smaller words." I held up a finger. "That's enough of you calling her ugly. It sounds ridiculous, and we both know it's a gross inaccuracy. Wait, that was still too big. You're wrong. Extremely wrong." Two fingers went up. "I have been keeping her busy. She's the manager of the fencing team now. If you can't work with the time I've afforded you, I don't know what to tell you. I can't tie her up. If she wants to go back to her room, I let her."

Although...the idea of tying Delilah up didn't sound so bad. Maybe then I'd be able to get a grasp on what the hell was up with her unexpected behavior. As the days passed and she interacted with me like normal, I only became more confused.

It was beginning to dawn on me that she truly wasn't waiting to be chased. This was no game. The girl wanted nothing to do with me, and that befuddled me.

I did not like not knowing what was happening around me.

But that was an issue for another time. First, I had to rid myself of the blustering gorilla invading my space.

"Fuck off." Charles scrubbed his face with both hands and violently shoved his fingers through his hair. Then he peered at me through narrowed eyes. "There's no blood in fencing, is there?"

I sputtered a laugh. "No. Why would you ask that?"

His hands balled into fists. "I fucking knew they were messing with me. The ugly one, I expect it—"

I wagged a finger. "Ah, ah, ah. We talked about this. There's no ugly one."

His nostrils flared. "And you care what I call her ... why?"

I shrugged like I didn't care, even though it rankled me more than it should have. "If you want to sound stupid, continue."

His breathing was labored and shallow. "Fine. *Delilah* is a bitch, so I expect her to act like a bitch. But Evelyn is sweet. Why the hell would she play along with her bitch-ass sister?"

I cocked my head, amused, wishing I'd been there for this particular conversation. "Perhaps you don't know Evelyn as well as you think you do."

"Maybe. Or maybe her fucking sister is too much of an influence on her." His sneer was ugly and tinged with violence. "If you want to see that money, get her out of my way."

The words were on the tip of my tongue. *Take your money and shove it up your hairy asshole.* But memories of my stepfather combing through my account, demanding receipts for every dime I withdrew, were too bitter to forget.

"What was this fifty dollars used for?"

I tried to come up with a plausible explanation, but I wasn't fast enough on my feet.

I wanted to tell him my favorite lady of the night had been running a Black Friday deal and I could give him her name if he liked. But Preston's sense of humor wasn't nearly as refined as mine. The last time I'd made such a joke, my ears had been ringing for days.

Ol' stepdad wasn't just a money man—he had a mean bitch slap and wasn't afraid to use it.

This time, I got lucky. Instead of my face, Preston slammed his hand down on the table, rattling the china my mother had set out for our lovely family dinner. She remained quiet, as always, her hands clutched beneath her chin, her eyes imploring me to have a good answer.

"I know exactly where it went. You're a sneaky little shit and always have been. If I find you withdrawing cash again, I expect to see the receipts for what you spent it on. Otherwise, you'll be cut off. Don't test me."

I had to swallow down my hatred and nod in agreement. I had to bide my time. Just a few more years, and I'd be out from under this asshole.

Suck it up.

Play the game.

It's almost over.

A little longer. Just a little longer. One more payment, then I'd tell Charles to go fuck a railroad spike.

"I'll see what I can do," I gruffed. "Now, remove yourself from my room."

He huffed and puffed, but when he failed to blow my little house down, he exited. Slamming my door because, of course, it wasn't like he could help himself. Neanderthal gonna Neanderthal and all that.

· · · • · • · · ·

I fell into step with Delilah after practice. No doubt she was headed back to her dorm to cockblock Charles. The idea delighted me, but I had things to discuss with her before I could let her go.

Holding the door open for her, she stepped outside, and I followed, taking my place beside her.

"What do you think about fencing?"

She snorted softly and tucked her thick mane behind one ear. "It's not as boring as I thought it would be. I could do without all the screaming."

"It's invigorating."

"It's obnoxious." Her lips curved into a small smile. "But I accept that some things are the way they are and won't change just because I don't understand them."

"Did you know if a fencer screams convincingly enough, a judge will award them the point for the touch when it's unclear who touched first?"

"I read that. It seems like a flawed system."

Spinning around, I walked backward so I could look at her. There was no artifice in her expression. She wasn't shitting me. She'd really read about fencing.

"You did research?"

"I did." Her eyes raked over me. "Don't you need to shower?"

I plucked at my sweaty T-shirt. "I will. I didn't imagine you would have waited around for me to hose myself off."

"You're right. Why would I?"

This girl continued to baffle me. Her reactions didn't make sense to me. I was aware I didn't come off as likable, but hell, she'd let me inside her. She'd *initiated* it. I would have assumed that meant she'd liked me on some level, but...no.

She didn't.

And maybe I was a glutton for punishment, but I had to know why.

Reaching out, I wrapped my fingers around her forearm and steered her off the path. She must have been stunned at the sudden change in course because she allowed me to guide her onto the grass and pull her down with me, so we were sitting in the shade of a tree.

The grass hitting her legs seemed to have woken her up. She snatched her arms away from me, tucking them close to her middle. "What's happening right now?"

"We're going to talk."

"We *were* talking. Now, we're...I don't know. What is this, Rhys?"

"Tell me why you're acting like we didn't have sex."

Her brow dropped, and she blinked hard. "Is this how you behave with girls you've had sex with? Absconding with them until they answer your questions?"

"No," I snapped. "It isn't how I act. That's why this is so fucking frustrating."

She pulled her bag over her shoulder like she was preparing to leave. "I don't know what to tell you. Why don't you tell me what you want me to say?"

My hand darted out, snatching her bag from her shoulder so she didn't get any ideas about leaving before I was satisfied. "I told you what I want you to say."

Her lips parted to release a heavy sigh. She eyed the bag but must have realized I wasn't letting it go, so she didn't try to fight for it. "This doesn't have to be a big deal. It was a one-time thing. Why must we rehash what happened?"

"You're telling me, if I offered, you wouldn't want to fuck again?"

Her cheek ticced. Her eyes slid to the side. "Yes. That is what I'm telling you."

There was something she wasn't saying, and I had to know what it was. She'd been on my mind since she'd walked past me in the hall after the retreat, and I needed her to get it out. Once I solved the puzzle that was Delilah, I would move on.

Well...as soon as fucking Charles deemed the job was done.

I took her chin between my fingers, turning her back to face me. Even then, her eyes wouldn't quite meet mine. A puzzler, indeed. "Why not, Delilah? What's so distasteful about me that you'd go there once but not again?"

She jerked her face from my grip, and her little plush mouth turned down into a frown.

"Did you have a good time, Rhys?"

"I—" I flashed back to her soft and pliant beneath me, warm pussy sucking me in, the scent of her, the sounds she made. "I came, so yeah. I had a good time."

Her lashes brushed the top curve of her cheeks as she slowly blinked. "Your needs are simple, huh?"

"Sure. I never claimed to be a complicated guy." I snagged her chin again, grazing the tips of my fingers along the silky skin on the underside of her jaw. She was answering questions with more questions. It was infuriating, but I kept my cool, stroking that impossibly smooth patch and using every ounce of my patience. "Did you have a good time?"

Her nose scrunched. "I'd rather not speak about this anymore. Can we leave it at that? It happened, now it's over, and I'm not interested in going there again."

She reached for her bag, but I held it behind me. No way was she leaving now.

"No, we can't leave it at that. Obviously. *Why* don't you want to go there again?"

"Drop it, Rhys. Honestly, I don't—"

"Tell me. Tell me, and I'll drop it."

"Stop."

"I will when you open your mouth and use your big girl words. That's not too much to ask, is it?"

She shot to her knees and wound around me, trying to snag her bag. I was faster. My arm shot out and banded around her waist. I yanked her down so fast she ended up sprawled in my lap, her tits pressed to my chest, her face inches from mine.

"You've lost your mind," she hissed.

"Because you're driving me mad, woman. Just talk."

"No!" She shoved at me, but I held her tight. This close, I caught her scent with ease. Forgetting myself, I leaned in and nuzzled the side of her hair. *Roses.* If I thought she'd tell me, I would've asked her what shampoo she used so I could buy some and huff it like an addict.

"Are you sniffing me?" She squirmed, and my dick reacted. How could it not?

"Yes. Are you going to talk?"

"No." She wiggled back and forth. "Stop it, Rhys. Just forget it."

"I will when you tell me." My nose slid along hers. "Tell me why you don't want to go there with me again. Explain it to me like I'm five."

"Stop." She shoved my shoulders. "You don't want me to, I promise you."

"Yes, I do. That's why we're here."

I would rip all my hair out if she didn't start talking. I couldn't remember a time when I wanted something more than I did right now. If I could have pulled the words from her mouth, I would have.

"No." Her lips clamped shut.

"Yes." I dug my fingers into her side to test if she was ticklish. She immediately folded in half, releasing a pained sound that was half laugh, half yelp. "Oooh, you *are* ticklish."

I dragged my fingers along her ribs, tickling her and torturing her. She was a worm on a hook, jerking back and forth, laughing, scrambling to get away, but caught all the same.

"Tell me," I whispered beside her ear.

"I won't." She arched, tears leaking from her eyes as I found a new spot on the dip of her waist. "Rhys, *please*..."

"I'll stop as soon as you tell me."

She bucked and cried, even though I was going light on her. I had no intention of hurting her. In fact, the barest graze of my fingers in certain spots turned her inside out. I would have been laughing with her if I wasn't so pissed off at how utterly stubborn she was.

"No, no, no!" Her head whipped back and forth as she jiggled on my lap. My dick was throbbing behind my zipper. I was being tortured as much as she was.

"Yes, Delilah. Tell me why, and I'll let you go."

She squeezed her eyes shut. Her face was flushed. Tears were streaming down her cheeks in earnest.

"It was bad, okay!" She turned her face away from me. "It was so, so bad."

It took me a second to register what she was saying. When I did, my hands fell to my sides, freeing her. She scuttled backward immediately, falling off my lap and onto the grass.

Her eyes opened and met mine. She should have been angry at me for holding her hostage, but that wasn't what I saw. Remorse filled her gaze.

"Don't look at me like that," I gritted out.

She slid a hand over her face and through her hair. "You shouldn't have made me say that. I didn't want to."

My dick died a quick death as I exhaled heavily through my nose. "Do you care to explain yourself?"

"Rhys, honestly, I've said enough."

"No, you haven't. You can't make a sweeping statement like that and not elaborate. Why was it bad?"

Her stare was assessing, scanning over me. "I'm not going to make a list for you, but—"

I barked a laugh, but there was no humor in it. "There's a list? Oh please, enlighten me."

She shook her head. "This isn't going anywhere useful." Then she climbed to her feet and swiped her bag from beside me before I could stop her.

I hopped up, needing to regain some semblance of the upper hand. It wasn't every day I was told I was bad at sex. Then again, I avoided post mortem conversations like the plague because I didn't care.

"I apologize that I'm not the lovemaking type, Delilah. If that's what you were expecting, you were barking up the wrong tree. But I—"

She rolled her eyes. "Come on. I don't think even the most delusional girl would expect anything close to love from you. Pardon me if my expectations are too high with thinking having an orgasm should be the bare minimum in a sexual experience. I don't need hearts and roses, but being reduced to nothing more than a Fleshlight isn't really an experience I care to replicate."

Blood drained from my head so quickly that I forgot what the word meant. "Fleshlight?"

She flicked her hand carelessly. "Pocket pussy. Whatever guys call fake vaginas they use to masturbate with."

"*Fuck*," I spat. "Are you shitting me?"

"Not shitting you. I wish you hadn't forced me to say this." She heaved a sigh. "I'm going to go now. I hope we can pretend this never happened."

She marched off, leaving me there like roadkill.

But that was my fault. I'd asked to be run over, and she had done it with panache.

CHAPTER THIRTEEN
Delilah

TODAY WAS THE FIRST match of the fencing season. We'd be taking a coach bus an hour away. Along with Mr. Chevalier, I made sure all our equipment was loaded and checked everyone off as they boarded.

And yes, I dallied.

I planned to sit at the front of the bus by myself. There were only eighteen members on the team, so it shouldn't have been a problem.

Mr. Chevalier gestured for me to climb on the bus ahead of him, and since I couldn't find another reason to delay, I trudged up the stairs.

I truly didn't know why I was so apprehensive. Rhys had left me alone the last couple days, though I'd caught him looking at me with a deep frown several times. It reminded me of the way Evelyn stared at people she was trying to decipher.

To my dismay, the front seats of the bus were claimed by gear bags. I walked down the aisle, and there was either a person in a seat or more bags. Every time I stopped and asked someone if I could sit with them, they shook their head and told me they needed the space.

I was left with no choice but to go to the back of the bus, where Rhys Astor was taking up the last two rows.

"Can I have one of your many seats?" I asked.

He took his time looking up from his phone and even more time removing his headphones. "What was that, Darlene?"

I put on my sweetest smile. "May I move one of your bags so I can sit down?"

He gave an unhurried glance at the seats surrounding him then met my eyes, shaking his head. "No. My stuff stays where it is." He patted the space right beside him. "I can make room for you right here, though."

"Come on."

He cocked his head. "Take it or leave it."

I turned back to the front of the bus. Chevalier was kneeling on his seat, tapping his watch to tell me to *hurry up, time's a-wastin'*. With a huff, I gave in since I was out of options and marched to the open seat. Digging my earbuds out of my bag, I crammed them in my ears and plopped down beside Rhys, squeezing my legs together so our thighs didn't touch.

He had no such qualms, spreading his long legs until his was nearly on top of mine.

We were on the road in minutes, and Rhys hadn't tried to interact with me in any way, so I began to relax. Florence + The Machine played through my earbuds. I closed my eyes for a moment, my mouth moving with the lyrics of my favorite song.

I was never unaware of Rhys beside me, his leg subtly bouncing against mine. The faint scent of his cologne. Each time he moved, reached for something or shifted. Rhys wasn't one to be still.

Without warning, one of my buds was plucked from my ear, and Rhys's head leaned against mine, the stolen bud now firmly in his ear.

"What are you doing?" I whispered above the music.

"Just curious what you're listening to."

"You could have asked."

"I could have. You're right." He tapped my lips. "Quiet now. This is my jam."

"You lie."

"I wouldn't lie about my love for Florence Welch." He tapped my lips again. "Now, shush, you."

I couldn't find it in me to argue. So, even though it was strange, we sat like that for the rest of the drive. Every once in a while, Rhys would turn to peer at me, then he'd settle again, his head against mine.

When the bus pulled into the lot of the opposing team's school, he reached across me to tap my phone, turning the music off. In the sudden silence, I gasped a soft breath. Rhys leaned forward, positioning himself almost in front of me.

His hand darted out, cupping the side of my face. At least, that was what I'd thought he was doing before my earbud was slipped from my ear and placed in my hand with the one he'd stolen on top.

His wicked lips quirked. "Never knew I was a dancer 'til Delilah showed me how."

My stomach swooped. He'd quoted Florence to me. Not even a song we'd listened to, but the only one with my name in it.

Why did Rhys Astor have to have this one extremely appealing quality that made me want to forget all the others?

With a low chuckle, he patted my shoulder. "Wish me luck, Delilah."

I cleared my throat and attempted to gather my scattered wits. "Is there a fencing equivalent to 'break a leg'? Is it 'get stabbed many times'?"

He snorted softly and fell back on his seat. "I haven't heard that one, but I'll keep it in mind during my bouts."

I frowned at him. He was so...shifty. His hands rubbed along his jiggling thighs, jaw sliding back and forth. "You can't be nervous."

His brow popped. "I can't be?"

Everyone else had started to get off the bus, so I hopped up, grabbing my bag and one of his. Rhys plucked it right off my arm before I could even take a step, shaking his head like I was a naughty puppy for even trying to carry his things.

I made my way up the aisle with Rhys on my heels. We came to a stop to let others off, and he curved his body around mine, bringing his mouth beside my ear.

"Why can't I be nervous?"

Goose bumps broke out along my neck and shoulders where his warm whispers touched.

"You know how good you are," I murmured. "Don't be coy."

He hmphed. "Ah, that's right. I'm good at *one* thing. I remember now."

I tipped my head to the side, my cheek almost grazing his nose. "You are. I doubt you've ever lacked confidence in that area."

"I don't know. Maybe I've always thought I was decent, but in reality, I have no clue what I'm doing."

I raised my shoulder. "You have demonstrable proof that isn't true. I saw your record. You're good, and I think you know that."

"Hmmm. Maybe."

And then, out of nowhere, he dragged his tongue up the side of my neck and over my cheek. I shivered and jerked away out of instinct. Not because it felt bad. By rights, I should have been disgusted, but I wasn't. Quite the opposite. My knees went weak, and I had to clutch the top of the seats on either side of me, so I didn't fall.

Rhys nudged me from behind. "Get a move on, Darcy. I have a match to win."

· · · • · • ◦ • · · ·

I wised up for the drive home, nabbing a front seat on the bus before everyone else boarded. When Rhys passed me, he shook his head and laughed.

I didn't know what he thought was so funny. I'd beat him at his own game.

Or so I thought.

When Mr. Chevalier climbed on, he took one look at me and jerked his chin. "Back in your original seat, Ms. Kastanos."

My brows slammed down over my eyes. "But...why? I'm happy to sit in the front."

A fencer across the aisle from me leaned over. "Team rules. If we win the first match, everyone stays in the same seats the rest of the season."

I sputtered. That was impossible. "No. But I—"

Chevalier held up his hands, cutting off my argument. "What can I say? Athletes and their superstitions. You can't beat them."

No wonder Rhys had laughed at me. He knew I'd be joining him in the back of the bus, and he hadn't had to put forth any effort to make it happen.

I allowed myself a moment of resignation, then I sucked it up and made my way to the back of the bus as if it had been my idea the whole time. No shame or hesitancy. If Rhys thought he'd defeated me, he'd gloat, and that would make all of this much worse.

He patted the seat next to him. "Nice to see you, princess. Your throne awaits."

I gave him a pinched smile and sat down. He immediately went into full manspread mode, taking up all his space and half of mine.

I dug my earbuds out, but before I could put them in my ears, Rhys snatched them from my hand and tucked them in the pocket of his jacket.

"What are you doing?"

He twisted, putting his back against the window so he was facing me. "How do you know it wasn't you who made it bad?"

"What?" My mouth fell open and closed. There was no question as to what he was referring to, but I couldn't quite believe he'd brought it up this way.

"How do you know it isn't your fault it was bad? Why am I getting the blame?"

I blinked at him. "Do you truly want to discuss this?"

"Obviously." He rested his hands on his stomach, idly tapping against the flat plane.

"And if I don't want to...?"

"I don't take an interest in many things. I'm not known for dropping subjects once I do. You can be sure I'll keep asking until you've answered."

I had a feeling that was the case. He wouldn't just let the awkward die a merciful death.

"You accused me of expecting to be made love to, and that simply isn't true. I knew what it was we were doing, Rhys. It didn't mean anything to either of us. A bit of fun to pass the time. Well, it started as fun. Then it wasn't."

His brows fell heavy over his intense eyes. "Explain."

"You're so demanding."

"This situation calls for it." He held his hand out. "Go on."

Puffing up my cheeks, I blew out a slow breath. He wanted this, so he was going to get the truth. "We didn't kiss. You avoided my mouth, actually. I could have looked past that because maybe you're like *Pretty Woman* and never kiss on the mouth."

A deep bark of a laugh cracked between us. "Are you comparing me to a movie whore?"

I grinned. "If it walks like a duck..."

"Point taken." He eyed me for a moment as his amusement faded. "Keep going. Tell me what else I did wrong."

"You asked for this. Don't act like I'm attacking you."

"Fine." His fingers drummed on his stomach. "Please, continue."

I decided to blurt out the rest so we could be done with this and move on with our lives. Maybe Rhys would take this as constructive criticism and do better with the next girl.

My stomach clenched at that thought, but I refused to acknowledge it.

"There was no foreplay. You barely touched me then you were slamming into me. And once you were inside me, it was like a race to the finish line. When I tried to get myself there, you didn't slow down or wait for me. You just kept going without any consideration for me. That would have been okay if you'd tried to help me out after, but once you got off, it was finished."

He watched me, unmoving, barely blinking. I should have stopped there, but I was on a roll.

"Those things had made it bad on their own. But the way you refused to look at me at all made me feel like a sex toy—and not in a sexy way. I felt like a receptacle. It was shit, Rhys. I was counting the seconds until it was over. I can't imagine it was much fun for you. How could it have been? Or maybe you have simple needs. Give you a warm puss—"

His hand covered my mouth. "That's enough. I've heard what you had to say."

My tongue darted out to lick his palm, but he didn't budge, only peering at me harder.

"I can't argue with any of your points. That night wasn't my finest form. Which is why I'm putting in a request for a second chance." He slowly slid his palm down to my chin. "Give me a second chance."

I giggled at his audacity. He truly was a lunatic. "Why on earth would I do that?"

"There is no way I'm letting you believe for the rest of your life that performance was my best. That's unacceptable."

There was no jest in his expression or words. This boy was serious.

"Rhys, please. This is silly."

"I don't think so. I've never been so serious about anything in my life."

"That's odd. I hope you're exaggerating."

He let go of my chin to shove his fingers through his hair. "Maybe I am. I can't think straight right now. I just won my first match of the season, and I could give a shit. This is the only thing I can focus on."

I wrinkled my nose. "Why would I agree to let you use me to get yourself off again? I can't see what's in it for me."

"Tell me what you want. Show me what would make it good for you. I'll do it."

I stared back at him. The strange thing was, my mind was just as scrambled as his. I should have said no without a second thought, so why was I hesitating?

"Hypothetically speaking only, before I'd let your knob near me again, you'd have to prove you're even capable of not being selfish."

"Okay." He nodded. "Hypothetically, how do I do that?"

"Do all the things you skipped the first time: kissing, touching, fingers, mouth..."

"Kissing, touching fingers...yes. I'm in."

"This is all hypothetical." I poked his hand. "And you forgot mouth."

He glanced away. His jaw ticced twice. "That isn't something I've done."

I gasped. "You're kidding. Why haven't you?"

"I'm not a whore about kissing, but I suppose I am about that. I've never been inclined to French kiss a pussy."

"Too personal?"

"Yes. The idea of getting down on my belly with my face between a girl's thighs has never appealed to me. Maybe it's because I was with the wrong girls." His nod was sharp and slight. "I will on you, though. You can teach me exactly how you like it."

"Why on me?"

He lifted a shoulder. "Because I know you're not going to fall in love with me when I eat your pussy so good you don't remember you have legs, much less how to use them."

My thighs instantly clamped together. "Big words for someone who didn't come close to getting me off the first time."

"I wasn't dedicated to the job then. Now, it's about pride, Delilah." He canted his head. "Besides, don't you think it's your responsibility as a woman to send me out into the world well trained?"

"I would roll my eyes, but I would most likely injure myself from doing it too hard."

He took my hand in his, bringing it to his mouth. "I'm committed to this endeavor. I won't ask to fuck you until I've mastered the art of making you come. You'll be my teacher, and I'll be your attentive student."

I shook my head. "I'm busy."

"You aren't too busy for me to lick your pussy."

"You're ridiculous."

"No, I'm determined. Think how jealous ol' Ivan will be when he finds out I'm making you come on a regular basis."

"I have no interest in making Ivan jealous."

"Sure."

"I don't. And hypothetically, if I were to say yes, I wouldn't want anyone finding out."

"Ashamed of me?"

A little. Yes. Maybe. I don't know.

"I'm private, Rhys."

"I am too. Have you heard any girls talking about hooking up with me? Or vice versa?"

I thought about it but couldn't recall rumors or whispers. And girls around SA would definitely be talking about Rhys Astor treating them like a pocket pussy.

"No. I can't say I have."

"That's because I don't fuck with SA girls." He nibbled along my knuckles then the flat of his tongue licked between my index and middle finger. "I made an exception for you, Delilah, and I would like to keep making an exception for you until I get it right."

"I don't understand why. As you've said, you've gotten along fine until now. Other girls obviously don't mind being treated as your receptacle."

"Hmmm." He tugged me closer to him until my chest was flattened against his. "You seem to have a misconception of me, and that's probably my own fault. I don't stick my dick in anything that moves. I'm too selective for that type of fuckery."

"You weren't a virgin before me."

Please, please, please tell me he wasn't a virgin.

He chuckled dryly. "No. Not a virgin. Although, apparently, I could pass for one."

I shuddered with relief. "Thank god. The last thing I want is your flower."

He burst out laughing. "Don't worry. I gave my flower away at the ripe age of fourteen."

"So young."

He raised a brow. "How old were you?"

I rolled my lips between my teeth, but he kept staring at me until I told him.

"Fifteen."

Another laugh. "Not much older than I was, huh?"

"Not much. That seems like ancient history now." Three years ago, to be exact. But who was counting?

He nodded. "For me as well. A lifetime ago. I'd rather focus on the future, which will involve me being under your tutelage."

"Hypothetically."

"Sure."

"I still don't see what's in this for me."

He licked between my fingers again. "If you teach me right, several orgasms and the pride of a job well done."

"I want to say no. This is absolutely nuts." But my thighs continued to press together, trying to ease the ache between them. There was no reason for me to be turned on. Rhys had proven to be a selfish, terrible lover. A part of me believed his determination, though. And since I'd already gone there with him once, it wouldn't do any harm to go there again. I wouldn't be adding an unwanted notch to my proverbial bedpost, and it wasn't like I was going to fall for him.

No, no. This was too crazy to contemplate.

He circled his finger in front of my forehead. "I see your mind working. You're thinking about it, aren't you? It's enticing."

"Just because I'm thinking about it doesn't mean I'll say yes. It's more than likely I'll say no."

His nose twitched, then his eyes drifted to my mouth. "Make out with me. Right here, right now."

A laugh slipped out of me. "What? Are you mad?"

"Yes. You've driven me mad. This is an unprecedented situation, and I won't rest until I'm on the road to a resolution. Let's kiss. That will be a start."

I shoved him away with less force than he deserved. "I'm not kissing you on the back of a bus with the rest of the fencing team rows away."

He sighed, his head falling back against the rest. "I don't know why you have to be so difficult. No one is looking. I saw you pressing your legs together, so I know you're into this, as much as you try to deny it."

"You've been speaking about eating my pussy. Naturally, she woke up and took notice."

His mouth curved into a sly grin. "You keep delighting me. I think you're a fucking firecracker, Delilah Kastanos."

I smiled back. "Thank you." Then I tapped his lips the way he'd tapped mine earlier. "But I'm still not making out with you on the bus."

"Tease."

"Maybe." I snatched my earbuds from his jacket pocket. "It's quiet time now. I have a lot to think about."

"Ugh, fine." He stole one of my earbuds back and tucked it in his ear. "What are we listening to?"

"Whatever I want."

A moment passed, then his mouth was grazing my jaw. "Exactly, Delilah. Whatever you want."

I suppressed a groan. But barely.

If he kept doing things like that, it was going to be a struggle to remember all the reasons I should've been saying no.

CHAPTER FOURTEEN
Rhys

I HAD A VISION I couldn't get out of my head. Delilah, a few years postcollege, out for a drink with her sophisticated girlfriends. On the second or third glass of wine, someone would bring up sex, as was wont to happen in those situations, if movies and TV shows could be believed. The subject would teeter to bad sex, and they'd trade stories. Delilah would remember this guy from boarding school. Someone she hadn't thought about for years. She'd tell them about what went on on the boat, and they'd laugh and titter with sympathy.

She wouldn't remember anything else about me. In her mind, I would be whittled down to the dick who had fucked her with no finesse and hadn't bothered to even attempt to get her off.

I shouldn't have cared how she would think of me in the future, but I could admit my ego was fucking fragile.

If I had anything to say about it, the stories Delilah would tell about me would fill her sophisticated girlfriends with envy. Maybe one of those girlfriends would be so envious she'd turn into a little sleuth and track me down.

I'd chuckle and say, "Oh, Delilah Kastanos? Sure, I sort of remember her. Give her my regards."

And the universe would be balanced once more.

The fact that I'd undoubtedly been a lousy lay in the past didn't bother me even a little bit. Those girls could tell their stories all they wanted.

I couldn't say why one circumstance got under my skin while the other slid right off. But it was a fact, and I didn't have the time to question it.

Not when I spent all my study time fixated on a future scenario that wasn't going to happen. I had a fucking test tomorrow, and all I could think about was how I could convince Delilah to say yes.

She'd left me hanging since the weekend. Last night, I'd broken down and texted her using the number I'd pilfered from Beckett's phone.

Me: *Making me wait isn't nice.*

Delilah: *I can only assume this is Rhys. How did you get my number?*

Me: *I have my methods. When I want something, I stop at nothing to get it.*

Delilah: *Fascinating.*

Me: *I sense sarcasm. That's not very becoming of a lady, Delilah.*

Delilah: *Wow, you called me by the right name on the first try. You really must be trying to get on my good side.*

Me: *If your good side is between your legs, then yes, yes I am. Give me an answer.*

Delilah: *Utterly charming.*

Me: *Answer me.*

Delilah: *Hypothetically, I'm still considering it. Leave me alone so I can actually think.*

Me: *Fine, but I won't wait forever.*

She hadn't replied, which had irked me beyond measure. Then, today, she'd rushed out before the end of practice, the little wily minx leaving me with no chance of cornering her after.

The text I'd sent her an hour ago had been read but not responded to. I couldn't imagine what was so goddamn important in her life she couldn't take the time out for some good, old-fashioned cunnilingus. I was beginning to take her avoidance personally.

With a groan, I picked up my notebook to go over my notes. I'd never hear the end of it from Preston if I failed a test, and one of my main goals in life was not having to listen to my stepdad's voice.

Not even a minute passed before my mother's ringtone interrupted me.

She was the last remaining person on earth who called instead of texted, and it was incredibly obnoxious. What could have been settled in a few back-and-forth texts always stretched into half an hour of unnecessary conversation.

I picked up because if I didn't, she'd continue to call. "Hello."

"Hello, Rhys. Am I interrupting anything?"

"Studying." I kicked my notebook off my bed. After this, it was a lost cause. Fuck AP history and the horse it rode in on. "But I'm finished now. How are you?"

"I would be doing great if the kitchen remodel was going as planned. You won't believe this, darling. The ship carrying the Travertine we ordered from Italy sank. Our countertop is at the bottom of the Atlantic."

"Along with some sailors, but that's neither here nor there, I guess."

"Rhys." My name came out like a sigh, the way I'd been hearing it for years. "For your information, I did inquire about the people on the ship. They were rescued, and none died. Only our marble went to a watery grave."

"Well, that's a relief. The part about the survivors. The part about the marble is truly tragic."

There was a long pause. I knew this jig. An admonishment was coming.

"You're teasing me, Rhys, and I don't think you're funny. Not everything should be made into a joke. It's okay to take things seriously once in a while."

"You're right, Mom." If I argued, I'd be on the phone much, much longer. It was better to agree and get on with things. "Other than the missing counter, is everything else good?"

"That's why I called. The kitchen should have been completed in plenty of time for Thanksgiving, but unfortunately, that's not happening. Plan *B* is Thanksgiving dinner at Tersiguel's."

"Ah, the French are well known for their turkey and stuffing."

She huffed. "You're teasing again. What did I just say about that?"

"It's unbecoming of a gentleman."

"Rhys," she groaned.

"I apologize. Tersiguel's is fine."

Sitting through dinner with my stepdad was always torture. Moving it to a new location wouldn't change that. He'd have to be on his best behavior, given we'd be in public, though, so maybe it wouldn't be quite so bad as normal.

"Good. Preston and I look forward to seeing you."

"Sure."

Another weighty pause followed by a sigh.

"I'll be at the academy this week. I'd like to see you."

I'd rather fucking not.

In another life, my mother would have been a PTA mom, on school committees, planning parties and assemblies. But she was married to Preston Barron, which meant her baby boy was shipped off to boarding school, despite living in the same goddamn town. There was no PTA at Savage Academy since the rest of my schoolmates' families were mostly hands off in their children's education.

But my mother couldn't help who she was on the inside. Once a month or so, she'd come to campus to bring the staff a catered lunch or titter about in the office, making copies to show her appreciation for a job well done.

Her care for me was unwanted. No matter how many sweet gestures and praising words she lathered me up with, I would never get over her betraying me and my father's memory by marrying Preston and allowing him to take over my whole world. Too little and much too fucking late.

I got off the phone with vague promises about seeing her after practice and absolutely no intention of following through.

I planned to be busy with Delilah anyway.

Grabbing my phone, I sent her a text. She'd had enough time to consider my offer.

Me: *Give me your answer.*

I stared at my screen, willing her to respond. She didn't, and I realized there was something wrong with my phone.

There was no time stamp beneath my text. Nothing that said it had been delivered or read.

I walked out of my room to where Felix and Ryan were hanging in the living area.

"He lives," Felix announced. "What's up, Astor? Why do you look like you want to murder your phone?"

"Because it's broken. Are your texts going through?"

Felix flipped over his phone and tapped the screen. "Seems fine. I texted my sister twenty minutes ago and she replied. Your texts aren't going through?"

I showed him the last text I sent. "Look at this. It doesn't say delivered. Something's obviously wrong with the network."

Ryan snorted a laugh, followed by Felix sputtering. I whipped my head back and forth, scowling at them both.

"Stop laughing and explain," I commanded. I *really* fucking hated not being in on the joke.

Ryan wasn't my friend. He was a dudebro soccer player who filled in the empty space in our suite. Of course, it was him who dropped the bombshell.

"You've been blocked, man. That's why your text isn't going through."

In disbelief, I turned to Felix. "Tell me he's wrong."

He held up his hands. "If I did, I'd be lying. You're definitely blocked." His eyes flicked to my phone. "A girl blocked you?"

"Obviously, it was a mistake."

Ryan snickered again. "Nah, don't think so. You have to want to block someone in order to do it."

"That can't be right. She has no reason to block me."

Felix clapped me on the shoulder. "Maybe she just doesn't want to talk right now and will unblock you in the morning."

I walked back into my room to the sound of Felix and Ryan laughing, but I barely heard them.

Blocked.

She'd blocked me.

As if she hadn't already annihilated me with her one-star review of my performance. It was becoming difficult not to take this personally.

Chapter Fifteen
Delilah

IN ENGLISH LITERATURE, WE sat on the floor on pillows. Since girls wore skirts as part of our uniforms, it was annoying, but I'd mastered the art of angling my legs so I didn't flash my classmates.

Luciana sat beside me with a sigh. "Can this year be finished?"

"Don't I wish."

She turned to me. "You look exhausted, poor thing."

I barely suppressed a yawn. "That's because I am, precious."

I'd been up until three a.m. studying for my sociology exam. Since I'd quit going to the library with Ivan, my study schedule had been upended, and I had fallen behind. I had planned to cram after dinner last night, but Evelyn had a stress-induced meltdown. She didn't have them often anymore, not like when she was little, but when she did, she needed me to be present.

So, I sat in her room with her until she was calm enough to fall asleep, then I curled up beside her and studied until I couldn't keep my eyes open.

"Thank goodness for Thanksgiving break," she murmured. "I'm going to be getting my nap on every single day."

"Oh please, we both know you'll be hanging out with Beckett the whole time."

She grinned. "I didn't say I'd be napping alone."

Speaking of the devil, Beckett sauntered in and took his spot beside Luciana. Rhys trailed behind him, parking himself on the cushion beside me, where Ivan normally sat, instead of sitting on Beckett's other side like he always did.

"Good morning, Dottie," he crooned next to my ear.

"You don't sit there."

"Hmmm." He tilted his body toward mine and smacked his backside. "Seems like I *am* sitting here."

"Don't be dense. That's Ivan's spot."

"Seats aren't assigned." He cuffed my chin with his knuckle. "I guess your boyfriend's going to have to find somewhere else to sit."

Ivan strolled in and paused when he noticed his seat had been stolen. He arched a brow at me, and I shook my head like I had no idea why in the world Rhys would be sitting beside me. Ivan's expression darkened as he crossed the room and crouched in front of me.

"Are you unwell, Delilah?"

"No. I'm fine."

He cocked his head, scanning me for evidence of my lies. I'd coated my dark circles with extra concealer, but they weren't completely hidden.

"Are you certain?"

Rhys cleared his throat and shifted so he was partially in front of me. "Did you not hear her say she's fine? *Do Svidaniya*, comrade."

Ivan's gaze hardened. "That is offensive, and your pronunciation is shit."

I touched his hand, hoping to defuse the situation and escape his scrutiny. "I'm really okay. We'll talk later, all right?"

Relenting, Ivan took the pillow on Beckett's other side, eyeing both Rhys and me for several moments. I shot him a smile, but it didn't feel convincing.

Rhys's scrutinizing gaze bored a hole in the side of my head, but I refused to give him attention. Not even when he trailed his fingers along my jaw and lifted up pieces of my hair.

None of our interaction had gone unnoticed by our friends. Reaching across Luciana and me, Beckett swatted Rhys's extended leg.

"Cut that shit out, man," he uttered lowly.

Rhys seemed to take that to mean he should scoot closer to me. "I don't know what you mean."

Beckett's eyes narrowed. "Do we need to have a conversation?"

"No thanks," Rhys replied cheerfully. "I'm good."

Beckett's attention slid to me, clearly giving up on his friend. "Tell me if he gets out of hand. I'll take care of it."

Rhys barked a laugh. "Nice, Savage. How about when Delilah gets out of hand? Are you going to take care of that? Because Miss Kastanos isn't the sweet little—"

I swiveled around to glare at him, and he cut himself off, biting down hard on his bottom lip.

"Don't you dare," I whispered.

"I won't," he mouthed. "I'm sorry."

His immediate apology knocked me off-kilter. I hadn't expected that from him, especially without asking for one.

"Thank you," I mouthed back.

The truth was, I didn't want to fight with Rhys. Life was complicated enough. If he could be apologetic, I could appreciate it at face value and accept it.

He tipped his chin down. "This isn't over, princess."

Oh, yes. There was the Rhys Astor I had come to expect.

···•·•••··

"What the hell are you eating, love?"

I held up my spoon. "Haven't you eaten porridge?"

Freddie Spencer, my friend and occasional platonic make-out partner, gagged. He was dramatic that way, which was why we all loved him. That, and he was a genuinely good person despite his royal British roots. You would never know he was something like eighteenth in line for the throne by speaking with him.

"Not since I grew teeth." He screwed up his face in disgust. "You're meant to chew your lunch, not gum it. I demand you go back and choose something else. How about a nice sandwich?"

I mimed gagging. "No thank you. Porridge is comfort food to me." Especially with dates, cashews, and honey drizzled in it.

Freddie and I were the only two of our friend group in the dining hall. Our schedules aligned, so it was often this way, though most of the time, Ev was here too. After last night, she needed quiet time, so she was eating in her room.

"Why do you need comfort food?" he asked.

I lifted a shoulder. "Who doesn't need to eat their childhood favorite from time to time?"

He eyed me with suspicion. "Is there something going on with you? Ev's not here, and you're eating vomit. Something's not quite right."

I giggled, my spoon halfway to my mouth. "Don't call it that. I'll gag for real."

He waved his sandwich at me. "This isn't a diet, is it? I'll never forgive you if you do something to lose your T&A."

I had to set my spoon down before I spilled my food all over myself. "What do you care about my tits and ass? It isn't like you're interested in them."

He cocked a crooked grin. "Hey, being gay doesn't mean I can't appreciate the female form and give it the occasional grope."

"You perv."

He blew a kiss at me. "I don't recall you objecting to me feeling up your boob last semester."

I feigned a scandalized gasp. "You said it was a science experiment."

"It was." He nodded. "An experiment to see if your tits affected the gravitational pull around my dick."

"I hope to read your conclusions in a science journal sometime in the near future."

"Don't worry, dollface. Just got to finish my report, then it's time to hit publish. But if you must know, there was a light lift."

I covered my face with both hands, head shaking. "Please, no more. I can't take it."

A tray clattered on the wood table beside me. I dropped my hands in time to see Ivan taking the chair next to mine.

He looked at Freddie. "You made her laugh. Good."

He shrugged. "She's gone batty. I was only telling her about an experiment I conducted, and the poor thing started chortling like an adorable wee piglet. I think she's lost the plot a bit."

I balled up my napkin and threw it at him. "I've had enough of you, sir."

He tossed my napkin back at me. "No you haven't."

Ivan turned sideways in his chair, completely ignoring my and Freddie's banter. "You're not coming to the library anymore."

"I know. I'm sorry I didn't tell you. I'm managing the fencing team now and have to go to practice directly after class."

He exhales heavily through his nose. "We will meet after."

I shook my head. "No, that's okay. I'm doing my own thing now."

"Why?"

One of the things I liked about Ivan was how blunt he was. There was no pussyfooting around, for politeness' sake. Maybe it was a Russian thing, or maybe it was simply Ivan.

Right now, I wished he would be a little less like himself so I could get away without answering.

"I do better studying on my own," I hedged.

"That isn't true. You did very well studying with me."

"Christ, man. Leave her alone," Freddie said. "She doesn't want to study with you any longer, clearly. Get the message."

I held up my middle finger. "Thanks so much, Frederick."

He whirled his hand as he mock bowed. "Anything for you, milady."

Ivan stared at me, his mouth pulling into a frown. "Is this true? You no longer wish to study with me?"

I sighed. "It isn't exactly that. I have other things going on now, and I don't want to spend time in the library anymore."

"With me," he added. "It isn't the library, it's me."

Freddie groaned, falling back in his chair as if he'd fainted. "Someone, anyone, put me out of my misery."

Ivan ignored him, glowering at me like we were now enemies. "I don't like being there by myself. There are girls who take my being alone as an invitation to join me, which it is not. And they talk and talk and talk. You were always quiet. I like your quiet. Come back, Delilah."

"I told you, I'm busy. I've been studying in my room. You should try it."

He huffed a humorless laugh. "Freddie also does not know the meaning of quiet. I can't concentrate."

Despite my frustration, I snickered. Ivan and Freddie were roommates. They'd been thrown together because they were both swimmers and seemed to get along pretty well, but their personalities were certainly opposite. Freddie only stopped talking in his sleep, whereas Ivan existed in silence, intermingled with short spurts of loud outbursts.

Freddie flicked his accusation away. "Go on. Pretend you weren't cackling at the story I told you about Charles Bloomberg screaming like a tiny girl when he accidentally sprayed Icy Hot on his balls."

"Funny, yes," Ivan agreed. "But you barged into my room to tell me this with no mind I was writing a paper."

Two dots of color appeared on Freddie's cheeks. "All right. So I could work on my comedic timing."

I patted his shoulder. "I think you're perfect, darling."

Ivan gruffed. "That is because you do not live with him."

Freddie recovered from his brief embarrassment. "You're no peach yourself. Every morning, it's like a bridge troll has taken over your body. Slamming doors and crashing into things while growling and cursing in Russian. It's all very uncivilized."

I grinned at them both. "It sounds like you two are perfectly matched."

Ivan nodded. "I would agree if he would be quiet."

Freddie cocked his head. "I'll be quiet if you'll stop waking me up an hour before my alarm is set to go off."

"Fine," Ivan agreed.

"Fine," chimed Freddie.

I pressed my hands together. "Look at us. We've reached a peace treaty without a diplomatic incident."

Ivan cupped my shoulder with his oversized hand. "Do not think I'm distracted from what I asked. Have you stopped coming to the library because of Rhys Astor?"

Freddie leaned forward on his elbows. "What's this now?"

"Nothing," I declared. "Rhys is nothing."

Ivan's stare pinched. "He was protecting you this morning. He walks with you and watches you. There is something. I don't know if he is for you, Delilah."

"Why not?" Freddie asked. "He's sexy in an unhinged, ginger way."

"Ginger isn't a character trait," I argued.

He lowered his chin, leveling me with an unconvinced look. "Isn't it?"

"Perhaps it can be," I relented.

"Ginger is...a hair color? Ivan asked.

"Yes. And a personality. Everyone knows gingers are the devil's work," Freddie pronounced.

Ivan's brow dropped. "Hmmm. This seems offensive."

"That's because it is," I told him. "But why do you think Rhys isn't for me?"

"Yes." Freddie steepled his fingers. "Why isn't Rhys for Delilah?"

Ivan glared at him. "Do you think he is worthy of her?"

"Obviously not." Freddie tapped his fingers together. "But no one is worthy of my queen."

I let my head fall on Freddie's shoulder. "Thanks, friend. Although, if that's true, then I have a very lonely life ahead of me."

"Does that mean there's something going on with Astor?" Freddie prodded.

"No." I lifted my head. "We're around each other because of fencing and that's it."

Ivan made a grumbling sound. "Does he know this?"

"Of course he does." I pushed back from the table. "As much fun as this has been, boys, I'm going to go get ready for my next class."

Ivan grabbed my fingers to stop me from leaving. "You are not angry with me?"

"No, of course not." I gave his hand a squeeze because it was true. Enough time had passed, and my crush on him had chipped away until there was nothing left. I didn't even feel a twinge when his hand closed around mine. "You should try one of the study cubes. That's where Ev does her schoolwork. It's the only place she can find true peace and quiet."

He nodded. "Thank you, Delilah. I will."

I waved at Freddie. "Bye, Frederick."

He blew me a kiss. "Adieu, my love."

I left the dining hall feeling lighter than I had in days. Things were settled with Ivan, and I was over the bruised feelings. We might not be study partners the way we were before, but there was a chance we could get back to that once fencing season was over. Either way, we'd still be friends.

I only made it a few steps out of the dining hall before Rhys stepped into my path.

"There you are, princess. Just who I was looking for." He slung his arm around my shoulders and brought me flush with his side. "We need to talk."

Chapter Sixteen
Delilah

"Do you know that you have driven me out of my mind?"

Rhys paced around the small space in his room like a caged lion while I looked at all his things. I figured I wouldn't have another opportunity to see inside his lair, so I was taking advantage. Rhys had a lot of books. Not schoolbooks, ones that had clearly been read for pleasure. His shelves were lined with the cracked spines of fantasy and science fiction novels. Some I'd read, others I'd never heard of.

He wasn't messy, nor was he especially tidy. His bed was unmade, the covers thrown back as if he'd just left it. There was a pair of plaid pajama pants on the floor beside it and a stack of folded laundry on his desk. Two empty water bottles sat on top of his dresser, a line of unopened sports drinks behind them.

I fingered a well-worn copy of *The Shadow of the Isle* on his nightstand and turned to him.

"Am I? Why is that?"

He stopped pacing to glower at me. "Did you know you blocked me last night?"

"Oh, right." I snapped my fingers. "I had forgotten I did that."

"So, it was on purpose."

"Yes. I had a lot going on last night, and I didn't want to deal with your texts."

He moved slowly, folding his arms across his taut chest. His jaw clenched and rippled. His cheeks tinged with red.

"I'm sorry, was I annoying you?" He asked this like the answer couldn't have possibly been yes.

"Yes. I told you to leave me alone to let me think and you didn't respect that. I would have just ignored you, but like I explained, I wasn't capable of handling you with everything else last night, so I blocked you. I actually did intend on unblocking you this morning, but it slipped my mind."

He stepped forward into my space. "What were you doing last night?"

"It's personal, Rhys, and it has nothing to do with you."

He dipped his head, bringing us almost face to face. "Were you busy with Ivan?"

I raised my chin, regretting following him to his room. "No, but if I were, it wouldn't be your business."

He took my chin between his fingers and tipped my face to his. "Just tell me, Delilah. Please. I need to be able to think about something else."

His plea softened me. I suppose it might have been jarring for him to realize he'd been blocked. But I'd been with Ev, and she had been my focus, so I hadn't been considering how he'd feel in the moment.

"I'm not going into details, but I was with Evelyn last night. That's all I'll say about that. I am sorry for blocking you, though. It wasn't done to hurt you or drive you crazy, I promise."

His eyes darted between mine, and the tension drained from his neck and shoulders bit by bit. His hand drifted from my chin to cup the side of my neck.

"All right. I'll accept that. Sisters trump a random guy who gave you bad sex."

I grinned. "Thanks for being so understanding.

"I have a sister of my own. It's not difficult for me to put myself in your position."

"You have a sister? I didn't know."

"I do. Catrin. She's older by four years." His thumb stroked my throat. "You don't know much about me, do you?"

"I know a few things."

Back and forth, the rhythm of his thumb lulled me. I had to get to class, but I couldn't seem to make myself move my feet.

"Let me kiss you, Delilah."

"I haven't decided yet," I said softly.

"What if I'm the best kisser you've ever encountered?"

"Do *you* think you're a great kisser?"

His hand slid back to my chin, and he pressed his thumb to my bottom lip. "I think I could be. Your mouth is inviting. I'd like to trace this little cupid's bow with my tongue."

"Hmmm. Your mouth is fine too, I suppose." He laughed at my paltry compliment, and I wrapped my fingers around his tie. "If I let you kiss me, it can't turn into anything more than that. One kiss, then I have to leave."

"Is that a yes?"

Yes. No. Maybe. I don't know.

After my shitty evening, lack of sleep, and the stress of getting everything done, I wanted one thing that would take my mind off all of it. Even if Rhys was as craptastic at kissing as he was at making me come, he would give me a brief reprieve from all that was waiting for me outside his door.

But something told me he could be a good kisser if he put his mind to it. His lips were full and dusky pink. Some of his freckles had crept onto them, and up close, they were cute. Charming. Enticing.

I wanted to find out what kissing Rhys Astor was like.

"Yes."

His arm shot around my waist, yanking me against him. He peered down at me for a long beat, then shook his head.

"No, this isn't going to work."

I frowned. "You're giving up already?"

"Hardly. I just realized I can't do my best work like this." He patted the top of my head. "You're way down there and I'm up here. Sure, we can stretch and bend, but that's no fun."

"This really sounds like you're giving—"

The air was knocked out of me as Rhys essentially tossed me onto his bed and landed beside me, his arm banding around my waist. He dipped his head, dragging his nose along mine.

"This is a far superior angle," he murmured.

"I'm not sure I want to be on your bed. This is only supposed to be kissing."

He pulled back, meeting my gaze. "I know that, and I'm not going to take anything not offered. The thing is, I have a deep-seated need to kiss the hell out of you."

I nodded, agreeing with that idea. "Then do it."

He eyed me with suspicion. "Will you kiss me back? This is a two-man job. You have to fully participate in order for it to be successful."

"I will." I reached for him, tangling my fingers in the back of his hair. "I am supporting your endeavor. Kiss me now so I can go to class."

His lips grazed mine. "There. How was that?"

I grinned against his mouth. "Devastating."

"That was only a warm-up." Another graze. "Obviously, it doesn't count."

I curled my fingers in his hair, which was much softer than I would have guessed. "Sure. But how many warm-ups should I allow?"

"I think I'm ready to go in for the kill." His tongue traced the dip in my top lip, and goose bumps flooded my arms. "Here I go."

His mouth pressed firmly to mine, and he cupped my jaw with his smooth, warm palm. My toes pointed inside my shoes when he slowly moved his lips against mine, coaxing mine to part. Then he slotted my bottom lip between his, gently sucking and nipping.

I'd expected tongue and lots of it, but Rhys was methodical in the way he kissed me. Second by second, he went deeper, flicking my lip with his tongue, then pulling back. Lips moving against mine, almost stroking me with his mouth.

It was so soft. Careful and restrained. Like a dream first kiss between two sweethearts. The opposite of what we were, but I sealed my eyes shut and pretended. I'd never been kissed this way, and I doubted I'd ever have it again.

My body rolled into his, our chests pressing flush together. He was curled around me, long legs going on for miles after mine ended.

In those seconds when he kissed me like I was the delicate bud of a flower he desperately wanted to bloom, I wasn't myself. Not the protective sister, the girl above name-calling in the halls, the daughter who'd been called "wrong" more than anything else.

Just me. The girl he'd begged to allow him to kiss her.

He pulled back, and my eyes fluttered open. I had no idea what I thought I would see, but it wasn't what I was met with. His gaze was laser-focused on me, and none of the gentleness from seconds ago was there.

"Well? Did I meet your expectations, princess?" The dry, bitter way he asked me that made my stomach curdle.

While I was thinking about how precious he made me feel, Rhys was concentrating on proving a point.

"If only you hadn't opened your mouth after." I shot up from the bed, yanking his hair in the process. My bag lay abandoned by the door. I grabbed it quickly and slung it over my shoulder.

"Delilah," he groused from behind me. "Why are you storming out of my room like I've wronged you?"

I flung my hair behind my shoulder and glanced back at him. "I'm fairly certain the only reason you dragged me to your room was to kiss me. That part is finished, isn't it?"

"So you're running out on me? After I kissed you so well you were holding on to my hair for dear life?"

I snorted. "The kiss was fine, but I have to get to class. And don't worry, I'll unblock you so you don't feel the need to kidnap me again."

With that, I flounced out of his room like my feelings weren't hurt.

It absolutely murdered me that they were.

I really knew better. I wasn't some doe-eyed virgin. But one dose of sweetness from Rhys, and I forgot who he was. Who I was.

Bloody hell.

It was lack of sleep. That had to explain it.

The elevator came quickly, and I boarded, smacking the button for the lobby. The doors were starting to slide closed when an arm darted between them. They reopened, and Rhys stepped in, nostrils flaring. I stepped back, and he followed until my back hit the corner and he had eaten up every ounce of space.

"Wha—"

"Goddammit, Delilah," he growled at me as he took my face in his hands and crashed his mouth onto mine.

My hands shot up, clenching his shirt. I meant to push him away. I really did. But then his tongue swept between my lips, and my intentions dissolved. He licked my tongue and ground his erection against my stomach. I mewled and kissed him back with the same fervor that had come from nowhere.

Behind him, a bell chimed, but he ignored it, kissing me and kissing me. Somewhere in the back of my mind, it registered that we weren't moving. We must've hit the lobby, and now the elevator was just waiting for us to get the hell off.

But Rhys was working on his own timetable.

I was no longer a little bud.

He'd ignited me into a wildfire, and with each lash of his tongue, he stoked my flames.

The bell chimed again, followed by the sound of the elevator doors opening. This time, there were voices on the other side.

"Whoa, what the fuck?"

"Is that Astor?

"Get it, Astor."

Rhys tore his mouth from mine and roared at the guys standing at the threshold of the elevator. "Keep your mouths shut and get the fuck out of here."

He blocked me from view with his much taller body as he whirled around and slapped a few buttons. In seconds, we were alone and ascending.

He hadn't faced me again, but I saw him reach into his pants to adjust himself. A flutter of pleasure tickled my chest and belly.

"They didn't see you."

I nodded, though I was still behind him. "I know. Thank you."

He slid his hand over the side of his hair and finally turned to the side, raking his eyes over me. "Don't lie to me."

My brow furrowed in confusion. "Okay...?"

"Tell me how it was."

"The kiss?"

"No, the State of the Union address. Fuck, of course the kiss." He shook his head. "Must you drive me mad every second of the day?"

"As it's unintentional, I can't control it."

Muttering a curse, he took my hand and dragged me off the elevator. We were two floors above ours, and I suspected Rhys had done that so the guys in the lobby wouldn't be able to guess who he had been with.

Which was thoughtful.

He put his hands on his hips and leveled me with a long look. "Are you going to speak or what?"

"I didn't know I had to give verbal feedback."

"You do. How can I improve if you don't tell me what I did right and wrong?"

"Well—" I shifted from foot to foot, which made me all too aware of the state of my underwear. I'd agreed to this...whatever it was, so I was obligated to be honest. "The kiss in your room was so sweet it took my breath away."

His frown didn't lift. "That must be a bad thing since you ran out the minute it ended."

My eyes rolled. "That's because you were obnoxious the minute it ended. It shocked me out of the lovely little spell your lips had put me under."

His head cocked. "A lovely spell?"

"Shush, you. This better not be a ploy to get me to boost your ego."

"I had to listen to everything I did wrong the first time around, so if you have good things to say, I want to hear them."

It hadn't been easy to tell him the bad things, but why was it so much harder to tell him how much I liked being kissed by him?

"You know those were hot kisses, Rhys."

"You liked them both?"

I nodded, and my fingers went to my mouth before I could stop myself. My lips were still tingling. "Did you?" I asked.

His frown finally began to unfurl. "Yeah." He huffed a laugh. "You inspired me, you know. That first kiss came from nowhere. I'm relieved it landed."

I laughed too. "You're so strange."

"So I've been told." His feet shuffled before he pinned me with a hard stare. "Too bad you like kissing a strange guy."

"It wasn't meant to be an insult. Only an observation. I have nothing against strangeness. And the first kiss landed in a big way." I rubbed my lips together. "Like I said, it was breathtakingly sweet."

He considered me, eyeing my mouth then the rest of me. "So, we're moving forward? You'll tutor me?"

My clit would have screamed, "Yes!" if she was capable. Fortunately, my mouth was in charge. Even through the tingles, my wits were present and accounted for.

"I have to think about it. Can you wait until after Thanksgiving? I'll give you a definite answer then."

His sigh was so heavy it was like I'd put a thousand pounds of feathers on his shoulders.

"All right. I'll wait, but I won't be happy about it, and since you have to be around me all the time at practice and matches, you'll suffer for it. Are you prepared for that?"

I hummed. "I'll think about that too."

He groaned. "You should think less, Dakota."

"That joke isn't wearing thin?"

He straightened his tie and slipped his pocket watch from his trousers, twirling it on his finger. "Not in the least." He jerked his head toward the elevator. "Come on, princess. I have to get you to class."

· · • · • · • · • · ·

True to his word, Rhys walked me to class.

Even truer to his word, over the next week, he groused and barked and was generally insufferable during fencing practice. He didn't ask me for an answer, though. No pressure came from him other than his piss-poor attitude.

He gave me time to think even though he was against it, and that made me teeter toward saying yes a little bit more.

By the time Thanksgiving rolled around, I still didn't have a definite answer, but I hadn't stopped thinking about his lips against mine and the look he gave me when he prowled into the elevator with me.

Once I got through dinner with Michael, I'd weigh all the pros and cons. I'd ask Ev what she thought too. I could count on her to give me the unbridled truth. She'd help me be logical about this.

But first, I had to see my brother.

Thinking about Rhys had stopped me from fretting about what seeing Michael would bring. But there was no more avoiding the inevitable.

I would have to sit across a table from my brother and do my best not to stab him with my salad fork.

I imagined that was exactly what the pilgrims had envisioned for the future.

Chapter Seventeen
Delilah

Evelyn and I were studying the menu of the restaurant Michael had chosen while we waited for him to pick us up.

"I won't eat. It's fine," she said.

"I doubt Michael will accept that. Let's make a plan. There has to be something you can swallow down."

She twisted her fingers as she gazed at my phone over my shoulder. "There will be bread. I can eat it as long as it isn't sourdough."

"Do you want me to call and ask?"

"No, no. They're busy. I don't want to bother them."

I sighed. "It isn't a bother. It's better to know what we're walking into rather than worrying over it for the next hour, isn't it?"

Her mouth twisted, and I knew she wanted me to, even if she wasn't going to say it. While she was distracted, I ran to the bathroom and made the call.

Michael had chosen some fancy French place for Thanksgiving dinner, which might have seemed odd, but I knew my brother. He'd most likely searched for the most expensive restaurant in the area and made reservations.

He knew our sister was a picky eater and through no fault of her own. It wasn't as if Ev enjoyed having sensory issues. She had spent years in occupational therapy to learn to handle them. But Michael came from the same school of thought as our parents. They were educated people, but they believed Evelyn should just *get over* being autistic.

And they wondered why I never wanted to live anywhere near them again.

The hostess sounded confused at my question about their bread but was polite in her response. She had to put me on hold to ask someone else, which took several minutes. When she came back to the phone, she described their rolls in detail. Once I heard they were not sourdough, I tuned her out and thanked her profusely before I hung up.

When I returned to the living room, Evelyn glanced up at me. "You called them, didn't you?"

"Of course I did."

"Of course you did," she echoed. "Did you ask to speak directly to the head baker?"

"I did not, darling. I only spoke to the hostess...who spoke to the head baker."

She blinked at me. "That wasn't necessary."

"It was. I'll not have you sit through an entire meal with Michael without a scrap of food because our idiot, narcissist brother doesn't understand not everyone in the world enjoys foie gras and veal."

She shivered. "Don't remind me of all the geese and baby cows who've died to feed the rich and French."

I waved her off. "I refuse to feel sorry for geese. They're mean little assholes."

She scrunched her nose at me. "Honk, honk."

"Exactly."

• • • ● • ● • • • •

Michael was waiting for us in front of our dorm in the back of a limo. I climbed in first, followed by Ev. It had been a year since we'd last seen our brother, but he couldn't be bothered to get out to greet us and barely lifted his eyes off his phone when we were sitting across from him.

"Happy Thanksgiving, Michael," I said as primly as I could muster.

Our brother had always been handsome. At twenty-one, he now dressed like a mini version of our father—open-neck collared shirt with a gold chain draped on his smooth, golden skin. His jacket and trousers were crisp and finely tailored, and his ankles were bare atop Tom Ford loafers. He had the same dimple in his chin as Ev and me. The same upturn at the corners of his eyes. Thick, wavy hair, almost black. A low dip in the center of his top lip. To anyone looking at us, it was obvious we were related. There was no denying Michael was our brother. But there were no feelings attached to that title. He was barely more than a stranger to me.

He finally laid his phone in his lap to look us over. "The twins are here." He waved his fingers in sarcastic celebration. "Would a parade be enough of a reaction for you, Delilah?"

"It would be a nice start," I quipped.

He chuffed, sliding his gaze to Evelyn. "I suppose it's out of the question since our dear sister can't abide loud noises. Or have you grown out of that phase?"

Ev whispered to the window in her most punk rock voice, "It's not a phase, *Mom*. It's a lifestyle." She turned her head slightly in Michael's direction. "No, you're right. Loud noises still feel like I'm having my skin peeled off centimeter by centimeter by fire ants. No parades for me. Thank you for checking."

I folded my arms under my breasts. "Did you come all the way to California to insult us or...?"

"Believe it or not, I actually did miss my two bratty sisters." He tapped his fingers on the back of his phone. "Didn't you miss me? Even a little?"

"Sure." I missed the brother I wished he was. I missed the tiny moments when he showed an ounce of humanity. I missed when he was small and hadn't quite dosed up on our family's poison. This version of him? I could have done without seeing for the rest of my life. "Thank you for coming to see us."

"Where else would I be?" He flashed a bright, fake grin. "It's lucky you live in an appealing locale. I can't imagine I would be visiting you in Connecticut or one of those other masses of land that barely qualify as a state."

Damn. Should have looked into schools in New England.

"We're so lucky," Ev agreed without any intonation.

Michael didn't know us, and he *really* didn't know Ev, so he had no clue how deeply sarcastic she could be. She tended to make fun of him straight to his face, and it was all I could do not to laugh.

"And you, Evelyn? Are you missing Europe and being close to Mom and Dad?" Michael asked.

"I haven't lived in the same country as my parents since I was seven." Her fingers twisted in her lap. Feet slid back and forth against each other. "I don't think about them, and I would be surprised if they spend any mental effort on me."

He puffed out his cheeks. "Are you taking drama lessons from Delilah? You know they sent you away to school so you could have the best care. Obviously, Mother would have preferred to have two daughters she could turn into her little princesses, but..."

He didn't have to finish. I knew what he was implying. Instead of two princesses, our poor parents were strapped with two wrongs.

· · ● · ● · ● · · ·

The ride lasted less than half an hour, but by the time the three of us walked into the restaurant, it felt like we were coming home from war. I was already out of fight, and we still had to get through dinner.

Ev and I stood to the side, expecting Michael to check in with the hostess. Instead, he broke out in a smile too warm to be familiar. I turned to see who was on the receiving end, and my breath caught. A slim man in a black suit strode toward us. My eyes traveled up him while my stomach plummeted.

"Roman's here. That doesn't make sense," Evelyn observed.

"No. It doesn't make sense at all."

Michael and Roman embraced, then the two swiveled to stand before us. Roman swept his dark gaze over me, his grin morphing from pleased to mischievous.

"Happy Thanksgiving, Ev." Stepping forward, Roman lifted my hand in his and pressed his mouth to my knuckles, peering at me from beneath thick lashes I'd always teased him about, saying it was unfair for a man to have been blessed with something he'd never appreciate. "Happy Thanksgiving, Delilah. Are you happy to see me?"

My fingers curled into his palm. The first boy whose hand I'd held and meant it. The one who broke my heart like it was nothing. "I'm surprised. I had no idea you were coming."

"Did you keep it a secret because you knew Delilah wouldn't have come if you hadn't?" Ev cut straight to the chase, as always.

Roman chuckled and straightened, keeping a grasp on my hand. If blood hadn't been rushing to my head, making me wobbly, I would have pulled away from him.

"Would that be so wrong? It's been more than a year since I've seen either of you. I missed my Kastanos girls. When Michael mentioned he was visiting, I couldn't resist."

Michael patted him on the back. "Come on, come on. We'll talk about this at the table. I'm starved and could use a drink."

Ev gave me a pinched look. "I've heard the bread is very good here."

I tried to smile at her. I really did. But my head was too cloudy to respond. I couldn't grasp what I was feeling the most. Attacked, certainly. Pissed, for sure. Caught off guard, one hundred percent. Wistful, a little.

Roman and I trailed behind them to the table. For a French restaurant on Thanksgiving, it was awfully busy. Waiters swerved around each other and between tables, while rich patrons clinked glasses and silverware. I was worried about Evelyn. Distracted by the presence of my first love and only heartbreak. Floating through the moment without really taking any details in.

I felt Roman watching me but kept my gaze on the back of my sister's head.

The last time I'd seen him in person, he'd had tears in his eyes, promising me he would wait for me forever. All I had to do was ask.

The last time I saw his face was in a picture taken later that night at a party. Roman had waited less than twelve hours to bang the girl he told me not to worry about, and her friends had made sure I was aware of it.

And now, I had to sit through a dinner with him in a fancy restaurant. If he or Michael believed I would pretend to be happy to see him, they thought wrong. I didn't have it in me to act. If I'd been warned, I might have been able to fake it, but they hadn't given me that much.

Roman touched my back between my shoulder blades. "You don't really mind that I'm here."

My feelings for Roman had ceased months and months ago. I used to think the way he made statements when he should have been asking questions was endearing. Now, I wanted to steal a waiter's pen to draw a question mark on Roman's forehead. Maybe he'd remember to use them through osmosis.

I tucked my hair behind my ear and peered at him. "Don't I?"

He cracked a grin. "Oh, it's going to be like that, is it? Should I remind you that you left me?"

"Knowing what I know now, I should have done it much sooner."

His hand closed around the back of my elbow. "She meant nothing to me."

I tugged free of his grasp. "I don't even know who you're talking about, but it would make this evening easier if you stopped touching me uninvited and didn't bring up ancient history. Unless, of course, you'd like to talk about the pilgrims."

He bit back his response as we arrived at the table. Michael and Evelyn were seated on one side, which meant I had no choice but to sit beside Roman.

Ev watched herself wrap her cloth napkin around her hand, let it unfurl, then wrapped it again. "I'm sorry I'm not sitting beside you, but I thought you would prefer to look at me during dinner. You know, since Roman had sex with that skank while you were trying not to cry so I wouldn't know how heartbroken you were to be leaving him. I might be wrong, but I'm guessing you don't want to see his face."

"Evelyn," Michael hissed. "What the hell is wrong with you? Have you no control?"

She barely turned her head. "I have plenty of control. But since you don't care enough to stand up for our sister, I will."

Roman held up his hands. "Calm down, Mike. It's fine. Evelyn isn't wrong, and while I'd hoped my presence would be a pleasant surprise, I hadn't expected to be met with open arms." He leaned toward me and dropped his voice. "Maybe by the end of dinner. I've missed holding you against me."

"Jesus," Michael grumbled. "Where's the fucking waiter? I need a drink if I'm going to be subjected to this kind of talk."

Evelyn was looking at the flickering candle in the center of the table. It was then I really noticed how dim the restaurant was. Each table had a candle or two in the center, making the light in the large, open space waver.

"We can blow it out," I whispered.

It took her a moment to raise her eyes to mine. "And sit in the dark?"

My brows popped. "It might be better."

Hers lowered. "It might be worse."

Roman leaned into me, draping his arm over the back of my chair. "I see you still coddle her," he murmured into my ear.

My spine stiffened. "Caring for someone's comfort is not coddling."

"I know how much you care for her. You gave up on us for her."

"And you made it so I would never want to come back." I scooted my chair to the right, making a fuss over it so the message was clear since my words didn't seem to be sinking in. Or he couldn't be bothered to listen.

"Speaking of coming back, have you made a decision about college?" Michael inquired as if his friend hadn't been in the middle of saying horrible things about me and Evelyn.

I cleared my throat. "We haven't heard from the schools we applied to. It's still early."

"Father wants you back in Europe. There's no reason for you to remain in the States."

Roman turned slightly in his seat. "Michael tells me you've both applied to schools in the UK. Since I'm living in London now, it would please me to no end if you ended up there."

It was jarring not knowing the man I'd once thought of as the love of my life had moved to an entirely different country. It went to show how far removed we now were from each other—and I didn't mean physically. Roman had his own life I knew nothing about, and I had mine, which I certainly wouldn't be sharing any details of.

"We only applied to those schools because our parents made us," Evelyn announced softly. "It's strange to me that you believe you're some kind of incentive to either of us. Is this denial or purposeful obtuseness?"

I kicked her gently under the table. She kicked me back a little harder. Roman may have thought the way I looked out for her was coddling, but it wasn't. We were a team and took care of each other. Her lack of filter in certain situations meant she would say what I often bit back.

Michael's face glowed in the candlelight, and not in a romantic way. He was lit with anger from within, holding on to the edge of the table so he didn't burst.

He dipped his head toward Evelyn. "I'll be speaking with Mother and Father when I get home. They're clearly unaware the treatment you're receiving at your current school isn't working."

She wrapped and unwrapped her napkin. "Because I say what I think?"

"Because you're a little shit with no manners."

She yanked the napkin tight. "Have you considered perhaps I'm just rude and it has nothing to do with me being autistic?"

I barely stifled a giggle. "I think it's a genetic trait."

Roman released a stiff-sounding chuckle. "She had you there, Mike. You're not exactly known for your manners either."

Thankfully, our waiter appeared, putting a momentary end to the painful awkwardness clouding our table.

Evelyn stared at the flickering candle and continued fidgeting with her napkin.

Michael ordered a double and demanded they *keep them coming*.

Roman chose not to take a powerful hint and stroked his thumb along my shoulder as he ordered for me.

I would have argued, but I became distracted when I caught sight of a group of three being led to a nearby table, one of whom was glaring at me.

As if this dinner couldn't have been worse, Rhys Astor was now seated two tables away, conveniently positioned to watch my every move.

Which he did without even trying to disguise it.

This was going to be the longest dinner of my life.

CHAPTER EIGHTEEN
Rhys

"RHYS." FINGERS SNAPPED IN front of my face. "Your step-dad asked you a question, darling."

Preston was a question man. He was riddled with them. I'd never believed he was fully human. The fact that he never ran out of questions only furthered my belief.

Today, they'd begun the moment I walked into their house.

Why are you late?

You always wear that godforsaken pocket watch but can't tell time?

You're wearing that to dinner?

Why didn't you win that first bout last week?

Do you really think I'm not keeping track of you?

Do you have any idea what I pay in tuition?

When I pointed out it was my father's money that paid my tuition, dear old Preston almost blew his stack. He didn't like to be reminded that the lavish lifestyle he now led was all due to my father. The house he lived in, the room he slept in, the woman he'd made his wife—it had all belonged to a better man first.

Of course, that had set the tone for our day. Now, we were at the ridiculous restaurant Preston had chosen, and the questions hadn't ceased. The thing was, I was all out of answers.

I might have danced the dance a little longer to make my mother happy, but I was too busy watching Delilah get groped by some handsome goon in a five-thousand-dollar suit.

I recognized the fine tailoring. In another world, I might have asked for a referral, but Jesus Christ, he could take his hands off her right about now.

I'd gotten a good look at the other guy at the table, undoubtedly the brother she'd told me she would be seeing for Thanksgiving. But the guy by her side was no relative. Though he was looking like he wanted to share a last name with her. *His* last name.

"Pardon me, I missed it." Shaking off the surprise of seeing Delilah, I focused on Preston's receding hairline. I'd found that spot a few years ago and hadn't looked him in the eye even once since. "I was distracted by the decor. Who knew the person who decorated the Beast's castle in Disney World also brought their skills to French restaurants in California?"

My mother almost stifled her laugh, but not quite, which got her a sharp look from dear ol' stepdad.

"That's a niche comparison," she quipped, knowing exactly what I meant.

We'd gone to Disney when I was eight. I could still picture the inside of the castle. Lavish decor meant to look like it had been transported from a town in the French countryside but was actually all sponge painting, Styrofoam, and particleboard.

That was basically what Preston was too. He looked the part, but he was hollow.

Preston cleared his throat. "I was asking about college applications. My contact at Stanford is eager to meet you."

I exchanged a look with my mother. She was supposed to have handled this. Stanford was Preston's alma mater, and I had no intention of attending. My father went to Savage U. I'd decided to go there in elementary school and hadn't once wavered.

"I don't see why I would apply there when I'm not going there."

Preston's nostrils flared. "You'll apply because it's a prestigious university you should be honored would even consider you. You'll apply because I told you to. You *will* apply because if you don't, we'll have problems."

His threats were relatively empty, minus the violence. My tuition to Savage Academy and the college of my choice had been paid for by my father. When I graduated from SA, I'd begin to receive a stipend from my trust until I finished college, then I'd have full access.

The fact was, Preston had no leg to stand on, yet he was more than capable of making my life hell if he felt so inclined.

And he would definitely feel inclined if I ignored his request.

"I'll get the application done tomorrow," I bit out.

"Thank you, darling," my mother cooed. "Your heart might be set on Savage U, but it's always smart to have more than one option."

I stared at her in disbelief.

Another fucking betrayal. She knew damn well how much following in my father's footsteps meant to me. For her to remotely encourage another path was a stab in the gut and akin to spitting on his grave.

They murmured back and forth to each other, and I looked at Delilah again, searching for a reprieve from the tension at the table.

Her hair was pulled off her face in a sleek, almost severe ponytail. The neckline of her dress was wide, the rounded tops of her soft breasts peeking over the ruffled edges. The urge to press my face there twisted my stomach.

Her gaze flicked to mine, and when our eyes connected, her mouth curved into the barest hint of a smile.

There was hardly any movement to it, but it was lasting. She watched me with something like amusement raising her cheeks. What was she so happy about?

If it was due to the prick beside her, I wasn't going to be pleased.

I expected better taste from her.

"All right, that's enough," Preston hissed. "Who is so important behind me that you can't give your mother or me even a moment's attention?"

I smoothed my napkin on my lip, slowly tearing my gaze from Delilah. "I see a friend from school."

My mother tipped in her chair to follow my line of sight. "Oh! That gorgeous girl two tables away?"

My nod was tight. "Yes. She's a friend of a friend."

She smiled at me. "Not a girlfriend?"

"That's none of your business."

Preston's slamming palm rattled the table. If we'd been at home, it would have rattled my teeth.

"Don't speak to your mother that way. If she asks you a direct question, you will answer it," he gritted out.

"It's fine," my mother started. "Rhys can keep things like that private. He—"

Preston's gaze darkened and began to shift to my mother. I hadn't witnessed him hit her or hurt her in any way, but I believed he had it in him. After all, if he could slap a twelve-year-old boy so hard he lost a tooth, what qualms did he truly have about hitting his wife?

Though my mother hadn't protected me the way she should have, I would always stand between her and harm's way.

"We haven't labeled it yet," I said. "We're taking things slow."

Why those words left my mouth, I had no idea. I should have continued with the "friend of a friend" bit. There would be more questions now, and I'd have to answer them or no doubt I'd be facing the consequences in the privacy of our home.

"If you're seeing her, she should be your girlfriend," Preston stated.

"We're new. Maybe she will be."

She'd sooner stab my eye out with a rusty spoon.

Preston scoffed. "That's how you cheapen a girl. If she isn't good enough to be your girlfriend, but she's good enough to mess around with, you're broadcasting her low value to your classmates. Is that what you want? Or do you not care?"

Mother laid her hand on his arm. "They're young, my love. Taking things slow is a good idea."

He placed his hand over hers. He was gentle about it. But my hackles still rose, alert for threat. He shouldn't have been allowed to touch her. My mother shouldn't have wanted it.

"Slow, yes." He picked up his wine and swirled it around the glass. "But if you don't commit yourself to something, you'll half-ass everything."

I glanced at Delilah again. She was leaning as far away from the goon as she could without falling out of her chair, his hand cupping her nape. I wondered why her brother hadn't interfered.

"I see your point." And if it were anyone other than Preston, I might have listened to it. "Actually, if you don't mind, I'm going to say hello to her. I'll be right back."

There was no doubt Preston minded.

But I was already on his shit list. Might as well go for the gold and add another reason for him to pop a few blood vessels.

I strode up to Delilah's table. They had their drinks but hadn't been served dinner yet.

Delilah was midmotion, her wineglass hovering close to her mouth. "Hi."

The prick stopped speaking midsentence and twisted his body toward me. I paid him no mind, giving Delilah all my attention.

"Hello, princess." I rested my hand on her shoulder and squeezed, then turned to Evelyn. "Happy Thanksgiving, Ev."

Her hands were in her lap, one busy strangling the other with her cloth napkin. Her chest rose as she sucked in a deep breath. Poor girl didn't look to be having much fun.

I understood completely.

"Happy Thanksgiving," she whispered.

The brother stood from his seat, his hand extended. "Michael Kastanos."

"Rhys Astor." I shook his hand, allowing him to appraise me all he felt the need to. He wouldn't find me wanting. Not on the outside, anyway. And in our world, appearances were nine-tenths of the law.

I grazed Delilah's cheek with my knuckle. "This one didn't tell me you would be having dinner here too."

"I only found out this afternoon. Michael likes to leave me in suspense." Delilah's brows drew together. She had to wonder what I was doing since she truly had no reason to inform me where she was going to be spending Thanksgiving.

But I liked the idea of her having a reason. More than that, I liked the uptight guy now offering me his hand thinking she did as well.

"Roman Drakos." We shook, and he stayed standing, unlike the brother. Up close, this guy was a lot older than I'd expected. Same age as the brother, who had to be midtwenties. Interesting. "How is it you know Delilah and Evelyn?"

"Classmates." I peered down at Delilah, stroking her jaw and neck with the back of my hand. "Of course, Delilah is a lot more than that to me now."

He froze, gawking slightly. "Is that so? She hasn't mentioned you."

Evelyn answered for me. "She wouldn't have, would she? Delilah hasn't spoken to you for over a year."

Ah, yes. I always knew I liked Evelyn.

Roman sank back to his seat, a deep frown pulling at his chiseled features. I wasn't sure who this guy was to Delilah, but I got the sense he was an ex. I didn't normally have self-esteem issues, but this handsome motherfucker might've made me feel inadequate if I had to stand beside him too long.

Delilah reached for my hand and clutched it to her chest, right above the soft swell of her sweet tits. She had my full attention.

"Rhys, this is our brother, Michael, and an old acquaintance, Roman." Roman sputtered at that introduction, and I had to bite the inside of my cheek to keep myself from laughing. "Michael and Roman, this is Rhys, my—"

"Boyfriend," I supplied, tightening my hold on her hand. "It's good to meet more of my girl's family and an old friend. Another piece that makes up the gorgeous puzzle that is Delilah Kastanos."

I bent down and touched my lips to her temple. She pressed her face against my lips, prolonging the kiss. She smelled of wine and roses. I had to stop myself from running my nose along her neck to get a stronger whiff.

"Are you aware my sisters will be moving back to Europe as soon as they graduate?" Michael asked.

"Nothing has been decided," Delilah snapped.

"It's okay, princess." I kissed her cheek, then returned to my full height. "Of course I'm aware it's on the table. But I have months to persuade her to stay on this side of the Atlantic, and honestly, I'm pretty sure my chances are high."

Delilah fluttered her lashes at me. "Keep being as sweet as you always are, and I could be talked into pretty much anything."

The sip Roman had just taken got lodged in his throat. He coughed and patted his chest. Michael's expression turned down in disgust, no concern that his buddy was actively choking.

Delilah reached around and thwacked Roman on his back. "Please don't die. You'll ruin everyone's dinner."

Roman was too busy hacking up a lung to hear what she'd said, but her brother took on the shade of red Preston often did when I didn't sufficiently fall into line.

Movement caught my eye, and I glanced over at my mother, finding her waving. Not at me, though. Delilah waved back, then my mother gestured for her to come there.

I sighed and addressed Evelyn. "Would you mind if I borrowed Delilah for a minute or two? My mother has seen her, and she won't rest until I introduce her."

Evelyn nodded, but she seemed far away, unfocused on anything in particular.

I held out my hand to Delilah. "Come with me?" She hesitated, flicking her eyes to her sister. "Don't worry." I pulled her to her feet and murmured next to her ear. "We won't leave her alone with them for long."

"This is strange," she whispered back.

"Play along. It'll be over soon." I tapped the ruby stud in her velvety earlobe. "I'll even kiss you again as a reward."

She started to sit back down, but I hauled her against me, making her laugh.

"Come on, you. Be good."

"Fine," she muttered. "You be good too."

"Never."

Then, I dragged Delilah along with me to meet my mother.

Chapter Nineteen
Delilah

Rhys's mother, Amanda, had dark-blonde hair and a wide, white smile. She was elegant in the way I expected of a rich woman in Southern California—obvious wealth in the form of diamonds and designer clothing, unnaturally smooth skin, a body toned to within an inch of its life. When she shook my hand, the sinews in her lightly muscled forearms rippled beneath her skin, and I imagined she spent her days playing tennis.

His stepfather also wasn't a surprise, though he didn't match Rhys's mother. He was tall, with pudge around the middle and a receding hairline. There was nothing memorable about his face. Bland was the only word for him. And while his clothing was obviously of fine quality, he looked like every other man in the restaurant.

Rhys's fashion sense may have been over the top, but at least he had style. There was no one else here in velvet smoking slippers, charcoal cigarette trousers, and a matching waistcoat.

He introduced me as his girlfriend, which sounded strange coming from him. But his mother had practically squealed in genuine delight, and Preston had managed to smile like he was pleased.

They insisted I sit down with them for a moment, and Rhys basically shoved me into the empty seat.

"I can't stay long, unfortunately. My family will wonder where I disappeared to," I said.

"We won't keep you," Preston answered. "Forgive us for being curious about you. We've never met any of Rhys's love interests."

Amanda fluttered her manicured hands. "Oh, we don't need to speak about the past. Let's focus on Delilah. Kastanos is a Greek name, isn't it?"

"Yes. That's where my family is from. My parents still live there, though they travel for much of the year, so it's really more of a home base."

"Will you be returning to Greece for college?" Preston asked.

"No." I shook my head. "Ideally, my sister and I will stay here. But we haven't decided."

Amanda's brows rose. "Sister?"

Rhys draped his arm over my shoulder like he did it every day. "Delilah is a twin."

Amanda grinned. "That's so fun. I would have loved having a twin sister."

"I can't imagine life without her," I replied. Then I remembered Rhys mentioning his sister. "It's too bad Catrin isn't here. I would have loved to meet her too."

The instant I said her name, the vibe at the table shifted. Amanda's smile fell like an anvil, and Preston hardened to stone. Rhys's hand on my shoulder curled like a claw, pressing into my flesh. I'd clearly stepped on a land mine. Now, I had to find my way off without losing a limb.

"Catrin hasn't been to a family dinner in several years," Rhys said quietly.

Preston's gaze was shrewd as he watched me with his stepson. "We don't talk about Rhys's sister. She is a painful topic for all of us."

"I'm sorry," I rushed out. "I only knew she existed. I had no idea—"

Rhys pulled me closer to his side. "It's fine, princess. You didn't do anything wrong."

Amanda picked up her wineglass and tossed most of the contents back. Since it'd been more than half full, she'd ended up chugging it. Preston's upper lip curled, but his displeasure didn't stop her. She set the empty glass down on the table with a thunk and delicately wiped her mouth with her napkin.

I pushed back from the table. "I should be getting back to my family."

Rhys stood with me. "I'll walk you back."

He guided me in the opposite direction I should have been going, and I allowed it because I was somewhat shell-shocked by how drastically I seemed to have screwed things up.

We ended up in the hallway leading to the restrooms, and Rhys pulled me into an alcove that had probably once held a pay phone. He tapped his lips.

"Kiss. Now."

"What?" I breathed out in disbelief.

"Yep." He lowered his face to mine. "Because I'm going to have to rejoin that table and put up with my mother and Preston's foul moods for the next hour or two while watching your ex feel you up every chance he gets. Give me something good to get me through."

That he considered a kiss from me so good it would give him incentive to survive a tense dinner did something to me. My stomach warmed. My chest inflated.

"Why don't you kiss *me*?"

"It's your turn, Delilah. Show me what you got."

I really didn't need convincing. Weaving my fingers through the back of his hair, I pressed my lips to his. The moment I did, his arm banded around my waist, and he dragged me against him. His tongue swept into my mouth, meeting mine and sliding against it. He needed no direction, and I decided then I was keenly looking forward to experiencing other things he might do with his mouth.

The sound he made when I nipped at his bottom lip heated me to my bones. Oh yes, definitely looking forward to more.

He rolled his forehead along mine, our lips ghosting over each other's.

"I'll take you back to your table. I might be wrong, but I doubt leaving Evelyn alone with those two is the best idea."

I took a step back from him, shocked I hadn't thought of my sister. Now that I was, an urgent need to get to her spurred me on. "Yes. Please. I should get back."

Rhys took my hand and guided me around the outskirts of the dining area so we didn't pass directly by his parents. When we arrived at our table, Michael was in Evelyn's face, waving a forkful of salad in front of her lips.

"Just fucking eat it, Evelyn," he hissed. "Stop being stupid. This shit isn't going to work on me."

"Michael." Without a single care whether I caused a scene, I knocked the fork from my brother's hand. "What is wrong with you?"

Roman shot to his feet, starting to circle around to my side, but Rhys held out his hand and gave his head a hard shake. That was a good thing since I was equally pissed at him for sitting there, doing nothing, while Michael tormented my sister.

"Delilah—" he started, but Rhys put his body between mine and Roman's.

"No," Rhys gritted out. "Sit back down."

And Roman did.

Evelyn was curled forward, trembling, her eyes shut. If I didn't get her out of here soon, she'd melt down. Of course, I should have known Michael would trigger her with his "throw her into the deep end and she'll swim" philosophy based on absolutely nothing but his own ignorant ideas.

"We're leaving." I tugged on Evelyn's hand until she got up. "Come on, Ev. We don't have to stay."

Michael's face turned beet red with fury, but he didn't let it out in volume or gesture. It shot from his eyes like streams of lava.

"Mother and Father will be hearing about this," he warned.

I raised my chin. "Good. Explain how you caused a scene in public. I'd like to hear your excuse."

Without waiting for his retort, I wrapped my arm around Ev's waist and hurried us outside. Once we were free from the restaurant, I pulled her to the side of the building, away from prying eyes and the sounds coming from within. Then I let her go, giving her the room she needed more than my embrace.

"I'm sorry," she whispered.

"You did nothing wrong. I'm going to order an Uber. Just a little bit longer, Ev, and you'll be back in your room."

A hand landed on my shoulder, making me jump and whirl around. Rhys held up both hands in surrender and took a step back.

"I'll drive you home. Stay here. I'll get my car. It'll be much faster than waiting for a rideshare."

I turned to Evelyn. "Is that okay? Or would you rather wait for a car?" She *hated* anyone seeing her upset and worked hard to appear as "normal" as possible all day long. Right now, she was overwhelmed, and there was no way she'd be able to mask her coping mechanisms in front of Rhys the whole drive back.

She shook her head. "Rhys is fine. We can go with him." She clutched her middle and rocked. "I really wanted the bread," she muttered dejectedly.

Despite the shitty evening, I let out a watery laugh. "I know you did."

Rhys swiveled on his heel. "Don't move. I'll be right back." Then he ran, quickly disappearing from sight.

Ev's back was to the building as she held herself, gently rocking forward and backward. Her jaw was clenched tight, and her fingers dug into her biceps.

I knew better than to try to speak to her. She needed space to process, so I gave it to her, standing beside her without touching.

In less than a minute, a car pulled up to the curb, and the passenger door of the back seat swung open. From within, Rhys called, "Get in, Kastanos twins. I'm taking you home."

I climbed into the back seat first, followed by Ev. Rhys eyed me through the rearview mirror, but I was thankful he didn't turn around to look at Ev.

He put the car in gear, but before he began to drive, he extended his arm back to us, a basket in his hand.

"Here," he gruffed. "I got this for you."

When the smell of freshly baked bread hit me, I realized he was speaking to Evelyn. She must have too, because she reached out and grabbed the basket, cradling it in her lap. Her "thank you" was barely audible, but Rhys nodded like he'd heard it.

She unfolded the napkins on top of the basket, revealing several rolls and a partial loaf of French bread. Her fingers curled around the roll, and she brought it to her mouth, tearing into it with more savagery than I was used to from her.

Her eyes fluttered closed as she chewed, and the tight knot of barbed wire lodged in my stomach unraveled somewhat. Rhys glanced at me again. I tried to smile, but it was wobbly at best.

I hated my brother. I'd thought it before, but now, I knew it was true. There was no way we would ever live anywhere near him. If I could help it, we would never even see him again. He brought nothing but misery and the reminder of what could have been but never would be.

· · • • • • • · · ·

Rhys rode the elevator with us to our floor and watched us walk down our hallway. I waved to him once I'd unlocked our door and Evelyn rushed inside.

"Thank you," I called.

He waved me off. "I didn't do anything." Then he got back on the elevator and disappeared.

I'd think about what he did and said later. For now, I had to make sure Evelyn was okay.

Music was already vibrating the walls of her bedroom. She was standing in the center, her dress in a puddle on the floor, wearing a sports bra and cotton underwear. Her head was tilted back, and her eyes were closed as she swayed.

"I'm okay," she said. "You don't have to watch me."

"You are?"

She opened her eyes and nodded. "I think the bread reset me."

I burst out laughing. "The bread?"

"The bread. Leave it to the guy who gave you the worst sex of your life to find the magic wand."

"Well, now I know it. Next time you get overwhelmed, I'll just stuff rolls in your mouth."

I had become the one who was overwhelmed. All the pent-up feelings I'd been holding back so I could be there for Evelyn came flooding in. I couldn't stop the tears, even if I'd had the energy to try.

She held out her hands. "Come dance with me."

"I hate your music."

"I know. Dance anyway."

I couldn't think of anything better than dancing in my underwear with my sister to her terrible, horrible music. Ripping off my dress, I moved my body, spinning to my hatred of Michael, swaying my hips to my anger at Roman. I twirled to the surprise of Rhys and bounced to the misstep of mentioning his sister. We jumped together to not being broken despite being wrong, wrong, wrong.

Evelyn outlasted me, but then she danced every night. I curled up in her bed and watched her sway and shimmy. She'd put on her headphones, so from my perspective, she looked funny dancing to silence. I smiled to myself as my eyelids slid lower and lower.

The last thing I saw before I fell asleep was my sister with her arms raised, her lips curved into a slight grin. Rhys's concerned expression flashed in my mind.

Who was Rhys Astor?

I closed my eyes.

I'm going to find out.

CHAPTER TWENTY
Delilah

ME: *ARE YOU AROUND?*

Rhys: *Yes. Are you going to sit on my face?*

I threw my phone in disgust.

But I laughed too.

The earth's axis had realigned. This was who Rhys was supposed to be. The quiet, thoughtful Rhys from two days ago was someone foreign.

I picked up my phone to text him back.

Me: *I was thinking I could come by your room to thank you.*

Rhys: *You don't need to do that, but you can come to my room. Everyone's away for the holiday so I'm all alone. Come to think of it, I'm a little scared and could use some company.*

Sitting on Rhys's face was out of the question. Did people really do that outside of porn? People with thick thighs, big butts, and double-digit clothing sizes?

I almost stopped to Google it but decided to save that for later. It seemed like a bad idea to enter Rhys's lair with that image fresh in my mind.

Since I absolutely, positively wouldn't be doing it.

Evelyn was happily knitting and listening to music, so I left her to it and rode the elevator to his floor. When the doors slid open and revealed his mischievous smirk, I let out a yelp.

"That took you a long time. I almost came looking for you." He snagged my hand and marched me down the hall toward his room, walking a little too fast, his grip a little too hard.

I let out a breathy laugh, almost running to keep up with him. "I think we need to practice this too."

He came to an abrupt stop, raising his eyebrows. "What?"

"Hand-holding." I wiggled my fingers in his tight grasp. "I've gotten the sense this is new to you too."

With that, his brow dropped. "Your sense is correct. I've never had any use for it." He frowned at our joined hands. "Tell me how you like it, then."

"Let go first."

"No."

"I thought you were going to be my willing pupil? It's a bad sign you're saying no to my first instruction."

"Fine." He released my hand but kept his close. "Show me."

Sliding my palm down his, I wove our fingers together, then used my other hand to curl his fingers around mine.

"There." I held up our hands. "Not like you're keeping me captive. Like you want to be beside me and go everywhere with me."

He clicked his tongue. "I'm just trying to go to my room."

"Hey." I gave his chest a shove. "You're the one who was holding my hand in the first place. I'm perfectly fine going without."

He made a disgruntled sound and started walking again, but he didn't let me go, nor did he squeeze me too tight.

Rhys could learn if he wanted to.

I dug my teeth into my bottom lip to suppress my grin.

He'd wanted to learn to hold my hand right.

Rhys swung open his door and pushed me into his room. He kicked the door shut and leaned against it.

"What were you doing before I texted?" I asked.

"Practice this morning. Just got back and showered." He ran his hand over his still-damp hair. "You should come to the gym with me tomorrow. It's empty and—"

I groaned, flopping down on his couch. "This again? I have to say, with all your prodding for a second chance, you sure aren't making me want to get naked with you when you keep pushing me to go to the gym. I've gotten the hint, Rhys."

"What the hell are you talking about, Desdemona?" Pushing off the door, he prowled toward me. "I don't give hints. That's not really my style. If I want to say something, I will."

He took the cushion beside me. "Explain."

I started to roll my eyes but stopped myself. Had I been wrong? It was true. Rhys wasn't one to beat around the bush. If he wanted me to lose some of my fat ass, he'd undoubtedly let me know.

And then I would let him know what it was like to live with only one testis.

I took a deep breath. There was no sense in getting riled about something that might not be true.

"You keep asking me to go to the gym. I assumed you were telling me I need to work out."

"Everyone needs to work out. That's common knowledge." His gaze swept over me. "If I had a problem with what you looked like, I sure as hell wouldn't get hard looking at your tits in your uniform. Your *uniform*."

I wrinkled my nose. "It's ugly as sin."

"Exactly my point. Yet you have me sporting wood more often than not. Does that not say anything to you?"

"Then why do you keep asking me to go to the gym with you?"

Sighing, he threw out his hands. "To spend time with you because you interest me—and to show off my athletic prowess. Mostly the latter, but a lot of the former too." He flexed, and though I didn't consider myself a muscle girl, Rhys's defined biceps made me want to lean in and bite them. "If you see me in action, I'll have a higher chance of getting inside you again."

"I see you in action at practice on a daily basis."

"And?"

Rhys was fishing for compliments, and it was sort of endearing.

So I gave him what he wanted.

"And your athletic prowess is unmatched."

He pressed a finger to my lips. "Honestly, you should stop. You're embarrassing both of us with your fawning. It's a bit much."

I slapped him away, laughing at his ridiculousness. He watched me from under hooded eyes, a pleased grin curving his lips.

"Thank you, by the way. I'm not sure if I said it the other night."

His smile fell, and he shoved his fingers through his hair. "Yeah, you did. You don't have to, though. All I did was drive you home."

"You did more than that. The bread—"

"Stole it off a table. I'm probably banned from that place." He cocked his head. "Is Evelyn good now?"

I nodded. "She's fine, and she was fine that night because of you. So, I will thank you for stealing that bread for her and driving us home without question."

"Sure." His fingers dug into the arm of the couch. "I hope you don't like your brother because I'm going to be calling him an asshole."

"Feel free."

"Your brother is an asshole, Delilah. I don't know what he was doing to Evelyn, but it was clear he was making her uncomfortable and being a general dick in her direction. Don't see that guy anymore."

I was indescribably grateful he didn't ask questions about Evelyn. If she were here, she'd most likely tell him she was autistic and everything about that night, including our brother, had overstimulated her until she shut down. But she wasn't here, and it wasn't my story to tell.

I added another entry to my list of things I liked about Rhys Astor. It was short but growing.

"I agree with you, and I won't be seeing him again if I can help it. He won't change, and that's sad, but it is what it is." I nudged his calf with my toes. "Did your parents give you hell for leaving early?"

"Not parents. Mother and her husband." His hand shot out, catching my foot, and brought it to his lap. Tossing my flip-flop aside, he cupped my foot in both hands and continued talking. "Hell is to be expected when I interact with Preston, no matter if I toe the line or act out. When I told them I needed to take care of you, though, my mother nearly swooned, which softened my stepfather in the moment. I had to sit through a long phone call yesterday, but at least I didn't have to look at his face while he explained all the ways in which I was a disappointment and future failure."

"Wow, what a dick. I'm sorry I was the reason you had to sit through that."

"I'm not." He squeezed my foot. "I would have heard the same lecture anyway. Preston isn't very bright or creative. It always revolves around *there's something wrong with you* and *you're bringing shame to the family.* That old song and dance."

"I always wonder how people like that land partners. Forgive me for saying it, but your mother is a fox."

Rhys snorted a laugh. "I don't know about that. But I *can* tell you exactly why she married Preston. She'd been utterly dependent on my father, who had taken care of her because she was the love of his life. Our family was his reason for being. That was the kind of man he was." He dropped his gaze to my foot, running the pad of his thumb over my painted nails. "My father died when I was eleven, and my mother had no clue how to stand on her own two feet. Along came Preston, who'd been a distant friend of my father's. He was always there, helping my mother with her accounts, reaching for things on tall shelves, making phone calls. He asked her to marry him six months after my father died."

"I can't believe she married someone who treats you like crap."

He shrugged. "The first of many betrayals. She traded the memory of my father and my security for a man who knew how to file taxes. Like you said, it is what it is."

"I'm sorry, Rhys. My parents have never cared much for Ev and me, so I've never expected it. But I can't imagine how it destroyed you to go from two loving parents to what you have now."

The laugh he let out was bitter and jagged. "It was jarring, I can tell you that."

"Did Catrin leave home because of him?"

His jaw rippled as he turned his head to look out the window. "You could say that. But we don't talk about Catrin, by order of Preston the Dick-Tator."

I was curious, but I'd be a hypocrite if I pressed him for more information. He'd already opened up to me more than I'd expected.

"Do you want to talk about something other than our messed-up families?"

"Hell yes." He yanked on my foot so hard my ass slid forward. Before I knew it, I was flat on my back and Rhys was looming over me, his knee pressed against the back of my thigh and butt, one hand braced beside my head. "I want to *do* something else."

I gripped his T-shirt in my fist. "I'm not having sex with you."

"I'm aware." He might have been aware, but he peered down at me with a hungry expression that told me he was eager for me to change my mind. "Come to my room."

My stomach swirled with a heady mix of nerves and desire.

"Promise you won't try to go further than what we agree to."

"*Never.*" There was fierceness in his growled vow. "You're in the lead, Delilah. This is your show. I'm asking you to come to my room. Everything that happens once we're in there is up to you."

I let go of his shirt to slide my hand to the side of his neck. "Then let's go to your room, Rhys."

CHAPTER TWENTY-ONE
Rhys

WE LAY FACING EACH other on my bed. Delilah was wearing nothing but a loose V-neck T-shirt, allowing me a generous glimpse of her tits, lacy bra and black lace boy shorts. Her lips were puffy from all the kissing we'd done over the last hour. Kissing and nothing else, although she'd lost her pants somewhere in there.

My fingers twitched to touch her, but we were going at her pace, not mine since mine had proven to be ineffective.

And I wanted to affect this girl, not because of money or to assuage my bruised ego. Because she was affecting *me*, and it was only fair I wasn't alone in this.

She dragged her finger along my bottom lip. "I think you've mastered kissing."

"Is it time to level up?"

She nodded slowly. "I want to show you what gets me off."

"Show?"

"Mmmhmm." Her thumb hooked on the band of her underwear. "I'll be doing the touching. Can you handle that?"

"I get to watch?" Half my body's blood supply had already migrated to my dick, but another flood surged below my waist. I might not survive long enough to graduate from Delilah's school.

"Yes. If you can look without touching..." She inched her underwear down her rounded hips. "Can you, Rhys?"

"You underestimate my restraint, princess."

"We'll see," she murmured.

She may have doubted me—hell, I sincerely doubted myself—but she tugged her panties the rest of the way off and kicked them to the foot of the bed.

She'd been naked beneath me once before, but it'd been somewhat dark, and I'd been in a goddamn hurry, so I never got a good look at her.

The sight of her smooth, creamy thighs meeting at her slick, bare pussy nearly undid me. It was a good thing she still had a shirt on. If I'd seen any more of her, I would have embarrassed myself. I couldn't guarantee I wasn't going to jizz all over myself as it was.

This girl had been in class with me, sleeping in the same dorm, living her life parallel to mine for over a year, and I'd never paid attention. All this soft flesh and addictive rose scent had been right under my nose, and I'd been too stupid to sit up and notice.

I was now. I couldn't look away.

I raised my hand and started toward the curve of her stomach, but she sucked in a breath, and I stopped myself, flicking my gaze to hers.

"Sorry. You're just—" I flashed her a sheepish grin. "I'm keeping my hands to myself. You should know it's the hardest struggle I've faced."

"Good." She reached between her thighs to cup herself. "Perhaps you'll learn some humility."

"If this is how I learn humility, I'm good with that." I wrapped my hand around the base of her throat and dipped down to press my lips to hers. "Touch yourself, princess. Show me everything."

At first, I watched her face. Her lips parted, and her eyelids slid low. Little panting breaths escaped her. Only when she let her eyes close fully did I pull back so I could see what was happening between her legs.

Pushing myself up to sitting, I scooted down the bed for a better view.

"What are you doing?" she asked.

"Watching. I want to see how you touch yourself." I rested my hand on the inside of her bent knee. "Is this okay?"

She nodded, so I pressed down, spreading her thighs apart, giving myself the view of a lifetime.

Two fingers were circling her clit, and beneath, her swollen pink lips glistened. My cock jumped with the need to get in there. But I knew if she let me, I'd lose my mind and bang her like a maniac, and we'd be right back where we started. Except I really fucking doubted I'd get a third chance.

"Light or firm?" I asked.

"Huh?" She raised her head, cracking open one eye.

"Pressure...light or firm?"

"Um—" Her head fell back. "I don't know, I don't know. Put your fingers on top of mine and feel."

Swallowing hard, I shifted to align my arm with hers and slid two fingers from her knuckles down to her nails. The devil on my shoulder urged me to keep on going, but that devil was easily silenced. Delilah was giving me her trust even though there was no way on Goddess's green earth I deserved it.

And I was taking it anyway.

"Do you like to put your fingers inside?" I murmured.

"No." *Pant, pant.* "My clit wants all the attention."

"Needy bitch."

Her laugh was breathy, and she turned her face into my arm. Her lips moved against my skin, kissing and breathing. With my free hand, I stroked her hair off her face and skimmed my knuckles along her cheek down to the exposed parts of her chest.

She arched into my touch, her body rippling like a wave as I dragged my hand over the length of her and settled on her thigh—the one place she'd given me explicit permission to touch. I'd pushed enough of Delilah's boundaries. From now on, I'd wait until she let me inside.

Her hips rose off the bed, following her own hand's movement. My fingers shadowed hers, swirling and pressing but not too hard. I memorized what she did. How she took care of herself so I could do the same.

"Are you going to come, princess?"

She nodded against my arm.

"Can I see your face? Show me what I missed the first time. Let me see how pretty you look when you come."

Her sweet little moan was a bullet in my bloodstream. Painfully arousing, knocking me back hard. Next time, I'd find a way to elicit those sounds from her myself.

She turned her face toward the ceiling, her neck arching, lips parting as she released more breathy moans. I pushed up on my elbow, hovering over her so I didn't miss a second.

Cheeks flushed.

Eyelids squeezing.

Chest heaving.

Nipples straining.

Our fingers circled with frantic precision, drawing out more moans and rapid pants as she snapped her hips up and down, up and down.

I held my breath. My toes curled over the edge of a sharp cliff for that last step. And then she was there, falling, and I exhaled, watching the glorious view of her ecstatic descent.

When her fingers stilled and her body relaxed into a loose heap of limbs, I collapsed beside her, resting my head on the pillow of her tits. I had been thinking about lying there since I first truly noticed the magnificence of her breasts, and it was every fucking thing I had hoped and dreamed.

I presumed she'd kick me off as soon as my head landed, but after no more than a beat, her fingers sliced through my hair in slow strokes. Since she wasn't making me leave the best place I'd ever laid my head, I banded an arm around her middle and yanked her a little closer.

"Feel good, princess?" I murmured.

"Mmmhmm. Like I could nap."

"Then nap."

"I have no pants on. I'm not sure I could sleep pantless in the same room as you."

The last thing I wanted to do was move, but I also did not want her leaving.

Yeah, my cock was rock hard, and if I had to venture a guess, I'd say it wasn't going to soften until Delilah was nowhere in the vicinity. If she left, I could take care of it and relieve the ache.

But then what? I'd be empty and alone.

Today, I didn't want to be alone. More specifically, I didn't want to be without Delilah.

"One second." I jackknifed upright, grabbed her underwear from the foot of the bed, and threaded her feet through the holes. She took over, wiggling them the rest of the way up. I skimmed my fingertip over the lacy band on her stomach. "There. Now you're safe from my nefarious ways."

"Thank you." She reached for me, hooking my shirt in her fist, and gave me a gentle tug. "Come back."

"Gladly." I touched my lips to hers, then put my head back where it belonged, and her fingers resumed their same route in my hair.

We lay there like that for a while, quiet and peaceful. My eyes began to slide shut, and her fingers started to slow.

"Don't be mad at me if I leave a puddle of drool on you."

Her chest shook as she giggled softly. "I won't be mad."

"That's because you're a sweetheart."

"Maybe grossed out."

I rolled my face on her tit, smiling despite being halfway asleep. "That's because you're a princess."

"Mmm. I thought we were napping."

"We are."

She sighed, vibrating my cheek. "Rhys?"

"Hmmm?"

"Tell me something vulnerable."

I was reluctant to lift my head, but I did, peering at her from beneath heavy lids. "What's going on?"

She shook her head. "Just feeling a little exposed after that. I was brave before, and now, I'm...not."

"So, you want me to even the playing field?"

She rolled her lips over her teeth and nodded once. "Please."

I hadn't stopped to think it might've been difficult for her to lie half-naked in my bed and put on a show for me while I stayed fully dressed, watching her every move. Especially after the last time we were in this position together.

I wasn't a person who was modest with my nudity, but there were other parts of me that never saw the light of day. Parts I'd been told, and told, and told were no good. Wrong. Never to be shown.

She needed it, so I'd give it to her. I didn't really know why yet, but I got the sense I could trust Delilah. So, I lay back down and showed her the wrong parts.

"Up until I was almost thirteen, I liked to cosplay characters from *Lord of the Rings* and *The Shadow of the Isle*. It was a thing I started doing with my dad. When he died, I dragged Beckett into it sometimes, but I did it on my own too. There was a period where it was easier to be Frodo or Fathaniel than myself."

She didn't laugh. Not for a second. One hand rested on top of my head, and the other played with my fingers draped over her hip.

"I noticed the book on your nightstand. It looks well loved."

"That was my dad's."

"A treasure, then." She wove her fingers between mine. "You stopped cosplaying?"

"Preston forbade it. Got sick of seeing me dressed up. He kept telling me there was something wrong with me. No kid of his was going to be a nerdy freak. Laughable since he's the biggest fucking dork in the state. If he reproduced, his own offspring would come out prematurely balding, ranting about rules and statutes."

The noise she made could only be described as a growl. "Let's hope we don't meet again. I might not be able to resist telling Preston he has mushy peas in his skull instead of brains."

"You'll stand up to my evil stepdad for me, princess?"

"I will. I don't like anyone being told who they are is wrong. I've heard it from my own parents, and it makes my skin crawl to know it's been said to you as well. And for a harmless hobby you did with your dad." She clucked her tongue. "Preston can go sit on a spiky dildo."

"Violence is becoming on you. I like it."

If this was how she reacted to Preston being a dick, I didn't want to know how she'd react to the even worse things he'd done. But Delilah didn't need to see that kind of ugly. I'd keep that stored in my gut, where it festered on a daily basis.

"I'm angry for you, Rhys."

"I know you are." It soothed my tarnished soul to have this beautiful, stable, well-adapted girl ready to pick up a spiky dildo and go to battle in my honor. "And I really fucking appreciate it."

"I can't believe you let him push you around like that. That doesn't strike me as something you'd accept."

"Yeah...well, I was a kid when he came into my life. An impressionable, grieving kid. It was easier to cow to my mother's new husband than fight."

"Prick," she uttered with more vehemence than should have fit in one little word.

"I don't want to talk about him anymore, all right?"

"Of course it's all right." She squeezed my hand. "Did I ruin naptime?"

"Not for me." I kissed her tit and sighed. "I'm going to pass out on this little slice of heaven."

"Okay." She started stroking my hair again, and I got the sense it was as much for me as it was for her. "Thank you for telling me that. You've made me feel very safe with you."

"You are."

I would devour her whole if I could, but I wouldn't hurt her if I could help it.

Charles's stupid face popped into the back of my mind, and I shoved him into the darkest corner where he belonged.

Chapter Twenty-Two
Rhys

BECKETT LET ME INTO his postage stamp room. He had a single this year, which he was happy about. But there was barely enough space to walk between the furniture, much less stretch his dick out.

I didn't know how he did it. I needed to roam. I would have gone mad in here.

"Your room smells like baby powder and a field of flowers. It's like—"

He glared at me. "If you compare my girlfriend's scent to a whorehouse, you're going out the window."

I clapped. "Oooh, a threat of defenestration? It must be serious between you."

"You know it's serious, asshole." He tried to stay hard, but after a second, his mouth wobbled, and he ended up laughing. "Defenestration? Really?"

I finger gunned him. "Word of the day calendar, my friend. Best investment I ever made."

"Your mother gave it to you for Christmas?"

"Yes. So, you can see why I call it money well spent. Although, when I pull fancy words out of my ass, I never fail to impress, so I can't say it was the worst gift of my life." Kicking my shoes off, I made myself at home on his bed, my back against the headboard, legs stretched out in front of me. "How was your break?"

It was Sunday night, and everyone was coming back from their trips. The only reason I'd been able to get a solo audience with Beckett was because I'd texted him demanding one. Otherwise, Luciana was a permanent fixture by his side. Normally, I didn't mind that, but I had delicate subject matter to discuss.

He sat down at his desk, arm crossed over his chest. "Good. Spent most of it at Luciana's place."

"Ah. Were Joshy and Gretch up to their usual hijinks?"

Beckett's parents weren't great, but they loved him in their own distant yet controlling way. Gretchen had made reversing the aging process her job. Josh basically owned the town of Savage River, which seemed to make him think he owned the people inside it, including his son.

When we were younger, I'd felt sorry for him. He'd hang out with me and my dad any chance he got. When my life fell apart and Preston entered stage left as the dastardly villain, Beckett's life had started looking better and better. Our roles had reversed, and it was me hiding out at his house whenever I could until we'd both enrolled at Savage Academy, getting the hell away from our dysfunctional origins.

Beckett shook his head. "As soon as the dishes were cleared from the table on Thanksgiving, they were headed to the airport. They spent my break in St. Croix."

"Wow. That's...harsher treatment than I've come to expect from them."

"Oh no, I wasn't abandoned outright." He chuffed. "They invited me, but the last thing I want to do with my free time is spend it sitting by myself at a resort while Josh golfs and Gretchen spas."

"Which they knew."

He nodded slowly, a sardonic smile tugging at the corners of his mouth. "You get the picture. I was invited, but not really. Spending time with Luc's family was eye-opening anyway."

"In what way?"

He unfolded his arms and leaned forward, elbows on his knees. "Did you know there are families who like one another? The Ortega-Whitlocks are like a fucking Hallmark movie. They ask each other questions and genuinely listen to the answers. The jokes they make are not at someone else's expense. In my entire time there, I didn't hear a single lecture."

"What?" I pressed my hand to my chest like a scandalized Southern church lady, but in actuality, I didn't know anyone with a home-life like that. That could also be because I'd never cared enough to ask, but that was neither here nor there.

"Right? I mean, I guess I knew they were like that, but being around it for days at a time blew my mind."

"Because it never stopped?"

"Yeah. They are always like that with each other. And it made me think."

"Think what?"

His eyes met mine, and there was determination there I usually only saw when he was on the soccer field...or when it came to Luciana.

"That's what I want. I want my kids growing up in a family like that."

I shrugged. "Then you'll have it."

He exhaled. "That simple?"

"For you? Sure. Not that I think having a functional family comes easy, but I know you. If you want it to happen badly enough, it will."

I believed it wholeheartedly. Beckett had a lot of good in him, and Luciana was a sunshine-y angel with a steel spine. If they stuck together—and Beckett would make sure they did—they'd have the kind of life they both wanted.

Maybe they'd invite crazy Uncle Rhys over from time to time.

"Thanks for saying that." He settled back in his chair, stretching his legs out. "Now, are we going to get to the issue you needed to talk about? Or are we going to keep putting it off?"

I flipped my hands over on my lap. "How is my asking about your Thanksgiving putting it off? I'm being a normal human like you're always encouraging me to be."

Grinning, he kicked my foot. "You did a very good job being human today. Now come out with it."

"All right. But I need you not to judge me."

He held up his hand. "You watched me eat paste in kindergarten, and I stood by while you picked up dog shit from the sidewalk with your bare hands. We're past judging each other.

"I was six and thought it was a stick. Do you really need to always bring that up?"

He chuckled. His laughs had come a lot easier since Luc became his, and it put an ache in my gut. I couldn't really even pinpoint why. It just was.

"I feel like I do. It'll be part of my best man speech at your wedding."

"Then it's a pity for you I'll never be getting married."

He rolled his hand. "We could go back and forth all night, but I'm curious. You've never come to me for advice before."

There was no one else I would have even considered coming to for this type of advice.

"This is about sex."

He shifted in his chair. "Don't tell me you knocked someone up."

"No, no. Nothing remotely like that. I—"

"What?" He was leaning forward again, his gaze intent on me. "I give you a hard time, but I'm not going to judge you. You know that."

"I do." I sucked in a breath and spit it out. "I need you to tell me how to go down on a girl."

A heavy exhale whooshed out of him. "You're kidding."

"No."

"You have a lot more experience than me. It's only been Luc, and not for long—"

"I know it's only been her. But in that department, you have one-hundred-percent more experience than I do."

He was silent for so long I wasn't sure he was going to speak again. My intestines squirmed and knotted. This was so fucking uncomfortable. But necessary. If Delilah let me in, I didn't want to look like a bumbling idiot. Not again. I'd be an idiot in front of Beckett, though. It wouldn't be the first time, definitely not the last.

He scrunched his eyes and rubbed the spot between his brows. "You don't go down on girls you have sex with?"

"I haven't, no."

"Why?"

I shrugged. "I've never been interested. Sex has been a means to an end."

His eyes popped open. "Something's changed?"

I nodded once. "I'm interested now."

"Is there a girl?"

I nodded again.

"Who?"

I cocked my head, my mouth pressed into a firm line. I'd really been hoping to get out of here without being asked this question. But this was Beckett, and he didn't give up so easily.

"*Who*, Rhys?"

"Why do you need to know?"

"You tell me about your French whores but won't tell me about a girl you're into?"

I threw my arms out. "I was obviously joking! I can't believe you thought I was serious about that."

He tossed his arms out in the same way. "How the hell was I supposed to know you didn't spend your summer banging whores?"

"Because I think you know me better than that."

"Christ. I guess I do." He shoved his fingers through his inky hair. "So who's the girl?"

"Can we just skip that part and you give me the information I need?"

He dropped his hand, eyeing me sharply. "It's obviously someone I know. Someone I wouldn't approve of?"

I blinked at him. He wasn't getting shit from me.

"Isla? Better not be Isla. Felix will kill you without a second guess."

I jerked back. "No, I'm not with Felix's baby sister. That might be worse than you thinking I'm really banging whores."

"Fine." His eyes narrowed. "If it's not Isla, then—*no*."

Understanding dawned on his face, but I remained impassive, staring back.

"Rhys, no. If you—tell me it's not Delilah."

"I can't tell you that."

He shot to his feet, his hands balled into fists. "I told you she was off-limits. You can't fuck around with my girl's friends."

"No, you told me not to talk to her because you knew I wasn't interested in her. Well, I *am* interested. I like talking to her. She's witty and much, much smarter than me. Plus, that accent. So...yeah, I'm going to keep talking to her." Beckett looked like he was about to protest, so I barreled on. "I also like kissing her, and I want to do more, but I need help, so I came to you. You can give me shit about liking one of Luciana's friends, or you can help me make sure I treat her the way she deserves."

He paced the two feet of empty floor, his hands clasped behind his neck. "You like Delilah?"

"Yes."

"And you want my advice..." He squeezed his eyes shut. "Fuck. I can't believe you like *Delilah*."

"Why not?"

He let his arms drop heavily at his sides. "I don't know. Is she your type?"

"Why would you think she isn't? Because she isn't thin? Is that it?"

"No. I didn't say that—and don't repeat that shit."

I smirked, but there was no humor behind it. "Your girl wouldn't like that, huh? Bashing her friend's body."

"Fuck off. I absolutely did no such thing. You're not going to repeat it because that isn't what I meant or what I said."

"But you're surprised I like her. There's a reason for that."

I was giving him a harder time than necessary, but his reaction wasn't one I'd enjoyed. Not because I thought he was truly ragging on Delilah. If I believed that, I wouldn't have been sitting on his bed quite so calmly.

"You know she doesn't look like the girls I've seen you hook up with."

"Sure." I raised my chin. "And I didn't like any of them."

"Which is why I'm perplexed by the idea that you like *anyone*. It has nothing to do with her not being attractive or thin enough. Objectively, I know Delilah is beautiful. There's no question about that."

"Damn right."

He sank down on his chair. "You actually like her."

"Yes."

"And you want me to give you advice on—" He cupped his face, letting out a laugh that bordered on hysterical. "Is this real life?"

"I don't understand why you're so out of sorts."

"This is all so out of left field. I got no warning."

"How should I have warned you?"

He exhaled, lifting his head to look at me. "I wasn't even aware you and Delilah were on speaking terms."

I arched a brow. "You've been busy living the dream, Savage. Delilah's the manager of the fencing team. I see her daily."

He turned toward the wall, his jaw rippling. "Wow. I'm a dick."

"No, you finally got the girl. I get that things change. I'm not your number one anymore." I chuckled, but my intestines were squirming again. My *joke* sounded more like the truth.

"Things change, sure. But not everything." He faced me again. "I'll do better. Consider my head out of my ass."

"Considered. Are you ever going to answer my question?"

"I don't know. It might've been easier if I didn't know *who* the advice was being used on."

"You asked."

"I did. That's my bad." He groaned, scrubbing his face. "All right, all right. I'm putting on my best friend hat—"

"You look good in that one."

"No interruptions, Astor. I'm not going to get through this if I have to think too hard."

I mimed zipping my lips.

He let out a slow breath. "You have to start with turning on her brain. Make her feel beautiful, like you're lucky to be with her. All that's true, and you know it, but she needs to know it."

Mouth shut, I recalled Delilah describing how I'd been with her. I hadn't done any of what Beckett was saying. No doubt, *treating her like a sex toy* wasn't going to be part of his tutorial.

"When she shows herself to you, look at it. Take a minute to admire what you're about to have. Let her see you taking in every inch of her."

I sat forward, listening to every word.

"Touch her first. And when you're touching her, tell her how good she smells. That you can't wait to get your mouth on her. Really get her ready. And when she is, when you go down on her, don't do it because she'll like it. Don't do it because it's what's expected. Do it because you can't go another second *not* doing it. She'll feel the difference, how badly you want her, how fucking honored you are to be there."

He rubbed his lips together. "I apologize if you were expecting me to give you technique advice, but that's really individual to each girl. You're going to have to find that out by experience."

"I'm relieved you didn't give me a step by step. There is no part of my brain that wouldn't reject the image of *you* going to munch town."

Beckett groaned. "Yeah, I didn't think it needed to be said, but I see I was wrong. Never say 'munch town' again."

"I can't make that promise."

"Didn't think you would."

I fell back against the headboard. "Thank you for the rest of it, though. I'm going to work really hard to ensure your voice isn't in my head when I implement it."

He didn't laugh, giving me a considering look. "Don't mess up, Astor."

I heard all the meaning behind those words.

Don't break Delilah's heart.

Don't screw up his thing with Luc.

Don't misuse his advice.
Don't think about him while I'm fucking.
Emphasis on that last one.
"I'll do my best, Savage. I'll do my best."

Chapter Twenty-Three
Delilah

RHYS SNAGGED ME BY the waist on my way out of the gym. "You better wait for me, Dawn."

"When you stop thinking that's charming, you can expect me to wait for you."

I shrugged his sweaty arm off me, though I didn't find it as disgusting as I should have. Even the damp spot he'd left behind wasn't so offensive.

"I expect you to wait for me because I'm ready to take our tutoring to the next level." He tugged me against him, then dragged his tongue up the side of my neck and cheek. "Come on, princess. You know you want to."

I turned to him, pressing my palms against his chest. "I'm going back to my room. Text me when you've showered and maybe I'll be free."

He groaned. "Stop being pragmatic and throw caution to the wind. You can't tell me you don't want to be eaten out."

My hand flew to his mouth, and my head whipped around, checking to see if he was overheard. Other fencers were still gathering their equipment post-practice, but it didn't seem anyone was within earshot.

"Must you say those things where anyone can hear?"

He licked my palm, getting it nice and soggy. I wiped it on his shirt and tried to glare at him but failed. Rhys could be an entitled prick, but sometimes, like now, he was more puppy than human, and it was impossible to get mad at his off-the-wall behavior.

"I must, princess." He gave me a gentle shove. "Don't wait. I don't want you to anyway."

"Your tricks won't work on me. I'm going."

"Good. I want you to."

"Prat."

He grinned, and the tips of his ear reddened. "I'm going to shower now, but you can't stop me from thinking about all the things I'll be doing to you later."

I burst out laughing, which I did quite often with this boy. "Leave me alone, Rhys."

I finally escaped him—he let me—and headed toward my dorm. There was no denying the uptick of my heart was due to his promises.

How was I here? My heart pitter-pattering for Rhys Astor? All because he'd given me terrible sex.

If the sex had been average, we wouldn't have been here, which was just strange. Everything about what we were doing was so far outside of anything I'd expected of my senior year, but maybe that was why I continued to wake up in the morning with a flutter in my stomach.

Not the crush sort of flutter Ivan had evoked.

There was no tinge of fear that came along with my anticipation of seeing Rhys each day. No worry over ruining something important because there was nothing to ruin. Whatever we were had been formed out of thin air on a docked boat. There was no pressure to be a certain way or worry over who was talking about us.

He was a secret I whispered to Evelyn in the dark. She asked me a thousand questions, trying to understand, and I asked her a thousand back because I didn't.

But I thought that was what made this exciting. Being with Rhys in the way we were was an uncharted path. He was my own private adventure.

My steps picked up as my chest warmed at the thought of him knocking on my door soon. He would definitely speed through his shower as quickly as he could. Rhys was nothing if not determined.

"Delilah."

I had one foot on the steps to the front door of my dorm when I stopped and turned my head in dread. I knew that voice.

"Roman."

My ex-boyfriend strode toward me, a half smile curving his lips. "Hello there. I almost gave up on seeing you."

"You should have."

I clutched my bag's strap and straightened my spine. It did nothing to add height. Roman still towered over me as he always had.

Chuckling, he rested an arm on the stone ballast beside me, casually cutting off my path. Though, if that had been his intention, I couldn't say. "You Kastanos girls know how to cut me to the quick. Evelyn said the same thing when I saw her earlier."

"Yet you chose not to listen."

His humor faded with a heavy exhale. "I couldn't leave California without a proper goodbye. The way we left things last time...I didn't want to do that again. Being at odds with you is unnatural."

"We aren't at odds. We're nothing. There's no need for any of this."

"*I* have a need. Will you give me five minutes? That's all I'm asking."

I'd loved this man and had been devastated when we'd ended. But his actions, plus time and distance, had dulled all those feelings until they were an old, dusty memory. I barely remembered the girl who had once pined for him. I *wasn't* that girl anymore.

But I could spare five minutes to honor the girl I used to be.

"Okay. I can give you five minutes."

He exhaled his relief, allowing his head to fall forward.

We both took a seat on the stairs, turning toward each other. I tucked my legs to the side and smoothed my skirt over my knees. Roman straightened the collar of his button-down shirt.

"I'm sorry," he started.

"Okay."

His mouth quirked. "You have no forgiveness for me, angel?"

I winced at the pet name. It wasn't one he'd ever used on me, which made me think it was the latest generic one he called all his girls. And I had no doubt Roman was plowing through all the pretty little English roses he could get his hands on. The two years we'd spent together in monogamy had been an anomaly for him. He'd bounced back to his true nature the second my plane had taken off.

"Does it matter?" I asked.

"It does. I certainly wouldn't be here if it didn't." He took my hand between his and rubbed his thumb along my knuckle. "You broke my heart when you left, and I made a bad, destructive choice."

"You were angry at me for leaving. That's why you slept with her."

He opened his mouth to protest and slammed it shut just as quickly, his head falling forward. "You know I didn't agree with your decision to transfer schools. I've always thought you were far too overprotective of Evelyn—"

I yanked my hand from his. "We don't have to rehash this. We'll never agree."

The look he gave me could only be described as bereft, but I didn't believe it. He'd given me an eerily similar one when I'd left, and yet...

"Are you happy here?" he asked.

"Yes. We both are. It was the right choice."

"Leaving me or the school?"

"Both," I answered honestly. "I was too young to be in something so serious with you. And you're too...*you*, to have continued as we were for much longer. I wish my memories weren't tainted by how it all ended, but there's nothing for that now. It's done."

He barely reacted to what I was saying. But that was Roman. He was so used to getting what he wanted my telling him I no longer wanted him was incomprehensible.

"And if you're in Europe? If we live near each other again?"

I lifted a shoulder. "If we cross paths, I'll say hello."

He blew out a heavy breath. "You're cold. I didn't expect this from you, Delilah. I thought you'd miss me like I have missed you."

"It was easy not to miss a man who was so clearly not who I'd fooled myself into believing he was. And anyway, it's been more than a year. I'm sure you've moved on ten times over. I have as well. All of this is tragically moot and far, far too late."

"You've moved on...to that fucking redheaded kid from the restaurant? He's a child, Delilah."

I burst out laughing. "If he is, then so am I, considering we're the same age. You're sitting in front of my high school dorm. Don't you feel a bit silly being here for reasons I've yet to uncover?"

His brow dropped, and he leaned into me, contrition replaced with bitterness. "You aren't a child. You weren't when I fucked you at fifteen, and you aren't one now. Don't try to rewrite history—"

"Sorry, sir, but Grandparents' Visiting Day isn't until next week."

Roman broke away from me, swiveling around to peer at Rhys, who was standing over us, swinging his pocket watch.

"We're busy here," Roman gritted out.

"Sure, sure," Rhys nodded. "But as I said, you'll have to come back next week for Grandparents' Day."

Roman scowled at me. "What the hell is this idiot on about? I'm clearly not a grandparent."

Rhys's hand flew to his cheek. "Oh, pardon me, sir. My mistake. It's just...you're so fucking old, I thought you had to be Delilah's granddad. I couldn't really imagine any other reason for you to be so close to a girl much, *much* younger than you are."

Hopping up, I grabbed Rhys's hand. "Come on, trouble. Roman and I were finished talking."

Roman sputtered, calling after me, but I kept moving forward, a cackling Rhys in tow. He was getting a hell of a kick out of the chaos he'd created.

He stayed on my heels all the way to my room, where he kicked the door shut behind him and snapped the lock. Then he leaned his back against it, tucked his hands in his pockets, and crossed his ankles.

"Explain that guy."

"An ex." I dropped my bag and toed off my loafers before sitting on the side of my bed and rolling down my knee socks. "I suppose I should say he's *the* ex."

"You do know he's exceedingly old, don't you? At the restaurant, I wondered if I was off in my estimation because of the lighting. But no, he's old."

I shrugged off my jacket and unbuttoned a few buttons on my top. "He's twenty-three. The same age as Michael."

Rhys's lip curled with obvious disgust. "Five years older? And...I'm assuming he was the one you were with when you were fifteen?"

I nodded. "In hindsight, it wasn't the best choice."

He straightened, tossing his arms out. "It's a felony, princess. *Jesus.* What was he even doing here? Is he like a serial killer who can't help but return to the scene of the crime?"

I tossed my shirt aside and crossed to my dresser, pulling out a T-shirt. Before I had the chance to slip it on, Rhys was behind me, his arms circling me, his palms cupping my lace-covered breasts.

"Am I the crime scene?" I leaned into his warmth, turning my head to the side.

"These tits are criminal, but don't try to distract me with them." He lashed at the crook of my neck with several long licks. "You were with him when you were fifteen and he was twenty?"

I nodded. "Yes."

"And your brother didn't beat him to a fucking pulp for going there with you?"

"No, Rhys. Michael isn't that kind of brother. His biggest reaction was annoyance when Roman brought me to social gatherings. It's difficult to snort coke off girls' tits when your little sister is present. Or so I assume."

His mouth was warm on my neck. "I don't find this funny. In fact, call Roman back here. I'd like to do what Michael failed to."

I turned so we were chest to chest. "He isn't important. He's the distant past for me, and he made it really easy to move on."

"I hope you were the one to dump his old, wrinkly ass."

I laughed even though Rhys was dead serious. "We broke up because of circumstances. Ev and I transferred here, and neither

Roman nor I wanted to do long distance, so that was that. He didn't want me to leave, but we couldn't stay."

"Hmmm." He trailed his thumb along my bottom lip. "Not that I'm not pleased you're here, but why couldn't you stay?"

"The situation at our school became...untenable."

He frowned at my hesitance to reveal the details. "I won't repeat anything you say. Ask Beckett. I kept his obsession with Luciana secret for five years."

"Because he would have killed you if you hadn't."

"True. I do respond well to threats of violence, so feel free." He pressed on my lip. "Talk to me."

I sighed and let it out. "Ev was being viciously bullied, and nothing was done about it by the administration. She never asked me to leave with her, but it wasn't a safe place for her. I made an escape plan for us. Savage Academy has a good reputation for snuffing out bullying swiftly, and the distance was enticing. I wanted her far, far away from that school."

There was something incredibly soft about the way he was looking at me. "So, you packed your bags, dumped your old-ass boyfriend, and moved across the world to protect your sister?"

I nodded once.

His head dropped to the curve of my neck, and he dragged his tongue along my shoulder. My stomach clenched, and I dug my fingers into his hair, holding him close.

"This is probably an inappropriate reaction, but I have never found you sexier." He rocked his erection into my belly. "Can I eat you out, princess?"

"Really? Is this a reaction to seeing me with my ex?"

"Nope. My plans had already been made before I saw you with that geriatric little bitch." He took my face in his hands. "I'd rather you not mention him again when I'm on the verge of burying my face between your thighs, though. If that's all right with you."

My laugh was breathy. "I can handle that." I broke out of his arms and backed up toward my bed, my heart lodged in my throat.

Lifting my skirt on the sides, I hooked my thumbs in the band of my underwear and tugged them down and off. Rhys watched, hunger turning his eyes nearly black.

Suddenly, I was nervous even though I shouldn't have been. Rhys was the one with something to prove here, but it was me who'd be laid bare.

"Take your shirt off." I licked my dry lips. "Please."

Snagging his shirt, Rhys yanked it over his head then prowled toward me. I backed up another step. My legs hit the mattress, knocking me off balance, and I landed with a bounce. Rhys was over me a second later, his mouth covering mine, and all my concern vanished under the slide of his tongue and the groan emitted when we connected. He kissed me like he'd been wanting to for centuries. Like he was starved for me. Angry at me. Wild for me.

His hands were all over me. In my hair, around my throat, kneading my breasts, practically massacring my bra to get to my nipples. He rolled them between his fingers, and I moaned down his throat. He nipped and sucked, kissing me stupid, touching me alive. My skin sparked and sizzled as he dragged his knuckles and fingertips along every bare place, stroking me, knowing me.

"Delilah," he murmured. "Can I?"

Rhys lifted his head, meeting my gaze. His lips were puffy and pink. The freckles on his cheeks were glowing from how flushed he was. His hair was poking in every direction, courtesy of my fingers.

He was handsome in a way that wasn't like anyone else. Not quite conventional, but real and gut-clenching. Looking at him this way, above me, aroused by me, desperate for me, gave me a heady sense of power.

"Are you ready for me?" he asked.

"I don't think I am, but I want you anyway," I answered.

He squeezed his eyes shut. "You drive me mad, woman."

I spread my legs wider, and he dropped his hips to settle between them. I rocked against the thick erection prodding me, and Rhys groaned, rearing away from me.

"Naughty little princess." He tapped my nose. "There will be none of that. I owe you many orgasms, remember?"

I rubbed my lips together. "I haven't forgotten."

With a grunt, he worked his way down my body, licking a path from my sternum to my belly button. Slowly, he slowly gathered my skirt to my waist, revealing my bare, slicked flesh beneath.

He closed his eyes and inhaled, his chest rising. "Fuck, you smell good." Then he lowered himself onto his stomach and pressed his warm palms on my legs, spreading me wide.

For a long, drawn-out moment, he didn't move. His nose was nuzzled against my inner thigh, and his eyes were locked on my pussy. I felt him breathing me in, slow and deep.

"What are you doing?" I whispered.

"Taking my time." He raised his brows, peering up at me. "Have you looked at yourself down here? You're exceptionally pretty."

One finger drew a line along my outer lip. "I like how you're made, princess. So soft and pink. Like a cute little Easter marshmallow."

"What does that mean?"

"Take my word for it. It's a good thing." Leaning forward, he kissed my pussy. "Yeah. A really good thing. Tell me what you want from me. Tell me how you like it. If you leave it up to me, I'm going to dive right in and get incredibly messy from the nectar beginning to drip between all this shiny pink."

"Nectar?" I repeated with a soft laugh.

"Don't mock me." He nibbled my thigh, sending goose bumps trailing along my legs. "Start talking."

I reached down to card my fingers through his hair and touched his stubbled jaw. I'd never done anything like this, but wasn't that why we were here? I was supposed to tutor Rhys to be a better lover, and that meant I had to find the words. It wasn't easy to just...*say* what I liked.

"Lick my clit. Flick your tongue on it. Suck it when I get close."

His finger lightly dragged from my clit to my entrance. "What about the rest of you? Can I taste that too?"

"Mmmhmm. But once I get close, stay on my clit."

"You're convinced I'll get you there?"

I was. He had me this turned on without even touching me. I was aching for his mouth. It wouldn't take much skill to bring me over.

"That's why we're here." My hips rose of their own accord, and Rhys took it as an invitation. Before I could say anything else, his tongue was on my flesh.

He drew back and stared at my pussy. "God*damn*, Delilah."

My heart stuttered. "What?"

He raised his hooded eyes to mine. "How am I ever going to do anything else now that I know what you taste like?"

He didn't expect an answer, and it was good I didn't have to speak. In the next beat, he dove back in, and I was rendered speechless, my lower half clenching into a ball of desire. Certainly, no one had ever said anything like that to me.

He was messy at first, pressing his face into me. It wasn't going to make me come, but I liked the way it felt so, so much. With my fingers in his hair, I closed my eyes and relaxed into his ministrations.

Each lap of his tongue, he groaned like he was the one being pleasured.

"That feels really good," I told him. "Please don't stop."

His grip on my thighs tightened, and he went at me with even more determination. Finally, *finally,* he moved to my clit, swirling and flicking, paying it exquisite attention.

My belly tightened, and all of me went hot. Fingers curling in his hair, I pressed myself to his mouth. He lapped my clit then sucked, pulsing his lips around it.

A loud cry escaped before I could stop it. Too aware my roommates could probably hear me but unable to keep quiet, I covered my face with my pillow and moaned Rhys's name.

It was so good.

So, so good.

I came and came, and he never let up. Sucking, kissing, making me fly.

"One more," he murmured.

"Yes," I answered. "Please."

"Can I put my tongue inside you?"

"Uh-huh. Yes. Okay. Please."

His chuckle vibrated, sending aftershocks through me. "So polite."

The next moment, he did as he'd asked, plunging his wicked tongue past my entrance. My hips snapped off the bed and plummeted just as fast. His thumb rolled my beaded clit while he fucked me with his tongue.

I'd never...never...never known this feeling.

Hadn't known it was something I'd like.

That would get me off.

Dear god, was I coming apart at the seams.

It took less than a minute before I was tumbling into another orgasm, rocking against his mouth, crying into my pillow. Sweat misted my skin. Tears leaked from the corners of my eyes.

He crawled up me, kissing the same path he'd made on his way down, then he knocked my pillow to the ground and took my mouth with his.

We shifted to our sides, tangled together while we kissed and held each other tight. Our legs were braided, and our arms were wrapped. He stroked my back and palmed my ass. I dug my fingers down the back of his pants and trailed along his spine.

Eventually, some of the wild heat cooled, and our kisses slowed into lingering pecks and lazy licks. We parted and stared at each other, too close to see the finer details.

Rhys grinned, the corners of his eyes crinkling. "I did it."

"You did, and I barely had to direct you."

"I paid attention to what you told me. Even a monkey can be trained."

"Shut it."

His gaze turned intense. "That was the hottest experience of my life, Delilah. I'm going to make a hobby out of eating you out."

I giggled. "It's a good thing I wear skirts on a daily basis, then."

"I'm pleased you're not arguing with me on this."

"Why would I? It seems I'm getting all the benefits from your hobby."

He chuffed. "If you think I didn't get anything from that, you weren't paying attention when I said it was the hottest experience of my life."

"Aren't you sorry you've missed out on doing that all these years?"

"No," he declared. "It was hot because it was you. Your taste, the way you had to smother your sweet moans with your pillow, how you unabashedly ground your pussy into my mouth... Princess, there is no way that could have been better with anyone else."

My lips parted. He meant it, I could tell, but I still wanted to argue. I couldn't let what he was saying settle inside me.

"But you didn't get off."

"Believe me, I will get off on that for years to come." He drew a line down my nose. "Stop fighting me on this. Do you think I'd say untrue things just to flatter you?"

"No. I don't think you would. I'm far too much work unless you're genuinely interested."

He laughed. "You said it, not me. But I'm just as much work, so I don't mind."

I sucked in a shaky breath and told him the truth. "I don't either."

Maybe I was high off two orgasms, but I was having all sorts of feelings for Rhys I'd never expected...and was more than a little wary of.

This was never supposed to happen with Rhys Astor.

Chapter Twenty-Four
Rhys

"You like me."

The flush in Delilah's cheeks deepened. "You like me too."

I pecked the tip of her nose. "You're all right."

"And you're sort of okay."

With a sigh, I rolled to my back and adjusted the bulge in my pants. I needed to break the thick tension before I risked doing something stupid. Trying to mount her like the wild animal she'd turned me into was at the top of that list. "Your poor old man ex is probably sobbing on his way to the airport right about now."

That did the trick.

With a laugh, she climbed over me to grab her T-shirt from the floor. "Must you mention him when I'm not even dressed?"

Delilah had a way of moving that wasn't like anyone else. There was an easy confidence in her limbs. She shimmied into her underwear and tossed her wrinkled skirt on top of the rest of her discarded clothing without a care in the world. I couldn't take my eyes off her and found myself wondering again how I'd been near her for over a year without noticing any of this.

"I'm still pissed he went after you when you were fifteen."

She blew out a heavy breath and perched on the end of the bed. "I do think he cared for me, Rhys."

That made me scoff. "If he really cared, he would have waited a few years."

"I won't defend him. If it had been my daughter with a twenty-year-old man, I'd raze heaven and earth." She touched her chest.

"However, my mother had told me again and again how lucky I was a man like him was interested in a girl like me. So, you see why I stayed with him for so long."

I shook my head with disgust. "Your mother had no idea what she was talking about."

"I know that now. She's a ridiculous woman. But if you hear something is wrong with you enough times, you internalize it."

I knew that all too fucking well. "You know he was the lucky one, right? Both to have you and not catch a charge."

She laughed. "Thank you for saying that. It doesn't matter. I've chalked Roman up to a learning experience. He's what I don't want, and I know that now."

Knifing upright, I looped my arms around her middle and dragged her down on the bed with me. She squealed with surprise but came willingly, settling her softness at my side.

She patted my face. "Has your ego now recovered after you succeeded in making me come?"

"Not quite. I have some work to do."

"I won't stop you." Another pat on my face. "How old was the girl who you were with when you were fourteen?"

I'd been hoping we could skip over that—especially after the big deal I'd made over her ex-fossil.

"She was a senior," I muttered.

Delilah pulled back, her eyes wide. "Oh my...*Rhys*. Are you, in fact, a gigantic hypocrite?"

"At least she was in high school too."

"Okay, sure. And what happened with this much, much older girl? Was she the love of your life?"

"Absolutely not," I said adamantly. "She's the reason I have nothing to do with girls at SA. Once I cut it off with her, she wouldn't leave me alone. It was a fucking nightmare, and my parents actually told me I should have been flattered by her attention."

Her mouth formed a perfect little *o*. "Do we have the same parents?"

"Cut from the same cloth, apparently."

My gut twisted at the parallels of our lives. I knew all too well how Delilah must've felt hearing those words from her mother. I'd heard much of the same.

"I let it go on with her for far too long because I was trying to be someone else. I was tired of being the nerdy *Shadow of the Isle* kid I'd been all my life. She was a popular girl, and I'd wanted some of that to rub off on me—make the people who'd known me before forget the times I'd shown up to school wearing my Fathaniel Flamen robes."

Her mouth quivered into a half smile. "I bet you were cute."

"Don't feel sorry for me."

She shoved my arm. "Don't you feel sorry for me?"

"I don't. I'm furious for you."

"Well, I'm furious for you too. And I really don't like that you've hidden away an important part of yourself."

I scoffed at that. "I don't need to exist in a fantasy world anymore. I'm not looking for a way out of who I am. There was a time I'd needed it to make it through, but that's long gone. I am who I am, and I've learned not to give a solitary fuck what anyone thinks."

"Hmmm."

"What's that 'hmmm' about?" I gripped her chin, tilting her face up to mine. "You don't believe me?"

"It isn't that."

"Then what?"

She rolled her lips between her teeth. I waited, keeping a hold of her chin until she answered. "Is it possible you abandoned the idea of fitting in with the crowd when it was never going to happen and adopted this...kind of abrasive outer shell? When you're not part of something, it seems like it's because you don't care to be, not because you weren't included. People can't tell you there's something wrong with you when you're telling them you already know there is and don't *give a solitary fuck what anyone thinks*."

My stomach plummeted further and further with every word, and a sick feeling crawled through my veins. I shot up out of bed, needing to be away from her.

"You don't know what you're talking about." I bent down and picked up my shirt, shoving it over my head.

"Rhys." She was behind me, her hand grazing my back. "I'm sorry. I shouldn't have said anything. Clearly, I have no idea—"

I spun around, unable to meet her eyes, which saw right the fuck through me.

"No, you don't. I didn't ask to be analyzed by you. What the hell were you thinking?"

"Nothing." She held up her hands. "Obviously, my brain has gone haywire, and I let my mouth run away from me. Please, I didn't mean to—"

I held up a finger. My face was burning. I needed to get the hell out of here. "It's enough. No more talking."

She folded her arms. "You're overreacting. I was wrong and apologized."

There she was. The steel-spined Delilah Kastanos, who had intrigued me from the moment I'd met the real her. I paused, staring down at her diminutive height, the wild waves haloing her head. Her bare thighs. Foot tapping impatiently on her carpet. Tits resting on her crossed arms. And finally, her flinty-eyed gaze. She may have apologized, but she wasn't really that sorry.

If anything, she was annoyed by my behavior.

And that stole a lot of the wind out of my angry sails. I couldn't even shove my foot in my shoe I was so flustered by the rightness of everything she'd said.

She reached out first like she knew she had to. My pride had only just repaired itself. I was too much of a fragile asshole to be the one to make the first move. But once her hand touched mine, I hauled her into me and folded myself around her.

"Did you have to bang the nail on the head so fucking hard, princess?"

Her arms were slower to wrap around me, but they did. "I don't like you storming off on me."

"I stayed."

"Almost didn't."

"Give me a minute, Delilah. I'm not used to caring when someone calls me out."

She sucked in a breath. "For the record, I don't think there's anything wrong with you."

Cupping the back of her head, I held her against my chest. My hammering heart gradually calmed as I inhaled her roses and she rubbed me with her cheek.

All I said was, "Thank you."

But it wasn't all I meant. That, I let rattle around in my head and reach its clutches down my throat.

For the record, princess, I give all the fucks what you think of me.

· · · · · · · · · ·

The first two weeks of December, time moved at the speed of light. With fencing and my tutoring sessions with Delilah, I barely made it back to my room before I was ready to crash.

But I'd learned something new about sweet little Delilah. When she had her period, she transformed into a hell demon. This morning, she not only forbade me from looking at her, I was told not to even perceive her. My offer of rubbing her stomach and feeding her grapes or chocolate like a manservant was shot down with a snarl and evil eyes.

Fair, I guessed.

That meant I'd wandered into my suite earlier than I had in quite some time. As I headed to my room, Charles's door flung open, but it wasn't him who emerged.

A girl I didn't recognize stumbled out, hair in a messy ponytail, uniform shirt misbuttoned, shoes in her hand. Charles followed her, his hand on the small of her back as he steered her toward the door. She giggled and whispered to him as he saw her out. His broad back blocked her from my view, but I did not miss the distinct sound of kissing.

He shut the door behind her and turned around, his eyes landing on me. His shoulders jumped, clearly not having seen me standing in the doorway of my bedroom.

"Rhys." He shoved his fingers through the side of his hair. "Didn't expect you so early. You're never here anymore."

I cocked my head in the direction the girl had gone. "Who was that?"

He waved my question off. "No one. A sophomore or something."

"Aren't you with Evelyn?"

He exhaled a heavy breath. "One has nothing to do with the other."

I folded my arms over my chest. "You fucking another girl has nothing to do with Evelyn?"

His hands went to his hips. A defensive pose. "I don't see what it has to do with you, but I'll explain anyway. Evelyn isn't ready to have sex, and I have needs. So, until she is ready to fulfill said needs, I'm slaking them elsewhere. It's a means to an end, that's all. No one's going to get hurt."

Oh, this motherfucker. "Except the girl who just left here and Evelyn when she finds out."

Felix poked his head out of his room. "What's Evelyn going to find out?"

I jabbed a finger at Charles. "That her boyfriend is screwing around."

Felix's head swiveled toward Charles. "I didn't think that was official, with all the girls you've been bringing back here. You're with Ev for real?"

Charles tossed his head back and groaned like we were bothering him. "Like I said, Evelyn doesn't want to have sex, which I respect. I'm all about consent. But we're not gonna be *together* together until then."

Felix held up his hands. "As long as she's aware." Charles didn't say anything to confirm that Evelyn was, but he scoffed with impatience. Felix's hands went to his hips. "She is, right?"

Charles groaned again. "What goes on between Evelyn and me is our business. I don't have to answer to either of you."

Felix knocked his head against his doorjamb. "I wish like hell I didn't know any of this. Evelyn's one of Bella's best friends. I'm not going to say anything, but if Bella happens to ask me anything on this topic, I'm also not going to lie to my girl. So, how 'bout you knock it off, Bloomberg? Then none of us have to cover up your mess." Felix closed his door harder than he needed to.

Charles turned to me. "And you? You're going to keep this between us?"

I scratched the back of my neck. He had me between a rock and a hard place, and he knew it. If I spilled this to Ev, he'd tell Delilah about the money. But I wasn't too keen on keeping this type of secret from either of them.

"You can't keep doing this to her."

He looked away, his jaw flexing. "Yeah. You're right."

"Am I?" I shook my head. "I mean, I know I'm right, but I didn't expect you to agree."

He turned back and crossed to my side of the room. "I like her, Astor. She's strange and sweet. I want to keep her—" He huffed, his shoulders rolling forward. "She won't let me call her my girlfriend, but that's all I want. I don't know. Maybe she senses I'm not all the way in. I have to be in to really have her. I see that now."

I cleared my throat, uncomfortable in the face of Charles's tender emotions. "Good for you. Be the change you want to see."

His eyes narrowed. "You've been going above and beyond with Delilah. You've more than earned your money."

"That isn't what it's about anymore, Bloomberg. I'm sure you're aware of that."

His mouth quirked into a sickening little grin. "Yeah, I kind of figured out you caught feelings." He clapped me on the shoulder. "Good for you. We're almost brothers-in-law now. Let's just hope nothing happens to ruin that. That would be terrible, wouldn't it?"

Charles's ham-fisted threat landed a solid blow.

"It's up to you not to screw up," I told him.

"The thing about me, Astor, is I'm perfectly willing to take you down with me if that's what it comes to."

"I got it." My jaw clenched, but I held back what I really wanted to say, kicking myself for ever giving him an ounce of power over me. I'd been too stupid to consider the repercussions, but here I stood while Bloomberg jizzed them all over my face. "But you heard Felix. I'm not the only one with a hand in the game."

He chuckled. "Yeah, yeah. Now that I think about it, it's cute we're all dating a girl from that suite. We should quadruple date. It would be adorable."

"Nope," I said immediately. "Never happening."

The rest of them? Sure, Evelyn too. But seeing Charles amorous all over her would have me projectile vomiting before appetizers were served.

He laughed even harder. "Okay, I hear you. You'll think about it."

I'd think about it in my nightmares.

CHAPTER TWENTY-FIVE
Delilah

RHYS: *WHAT ARE YOU doing?*

Me: *Hanging with Luc. You?*

Rhys: *Family matters to attend to. Will you be sitting on my face later?*

Me: *As lovely as that invitation is, I'll pass.*

Rhys: *Ugh, fine. Be a pillow princess.*

Me: *Is that a term straight people use?*

Rhys: *I don't know, but let's be real, it's what you are. My princess lies back and relaxes while her knight in shining armor does all the work.*

Me: *That sounds like a complaint.*

Rhys: *Never. It's an honor and a privilege to serve your pussy.*

Me: *I can't tell if you're being sarcastic, and now, I feel weird.*

A request for a video call popped onto my screen. Shutting the door to my bedroom, I accepted. There was Rhys's concerned face.

"Have I ever been indirect with you?" he demanded softly.

"Not that I know of."

He scowled at me. "No, I haven't. Say it."

"No, you haven't."

"If I had any problem spending time between your thighs, eating you, I would say it."

Someone coughed in the near background, which was when I noticed Rhy was in a moving vehicle.

I gasped. "Are you in an Uber?"

"Yes. What does that have to do with anything?"

I fell back on my bed. "You haven't a clue?"

"Do you really care if my driver knows I could eat your pussy morning, noon, and night and not get tired of it? He doesn't know who you are, and you'll never meet. There is no need to be embarrassed."

"You've killed me." I tossed my arm across my face. "Please, please stop."

He chuckled. "Are you convinced?"

"Fine, yes. If you stop now, maybe we can add to our tutoring sessions later."

When he didn't speak, I uncovered my eyes to look at him. He was staring back.

"There's no need to rush," he said softly. "What we're doing is satisfying. I wasn't trying to imply in any way that I need more than you've given me."

"What if I need more?"

We'd been doing this for a few weeks. Rhys never pressed to take things further, and he had become a master at making me come. Over and over until I had to beg him to stop sometimes. I wanted more, and I had for a while, but I was nervous about changing things. Nervous it would be like it had been on the boat. This time, though, it would break my heart a little if he acted like I was nothing more than an object.

Christmas break was next week, and we wouldn't see each other until after New Year's. I knew I would miss him, which was still hard for me to wrap my head around, but I wanted to take the next step before we parted. A gift to both of us.

Rhys exhaled a jagged breath. "If you need more, I'll give it to you."

"Okay," I whispered, suddenly shy in a way I hadn't been when we were hardly more than strangers at the start of this.

He smiled at me, then his eyes slid to the side. "Look, I need to go, but we'll talk as soon as I get back to school. Be a good girl today, all right, princess?"

"Sure. You be good too."

He winked. "I make no such promises."

· · · · · ● · ● · · · ·

Luciana convinced me to leave the academy and go with her to town to do some Christmas shopping. Bella and Freddie came too, but Ev stayed behind, though she sent me with a list of things she wanted me to buy.

Savage River had a cute little Main Street with a couple restaurants, a café, and many independently owned shops. We stopped at the bookstore first, grabbing stacks of books for ourselves and for gifts.

"What are you getting for Felix?" I asked Bella.

She rolled her eyes and huffed. "I have no idea. We haven't put a label on what we are, and he gets skittish if we talk about anything remotely emotional. Will he flip out if I buy him a gift? Is that too girlfriendy?"

"I don't think it's too girlfriendy, love," Freddie answered, looping his arm around her shoulders. "Your love language is gift giving, and you have to be yourself."

She groaned. "Don't let Felix hear you sayin' anything about love."

"It sucks you have to consider words like that so carefully," Luc said.

Bella balled her fists. "He drives me crazy, but if I try to pull back, he gets pissed. I don't even know with that boy."

"He likes you," Freddie declared. "And it's very clear he's too dumb to admit it."

Bella snorted. "That's a fact. I just know I'm not bangin' him until he gets his head out of his ass, you know? Be with me or not. I'm not gonna be in limbo with you. I have better things I could be doin' with my time."

But as the last few words left her mouth, her voice cracked, and her eyes welled with tears. Luc declared a state of emergency, and we bundled her off to the café for sweets and coffee.

The four of us found a table by the front window and covered it with pastries we all picked at while Bella unloaded her frustrations with Felix. I'd never seen her sad over a boy, so I knew it was serious—on her end, at least.

"Perhaps with some distance over break, he'll gain clarity," I offered.

Bella shrugged. "Why does it get to be up to him? That's what's not fair."

I offered her a chunk of chocolate chip muffin. "I know, babe. How can he not see what a catch you are?"

Freddie cuddled her into his side. "I've some mates coming in from England for New Year's. I can set you up with one of them. We'll post salacious pics all over social media and make Felix swallow his tongue."

Bella buried her face in his shoulder and groaned. "It's so bad, Fred. Normally, I'd be all over that, but I don't *want* him to see me with another guy. The idea makes me ill."

He cooed at her and stroked her back. My stomach was sick for her. I didn't have any advice, but I made a mental note to ask Rhys what Felix's deal was. If he was seeing other girls, I'd boot his testicles into his throat.

Luciana leaned toward the window. "Is that Rhys over there?"

I tried to find where she was pointing, squinting my eyes. "Surely not. He said he had a family do this afternoon. He's home—"

I finally landed on a man on the other side of the street. His height and red hair made him stick out like a sore thumb, but still, I wasn't sure it was him until he turned and I saw his unmistakable profile.

The strangest thing was he was holding a small child. A toddler, probably, though I couldn't quite estimate his age.

"Someone allowed Rhys Astor to hold a baby?" Freddie asked.

My brow pinched. "Yes. I don't know why he's—"

A pretty blonde woman approached carrying two shopping bags. The child reached for her. She grinned at him and tickled his belly.

"Oh, who's this bitch?" Bella muttered before flailing her hands. "Sorry, I'm in a bad mood. I have no proof she's a bitch."

"That's my sweet little Southern belle," Freddie said.

Rhys kept the child in one arm and slung the other around the blonde's shoulders before the three of them strolled down the sidewalk. A boulder lodged in my throat.

"Okay, seriously, who's that bitch?" Bella growled.

I turned back to my table of friends. "I don't know, but that was strange, wasn't it?"

Luc laughed, but it sounded somewhat forced. "Probably a family member. It's not like Rhys has a kid. I mean, that would be crazy. And Beckett definitely would have told me. He doesn't keep secrets from me."

"That kid looked like he was three." Bella tapped her chin. "Would Beckett have just out of the blue mentioned Rhys's three-year-old son?"

I covered my face with my hands. "I would think Rhys might have told me."

None of them said anything for a long time. When I made myself look up at them, three pairs of eyes peered back at me, all with some levels of sympathy in their gazes. As if they'd decided Rhys was indeed a father and had hidden it from me.

"Well, I'll just ask him," I said. "We're seeing each other later, and I'll ask. Then I'll know, and it won't be a mystery."

"That's right." Freddie pulled me into his other side and kissed the top of my head. "Don't get upset over something when you don't know what's really going on. That very well could have been a friendly stranger who'd asked Rhys to hold her child and—okay, no. Even I don't believe that."

"Not helpful, Frederick," Bella drawled. "Work on your pep talks."

He gave her a jiggle. "It isn't my fault all my ladies have such complicated romantic lives. I'm only seventeen, for heaven's sake. Life has not prepared me for all this drama."

"Oh, please. Drama is your main food group," Luc teased.

"Other people's drama. People I don't know," Freddie corrected. "I don't like when my friends are going through it. I'm a sensitive soul."

"I'm not going through drama," I argued. "I have a question to which I'll have an answer by this evening."

Freddie raised a brow. "And you'll send the answer in the group chat as soon as you have it, correct?"

"Of course, darling."

I floated through the rest of the day, shopping with my friends and laughing at Freddie, but never far from my mind was Rhys, the child, and his arm around the lovely blonde woman.

· · · · · · · · · ·

Rhys charged into my suite, took me by the shoulders, and licked the side of my face.

"Sweet as always," he murmured beside my ear.

"Shut up, trouble." I shoved him away and started for my room, Rhys nipping at my heels.

Bella poked her head out of her room and gave Rhys a major side-eye. He jerked his chin toward her.

"What's up with the face, Belladonna?"

"You should have seen the one I made at you earlier, Rhys-ling." Without another word, she swiveled on her toes and flounced back into her room.

"Does your roommate always talk such nonsense?" he asked.

"No. Not at all."

My plan was to get my question out of the way as soon as possible. With the nerves swirling in my belly, I couldn't stand to carry on much longer.

Rhys roamed my room while I leaned against the door.

"What did you end up doing today?" he asked.

I nodded to the bags I'd piled next to my desk. "Christmas shopping on Main Street with Luc, Freddie, and Bells."

"Oh?" He raised a brow. "I didn't know that was your plan."

"It was a spur-of-the-moment thing." I pushed off the door and moved to my bed, perching on the edge. Rhys quickly flopped down beside me.

"Did you buy anything good?"

"Not anything you'd be interested in."

He poked his bottom lip out. "Not anything for me?"

"Do you want a gift from me?"

"Well, if I say yes, I'll seem greedy. If I say no, then I won't get a present, so I'm torn on how to answer."

I narrowed my eyes. "I saw you today."

"You did?" The corner of his mouth hitched. Not quite a smile, but he was trying. "We had the same idea, huh?"

I sighed. He wasn't going to tell me. I'd have to be the one to get it out of him.

"I thought you were with family today, Rhys."

He nodded. "I was."

My stomach sank. "The little boy...is he yours? Are you a father?"

Rhys looked at me for a long, drawn-out moment, his deep-brown eyes skating over my face. I wanted to scream for him to answer me. To tell me the truth. But I waited, chewing on the inside of my cheek.

His mouth opened...and he burst out laughing. "Wow, not what I was expecting." He swiped at his eyes. "Hell no, I'm not a father."

I failed to see the humor. "The little boy had red hair like yours."

"Runs in the family." He took my hands in his. "The woman and the boy are family members, Delilah. I spent a few hours with my family in Savage River today like I said. I didn't lie to you. I don't do that. Not with you."

The knot in my chest unfurled. Of course he wasn't a dad. It made sense, and I felt immensely silly for thinking it might have been true.

He brought my hands to his mouth and nibbled to my knuckles. "Were you worried about this all day?"

"Not worried." My eyes fluttered closed, and I sucked in a breath. "That isn't quite the right word. I would have been disappointed if you'd kept something like that from me."

"I didn't." He put my hands on his chest and slid his fingers into the sides of my hair to hold my head. "Will you show me what you bought today?"

"Do you actually want to see, or are you humoring me?"

He cocked his head. "Do you think I'm only here for the delectable pussy? Because that's not it. I want your company. I find it hard to stay away from you. Let's listen to some Florence and look at your loot."

We'd both talked a big game earlier in our texts, but neither of us made a move to turn things heated. The rest of the evening was spent exactly as Rhys had said. I showed him what was in my bags, and he tossed it all around like the chaos demon he was, then we lay together on my bed, singing along to our favorite songs. His hand clasped mine, and I sank into the knowledge that whatever this was, it was *more*.

CHAPTER TWENTY-SIX
Rhys

ALL SEASON, I'D BEEN winning my matches for Delilah. To impress her with my prowess since I severely lacked it in other ways. To make her proud of me. To show off. Most importantly, to turn her on to the point she'd willingly sit on my face.

So, when I very nearly lost against an opponent I should have easily beaten, I not only disappointed myself but Delilah too. That was how it felt, at least.

A twisted fucking dagger of disappointment lodged in my gut.

I shouldn't have even been challenged, but my thoughts had been elsewhere. Break was coming up, and I'd be spending a solid ten days at the Astor residence. Just me, my mother, and Preston. No Catrin. No warmth. No holly jolly Christmas.

That was weighing on me, but it wasn't the only thing.

The money I'd taken from Charles had become a telltale heart, thumping with the rhythm of my guilt. I'd done what I had to do and didn't feel an ounce of remorse for that. It was the deception that was getting to me. I didn't enjoy being guilty. It wasn't a feeling I was familiar with. But there was not a chance in hell I would admit to Delilah what I had done.

Knowing that with absolute sureness hadn't stopped all of this from driving me to distraction.

Thus, nearly losing the match like a chump who'd just signed up for the team last week.

I was slumped in my seat on the back of the bus, leaning against the warm window, when Delilah sat down beside me. I couldn't look at her, talk to her, listen to her voice. I needed to wallow in my pit of self-disgust.

In my periphery, she held something out to me. I glance down, finding an earbud in her palm. After a beat, I took it, fitting it in my ear. The Front Bottoms were already playing.

When the bus started moving, I took Delilah's hand in mine and rested my head on top of hers. With her, the reasons I had to feel like a piece of shit faded. It wouldn't last. Eventually, she'd take her earbud back and slip her hand from mine, and I'd still be walking around under Charles Bloomberg's guillotine.

Delilah pressed my cheek to turn my head so she could speak into my empty ear. "You're feeling sorry for yourself, aren't you?"

"You saw me out there."

"I did. You were a mess."

I pulled back, on the verge of snapping at her. I couldn't do it, though. She wasn't wrong, and hell, I liked that she didn't lie to me.

"My head wasn't in it."

Her fingers slid into my hair, and she drew me down to her to press a soft kiss on my lips.

"I could tell. Want to unload on me?"

"There's nothing particularly interesting to say. School, family, life. Not very original."

"Still, if you need to talk—"

"I don't. I need not to lose my next match." I rolled my forehead on hers. "Will you make out with me?"

A puff of air blew from her lips, hitting mine. "Right here, right now?"

"Mmmhmm. With the rest of the fencing team rows away. What do you say?"

"Have you gone mad?"

"Yes." I took her by the nape and hauled her into my chest. "Yes?"

"Mmm...yes."

With Delilah's music in our ears, my team in front of us, the road beneath us, I made out with my girl for the rest of the ride home.

We were still kissing when we pushed into Delilah's room and I kicked the door closed behind us. She ripped her lips from mine, but only to remove her shirt and kick off her shoes. I tossed mine aside too, then I was on her, my hands on the softest skin I'd ever felt, her body flush with mine.

I walked her to the bed, knocking her down. She squealed, and I pounced, crawling over her like a prowling predator.

"Do you know you make it easy?" I uttered in not much more than a whisper.

Her fingernails trailed along the ridges of my abdomen. "Make what easy?"

"Everything." I dipped down to take her mouth again, falling to my side and taking her with me. She ended up half sprawled on top of me, her skirt flipping up to expose her little lace boy shorts and plenty of plump ass cheek.

I kneaded her roundest spots—tits, ass, hips. It wasn't just that she was soft, she felt like everything good. All the glowing memories I still had, the times I felt safe, content, when I won, cool sheets, laughing with the person who got my humor, thunderstorms, mewling kittens, sunrises on the beach. That was Delilah, how she felt and made me feel.

Clothes were discarded, unneeded. Once bare, our hands were everywhere, hers on me, mine on her. Of course, there weren't many times my hands weren't on this girl.

She held on to my shoulders and tangled her feet with the backs of my calves. "I want to do this with you, Rhys."

A shot of pure fear streaked through me. Not that I was scared of Delilah. It was more that I was afraid of screwing up yet a-fucking-gain.

But I wanted to make it right this time. Good for her and me. And I had a feeling it would be a lot better for me now. Things were different. I understood now. Delilah had shown me the way.

"I'm going to get you there first, princess."

She didn't argue as I worked my way down her body, sucking her milk-chocolaty-brown nipples that were so goddamn sweet I had to stop myself from taking a nibble out of them. They were perfect. Big and pebbled. I liked to study the way they reacted to my thumb brushing them when they were soft.

Lucky me, Delilah let me. She trusted me with her body, and she was right to. I might've been a screwup and would undoubtedly mess up in a way to make her hate me in the near future, but I would never hurt her.

Pushing her thighs apart, I worked my way between them, spreading her with my fingers, and dragged my tongue from her opening to her clit. Her breathing shuddered, and she wiggled, pressing herself deeper into my mouth.

I knew her now. What she liked. What her noises meant. How to kiss her, touch her, make her cry my name.

I could make her come in no time. Her clit was a little slut. Give it some attention, and it bloomed for me.

Tonight, I went slow with her. Not teasing—Delilah didn't like that—but savoring. I built her up with precise swirls of my tongue on her slick, sweet flesh. Held her ass to lift her to my face as I wrapped my lips around her clit and suckled.

Delilah's moan vibrated, and her inner thighs quivered on either side of my head. Her fingers worked into my hair, holding me against her. Her gentle, wordless requests got to me, making me work harder for her. Her pleasure was mine.

Before this girl, I had no idea I could care about another person's pleasure more than my own. She kept showing me the way. Leading me to the truth.

In this case, the truth was between her thick thighs. The truth was the dark-pink flesh that slickened when I took care of it. The pearly clit that throbbed and grew when I licked it right, her hands cupping my face and stroking my hair. My name on her lips. Her hips rose to the pleasure I was responsible for.

"Rhys," she cried. "I'm—oh..."

A burst of flavor hit my tongue, and she ground into me as she came undone, wholly and completely. I pressed my cock into the mattress, needing the pressure for an ounce of relief.

But there was no relief. The ache in my cock intensified as her moans slowed and softened.

"Come here," she whispered. "I want you inside me."

Closing my eyes, I rested my forehead on her lower stomach. Why did she have to do this to me? As if I wasn't already out of my mind from her body and taste, she had to say things like that? Did she want me to come all over myself before I came close to getting inside her?

"Rhys," she pleaded. "Come here, trouble. I really want you."

"I can't leave you wanting, princess." Spurred into action by a request I couldn't deny, I climbed back up her, stopping to suck her nipples again, lick her neck, then cover her mouth with mine.

Settled between her legs, I pressed my dick against her folds. We kissed because that was what we knew, what we were certain of, as I nudged her swollen clit with the head of my cock.

She sighed into my mouth and raised her legs higher, her feet at my hips. I pressed in again, hitting her clit, making her moan.

"Rhys, you're teasing," she accused.

"Do you know how good you feel?"

She shook her head. "No. Tell me."

I murmured my innermost thoughts into her mouth. "Before, I was thinking you feel like everything good that's ever happened to me. But it's more than that. You feel like wishes that have yet to come true."

She arched, rocking with me. "What kind of wishes?"

"World peace. You know, small things like that."

She blinked, her face so close to mine her long lashes tickled my cheeks. "I feel like world peace?"

"Mmm. Crazy?"

"Not the craziest thing you've ever said to me." Lifting her head, she pressed her lips to the base of my throat and swirled her tongue over my Adam's apple. "Grab the condom."

My heart threatened to beat its way out of my chest. This was it.

I grabbed the condom from her nightstand and ripped it open. Sitting back on my knees, I rolled the latex over my length, squeezing my base.

Then I looked at her.

Inky waves spilled over her pillowcase.

Kiss-bitten lips.

Fluttering eyelashes.

Heavy, round tits with the prettiest peaked nipples.

Flaring hips.

Open thighs.

Beauty. Sexy. Too much. All mine.

Jesus, fuck. I'd had this girl beneath me once, and I'd been too detached to recognize all this. I noticed her now. I couldn't look away from her.

When we started this, there was a while I worried I'd mess up again—worried I'd detach again. Not on purpose, but because I wasn't capable of being with someone else on more than a physical level. I hadn't known if I was built to care.

I knew now.

She held her hand out. "Rhys."

"I'm taking my time, Delilah. Don't rush me."

She took my hand and tugged me down. I cradled her face, just looking at her again. Her mouth curved, and she reached between us, sliding her hand along my sheathed cock.

"You don't have to do this." She aligned me with her entrance. "I'm a sure thing. I want this."

"Do what?"

"Act like this matters."

"Delilah." I shoved my fingers through the side of her hair to cup her head. "It does matter. We surpassed me being here to prove something weeks ago. You know that, right?"

One beat, then she nodded and breathed a sigh. "I thought so. Now I know."

"Now you know," I echoed.

Once we were on the same page, I started to ease into her. We both held our breaths as I sank inside. Her inner walls rippled, pulling me deeper and deeper.

When I was all the way in, I had to pause, rubbing my nose along hers. Her legs slid up and down my hips, and she held on to my shoulders.

"Good?"

She nodded. "So good. Move for me, please."

Licking her top lip, I reared my hips back and slowly pushed in again. We found a rhythm together. I paid attention to the noises she made and her expression. We didn't stare into each other's eyes like a pair of weirdos, but my gaze was on her. All over her. Her bouncing tits and parted lips. The perspiration misting her forehead and fluttering pulse in her throat. I *needed* to see her reaction to my pelvis grinding against her clit when I filled her all the way.

"That's my princess," I gritted out. "My sweet little princess."

"Rhys," she panted. "Keep going. Just like that."

"Not gonna stop. Never." It was a lie. My control was a taut string, and Delilah's snug heat was fraying it with every stroke. This would end far before I was ready, but I'd make it as good as I could for the both of us while I had her.

"Yes." Her neck arched, and I latched on to the base, licking and sucking her delicate skin. She cupped my nape, scratching her nails through my sweat. "Please, Rhys."

I kept up my slow, deep pace, retreating, then plunging in, rocking against her clit. Watching her through it all. Making sure she was into it. That she liked what I was doing.

This was brand new. My first time being present and aware of my partner. The first time it meant something more than getting off.

The pleasure was unmatched. She fit me like a glove, so tight and warm, it was all I could do not to let my eyes roll back in my head. But the visual of her beneath me was far too riveting to look away from.

And she was touching me like she liked me too, scraping her nails over my nipples and down my flanks. Couldn't be on the same level as I liked her. That was impossible. Then again, Delilah liking me at all, letting me in again, had seemed like an impossibility until only recently.

But here we were, and I was sliding all the way to the end of her, kissing her like she was my oxygen source, so fucking hungry for her.

Pulling back from her mouth, I stared down at her until her eyes fluttered open and met mine. Hers were glassy and unfocused. Her pussy was slicker, tighter, and her breaths were coming quicker.

"Close?" I murmured.

She nodded and lifted her hips to meet mine. "Close."

Pushing up on my knees, I reached between us to roll her clit under my fingertip. The moment I did, her pants became keening, and her pussy clamped down on me until it was difficult to do more than gentle thrusts.

Locking her ankles around my back, her arms fell limp over her head as she came, my name spilling from her lips. It sank into me, repairing something in me that had been damaged for so long I'd forgotten what it was like to be fixed. Those seconds of Delilah falling apart with me inside her, crying for me because I'd made her feel so good, were euphoric.

I'd do anything to get her to this place again. To watch her like this, lost in pleasure *I'd* given her. I'd never known anything as gratifying. We were only in the middle, and I wanted to start all over again.

She reached for me, pulling me down over her. Her mouth beside my ear, she nipped at my lobe. "I want you to come inside me. Fuck me how you want to."

I pressed my cheek to hers as I shuddered. "Can you take it hard?"

"*Anything* you need, Rhys. Give it to me." There was fire in her words, vehemence I couldn't argue with.

"You're going to get what you asked for, princess."

Shifting down, I hooked her legs over my arms and pushed them up and out, spreading her wide for me, then drove into her hard, testing her reaction. From her gasping breath and curling fingers, she had no objection.

I let myself go. Not in the way I used to, fucking mindlessly. No, I fucked my girl with precise attention. Powering into her with my fierce desire for her. Kneading her tits and telling her how gorgeous, sexy, hot she was.

Her nails dug into my shoulders and biceps, and she met me thrust for thrust. Her cheeks flushed a deep pink. Lids at half-mast, lips kiss-swollen and puffy, she was a wild, untamable creature. My precious princess with a pussy that didn't quit. So tight and hot I would be thinking about her perfection on my deathbed.

Never forget this. Never give it up.

Delilah's mouth fell open, and she was crying out again, her inner walls clenching tight around me. And that was it.

All she wrote.

I couldn't hold back a second longer.

I pushed into her until our pelvises were flush and spilled deep inside her, just as she'd asked. Rutting against her, I came and came, relief and extreme pleasure mingling, coming out of me in echoing groans I made no attempt to muffle.

When she'd wrung everything out of me, I rolled us to our sides and took her mouth with mine. Her arms wrapped tight around me, and we went at each other, just as hungry as we'd been at the start of this.

I took her face in my hands, kissing her mouth and licking the salt from her skin to get to the sweetness underneath. Slowly, gradually, urgent kisses became softer, more time in between, until our lips were ghosts haunting one another.

The condom meant I had to pull out of her before I was ready. Once I got rid of it, I curled around her and buried my face in her hair.

Part of me braced for her to get up and get dressed like she had the first time. Then, I hadn't considered stopping her. This time, we were in her room. She couldn't escape me, and I wasn't leaving.

"Well?" I pushed her hair off her face. "How was it, Dillydally?"

She laughed against my shoulder. "That's even less charming when we're naked."

"You didn't answer my question."

After a beat, she propped herself on her elbow and trailed her nails over my chest.

"I think you've ruined me, trouble."

I cocked my head. "How so?"

"Because"—she poked the center of my sternum—"that was, without equivocation, the best sex I've ever had. I refuse to believe it can be better than that."

"For me too."

She grinned. "Well, of course. But you've been having Fleshlight sex. Obviously, putting forth a little more effort would make it the best you've ever had."

"Hey." I gripped her ass and yanked her flush with me. "First, I never want to hear you mention having sex with anyone other than me."

"I won't. I've already forgotten...what was his name? I can't remember."

Her ass got a light smack for that. "That's better. Secondly, effort had some to do with it, but it was more than that. It was the best because it was with you."

"Rhys." Her mouth quivered. "You give me two orgasms then say the sweetest things to me? What the hell are you doing, trouble? You're getting me hooked on you."

"Right where I want you." I smacked her again, making her squeal. "Thirdly, I firmly believe it can be better than that."

Her brow dropped. "That isn't nice."

"You misunderstand me. You and I can do better. Next time, I want you to ride me. Then I want to take you from behind. And I'm still holding out for you sitting on my face."

She giggled, her head falling against mine. "Shut up. I don't like you."

"Yes you do."

I felt her smile against my cheek. "You're right. I really do. Can we promise not to mess this up?"

My heart thrashed with wild panic for a moment before I forced it to calm with a deep breath and the threat of eviction.

"I'm going to try, princess. I'm going to try my fucking hardest."

I would do what I had to do to keep that promise.

Chapter Twenty-Seven
Delilah

"Wake up."

I rolled to my side, burying my face in my pillow. "I will not."

Rhys wrapped himself around my back. "Wake up, Denver. It's my last day with you, and I need a lot of attention."

"Have you moved on to city names now?"

He pushed on my shoulder, and I allowed him to roll me to my back. Cracking an eye open, I peered at his sleep-mussed hair and heavy lids.

"Must you continue with this charade? You like it. You're charmed by me."

I was. God, I was. Rhys had spent every night in my bed since we'd slept together last week, and I fell deeper and deeper each time he held me, made me laugh, cared for me. We were leaving for winter break this afternoon, and it would be nearly two weeks until we saw each other again. Before, I'd been dreading the time with my parents. Now, I was dreading being away from Rhys.

Even thinking that still messed with my mind, but I had accepted it.

"Fine. I do." I patted his scruffy cheek. I loved his red-and-blond stubble, and he'd let it grow longer than usual to amuse me. "What shall we do today?"

"Hmmm." He dipped down to rub his nose along mine and kiss my lips. "I thought I'd take you out to the finest establishment for breakfast."

I smiled. "The dining hall?"

"You know it. Only the best for my princess." He kissed me again, his tongue parting my lips and plunging between them. This boy showed no regard for morning breath. Asking him to wait for me to brush my teeth was a fool's errand, so I'd stopped that. To be fair, as with most things Rhys Astor did, this had grown on me. I looked forward to having the hell kissed out of me first thing in the morning.

I pulled back from his mouth and scratched his stubble. "I want to give you your Christmas present."

He glared at me. "You shouldn't have gotten me anything."

"Don't worry. It's small. And it's sort of for me as well."

"No castle?"

I laughed as I sat up, swinging my feet to the ground. "Don't ruin my gift for next year, trouble." I padded over to my dresser and picked up the envelope I'd tucked between two books.

Spinning back around, I hid it behind my back. Rhys had sat up, and he held his arms out, beckoning me to him. I went, and he pulled me down on his lap. I wasn't sure I should have been sitting on him, but Rhys did what he wanted, so I didn't try to get off.

"Here." I held out the envelope.

He took it tentatively, his brows raised. "What did you do?"

"I got my boyfriend a present for Christmas. It's not criminal."

His eyes jerked to mine, and I realized what I'd said. I'd been thinking of Rhys as my boyfriend, but we certainly hadn't labeled ourselves yet. I refused to take it back, but I held my breath to see if Rhys denied it.

"No." He shook his head. "It isn't a crime for my girlfriend to get me a gift."

My toes curled with happiness, but I played it as cool as I could. "Open it."

His head canted, looking me over. "You think you're slick, sliding that in there, huh? Well, you aren't the first one to say it. I've been referring to you as my girlfriend for weeks. Just not to your face."

"Weeks?" I laughed, but I believed him.

"Weeks," he confirmed and shook the envelope. "This feels like tickets."

"Don't try to guess. Open it and find out."

He ripped the envelope open like a maniac and slipped the pair of tickets out, reading the words on the front. He looked up, his brows pulled into a taut line.

"How the hell did you get these?" he asked. "Floor seats...how?"

I shrugged. "Sometimes it helps to be a Kastanos."

My parents had connections everywhere, including the music industry. Several phone calls to a few different people, and I acquired floor seats at the Florence + The Machine show in February.

"Thank you, Delilah." He held up the tickets. "This is so fucking thoughtful. Beckett and I will have a really good time at the concert."

I shoved at his shoulder, snorting a laugh. "Good. That was exactly my plan when I bought them. I hope you'll buy me a T-shirt."

"If I have time." His arms wrapped around me, tugging me snug against him. "For real, thank you, princess. I can't wait to do this with you."

"Me too." I touched my lips to his. "You're welcome."

He patted my hip. "Your turn. I also got you a gift that's for me too."

I moved to the bed so he could get up to dig in his duffel bag. "I'm glad we're both equally greedy."

He looked at me over his shoulder. "You say greedy. I say smart." He stood with a box in his hands. "I even skipped the wrapping paper to save a few trees."

I held out my hands and wiggled my fingers. "Give me my gift."

He clutched it against him. "Oh, maybe you *are* greedy. Look at you, practically salivating."

I scrunched my face at him. "Don't tease me, or I'll take Luciana with me to see Florence."

"This is a side of you I never expected to see." He flopped down beside me, shoving the box my way. "Here you go. If you hate it, pretend for me, okay?"

Rhys had given me books. Not just any books. The outer box was painted with a scene from The Meadow on one side and a winter waterfall on the other. It held the three *The Shadow of the Isle* books.

"It's beautiful," I breathed.

I hadn't read these books. He knew that, the same way I knew how important these stories were to him. And he was sharing them with me. Sharing them in this package that was so beautiful, I'd be happy just to look at it.

My chest warmed. My heart pounded for him. Oh, was I falling hard.

"They're fully illustrated in watercolor." Rhys tapped the box. "I thought, if you want, we could read them together. I understand if you don't want to—"

"Rhys," I blinked back tears, "I love this so much. I do want to read them with you. I—yes, I would love that."

He released a heavy exhale and leaned down to kiss me. His lips were soft, fitting between mine as he gently suckled, the tip of his tongue lapping at my upper lip.

"Something to look forward to," he murmured.

"A lot to look forward to."

· · · • · • · · · ·

Rhys nipped at my ear while I tried to eat my breakfast.

"Eat your bagel, not me," I whispered.

"You taste better, though."

Our table was filled with our friends. I was trying to chat with Freddie on my right, but Rhys kept distracting me. He was clingy today. And though I was better at hiding it, I was feeling very much the same.

This was new for me. In my past relationship, I'd been happy to be together, but it hadn't hurt to part. With Rhys, my stomach was already a little queasy. It sucked.

"Hey, Astor." Charles Bloomberg's voice boomed over the din of conversation as he strode toward our table.

Rhys stiffened, his eyes narrowing as he focused on Charles. When he drew near, Rhys raised his chin. "How can I help you, Bloomberg?"

Charles scanned the table, pausing on Evelyn. She refused to look up from her plate. Ivan, in the seat beside her, shifted so he partially blocked her from Charles's view. Charles chuffed, a snarl distorting his mouth, then turned his attention back to Rhys and slammed his meaty paw down on the table between Rhys and me, a sheet of paper trapped beneath it. Rhys pushed back in his chair and rose to his feet, but Charles's focus was on me.

"Merry Christmas, Delilah. This year, my gift to you is the truth."

"What the fuck?" Rhys gritted out. "Get away from her."

Charles barreled on, lifting his hand from the paper. His voice was harsh in my ear, spitting every word like bullets. "You deserve to know how much Rhys earned to be your boyfriend." I went still, and it seemed like everyone around us did too. Voices died, but Charles's grew louder. "This is my bank statement. I helpfully highlighted the withdrawals I made."

"What are you talking about?" I didn't understand what was happening—or maybe I didn't *want* to understand. I looked to Rhys. He stood beside Charles, his fingers desperately raking through his hair. "What does this mean?"

He shook his head. "I'll talk to you. I'll tell you everything. Just come with me. Don't listen to him."

Beckett was suddenly beside Rhys, his arms crossed as he murmured, "What the *fuck*, man?"

Charles sneered at Rhys, ignoring Beckett. "Fuck off. The minute you decided to go to Evelyn, our deal became void. *I'm* going to be the one to tell Delilah exactly why you're with her, and it isn't because you're madly in love with her."

Charles turned back to me, jabbing at the paper on the table. "Three grand. That was Astor's price to keep you busy during the senior trip. Turned out, it was a veritable bargain. He upped the ante when we got back, demanding five to hang out with you. All in all,

Astor made eight Gs and got his dick wet along the way. If I were you, I'd be pretty fucking insulted, Delilah."

"What the actual *fuck* did you do?" Beckett uttered.

"Jesus, Beck, it's not—" Rhys started but didn't bother finishing.

My eyes met Evelyn's on the other side of the table. She whimpered, tears streaming down her cheeks.

Well, no. *She* hadn't whimpered. *I* had. I didn't understand any of this. There was no reason for me to believe Charles Bloomberg, but Rhys wasn't denying it. There was a truth ringing in his words. A violent, vicious truth.

Rhys had never shown interest in me because he *hadn't* been interested. Then, he came out of nowhere, hounding me at every turn.

And he'd been paid to do so.

While I was trying to find a way to wake up from this awful, hateful dream, a scuffle broke out behind me. Rhys was saying my name, yelling it, I thought, but everything became silenced by the static roaring in my ears.

Across from me, Ivan rose to his feet, his chair hitting the wall behind him. Our other friends were talking, moving, but they were blurs. Evelyn was the only one in focus. She stared at me, and I couldn't tear my eyes from hers.

Someone bumped my chair from behind, sending me flopping forward. My stomach collided with the edge of the table, knocking the breath out of me, and my brain jostled around in my head like a ship in a storm, my thoughts thrown around with it. Somewhere in the back of my mind, I heard my name, felt hands on me, but I couldn't focus.

There was only Evelyn. Tears on her cheeks. Her eyes on mine.

"*Help*," I whispered.

"*I'm coming*," she mouthed back.

Then she moved, rushing around to my side of the table. In a blink, she was beside me, taking my hand in hers, pulling me up.

For once, I let her take the lead. She tugged me toward the door, and I followed, dizzy, focused solely on the warmth of her hand around mine and how tightly she held on to me.

An anchor. Keeping me steady in the storm.

We almost made it to the door when a hand landed on my shoulder, whirling me around. Rhys was there, red-faced, the collar of his shirt torn. So un-Rhys-like.

I blinked at him, at the unfamiliarity of this boy I'd trusted with my body and my heart. Less than an hour ago, we'd been planning on reading books and going to concerts. Had that been real? Would I open the books and find them blank?

Who even was he?

A swindler. A phony. I didn't know this person.

Beckett loomed behind him like a bodyguard. Only, it wasn't clear if he was protecting Rhys or me.

"Delilah, princess, I'll explain everything. It isn't what you think. Charles is making it sound so much worse than it was—"

I found my voice buried under layers of disappointment. "Did you take money from him to be with me?"

His mouth flapped like a fish out of water. "I—there were reasons. If you give me a chance, I'll tell you what I should have weeks ago."

"It's a yes or no question." I could barely look at him, but if I didn't, I'd have to see our classmates watching us, hearing every humiliating word.

They all knew.

Everyone would whisper. Tell the tale of how something was so *wrong* with me Rhys had to be paid in order to be with me. Shame, I knew all too well, weighed me down until it was almost unbearable to stay standing.

Rhys's lips slammed into a tight line, and his eyes raked over me with a desperation I could not place and did not care to try.

Finally, he answered. "Yes, but—"

Stepping in front of me, Evelyn shoved at him with a strength I hadn't been unaware she possessed.

"No," she snapped.

"I'm talking to Delilah." If he hadn't said this as gently as a lamb, I might have slapped him. But even now, exposed and everyone knowing the truth, he was being kind to my sister. To me, it was an insult to brutal injury.

"And I told you no. You can't speak to her right now." Evelyn jabbed her finger in the center of his chest. "You are no better than Charles. Do not delude yourself into thinking you're above him. You are both underhanded and have no scruples, you simply hide it slightly better."

Beckett stepped up behind Rhys, wrapping his arm around Rhys's chest.

"Ev"—I squeezed her hand—"let's go."

Rhys didn't try to break free from Beckett to stop us from leaving, and that was the last thing I'd ever be grateful to him for.

Chapter Twenty-Eight
Rhys

Rage like I'd never felt before burned in my gut as I watched Delilah walk away from me. Since I couldn't light myself on fire, I was going to direct it at the next best thing.

Beckett let me go as soon as Delilah was out of sight. I felt his disgust and disappointment in me, mirroring my own. But I couldn't deal with that yet. Not with this inferno inside me, desperately searching for an outlet.

Charles Bloomberg was exactly where I'd left him, lording over our table like he was something special. Only now, he had his hands up, protecting himself as Bella went at him.

"You cheatin' little bitch!" she seethed. "It was *me*. I'm the one who made Evelyn aware of how filthy your dick is. Rhys had nothing to do with it."

Felix wrapped his arm around her waist, dragging her back a step. "Calm down, baby."

Charles lifted his chin. Now that Bella was being held back, he dropped his arms and got cocky. "Get your bitch in check, Santos."

"What did you say?" Bella screeched. Her feet were off the floor, kicking and scratching at Felix to break his hold. "You're a fuckin' cretin, Bloomberg. You really think I wouldn't tell my girl what I saw?"

Charles focused on Felix. "You should have warned me Bella saw shit. I could have covered—"

"Get outa here," Felix uttered. "You made your point. Go, so we can all calm down."

Bella writhed in his arms until she was sideways. Her flushed face turned crimson when she lighted on me. "Oh, fuck you too, Astor. You and Charles belong together in your pile of teat-suckin' mama's boys who couldn't give a girl an orgasm if they tried. And we all know you don't try, you two-pump chump."

Felix's hand clamped over her mouth, and he started to drag her backward again. His eyes widened seconds before he released a high-pitched howl and dropped her entirely, clutching his hand to his chest.

"You bit me," he accused. "What the fuck, Bells?"

"Don't try to control me," Bella hissed at him before rounding on me. "You can go to hell, Astor. I hate Charles with the heat of a thousand suns, but he did everyone a favor exposin' just what kind of sociopath you are."

Then she flipped me off and sauntered out of the dining hall. Felix ran after her, yelling about needing a rabies shot.

Charles flopped down in a chair, chuckling under his breath. "Holy shit. Poor Santos."

I took a step toward him, murder simmering in my veins. Maybe Bella was right. Maybe he'd done Delilah and everyone else a favor, but I'd never accept that.

Charles hadn't been looking out for her. He'd done what he did to ruin me.

Because he'd watched me closely enough to understand me being with her had had nothing to do with money and taking her away would tear me apart at the seams.

My path to Charles was blocked again. This time, by a tattooed Russian who wasted no time slamming his fist in my gut.

Black spotted my vision as the air evacuated my lungs. Doubling over, I clutched my middle, not out of protection but instinct. Ivan snagged the back of my shirt and yanked me upright, dipping down so his face was in mine.

"I know what you are, Rhys Astor. Never good enough for Delilah." He was deadly calm. No anger, no violence. He could have been out for a Sunday stroll, commenting on the weather. His fist barreled into my stomach again, his expression never changing. "You will stay far away from her."

Gasping for air, I steeled my spine and met his flat gaze. "She's not your business. You missed your chance."

He fisted my collar and peered into my eyes. "You don't have any idea what my business is. Don't pretend to know anything about me." With a grunt of disgust, he shoved me away, wiping his hands on his pants.

Ivan walked out of the dining hall, and an irrational part of me demanded to know if he was going to Delilah. Jealousy roiled in my gut. If he did go to her, she'd let him in. But not me. Never me again.

Beckett clapped a hand on my shoulder. "You deserved that."

I swiped the saliva from my mouth. "No doubt. Are you gonna give me more?"

His hold slipped to my nape. "Nope. We're getting out of here, and you're going to explain to me why the fuck you just shit all over a person who is very fucking important to my girl."

"I'm not done with Bloomberg."

He gave me a shake. "You walk out of here with me right now, or *I'll* be done."

Ivan's punches had knocked the demon's hold on me loose, so I was able to hear what Beckett was saying. I may have been self-destructive, but not so much I would blow apart my only true friendship.

Heaving out a breath, I gave a sharp nod. "Fine. Let's go before I lose my fucking mind."

• • • • • • • • • •

Beckett was silent until we entered his room. Pulling his chair out from his desk, he motioned for me to sit.

I did.

Beckett paced the two feet of floor space for a long moment before he gingerly took a seat on the edge of his bed.

"What the fuck, Rhys? Tell me Charles is making shit up."

I lifted both shoulders. It was all coming out now. No sense in furthering my lies or prettying up what I'd done. "He isn't making anything up. It's true. He offered me money, and I needed it, so I took it and did what he asked."

"You fucked Delilah for money?"

"No." I jammed the heel of my hand into my eye. "The idea was to keep her distracted, that's all."

"Not good enough," he gritted out. "You never should have entertained Charles."

"I *know* that." I slammed my hand into my forehead. "Don't you think I know?"

"Then why? Did Preston cut off your haberdashery fund or something?"

"No, and I'm insulted you would think I'd become beholden to Charles over something so unimportant."

"Pfft." His stare was hard and unforgiving. "I can't think of many things you value more than your wardrobe."

I winced. "Glad to know what you think of me."

He threw his hands out. "What am I supposed to think? You took money and fucked my girl's best friend. That's about as low as you can get—"

I was in the wrong. There was no doubt about that. But I could not abide by Beckett's proclamation that I'd fucked Delilah for money. Not because it was insulting to me but because it belittled her.

I needed it all to stop. Beckett's voice. His doubts in me. The things he was saying about Delilah. It couldn't go on. Not for another second.

Grabbing the first thing my hand landed on, I picked it up and threw it across the room. The heavy textbook landed against the wall with a crack and collapsed to the floor like a broken doll.

"I won't say it again." My jaw clenched as my molars ground together. "I did not get paid to fuck her. Everything that happened between us was real, and I broke my girl's heart. I didn't do that for my fucking wardrobe, Beck."

His nostrils flared as he exhaled. "Then why? Explain it to me. From where I'm sitting, this doesn't look good."

I met his gaze. I'd told him a lot. He knew all about Preston and my mom. The darkest secrets of our family. But I'd been keeping something from him, *from everyone.*

"Catrin has a son."

He jerked back like I'd hit him. "You're in contact with your sister?"

I nodded once. Sharp and precise. "For the last year. I see her when I can, which isn't often. She's doing well now, but she doesn't have much money. When Charles made the offer, all I could think about was helping her."

Groaning, he scrubbed his face hard with both hands. "I don't know what to say."

"Nothing to say."

"A kid. *Fuck.*" He dropped his hands and scrutinized me with a pinched brow. "So, your reasons are noble. I don't think that changes anything."

"No." I'd been banking on my noble reasons changing everything. Now that I was toe to toe with reality, it was obvious one disaster didn't wipe out another. There were just two disasters. "She'll never speak to me again, will she?"

He blinked a few times before shaking his head. "I don't think so."

"I don't think so either."

His eyes narrowed. "Are you going to give up like that? No fight?"

"You want me to fight for her after you just told me she'll never speak to me?"

"I said I don't *think* she will. Is that a reason not to try? If she's not important to you, I understand. Walk away. If she is, then you have to try to make it right, even if it feels like a losing game. Doesn't she deserve to see you fighting for her?"

"She's important to me," I intoned. "I've told you this."

"Act like it, then. When I messed up with Luciana, she told me she'd accept nothing less than me down on my knees, and I gave that to her. If she doesn't forgive you, at least she'll know you cared enough to try."

"I don't even know where to start."

"Start with apologizing."

Yanking my phone out of my pocket, I pressed on my message thread with Delilah and tapped out a message that wasn't good enough, but it was something.

Me: *There were reasons I took the money, and I want to tell you about them so you can decide if they're good enough. I'm sorry.*

She responded quickly.

Delilah: *Was any of it real?*

Me: *Yes. All of it. Let me come to you.*

No reply.

No reply.

The seconds turned to minutes. Still, no reply.

Me: *I'm sorry, Delilah. Please let me come talk to you.*

My message wasn't delivered, and this time, I understood why.

"She blocked me."

Beckett nodded. "Not surprised. You told her you were sorry?"

"Of course."

"She knows, then."

I tossed my phone down and took out my pocket watch, rubbing the engraving with my thumb. "Tell me what to do now."

"Give her space. Let her cool down over break—"

"I don't want to. That's too long."

Beckett chuckled. "It's not really about you right now, is it? Time to put Delilah first."

"Yeah." Jaw clenched, I turned away from him. "Are you finally through with me?"

Silence stretched on for so long I took it as my answer. I'd always expected this day to come. Through thick and thin, Beckett was the one who'd stuck by me. He'd put up with my oddities, had let my temper roll off his back, defended me when anyone came at me. He knew my secrets, and I knew his. I considered him a brother, but I was also all too aware he had a *real* brother. I was just the weird friend who was always around like a barnacle that could be scraped off.

"What kind of question is that?" He pressed his hands together. "I stuck by you through your Frodo phase. You think I'm going to leave you over this?"

"You'd be smart to. I'm a liability."

"No." He shook his head. "Let me be pissed off at you without needing to reassure you you're stuck with me for fucking life. I'm insulted you think so little of me."

"It's myself I think so little of."

His sigh broadcasted his impatience. "I'm not going to offer you pity. You know where I stand with our friendship. I'm not going anywhere. But I'm not happy with you, and it's taking a lot for me not to smack the back of your head. Luckily, Ivan took care of the physical violence."

I huffed, pressing a hand to my sore abdomen. "Lucky, indeed."

Beckett peered at me for a long time. "You really care about this girl."

"I really do."

He touched the tips of his fingers together. "Don't wallow, and don't be a dick. I'll help you in any way I can—"

"But you have Luciana to consider."

He nodded without any remorse. "This is tricky for me, you dick."

"You can still walk away from me. I wouldn't blame you."

He flipped me off. "Pretty sure we just finished talking about that."

"Got it." My hands balled into fists on my thighs. "I don't know what to do. She's right down the hall and I can't get to her."

"She's down the hall, safe with her sister and friends. This isn't about you right now. You need to see her, but she doesn't want to see you. Let her be for now and deal with it."

"Easy for you to say."

"You're right, it is. And if I were in your position, I'd hope like hell you'd be giving me this same advice."

"You've always been the rational one."

"Not when it comes to my girl."

For the first time, I understood Beckett's level of obsession with Luciana. Mine was newer, but it was no less true.

I'd managed to get her to fall for me. To like me. To make future plans with me.

And I'd lost her anyway.

I slammed my fist down on my leg. "I'll give her the break, but once we're back, my gloves are coming off. I'm going after her."

He held up his hands. "I know you will, Rhys. And as long as you're keeping her best interest at the forefront, I'll do anything I can to help you."

My mouth twisted. "Anything that doesn't screw up your thing with Luciana."

His brow twitched. "That goes without saying."

It went against everything in me, but I'd use the shallow well of patience I possessed and wait. I didn't deserve another chance when I was already on my second one with her, but I was a selfish, greedy bastard. I'd take everything I could get, and when it came to Delilah, I'd come back for more.

Chapter Twenty-Nine
Rhys

FIVE DAYS AT HOME, and I was ready to climb the walls. Misery dug into my limbs, making every movement an unbearable task.

Preston and my mother were too busy to notice I'd become one with the sofa. They had parties to attend, dinners to serve to people I didn't know, a holiday to bastardize.

Presents sat unopened under the tree two days post-Christmas. They were just for show. My mother had given me a gift card to my favorite tailor, and Preston had gifted me a fine talking-to.

It'd gone in one ear and out the other. He didn't care, so long as he got the disappointed words out. I had no doubt he was counting the days until I was gone for good.

Take a number, pal.

A heavy dose of whiskey and weed was getting me through the mind-numbing days.

I stared at the twinkle lights on the tree. Normally, it would have all been packed away by now—Preston didn't abide by clutter—but my mother was hosting another party tomorrow night, so the decorations would stay up until then.

After that, a mini army would come in like Cinderella's mice and stow it all away while we slept.

The melting ice in my glass clinked as I took a deep pull. The door from the garage slammed shut in a distant part of the house, followed by my mother's heels clacking against the floor.

They were home from another party, and I hadn't moved—other than to refill my glass and bring my vape to my lips.

My next talking-to would be commencing soon. I could sense it in my bones. I wanted it. Welcomed it. Anything to fade Delilah's crumpled, burning face from my memories. If only temporarily.

"What is that smell?" my mother asked. I could picture her lifting her nose, trying to identify the scent coming from the living room where I'd set up camp.

"I know exactly what it is."

Oooh, Preston is gonna be big mad.

I tried to sit up, but my body wasn't cooperating. I was slouching, having almost lain down, when Preston prowled into the room, my mother on his heels.

He scanned me up and down, and even as blurry as he was, his disgust was evident.

"You're smoking weed in my house? Where do you get off?" He kicked my bare foot with the toe of his dress shoe. In the recesses of my mind, I registered the impact, but I didn't really feel it.

I tipped my glass toward my mother, who was all done up in red sequins. Tasteful sequins, of course.

"Don't you look lovely," I said. And I meant it. "Was it a very merry Christmas party? That *is* where you were, right? Celebrating sweet baby Jesus's birth?"

"Rhys." Her hands flew to her mouth. "Are you drunk, darling?"

"Mmm..." My brow pinched as I looked at my glass. "That's an affirmative. I haven't actually been sober since I arrived home. Nicest visit I've had in a long time."

Preston kicked my foot again, and the sting cut through my fog of inebriation enough for me to draw it away from him. In slo-mo, of course.

"Preston!" Mother squeaked. "He's barefoot."

Dear ol' Stepdad ignored her. Then again, we both knew it was the only protest she would make. My mother had witnessed her husband box my ears and slap the shit out of me, all without saying a word. Why start now?

"Just what the hell do you think you're doing?" Preston demanded.

I scratched my head, squinting at the gold-wrapped presents that were just boxes piled beneath the tree. "If you really want to know, I was sitting here, looking at the tags on the fake gifts over there. I see my name, yours, and Mom's, but there's a name missing. Out of curiosity, is Catrin not considered part of the family anymore? Not even for show? Do your friends know about the daughter you kicked out of my dad's house when she was barely sixteen?"

Like a lightning strike, Preston grabbed me by the collar of my shirt and dragged me to my feet. For a spindly-armed doughboy, he was surprisingly strong.

Not surprising to me. I'd taken the brunt of his blows. I knew what kind of power lay within his spaghetti limbs. Enough to make my ears ring for days.

"Are you referring to that drug addict who habitually stole from us? Who robbed our silver and brought her dealer boyfriend into *my* house?"

Spittle gathered in the corners of Preston's mouth as he shook me. He was angry at me, but I couldn't really find it in me to feel anything at all. I knew what was coming for me. I'd been asking for it.

"My father's house," I corrected with unconcealed contempt.

"You little shit." Preston slapped the side of my head, whipping it sideways. This was child's play for him. Barely rang my bell. "This is my house now. You will respect that, or you can get the hell out too."

I cocked my head, peering around him to look at my mother. "Are you going to say anything, Mom? Do you even remember your other kid?"

Her eyes were glassy, and her hands were still at her mouth. Not reaching to defend me or pull Preston off. If she'd acted, I would have been shocked to the core. It would have been the first time.

"Rhys, darling…"

Whatever she was going to say became lost when Preston shoved me into the wall. "We're talking right now. Your mother isn't going to save you from this conversation."

The corner of my mouth hitched. "Don't I know it."

He pressed into me, his nose almost touching mine. I smelled the garlic and wine on his breath, but I didn't think he'd take too kindly to my pointing it out.

"Jesus, Preston, did you forget to ask Santa for a toothbrush?"

Oops.

His open palm slammed into my face, knocking my head into the wall. There was a crack behind me, which told me I'd done a number on the plaster.

I'd been accused of being hardheaded, and I guess this proved it.

"What the hell are you laughing at?" he seethed.

"You. You're funny."

Another palm to the face, which actually seemed pretty fucking ridiculous, but goddamn, did it smart. All the blows to my head were starting to stack up.

Still, I wasn't done, and neither was my raging bull of a stepdad.

I raised a brow. At least, I tried to. I couldn't really feel my face anymore, but that had been my intention. "Is that all you got?"

His hand moved down to my throat. "Not even close. You're going to learn one way or another."

Preston showed me what he had, proved he'd been holding back over the years. His fist was loaded with his built-up resentment as it collided with my cheekbone then my temple.

It felt good. Sharp. In blinding color, the ache in my chest and belly migrated to my face. My pulse pounded. My ears roared. My body jerked, fighting against my will to remain still and take it without defending myself.

What defense did I deserve? If my own mother couldn't find it within herself to protect me, why should I? Besides, Preston was only giving me what Delilah should have. Pain for pain.

He tuckered himself out, backing away from me, panting from exertion. Without him holding me up, I slid down the wall and landed on my ass.

I groaned from the impact. Another bruise to add to the tally. I'd have to sit on one of those hemorrhoid pillows.

Someone let out an obscene cackle. They probably wouldn't have thought this was funny if it was their blood trickling down their chin or their tailbone vibrating from impact.

Oh, wait. That was me cackling.

I guessed it was kind of funny. Preston had gotten the workout he'd desperately needed and had winded himself from beating me up. He probably felt like a big man now. I bet his puny, shriveled-up dick was standing up like a little worm.

My mother stepped forward as if she was going to come to me. "Rhys, why—?"

Preston grabbed my mother's arm, yanking her into his side. "Leave him alone, Amanda. He needed that lesson."

Her steps faltered. "But he's bleeding—"

"Good. Maybe now he'll finally start showing this family some respect." He pointed his finger at me. "Clean yourself up and sleep off your bender. I expect you to wake up with a completely different attitude tomorrow, or you can go back to school early. That's up to you."

They left me there, bleeding from my mouth, my eye swelling, dizzy and laughing. Still laughing because if I let myself stop, I'd go the other way.

Once I could get my legs under me, I was out of here. There was no need to be in this house another day. Preston had succeeded in wiping away every trace of the life I'd had in the before. This place was tainted, my mother too.

I was getting out of here tonight.

Fuck it all.

I'd crawl if I had to.

CHAPTER THIRTY
Delilah

TWO INTERNATIONAL FLIGHTS IN less than a week had taken a toll on me. And that was after life had already taken its toll. All I wanted to do was curl up in my bed and sleep for days.

But first, I had to unpack. I wouldn't be able to properly rest with a suitcase stuffed with clothing. My mind would be stuck on the mess I'd have to deal with later, and any sleep I got would be restless.

Evelyn wandered into my room as I shook out one of my new dresses, the tags still attached. "That's pretty. It's a shame you didn't have a chance to wear it."

I shoved it on a hanger. "If only our parents weren't cunts."

She flopped on my bed, propping herself on her side. "That's too much to hope for."

"Yes, it is. Sadly."

"You can wear it on a date."

My laugh was sardonic. "Oh, I'm not dating before this dress is out of fashion."

"Neither am I. I don't think I understand boys well enough to date any of them."

Charles Bloomberg was a gigantic dick. He'd been sleeping around while claiming to be *so into* Evelyn he was willing to wait for her to be ready for sex. But he'd sworn up and down he'd never kissed any of the girls he'd fucked. That was reserved for Ev, his special girl. And when she fucked him, that would be just for her too.

She'd spilled all of this to me on our flight to Greece; the same day the truth about why Rhys was with me came out. Bella had told her what Charles was doing the night before, and Ev had promptly dumped him.

"Why didn't you tell me last night?" I asked.

Her pinkie grazed mine on the armrest. "You were so happy with Rhys. I wanted you to have one more day of it before I spoiled it."

"Look how that turned out." I hooked my pinkie with hers. "You wouldn't have spoiled anything anyway. You're my co-pea. We don't keep secrets in this pod."

"It made me feel better to know you had something good. At least, what we thought was good."

"Rhys isn't good."

She shook her head sadly. "I thought he was. When he went back for the bread..."

"He had selfish motives for doing that."

"I know. What a disappointment."

"Yeah."

"I never liked Charles, but I did like Rhys."

I sighed. "Same."

Evelyn kept me company for a while as I unpacked, then she got bored with me and wandered off, murmuring something about needing a drink. When I was alone for the first time in almost a week, the knot in my stomach tightened to the point of breathlessness.

I pushed my balled fist into the center of my belly, hoping for relief, but there was none. My sadness and humiliation festered in my core, and there was no ridding myself of it without facing it.

As badly as I'd hoped otherwise.

If our parents hadn't been so terrible, Ev and I would have still been in Greece with the sun and beach as a distraction from everything that had happened. I shouldn't have hoped for anything more than the usual from them, though. They had failed us both most of our lives, and we were used to it.

So why did it still sting sometimes?

Evelyn stuck her head in my room. "There's a strange scratching sound coming from the door."

Distracted, I said the first thing that came to mind. "Ignore it. No one's in the dorm. It's probably a rat."

I meant it as a joke, but Evelyn grimaced. "There are rats in the dorm? Surely not. I know they're supposed to be very intelligent, but I haven't been able to look at them the same since I read *1984*." She chewed on her bottom lip, then softly sang part of a line from a song. "*...all my rage, I'm still just a rat in a cage...*"

"Ev, babe, I was joking. There aren't any rats here."

She glanced toward the door. "I'm going to check. If it turns out to be a rat, you'll have to sleep in my bed tonight. Perhaps tomorrow night too."

The rat cage scene in *1984* had traumatized us both, but Ev never forgot things like that. I should have known better than to joke about rats.

Guilty, I followed her to the door, arriving as she opened it.

"Oh!" She jumped back, and a body tumbled into our suite. "It *is* a rat."

The prone form spoke. "I've been called worse."

There was no mistaking Rhys Astor, though the sight of him sprawled face down on our floor wasn't exactly a familiar one.

Evelyn toed his shoulder. "What are you doing scratching on our door?"

"Not scratching, writing a note." He pushed up on his hands and knees, his head hanging low between his shoulders. "You weren't supposed to be here."

This boy was wasted. His words were slow and slurred, his movements sloth-like.

"What are you doing here?" I asked before I could stop myself. "You aren't supposed to be here either."

With a shaky groan, he pushed back on his knees and raised his head. My stomach dropped like a lead balloon. He'd been beaten black and blue. One of his chocolaty-brown eyes was only open a slit, the rest of it swollen and puffy.

"You look terrible." Evelyn crouched down in front of him. "Your face has to hurt quite a lot."

"It does indeed." His brow crinkled. "Are there three of you now?"

"Only one, I'm afraid." She peered closer at him. "Your vision is affected. Is that from the alcohol or the injuries?"

"Probably both." He grunted as he tried to get his feet underneath him. "If you'll give me a hand, I'll leave you alone."

Ev looked back at me. "I think we have to help him. He's rather pitiful."

"Fine." I stepped forward and grabbed his outstretched hand. Ev stood up and took the other. Together, we tugged him to his feet. He swayed and closed his eyes, his head falling forward again. "Don't pass out."

He chuffed but didn't lift his head. "I'm not certain I have a choice in that."

Ev and I exchanged glances. As angry as I was at Rhys, I couldn't let him wander off on his own and potentially die.

I sighed, accepting I would have to help him, even though I could barely stand to look at him—and not because of how banged up he was. "Come lie down. I'll get some ice."

"Delilah," he croaked.

"Shhh." I held up a finger. "No speaking."

He shuffled along with me and Ev, stumbling every few steps. Fortunately, we didn't have far to go. Between the two of us, we managed to wrangle him onto my bed, and I made a swift exit, ignoring the pang in my heart from seeing him there.

Evelyn followed me out, watching me as I grabbed our first aid kit from a cabinet and filled a baggie with ice from our mini fridge.

"Shall I take care of him?" she asked.

"No." My answer snapped out of me without thought. I should have let her. But the idea of someone else taking care of him made me even angrier than I already was. And I was spitting mad. "I'll do it. It's fine. I'm fine."

She frowned at me. "You don't appear fine."

"I'm not, but I don't want to talk about it."

"Okay. I'm going to my room now. I'll have headphones on, so if you need to make noise, I won't hear."

My mouth slackened. "I'm not having sex with him."

"Oh no, I know you won't. I was thinking of murder."

A long beat passed before her mouth twitched and we both started giggling. It felt like ages since we'd laughed.

"I don't think I'll murder him tonight."

She shrugged. "I wouldn't blame you."

· · · • · • · · · ·

Rhys was where I'd left him on my bed. I'd assumed he'd passed out, but when I bent over him and held my finger beneath his nose to check if he was alive, he grabbed my wrist, holding my hand to his cheek.

"Rhys," I squeaked. "You're alive."

"Barely. If you'd like me to die, I will."

"Okay, have at it."

His forehead crinkled, and he pressed my hand even harder to his cheek. "I'm sorry."

No, no. I couldn't let him soften me up with cuddles and pained expressions. Rhys had proven he could manipulate me for his own gain. There was no reason to believe this wasn't more of the same. I reminded myself of the money he'd accepted from Charles. Closing my eyes, I pictured our classmates watching my staggering humiliation, and that was enough to harden myself to him. He could look sad all he wanted. It wouldn't penetrate the fortress my parents had supplied the foundation for a long, long time ago.

I yanked my hand from his grasp.

"So you've said. That doesn't change anything. The only reason I'm allowing you to be in my presence is that I have morals and they won't allow me to send you on your way. I would very much prefer it if I never had to see you again."

The grunt he made was laced with agony. "I know that. You're a much better person than I am."

"Be quiet," I uttered harshly. "I don't want to hear you saying things like that. It only makes me angrier."

"Okay." He swallowed hard. "I'm gonna shut up."

He closed his eyes, and I got to work on his face. Even though I could have punched him with all the fury burning in me, I was gentle as cotton balls as I wiped the dried blood from his skin. His lips were rolled between his teeth, and his forehead was etched with lines, but he didn't voice his pain. He stayed quiet, just as I'd demanded.

I dabbed disinfectant on the cut beside his eye and one near his mouth then applied bandages. He didn't really need them, but it made me feel better to do something.

When that was finished, I carefully placed the bag of ice on his swollen eyebrow. He winced, trying to move his head away, but that seemed to pain him even more, judging by the guttural groan he released.

"Are you hurt somewhere else?" I whispered.

"Back of my head. Probably have a bump."

"Okay." Biting my lip, I tried to figure out how to move him on my own. "I'm going to roll you to your side, but you need to help me."

"Hmmm. So sweet, Delilah." His lids were so heavy and low I wondered how much of me he really saw. "I missed you."

I bit down even harder on my lip and turned away from him. "I told you not to speak. I don't want to hear your voice."

"Sorry," he mumbled.

Sucking in a deep, ragged breath, I shoved my fragile feelings aside to concentrate on the job I was doing and nothing else.

Together, we got him on his side, though he made the decision to roll toward me instead of away like I'd intended. I felt around the back of his scalp and quickly found a large goose egg that made him hiss when I prodded it.

"God, what happened to you?" I hadn't meant to ask it. It made no difference to me why he was in this state.

"Preston gave me a belated Christmas present," he said through clenched teeth.

My limbs froze. "Your stepdad did this to you?"

He made a weak chuff. "He outdid himself this time, didn't he?"

Tears pricked at my eyes. They couldn't be helped. As angry as I was at him, he didn't deserve this. Not from a man who should have been keeping him safe. And where had his mother been? Had she stood by, watching? The idea was too devastating to contemplate. All of it was. I had to get back to work, to do something tangible, or I'd let my tears loose and flood this entire dorm.

"Let's put the ice there. I think that's where you need it." I was so out of my depth. I'd never taken care of more than a skinned knee or paper cut. But I carried on like I knew what I was doing. Leaning over Rhys, I propped a couple pillows behind him to wedge the ice against his head, barely noticing his face was against my stomach until he nuzzled me and his arm hooked around the tops of my thighs.

"Rhys, no!" I swatted his shoulder and jumped away from him. "No, you don't get to do that."

"I know." He pressed his face into my pillow. "But you were close, and you feel so fucking good."

"Sure. How much did Charles pay you to say that?"

"Negative a million bucks. I said it from my own brain." He reached for me again, but I was too far from him now. "Miss you."

"Keep missing me." I skirted around the room toward my door. "I'm going to sleep with Ev tonight. Just...don't die in my bed."

"Okay, princess." His shoulders shuddered then went slack. "Love you."

I stared at him in disbelief. He hadn't said that, had he?

Seconds later, soft snores broke the prolonged silence. Rhys had fallen asleep, and surely, he hadn't known what he'd been saying before.

Even if he had, even if he'd been stone-cold sober, I'd never believe he meant it. How could I? Rhys Astor was a liar, and that was all he'd ever be in my eyes.

On my way to Ev's room, I spotted the crumpled paper Rhys had been writing on before he'd fallen into our room. Despite my wariness, I picked it up and read the incomplete message.

Delilah,

Princess,

I'm sorry.

I'm sorry.

I'm sorrrrrry.

I'm sorr

I'd give the money back if I could, but it's gone. All gone. My deeds were noble, but my princess got hurt, so maybe nobility can go fuck itself.

You are the prettiest girl in the world. People should pay millions to even look at you. I'm not even kidding, Delilah.

My, my, my Delilah.

Why, why, why Delilah

If loving you is wrong, I don't wanna be

That was where it ended, but I could fill in the blanks myself.

As calmly as I could manage, I folded the note neatly into a small square, placed it in the freezer, and walked to Ev's room. She was in dance mode, so I tucked myself into her bed and watched her sway to the music only she could hear through her headphones.

Then I let a few tears fall. I'd been trying so, so hard to keep all my sadness and anger inside, but this was too much. Too, too much.

Betrayed by Rhys, being unwanted and abandoned by our parents the second Christmas dinner was eaten, and now, Rhys showing up barely conscious on my doorstep? I was on the precipice of screaming and screaming and screaming until I couldn't scream anymore.

But I couldn't do that. I had to be the pillar. Ev was in front of me, and she would always keep me going, but there was no one behind us. Falling apart wasn't for me.

Quietly, I cried and watched my sister dance while the boy who'd broken my heart slept in my bed.

Soon, it would be the new year, and this would pass.

I only had to keep going.

CHAPTER THIRTY-ONE
Delilah

RHYS WAS GONE IN the morning, and I was more surprised than relieved. It annoyed me. I should have been relieved most of all.

At least I knew he wasn't dead.

Dealing with a corpse during the holidays had to be a pain in the ass.

Ev was busy knitting, so after I ate breakfast, I threw on leggings and a sweatshirt and went for a walk around campus. Maybe five percent of our classmates were here too, but I wouldn't have known it since no one crossed my path while I was out.

It was a good thing for everyone else since my mood was rather bloodthirsty. Overnight, I'd gone from deep, deep melancholy to homicidal. If someone looked at me funny, they were bound to get it.

But I made it around the entire campus, only spotting one person in the distance. My legs were properly tired as I climbed the steps in front of my dorm. I was digging in my cross-body bag for my key card when the door swung open.

Startled, I looked up, instantly scowling as Rhys stepped out, letting the door fall closed behind him.

He looked awful in the cold light of day. The eye that had been partially swollen shut had completed the process overnight. His bruises had deepened too. On top of that, he was disheveled in a way foreign to him. Rhys was always turned out and styled, but his rumpled T-shirt and gym shorts had seen better days.

"You're alive, I see." I nodded as I looked him over. "That's good."

His soft chuckle held a bitter edge. "Is it?"

"I don't wish you dead. I just wish you would disappear."

He flinched, shoving his hands in his pockets, and I wondered if he had his pocket watch. Then I decided I didn't care.

"You aren't supposed to be here." He started to rub his forehead, dropping his hand at the last moment. "I didn't expect you and Ev to be in your room last night. Shouldn't you be in Greece?"

"Once our parents revealed they were headed to one of their friends' yachts the day after Christmas, we decided not to stay. Being unwanted is worse than being alone." I jerked my chin toward him. "You aren't supposed to be here either."

"No." The corner of his mouth hitched, but it wasn't really a smile. "It feels that way."

I huffed. "I'm not interested in listening to you pity yourself. It doesn't move me, Rhys." I gestured to his injured face. "That doesn't either."

He laughed. "Do you really think I got myself beaten up to gain your sympathy? I didn't even know you were back."

"Which means, if you had known..."

"Sure." He rolled his shoulders. "As you know, I have no scruples. I'd get my ass beaten for a chance to spend the night in your bed."

"You're ridiculous, and I don't believe a word you say. Will you please move away from the door? I don't want to be near you."

"Delilah..." He shook his head. "Do you have five minutes? I would really like to explain what I needed the money for."

Now, it was me who flinched. It wasn't the reminder that he'd been paid to be with me that had felt like a physical blow. It was hearing him say the words.

"No. I don't care why."

He licked his lips, and his nose twitched. "I get that you're not going to forgive me. But if you'll let me explain where the money went, maybe you'll understand what I did had nothing to do with you or anything about you and everything to do with me."

I stared at the building over his shoulder. He wasn't going to move until I heard him out, but I couldn't bring myself to agree to listen. So I waited, bracing myself for what he had to say.

He exhaled and shuffled his feet. "The kid you saw me carrying in town? That's my nephew, Owen. Catrin's kid. I didn't even know he existed until last year. That was because the last time I saw Catrin was when Preston physically tossed her out of our house. She was messed up on drugs. Oxy, Percs, whatever she could get her hands on. From what she's told me, she stayed messed up until she got pregnant, then her turnaround was swift and complete. She pulled herself together for Owen. But she struggles. Living around here is not cheap, but she manages—and by manages, I mean she's one parking ticket away from disaster. They live on the edge, and she works herself sick…"

I didn't know what I'd thought he'd say, but it wasn't this.

"I asked you about him," I intoned. "Another lie on top of all the others."

He licked his lips, wincing slightly when he touched the split on the bottom. "I didn't tell you he's my sister's kid because he's a secret. Beckett wasn't even aware of his existence. Catrin is terrified Preston and our mom will take Owen from her if they find out."

"Perhaps walking around on Main Street isn't the brightest idea."

"No." He shook his head. "It isn't, and I heartily discouraged it. We were there for ten minutes to go to one store. We thought we were in the clear—"

"If I saw you, anyone else could have. You shouldn't do that again."

"We won't." His shoulders curled as he exhaled. "I paid her rent for the next five months so she can have some breathing room and save money. That's where the eight grand went."

"That was nice of you, but I find it difficult to believe you needed to go to Charles Bloomberg for money."

Another jagged exhale. He braced his hands on the back of his neck. "One time, I withdrew two hundred dollars from my account to give to her. Preston spotted the withdrawal immediately and demanded receipts. When I couldn't give them to him, I know he suspected I gave the money to Catrin, but I wouldn't say, and he kicked me in the shin so hard, I thought he broke it. Turned out, he only chipped the bone."

I winced. That had to have hurt so badly. "Why don't you fight back?"

He shrugged. "He usually only gets one or two hits in before he stops himself."

I gestured to his bruised face. "This is more than one or two hits."

"This is the result of me goading him. I was asking for it."

Why, why, why? But I didn't ask. Rhys was no longer my concern.

"Anyway, I got smarter after that. I bought clothing for myself, then returned it for cash. I couldn't do it often, and it wasn't much, but it was all I could do. And it wasn't really for her. It was Owen. Catrin made the choices that brought her to where she is, but not Owen. He didn't ask to be born into all of this, and I'll be damned if Preston gets his hands on him."

I blinked at him, gathering myself—and my will—so I wasn't moved by what he was telling me. The way he spoke about his nephew would have gotten to me in a huge way if he'd told me this two weeks ago. Before I knew the truth.

"I get it now. You love your nephew very much and want a better life for him."

Rhys nodded, a light of hope flickering behind his somber gaze.

I went on, needing to snuff it out as quickly as possible. "You love him so much you were willing to sacrifice my autonomy, pride, self-esteem, and heart. It would have been bad enough if you'd only hurt me. But that wasn't the end of it, was it? You also took no issue with trampling all over my sister to keep up your ruse." I folded my arms over my chest. "You knew Charles was sleeping around and kept it hidden, didn't you?"

He held up both hands. "I told him he had to stop. He said he and Ev weren't in a committed relationship, so I thought..." He didn't bother finishing. We both knew exactly who he was thinking about when he chose to keep that information to himself. And it wasn't Ev or me.

"Answer me this, Rhys. Would you have told me or Ev about Charles sleeping around if he hadn't been holding something over your head?"

He rolled his lips between his teeth. "I don't know."

"I do." Completely done with this conversation, I took out my key card and swiped it over the sensor. I had to reach behind Rhys for the door. Jerking it hard, it opened into his back.

As I slid through, his fingers wrapped around my wrist. "You're right. Everything you said is right. I made a selfish decision before I really knew you, and it snowballed into something I had no control over. But everything that happened between us was real. More real than anything I've ever had. I *will* make it up to you, Delilah."

I met his gaze, and it hurt. Much, much worse than I'd expected it to. I'd fallen so hard for him, and he'd let me. He'd seen me falling and allowed it to happen, which was too cruel for me to even comprehend.

"You can't make this up to me, Rhys, because I don't think you really understand what you've done." Tears welled in my eyes, and there was no hope they wouldn't fall. Last night, I'd been able to hold them back until I was away from him, but having him this close, pleading with me for something that was gone, gone, gone...it was far too much.

"Tell me," he whispered.

I sucked in a shuddering breath. "I feel disgusting. Grubby and unclean. My skin is too tight, and I am so fucking aware of every ounce of my body. The way my thighs rub and my belly rolls when I sit down. I can't stop naming how many things are wrong with me. And the list is long. So, so long. I don't want anyone to look at me. Never, ever again, because I know they're seeing how disgusting and unlovable I am. I must be, right? My own parents don't want to be with me, and the boy I thought I could...you had to be *paid* to even see me. I don't know how I'll ever get over this. How will I ever let anyone else touch me or see my body when I am so hideous and gross? I just feel—"

I lost my voice to tears then. Rhys was blurry, but his aghast expression was unmistakable.

"Delilah." My name was stretched into a long, agonized plea. "No. No, that shit is not true."

I ripped my hand from his grasp. My calm had withered, and I let myself scream the screams that had been stuck in my throat for far too long. "You needed eight thousand dollars to be with me, Rhys! It *is* true. Nothing you say means anything because you did that. You've humiliated me and betrayed me in one of the worst ways I can imagine. I will *never* look at you the same—even worse, I'll never look at myself the same."

He shook his head hard. "No. This is wrong. All fucking wrong."

"I know it is!" I yanked at the hem of my shirt, balling it in my fists. "We were supposed to be looking forward to seeing each other, to reading your books together, and you *ruined* it. You have to stay away from me. I can't bear you looking at me." My hands flew to my flushed cheeks, damp with rolling tears. "I want to rip my skin off so you can't see it. Do you get it, Rhys? Do you understand what you've done?"

He said my name, called me princess, but I was gone. Running from him—from the scene of our crime. He didn't let me go this time, though. He couldn't give me that.

He stayed behind me as I waited for the elevator and got on with me when it arrived. Never looking at me, just standing there.

My jaw was trembling so hard my teeth clattered. I'd been holding these words in since the scene in the dining hall, but I didn't feel any better. My insides were scraped raw, and I was swaying on my feet from the flood of adrenaline.

Why had he followed me?

Did he still not get it?

"Go away," I whispered.

"I'm making sure you get to your suite, then I'll leave you alone. I promise," he whispered back.

I slid my eyes to the side. His jaw was clenched as tightly as mine, and his balled fists were shaking at his sides, but he kept his gaze off me, studying the ascending letters above the door.

Then he kept his promise, following silently behind me to my door. Before I closed it, my eyes brushed over his.

"I'm sorry," he said.

"That's not enough."

I closed the door on him, wishing I could shut him out of my heart and memories just as easily.

CHAPTER THIRTY-TWO
Delilah

I WALKED AND WALKED and walked.

To Evelyn, I used the excuse that I needed to be outside to think. If she saw through me, she didn't say. And it was partially true.

But the crux of my need to walk was to rid myself of this unbearable feeling of disgust with myself. When I sat still, I was so aware of my body my skin crawled.

After my first day of walking alone, Rhys began to show up on my path, vacillating between being my shadow and haunting from a distance.

He didn't talk to me, but he was there, always there, watching over me. It must have been some form of penance. Though, I couldn't really imagine Rhys succumbing to a guilty conscience.

I wouldn't ask him why he dogged my trail day after day, so if that was why he was out there with me, I'd never find out.

Rhys didn't confine his haunting to my walks. The day after we'd had it out, I'd opened my email to find one sent from him and couldn't stop myself from clicking on it.

There was no message, just a voice recording.

I walked away from my desk for an hour. If I could have shoved my laptop into the freezer beside the folded-up note, I would have. But that would have been reckless and silly.

After an interminable hour passed, I gave in and clicked play.

Rhys's voice assaulted my ears, and I almost hit stop, but this wasn't some plea for me to forgive him or another explanation that didn't change anything.

The words weren't his. It only took me a second to recognize where they were from. The word "dragon" in the first sentence was an easy clue.

If Fathaniel Flamens hadn't wandered from the safety of The Meadow, he wouldn't have stumbled over the tail of the slumbering dragon.

The citizens of The Meadow wouldn't have been surprised to see Fathaniel Flamens stumbling. Since his father departed for the Great Black Wall nine years before, Fathaniel had been absent-minded, rarely watching where he was going.

They would, however, have been greatly surprised at the presence of a dragon, for dragons had been extinct an entire millennium.

I pressed my fist between my breasts.

He was reading *The Shadow of the Isle* to me. It struck me in the raw, aching gash in my chest. Now that I knew what this was, I wanted to hit stop even more, but I didn't.

Instead, I went to my shelf, slid out the first volume from the box set he'd given me before everything had changed, and opened it so I could follow along with his voice. It was harder to do with tears blurring my eyes, but I managed.

Rhys read to me for a long time. At least an hour, but I lost track, settling on my bed with his book and words dripping like acid-laced honey in my ear.

At the end of the last chapter, there was a pause, then he spoke again. "I would give anything to be reading this with you. To see your expressions at my favorite parts of the story. To tell you the things my dad and I talked about the first time we read this together. I don't know how to make this right, but I made you a promise. I told you we'd read this together, and this is the only way I could think of doing that."

Silence took over, and I gently closed the book. I wished all those things too, but Rhys had made it impossible.

· · · · •· •· · · ·

After that, there was an email in my inbox each day. Though I was tempted to read ahead of him, I made myself wait. As we got deeper into the story, I fell in love with it. When I saw him on my walks, it was on the tip of my tongue to tell him what I thought of it, but I bit those urges off with viciousness.

He'd continued leaving me a message at the end of his recordings, and I listened because I hated myself just the right amount and missed him more than I should have.

"You want to know something? Catrin left me alone in that house. She knew what kind of man Preston was, but she still left me for years. She didn't get in touch with me until she needed money." He broke off, his inhale like shattered glass. "Sometimes, I hate her. But Owen...I'm not a kid person, but he's the shit. I wish you could meet him. You'd see."

And then:

"I was *aware* of you, Delilah. I knew you existed. But I never saw you because I wasn't looking. You think it's because there's something wrong with you that made me overlook you, but that isn't true. It's me who's wrong, and I don't want anyone to know me because then they'll see. But you saw, didn't you? You got the full force of my wrongness shoved in your face. I'm sorry for that, but I will never be sorry for *us*. That's for selfish reasons, though. When I was with you, I felt right. I haven't felt that way since my dad." He huffed a laugh. "You know that saying 'two wrongs don't make a right'? I don't believe that anymore because your wrong, and my wrong, very fucking certainly made a right."

· · · ● · · ● · · · ·

That message sent me on a long, long walk around campus. It was New Year's Eve and Ev and I planned to watch stupid movies until midnight. I couldn't let her down. Otherwise, I would have taken to my bed like a Victorian lady.

So, I walked until my legs were shaky, replaying Rhys's words in my head—which had as much to do with the shakiness as fatigue did.

We *had* been right. Or, at least, it had felt that way. But it wasn't real, no matter what he said. If he truly had feelings for me now, they were based on a false pretense.

And yet...something had cracked inside me. My re-solve wasn't quite as concrete as it had been before I'd started listening to Rhys's messages.

I had to stop. They were only making this harder for me. I couldn't be with him. We would never be able to recapture what we were before the curtain had been lifted.

If only I could convince my hollow heart that he couldn't be the one to make it full again.

· · · ● · · ● · · ·

Ev was sitting cross-legged on our small couch when I arrived back at our suite. I stopped in my tracks when she turned to me wearing a New Year's crown with a noisemaker perched between her lips.

"Where did you get that?"

She blew the noisemaker once and tossed it aside. "Rhys brought us a care package. Crowns for both of us, champagne, glasses, and these dastardly noisemakers that make me want to carve my ears out. He said to tell you happy New Year. I gave him the half-knitted sweater I'd been making him and told him to finish it himself."

I collapsed next to her, and she plopped a crown on my head. I wanted to tell her my thighs were too lumpy to be deserving of a crown, but she would try to talk me out of that thought, and I didn't want to be talked out of it.

"What did he say to the sweater?"

"He thanked me, of course. He also said he's going to learn to knit since he has nothing else to do besides pine over you and self-flagellation." Her nose crinkled. "He's dramatic, isn't he? And he keeps making me like him."

Resolve chip, chip, chipping.

"He has that way about him." I straightened my crown. "I'm really struggling, you know."

She shifted her body to face me. "I've been letting you work it out on your own, but I'm not sure if that's a mistake. It's hard to tell. You look awful, but I think that comes with heartbreak. Is it more than that, though? Tell me if it is. We're co-peas, right? We don't keep things from each other."

I pressed my lips together so hard my chin wobbled. I had to get this out. Keeping it inside was driving me mad. "I keep hearing Mom's voice. What she'd say if she found out about this. *'Of course he had to be paid to be with a girl who looks like you. If you'd lost fifty pounds like I'd told you, you'd have your pick of boys. But the way you are now, what can you expect? You have to take what you can, Delilah.'* I know it's wrong, but I *feel* it. It feels real, Ev, and I can't shake it."

She reached for my hand, which she rarely did, so I knew it was bad. "Our mother also called me slow. She said I'm lucky to be pretty, so I'll find a husband who will overlook my other defects. When I was being bullied in Spain, she told me I should have expected it since I'd refused to even try to fit in." Her fingers squeezed mine. "Is any of that true?"

I shook my head hard. "No. Absolutely not."

She blinked at me. "Can you explain why you would believe anything that woman says about you, then?"

I swallowed hard, delaying answering her. It would mean admitting she had a point. And if I admitted that, then I also had to admit it wasn't really my mother's voice in my head. It was mine.

Fingers curled into a ball, I pressed my fist to my chest. "I don't know how to rid myself of this feeling."

"Stop feeling it. It's useless. You're not any of the things our mother said, and neither am I. Both have to be true for one to be true. Don't take my truth from me by leaning into her lies."

I shook my head. "I won't take it from you."

"Then stop, Delilah. Your anger should be directed at Rhys. Perhaps Charles too. Not at yourself."

"It's not anger," I protested.

"I'm not always the best at naming feelings, but I know anger when I see it."

"Aren't you mad too? Rhys should have told you about Charles."

She lifted a shoulder. "He didn't want to lose you. I can't blame him for that. You're wonderful. If you don't want boys to do stupid things to keep you, you should endeavor to be a little more intolerable."

"Evelyn," I groaned. "You're no help."

"I'm only answering your questions. As for Charles, he was a mistake from the beginning. I wonder if you're not disappointed in me for bringing him into our lives?"

"I'm not. Everyone is allowed one or two terrible boyfriends. I had Roman, and you had Charles. I think we're at our quota."

She crossed her arms and smirked.

I raised a brow. "What?"

"Nothing, really. It's just that you didn't mention Rhys as a terrible boyfriend."

Because he hadn't been. I'd adored spending time with him and how he made me feel. But that was over now. Wasn't it?

Yes, yes. It had to be.

Instead of saying those things, I reached for the bottle of champagne on the coffee table. "Shall we crack this open?"

Her mouth quirked into a half smile. "It's not midnight yet."

"Yes, but if you're truly going to make me watch *Party Girl* for the dozenth time, then I have to be half drunk."

Ev grabbed the glasses while quoting her favorite movie. "I would like a nice, powerful, mind-altering substance. Preferably one that will make my unborn children grow gills."

"Oh, please. Turn on the movie and get it over with."

She giggled. "Happy New Year, my love."

I managed to laugh too. "Happy New Year, babe."

New year, clean slate, starting fresh.

Though the clock hadn't struck midnight, I made a resolution: no more taking my heartbreak out on myself.

What I should have vowed was not to make poor decisions while half-drunk on champagne. That would have been much, much more useful.

......•....

It was half past midnight when Rhys opened the door to me. He was as rumpled as he'd been days ago, eyes heavy-lidded, hair sticking out in every direction. My chest warmed, and my mouth went dry. If I'd thought about what I was doing, I would have ended this, and I didn't want to end this.

I just wanted to feel something other than sorry for myself.

I walked in without being invited, pressing my chest flush with his. "I don't want to talk."

Chin dipped, his eyes searched mine. "What do you want, princess?"

I slid my hand to the back of his neck. "I'm tired of feeling so fucking bad. Make me feel good for a few minutes."

I tugged on him, and he easily came, ghosting over my lips with his. It was sweet, exactly what I didn't want.

"You taste like champagne. Are you drunk?" he murmured.

"One glass. I know what I'm doing."

He kissed me again, soft as a feather. My nails dug into his nape, drawing him into me so I could nip at his bottom lip.

"Harder," I uttered. "Kiss me like you mean it."

That was all it took. Rhys's lips covered mine. His kisses were deep and drugging, and our hands were all over each other. Rough and unforgiving, ripping fabric from each other's skin until we were all heat and desire.

Fabric puddled at our feet. Rhys slid my T-shirt over my head, leaving me in my bra and underwear, and I became too aware of the round parts of me touching the solid parts of him. Before I could spiral, Rhys yanked me hard against him, kneading my ass and cradling the back of my head as he plundered my mouth with his tongue. He stole my breath and self-hatred, replacing it with his desire and arousal even my scattered mind couldn't beat back.

Backing me into his room, he shoved whatever was on his desk off so he could prop me on it. My legs circled his waist, holding him against me.

Leaning over, he flicked a lamp on, the pool of light flooding over my bared skin.

"No," I yelped, squeezing my eyes shut. "Turn it off!"

"Princess..." To his credit, he complied. Darkness spilled behind my eyelids.

When both of his hands were on me again, they'd gentled. He knew. Nothing had changed. I couldn't bear for him to look at me. Not anymore.

"Don't talk and please don't treat me like I'm precious."

I meant I *couldn't* talk about it. Not with him or about this. Not when I wanted to forget all of this more than anything.

His brow furrowed. "You *are* precious."

"Rhys."

My nails dug into his shoulders, urging him on, begging him to *stop*, please, please stop.

Another second of hesitation, then he was on me again, palming my breast through my bra, stroking the length of my back with his other hand, giving me what I needed.

Our cores were aligned, hot and swollen for each other. I rubbed against him, frantic to feel anything other than what was going on inside my head.

It wasn't just that, though. I wanted him. I wanted Rhys like I'd wanted him for weeks. His hands on me, his cock inside me, his mouth on mine. I'd ached for it, and not having him had become unbearable now that he was within reach.

I didn't trust him anymore, but this...I could count on him to give me some reprieve from my thoughts and all that existed outside these walls. We'd worked at this together. Our bodies were capable of giving each other exactly what we needed.

The hand on my back plucked my bra strap, unhooking it with deft fingers. He slid my bra off with swift precision then bent forward, sucking my nipple deep into his mouth.

My head fell back as he feasted on my tits, hard and unyielding. He held them both to his mouth, licking, biting, sucking, with none of his normal, gentle finesse. He was devouring my flesh, suckling like he was starved for me.

Dizzy with need, I carved my fingers through his hair, pulling him closer. My lips parted, moaning to the ceiling.

My panties were so wet they were stuck to my skin, and Rhys hadn't touched me there yet. Not with his hands anyway. The ridge of his cock rocked against me through our underwear. Two thin pieces of cotton separated us. It wasn't much, but I was ready for him, and I wanted to shred the fabric with my fingernails.

My fingertips pressed into his waist and slid down to the band. He grunted with his mouth full of my breast, and I went farther, slipping inside. His cock was thick and hard, the head weeping. Using my palm, I spread the precum down his length, pumping him a few times.

He grunted louder and ripped his mouth off me to grab the sides of my head and tip it back. "What are you doing to me?"

"I want you inside me. Stop playing."

Even in the dark, I could read his displeasure. "I'm not fucking you unless you come."

I raised my legs on his sides. "Then make me come. Do it."

Reaching between us, he skated his palm up the inside of my thigh and tugged my panties to the side. My legs fell open, hitting the desk on either side. Rhys rubbed my clit and licked my neck while he cradled my head in his hands. The space between our bodies was paper thin. No room for me to move or run if I finally wised up.

His fingers curled in the back of my hair. I thought he would kiss me, but he rested the tip of his nose on mine and stared at me while he rolled my slick clit beneath his fingertip.

So close he was only a blur, but it was still too much. My eyes began to shut, but the hand on the back of my head gave a sharp tug, whipping them open again. He shook his head, his nose rubbing mine.

It was the intensity of his unyielding gaze that gave me the last push I needed. My hips rose and fell to the rhythm he set, and I breathed my pleasure into his mouth when he crashed into me at my first cry.

Before I began to come down, Rhys slid me off his desk and guided me to his bed without removing his mouth from mine until I was falling.

My back hit the mattress, then Rhys was over me, kneeling between my knees. His fingers hooked my panties, dragging them off in one swoop.

"Condom," I panted.

He cocked his head, staring down at me. All of me. My arms twitched, wanting to cover myself. But if I did, he'd know. He'd look at me the same way I looked at myself, and that was the last thing I wanted from him. I was here to forget, not to call attention to what I wished wasn't true.

"What's the hurry, princess?"

I raised my hips. "I need—"

"Me?"

"You inside me, yes."

He delayed another moment, his fist wrapped around his cock, stroking as he looked me over. And god, did he look me over. So much desire beneath his heavy lids, it couldn't have been faked. Rhys wanted me. The curve of my stomach and breadth of my hips didn't deter him. He was looking at me like they were part of the attraction.

I squeezed my eyes shut. I wasn't here for this.

"Rhys," I whined, rocking again. "Now."

With a grunt, he moved quickly, jostling me. The drawer beside the bed opened and closed, then there was crinkling. Next, he would fall on me, stare down at me as he slid in, and I couldn't take it.

While he was busy with the condom, I lifted my legs and rolled to my front. Gripping the headboard, I pushed up on my knees, ready for him.

"Princess," he gritted out. "What are you doing to me?"

I arched my spine, luring him in. "Hard, Rhys. Give it to me."

The mattress rocked as he got into position, his palms sliding over the curve of my ass to hold my hips. His cock nudged at my opening, lining up where I needed him.

"Rhys," I breathed.

He wasted no time, jerking back then thrusting into me, filling me with efficient, brutal force. We both groaned, grinding into each other.

"More," I demanded softly.

He gave it to me. Fingers digging into the give of my waist, he powered into me. And I met him, my ass grinding into his pelvis, soft slamming into hard. That was us, a study in contrasts. But when we came together in exactly the right way, we fit.

My nails turned into claws, working to shred the headboard as Rhys wrecked me. One hand traveled up my side to my tit, grabbing it roughly, rolling my nipple just shy of painful. I had to stop myself from putting my hand on top of his—from threading my fingers with his so we could touch me together.

No, I wouldn't get lost in what used to be. All we had was now, and we were no longer tender touches and sweet words.

His hand skated down my torso. When he neared my stomach, I froze for a second, and he powered into me harder, the other hand sliding to my shoulder, applying firm pressure, plowing through my self-doubt, rendering it into rubble.

"Face down, Delilah," Rhys uttered. "Let me give you what you want."

As I lay on the pillow, my ass in the air, he gripped my hip and braced his other hand on the center of my back. Once he had me where he wanted me, he let loose.

If I thought he'd gone at me hard before, I'd been wrong. Rhys became an animal. His slamming thrusts banged my ass like a drum. Grunting and slapping of skin were his sweet nothings. If I had wanted this to stop, he would have had to let me. There was no way I could have gotten away from him now.

I hadn't known it, but *this* was perfect. My will had been handed over, and he was clenching it in an iron fist while stroking me with a velvet glove, turning my choice to come here into his choice to keep me under him.

My inner walls clenched, which was impossible but true. The slap of his flesh against mine vibrated my clit, but there was no direct contact, which I'd always thought I'd needed to come.

Instead, I needed Rhys Astor going wild over me.

Moaning uncontrollably into the pillow, my insides squeezed and fluttered as I came around him without a single warning. He cursed under his breath, and the hand on my back slipped into my hair. Instead of becoming rougher, he stroked me through it. If I hadn't been buried under a tidal wave of pleasure, I would have told him not to touch me like that.

But I couldn't think.

Only feel.

Exactly why I was here.

Rhys's movements stuttered, going faster, deeper, then slowing at the end of me. Small, jerking thrusts, then he held himself deep, his arm banding around my middle. He tugged me hard and fell back with me in his arms.

I was on his lap, facing away from him. He had his feet on the floor, both arms wrapped around me, his face buried in my hair. His moans were breathy in my ear, his cock buried to the root. I was boneless. Sated. The world around us was flat and smooth. We were the textured, curved Technicolor truth.

At least, we had been, until his lips grazed my neck and shoulder, soft and sweet. Then he murmured my name and sighed like he was relieved.

My eyes sprung open. I looked down at his sinewy arms banded around my rounded stomach, and my skin itched with the urge to vanish into thin air.

What had I done?

Chapter Thirty-Three
Rhys

I WOULD HAVE BEEN stupid to think Delilah showing up at my door meant she'd magically forgiven me. Hell, I would have been pissed at her if she had.

But a boy could hope.

Goddamn, I hadn't realized I still had hope left in me.

The thing was, it was impossible not to have an inkling of it when I had my girl in my arms and I was on the verge of feeling right again. The kind of right I never knew existed before her.

My hope slid back to the land of pure imagination when I pulled out of Delilah—out of necessity, not desire—and she leaped to her feet to find her clothing.

I tossed the condom and slipped on my briefs, tracking her as she tiptoed through my suite, gathering her scattered clothes.

"You know, I'm feeling a little used, princess."

She spun slowly, color brightening her cheeks. "It isn't as if you didn't get anything from that encounter."

"Hmmm." I stalked toward her, cracking my knuckles one at a time. "The days of me being sufficiently satisfied by just getting off are long gone. You tutored them out of me."

"That's fine." She jumped as she yanked on her shorts. "You got me off too, so it was a job well done."

She fumbled with her shirt, dropping it to the ground. I grabbed it before she could, holding it hostage against my abdomen.

"You're really just going to walk out on me?" I asked.

"Yes." She held out her hand, but I had no inclination to give her her shirt since it was the only thing keeping her here.

"Why did you come in the first place?" There was a strange ache in my chest that nearly stole my breath. "Was this a backward punishment of some sort?"

"No, Rhys." She shoved her thick hair off her sweat-dampened forehead. "Did that feel like a punishment to you?"

"It didn't, but this"—I gestured between us—"really fucking does, Detroit."

She cringed at my nickname for her, but I couldn't help it. She was still mine, as far as I was concerned, and I was unequivocally still hers.

"No, that isn't cute at all anymore." She lunged for her shirt, successfully slipping it from my grasp.

Since I couldn't keep her in my room by holding her clothes hostage, I propped myself against my door, blocking her exit.

"I don't want you to leave."

"I've noticed." She twisted the hem of her shirt around her fist. "I don't want to talk."

Scoffing, I dropped my chin against my chest. "I got that loud and clear, but I do want to talk. Have you been listening to my chapters?"

Her eyes slid to the side, and I braced for a lie. "I don't know what you mean."

There it was. Inside, I did a victory dance. Small, but I felt more beaten down than after a session with Preston. I'd take any win I could get.

"You do. What about the messages at the end?"

She continued looking away from me. "I'm confused. What messages?"

She'd listened. I'd poured thoughts out to her I'd never given voice to before. It was less difficult to do via voice recording, but not easy by far.

And now that I'd given her my thoughts, I wanted hers back. Delilah wasn't someone who had trouble expressing her opinion, but things had changed.

I'd changed things.

"Avoidance is unbecoming on you, Daytona. I thought you were a straight shooter. You're being awfully cowardly right now."

Her head whipped around, and she pinned me with a narrow-eyed glare. "I have to be on guard with you. I don't know what your current motives are."

"Remember, you came to me."

"Yes, and I would like to leave."

"I'll let you go." She took a step toward the door—toward *me*—and I held up a finger. "First, answer a question."

Her jaw hardened, working back and forth. "If it means I'll be able to leave, then go on. Ask me."

I hadn't actually had one single question in mind. I had dozens I wanted to ask and demand answers to. I had to sift through them and decide which was most imperative to ask.

"Rhys," she sighed, impatient with me. "Come on."

"Okay." I went to her, crowding her space. That left the door open for her to sneak out, but my need to touch her one more time superseded all else. Besides, I couldn't hold her hostage here until she forgave me.

Well, morally, I had no problem with that. It was the realist in me that understood it would never work. My roommates would be back soon, and Felix or Ryan would put on their good guy hats and call the cops if they found out I had chained Delilah to my bed. Not to mention, Beckett wouldn't take kindly to it, Delilah either. I seriously doubted she would develop Stockholm Syndrome quickly enough for my liking.

I'd just have to win her back the old-fashioned way.

"What will it take for you to forgive me?" I took her face in my hands, stroking my thumbs along the corners of her plump lips. "I'm willing to do the work, you know that. Taking things slow isn't a problem for me either."

"I don't—" Her lashes fluttered, blocking her gaze from mine.

"I can't go back to who I was before you, princess. I need to be with you, and I will do anything to get you to the place where you feel the same again. Tell me how to do that. Give me a clue."

Her deep inhale made her shoulders rise and her chest press against mine. "Don't you think if I knew how to go back, I would? I've had enough time to think about us, and I believe it was real. At least the last few weeks."

"All of it," I uttered with vehemence. "Every word I said to you was real. If I'd been trying to charm you, I would have done a much better job at it."

A soft sob erupted from her lips before she clamped them shut between her teeth.

"I don't want this. I don't want any of it. I loved being with you and being without you has been misery, but I can't see how to find a way back." She dug her nails into my bare chest, and I welcomed the pain, knowing I deserved it all. "What you did destroyed us before we even got started, and I'm left here, trying to hold myself together when I'm broken, Rhys."

I shook my head, firming my hold on her. "No. You're sad. There's nothing broken about you."

"You have no idea. Saying it doesn't make it so. I *feel* broken and gross and unworthy. If I feel it, isn't it real? No matter how much you deny it."

My stomach became a bag of demented gummy worms. This was a side of Delilah I had never seen. After Ivan in the library, she'd held her head high, but she was slipping now. Going low, and I didn't fucking know how to stop her.

"Delilah...I'll treat you so fucking well if you let me."

"You did. You treated me well, but then—"

"Yeah." My forehead fell against hers. "I'll make it right."

"I wish you could." She pushed off me, and I let her get away. "I'm not going to come back here. This was a step backward, and I can't do this again. Our friends will be returning, and everyone who heard what happened."

Another break, and she squeezed her eyes shut.

"No one's going to say anything to you." I would carve out eyeballs and tongues if they looked at her funny or said a word that even mildly hurt her feelings. Of the two of us, I was the loser. If that wasn't obvious, then I'd make it obvious.

She started for the door, giving me a glance over her shoulder. "Are you planning on being my bodyguard?"

Two strides, and I was behind her, pulling the door open. Before I let her go, I banded my arm around her and pressed my chest against her back.

"It's funny that you doubt me. You know I have the tendency to be unhinged, and when it comes to you, I will absolutely stand between you and a bullet. You have nothing to worry about from our classmates."

I touched my lips to her temple and took a long drag of the rose scent I'd resorted to huffing off the T-shirt I'd been wearing the last time she'd laid her head on my shoulder.

She let her head fall against me and sighed. "I wish, I wish, I wish," she whispered.

"I wish too," I murmured into her hair.

Her fingers closed around mine, and for a fleeting moment, I thought I'd gotten somewhere. Then she lowered my hand, freeing herself from me, taking herself away.

She spun around to face me. "Happy New Year, Rhys."

I leaned against the jamb, my hands twitching to grab her and try the whole hostage thing.

"Happy New Year, princess. I'll see you Monday unless you feel like giving me another midnight visit before then."

She huffed, but her mouth slightly curved into a microscopic grin. "Don't be charming."

"I would never."

It curved a little more. "Bye, then."

She left me bereft.

Be-fucking-reft.

It took me a minute of leaning there, watching her evaporate, tumbleweeds rolling down the hall in her place, to catch my breath and slow my racing heart. Once I did, I went into my room, sat down with my phone in hand, and typed out a plan. Then I enlisted the people I trusted to help me enact it.

Getting Delilah back was the ultimate goal, but no matter what, no one would be allowed to make her feel bad about what I had done. She would feel safe walking the halls and showing her face.

I would make sure of that.

Chapter Thirty-Four
Delilah

OUR SUITE WAS ALIVE again.

Bella had lit it up the second she'd returned from break. She'd left Savage Academy pissed, and her time in Texas hadn't eased it. If anything, she was more livid than ever.

Her anger was directed squarely at all the boys in Rhys's suite, but mostly Felix. She'd blocked him on every social media platform, and he'd stolen his sister Isla's phone to text her.

I wouldn't admit it, but I was happy to listen to her relationship drama. I would never begrudge Luciana for what she had with Beckett, but it was reassuring to know I wasn't the only one who was floundering when it came to boys.

The four of us were buzzing around our suite, getting our things together before first period. I'd been slightly nauseous all morning. Facing the people who'd witnessed my humiliation wasn't something I was looking forward to, but once I got through today and everyone saw I was doing fine—due to really good makeup and the ability to fake it—I hoped they would lose interest.

Luc straightened her ponytail and turned to Bella. "What are you going to do when you see him today?"

Bella held up her middle finger. "This is all he's gettin' from me. I'm through with him. It's lucky we never defined what we were. We don't even have to break up." She folded her arms across her chest. "What I wanna know is, what are we doin' about Charles?"

I blinked at her. "What do you mean?"

"The girl he was bangin'—" She waved her hand toward Ev. "Sorry to be indelicate."

My sister shrugged one shoulder. "It doesn't bother me. I'm relieved not to have to be near him anymore. He smelled of mothballs. It was off-putting."

Bella snapped her fingers. "That's because he's ancient. Dude was redshirted by Mama and Pops, so their strapping lad could be the *biggest boy* on the football field."

I paused in readying my book bag to frown at her. "What on earth is a red shirt? Is that an American idiom I'm not familiar with?"

"It might be an American thing." Bella swiped ChapStick across her lips and popped them together. "Sporty parents hold their beloved babies back from starting school for a year or two, so they'll be the oldest and biggest in their class. Guess how old Charles is."

"Nineteen," Luc chimed.

Bella finger gunned her. "And a half. He'll be turning twenty two months after graduation."

I shuddered. "Who let this grown man walk among us? And kiss my sister?"

"Oh yes. I understand the mothballs now," Ev stated, unbothered. She really was over whatever momentary infatuation she'd had for him.

Luc swung her backpack onto her back. "All right. He's old, but why does that matter?"

Bella pushed her feet into her flats. "Back to what I was sayin'. The girl Charles was bangin' the day I saw everything is a freshman."

Luc's nose crinkled. "Oh, gross. Talk about cradle robbing."

"Mmmhmm. I recognized her from the JV field hockey team." Bella flipped her curls behind her shoulders. "Her name's Samantha. She's from Utah, where her dad is a super conservative US senator."

"Samantha had bad taste in men," Ev said.

Bella pointed at her. "That's because the poor thing is only fourteen. She doesn't know any better."

"Fourteen?" Luc questioned.

"Fourteen," Bella confirmed.

The four of us exchanged glances. Fourteen was *young*. A senior going after a freshman was bad enough, but the fact that Charles was nineteen going on twenty made it grotesque.

"That's..." Ev's mouth twisted as she searched for the word.

"Criminal," I supplied.

"Exactly," Bella said. "I was thinkin' maybe I'd have a chat with Samantha. See how she thinks her daddy would react if he found out about what went down. I don't want her to get in trouble, but I *really* want that asshole to pay. Preferably by castration."

"Oh." Ev perked up. "I don't think testicles are removed as punishment anymore, but chemical castration is available."

Bella bumped her shoulder. "Now you're talkin'."

The four of us headed out, and Bella fell into step beside me, hooking her arm through mine. "I want to tell you something, but I don't want to set you back on your road to gettin' over Rhys."

My chest constricted just from his name. I was nowhere near that road. I'd seen it in the distance and taken a U-turn.

"You've made me far too curious. You have to tell me."

"I know Charles's birthday because Rhys told me. He'd also mentioned I should pop by their room that day. I had braced myself to walk in on Felix steppin' out, so I was not prepared for the sight of Charles Bloomberg's balls swingin'. They're huge and dangly, by the way."

"That's far more than I ever wanted to know about him." I sucked in a deep breath, understanding exactly what she was telling me. "He couldn't tell Ev himself, but he made sure she found out."

She nodded, watching my reaction. "Yep, honey, that's what he did."

Suddenly, it was hard to breathe. My face grew hot, and I was panting. Dizzy. Bella stopped with me, pulling me to the side of the hallway. She blew in my face and ran her hands down my arms.

"Shhh. I know it's gotta be confusing. He's a dick, but he also tried to do the right thing in his own Rhys way."

I shook my head and bent at the waist, trying to pull myself together. "I don't know how to get over him."

"It's fresh." She twirled one of my waves around her fingers. "I'm tellin' you now, none of us would judge you if you decided *not* to get over him. Whatever happens, we're here."

She didn't have to tell me that. One thing I would never doubt was my girls always being at my back. I'd been unlucky in many ways, but not with my friends. They were the best.

I took a minute to calm down, then Bella and I continued to the elevators. There, Ev and Luc waited, along with Freddie and Ivan.

I exchanged cheek kisses with them both. "What are you doing on our floor?"

Freddie puffed out his chest. "I'm your big, strong escort to class."

Ivan's mouth hitched. "I'm his backup."

Freddie slapped his shoulder. "Are you implying I'm not capable of protecting my beloved Delilah on my own? I'm incredibly powerful, you know, and quite nimble."

Bella stroked her chin. "Experts say nimbleness is the key trait to look for in a bodyguard."

Ivan folded his arms over his chest. "Not skill with weapons? Fighting technique?"

"No." She poked his chest. "Nimbleness. Write that in your diary so you don't forget it."

Once we were outside, Ivan and Freddie walked on either side of me while Beckett, Luc, and Ev were in front. Ryan and another guy from the soccer team, Valentino, were right behind me.

This formation felt purposeful, like they'd been tasked to protect me, which was a strange thought. I wasn't a celebrity, and my parents were just as wealthy as everyone else's on campus. Why would I need protection?

Then we passed a group of girls who started snickering, and my group closed ranks around me, tightening my circle so I couldn't see them, and they definitely couldn't see me.

The boys walked with us to class before breaking off and going their own way. Beckett went ahead of Luc and me into English lit and arranged our floor pillows so he would be slightly ahead of me. Ivan sat on my other side, even with Beckett.

There was no denying that it was purposeful. It also seemed well coordinated, and I couldn't understand it.

I let it go, though, because Rhys walked in the door. His head swiveled, quickly and precisely homing in on me. My breath snagged on the fist in my throat, my reaction to him as involuntary as blinking.

We surveyed each other as he slowly approached where our group was sitting. His bruises had faded, but there were still shadows beneath his eyes and a slight edge of unkemptness to his clothes. His collar wasn't as crisp as normal. One button was only halfway through the hole. One shoe was untied.

When I met his gaze again, he was grinning like he was pleased I'd given him such a thorough sweep.

I wished I could smile back at him, but just because I cared what he looked like and how he was doing didn't mean we could be together again. The caring wasn't a choice. Everything else was.

Someone snorted on the other side of Luciana. "Oh my god, how pathetic."

Another piggish snort. "Right? He was *paid* to have sex with her, and she's still all googly-eyed over him. It's honestly so embarrassing."

Beckett shifted so I couldn't see around him, but I already knew who was speaking. Clarice's and Veronica's catty judgments were far too familiar.

"For real. And after she threw herself at Ivan," Clarice chimed. "Pathetic. She's shooting so far above her pay grade."

My head dropped so no one would see that my face was on fire. I'd known this would happen, thought I'd mentally prepared myself for it, but reality was far more bitter than the way I'd imagined it going.

Rhys cleared his throat. I couldn't bear to look at him or anyone else since they'd all undoubtedly heard them too.

"Enough," Rhys uttered lowly. "Shut the fuck up before we have problems."

Clarice rolled her eyes. "As if you could cause me a problem."

"Clarice," Ivan boomed. There was no other word for his thunderous voice, and judging by the sudden silence in the classroom, it wasn't only Clarice's attention he'd caught. "I have asked you twice to stop sending me nude pictures. I was disappointed to receive another one this morning. I am not interested in"—he scratched his head—"ah, yes, playing naked ponies with you, as you said. Please discontinue—"

Clarice screeched her indignation. "I don't know what you're talking about. I only texted—"

Ivan held up his hand. "Shhh, shhh, shhh. No need to be embarrassed. Surely, there is someone interested in naked ponies with you, but I am not."

Everyone around us was either laughing or asking Clarice to clarify exactly what naked ponies entailed.

Ivan patted my knee. "Don't cover your face. You did nothing wrong."

I dropped my hands and grinned at him. "Naked ponies?" I whispered.

His brow crinkled. "She is a very strange girl."

My mouth fell open. "I assumed you were making that up. Weren't you?"

He shook his head then nodded, a devious grin playing at the corners of his mouth, which made me laugh.

"You're not going to tell me?" He shrugged, and I hit his shoulder. "You goose."

He patted my knee again. "She will not bother you again."

"Thank you," I murmured, turning to scan my classmates. But I was looking for *him*. I found him a few cushions away, watching Ivan and I interact. He didn't look especially happy, but it wasn't my job to make him feel better.

He would have to do that himself.

· · · • · · • · · · ·

By the end of the day, I was certain I had bodyguards. After each of my classes, there were at least two soccer or fencing boys, but more often four escorting me to class. And they'd somehow finagled their way into sitting at the desks on either side of me, so I was never, ever alone.

People murmured, but no one was out and out rude like Clarice and Veronica had been.

Day one wasn't nearly as bad as I'd expected it to be. Day two was even better since all malicious laughter and sniveling little comments had been shut down hard the previous day.

Day two was also worse since fencing practice resumed, and I had to spend two hours trying not to watch Rhys in all his glory.

Fortunately, there were only a couple more weeks left in the season, so this particular torture would be over soon. Then, we wouldn't have a reason to be in close proximity. We could go back to existing separately within the same universe.

We'll never go back.

A loud scream made me jump. I had never gotten used to that. Mr. Chevalier didn't even flinch, while my shoulders were almost always bunched around my ears during practice and matches.

My hand was knotted on my chest when Rhys ripped his helmet off and walked over to his water bottle. He tipped his head back to drink, his throat bobbing as he swallowed. My heart had already been hammering, but Rhys Astor, dripping with sweat, wearing his fencing attire, made it thrash like a feral animal.

When would this go away? He'd hurt me, betrayed me, but the inexplicable pull to him was still lodged deep in my chest.

Like he knew I was watching him, Rhys turned to me, leveling me with a steady gaze as he wiped his forehead and the back of his neck with a towel.

Then someone screamed, and I flinched so hard my head hit the wall behind me.

"Oof." My eyes closed as I rubbed the sore spot on my crown. I should have been braced since it kept happening, but I couldn't stay on constant alert. It was too exhausting to try.

Warm hands engulfed my shoulders. "Did you go and hurt your-self?"

My eyes flashed open. Rhys was crouched in front of me, his head tilting left and right as he searched for signs of injury.

"I'm fine. It's merely a flesh wound."

The corner of his mouth slowly hitched. "Does Evelyn make you watch Monty Python films?"

"What makes you think *I* don't make *her* watch them?"

It was her. All her. Ev and I were a lot alike, but our taste in music and movies made us seem like we came from two different planets.

His smile widened. "Do you?"

That earned him a hard glare. "Don't be charming. And don't gloat."

"Because I'm right?"

"Shut up, Astor."

His smile slipped in increments as he reached for the back of my head, sliding his hand over my hair and curving down to my nape. "Are you really okay? I saw you hit your head."

"I truly am fine. You didn't have to interrupt practice to check on me."

"I did." He squeezed my nape, then slid his fingers up through my hair, pausing over the spot I'd hit. "You've already got a little goose egg."

"I bet I'll survive."

His expression grew even more serious. "Take care of yourself, Delilah. I like you exactly as you are, and I won't take kindly to you injuring yourself."

"Astor!" Chevalier called from the other side of the room. "Enough flirting. Get moving!"

Rhys hopped up, brushing his fingers over the top of my head, then strode away, pausing only to grab his helmet from where he'd stashed it.

With a sigh, my head lolled back against the wall, landing right on the same damn spot.

Shit. Why? But I knew exactly why. Rhys Astor had stolen my attention to my own detriment.

When would this boy stop wrecking me?

Later that night, he proved it wouldn't be anytime soon.

I listened to his chapters of *The Shadow of the Isle* and held my breath for his message that always came afterward.

"Hi, princess. Are you still listening? You have no idea how badly I want to sit you on my lap and ask you what you think of my favorite book. It's going to happen. I have to believe that."

There was a pause, shuffling, then he spoke again. "My mom fell in love with my dad when she saw him fencing for the first time. She used to tell me fencing was a gentleman's sport, and my father was the ultimate gentleman. When I started, she was there for every practice, cheering for me at every match. She was my biggest fan, and when my father and I practiced together, I sometimes caught her with tears in her eyes."

Another pause, and I fell back on my pillows, barely breathing as I waited for him to go on.

"She hasn't been to a match since Preston came into our lives. In my head, I excused her absence, telling myself it was too hard for her to watch because of my father. But that excuse doesn't hold much water anymore, does it? When she sent me a bouquet of roses after I won the regional finals my freshman year, I came around to the truth. My mother doesn't care. She can't possibly. Sending me roses like I'm the bad blind date she's letting down easy."

He heaved a breath, and I found myself copying him. His story was all too familiar.

"I'm not telling you this for sympathy. I don't want you to pity me, but I do want you to understand I have been alone for a long time. I dug my own grave to give Owen the dirt he needed to reach higher ground. He's important to me, and I will claw and fight so he never feels alone as I did...do. The thing is, I can't put you in the grave with me again. Seeing you so low has changed me in a way I don't think I can put into words yet. I know I would rip the world apart so you never cry from being hurt again. Like Fathaniel Flamen when he rewrites the path of the stars, changing the course of all humanity so Binboa doesn't get scorched by the eighth moon of Glavspor. I'd rewrite the stars for you too, princess."

My grin grew so wide I had to clamp down on my bottom lip with my teeth to remind myself I wasn't happy with him.

But he'd rewrite the stars for me. How could I not smile at that?

It was useless. He wasn't going to let me get over him, was he?

CHAPTER THIRTY-FIVE
Rhys

THE TOURNAMENT TODAY WAS a two-hour bus ride away, and I'd been looking forward to having Delilah as a captive audience. It was as close to an actual captive as I was going to get, *for now.*

I reserved the right to lose my mind entirely in the future.

Delilah was the last one to board the bus, and instead of making her way down the aisle like she was heading to the gallows, she stopped by Chevalier's seat to talk to him. From my vantage, I could see the top of his head shaking, then his profile as he looked up at her.

I almost yelled, "Speak up!" but I sensed Delilah wouldn't appreciate me drawing that kind of attention to her.

I'd been trying as hard as I was capable. To allow her space and time while also hovering in case she changed her mind at the drop of a hat. She hadn't so far, but the madness that lived within me demanded I stay as close to her as she would allow.

Some days had been closer than others, though I hadn't received another midnight visit. Some squeaky clean, pocket-protecting wearing, simp-ass bitch part of me was relieved she hadn't come by. We'd grasped and clawed and used each other on New Year's, but that wasn't what I wanted from her. The grasping and clawing, sure, but using? No. Not like that. We were far beyond that, and I wouldn't take a step back.

So, I waited for her. Protected her. Watched over her. Gave her the space she needed to forgive me while still toying with the plan of locking her in my room.

When Delilah sat down next to Chevalier, I stood up like a fuck-ing puppet on a string. What was she doing sitting by him? We had rituals. Superstitions. Not that I believed in them, but Chevalier did. We didn't switch seats during a winning season. That messed with the vibe.

I expected her to get up. Like maybe they were talking, but she wasn't going to stay there.

Except she did. The bus started rolling out of the parking lot, and she was still there, in the wrong seat. Rows and rows away from me.

This would not stand.

If she thought she was going to sit in the front on the way home, she didn't know me very well at all.

· · ● · ● · ● · · ·

The fencers at Willow Lake Prep were children. Even the seniors were puny little knob gobblers. I was surprised any of them had the strength to keep their sabres above waist level, much less parry or block with any success.

Yet my spindly-armed opponent was beating me.

It was all I could do not to block their unskilled, elementary parries I'd mastered as a child. Letting my opponent have priority took every ounce of my willpower. He was so slow on his feet it had to be obvious to the judges I wasn't trying. I didn't want it to be obvious. I simply didn't want to win.

Chevalier stormed up to me after losing my first bout. "What was that, Astor? Did you throw that bout?"

I shrugged, my helmet under my arm. "I'm off. Something changed, and I don't feel right. Maybe the next bout will go better."

His brow dropped low over stormy eyes. "What do you mean? What changed?"

I scratched the side of my head. "I can't put my finger on it. I've been off since the bus ride. But I'll try to pull myself together. Can't let the team down."

We both knew I carried our team. Sure, there were other talented fencers, but I was the most consistent and could be counted on to bring home the win.

Me fucking up would screw us all.

It wasn't that I wanted to let my team down. I didn't. But I *was* off. I had been for some time. It might have been the wrong way to go about it, but I couldn't see any other way to make things right again.

·········

Delilah was the last one on the bus again. She stopped by Chevalier's seat, and I could see him shaking his head the way he had this morning. She bent down, speaking to him as privately as possible given the location, but he continued to shake his head.

She straightened and faced the back of the bus. After a deep inhale, she marched down the aisle.

I turned toward the window, playing it cool as a cucumber. I felt her take the seat beside me but acted like the parking lot was the most interesting thing I'd ever seen.

It was enough to breathe in her roses and have her near. I'd look at her soon, but not yet.

"What was that first bout?" she hissed. "You threw it."

Slowly, I turned to her. Her cheeks were flaming red, and she was gnawing her bottom lip to death. Reaching across to her, I cupped her chin and pressed my thumb beneath her mouth until her lip was free.

"My head wasn't in it," I explained.

"I would believe that, except you didn't even attempt to gain priority and let him push you off the back of the strip twice. It was blatantly obvious what you were doing."

I wouldn't lie to her again, but since she hadn't asked a question, I didn't reply to her accurate assessment of my performance. Internally, I was pleased beyond measure how well she'd come to understand my sport, though. So fucking pleased.

"What did Chevalier say to you just now?" I asked.

Huffing, she pulled her face out of my grasp. "He told me I had to return to my original seat, which I'm sure you know."

"Why would I know?"

"Because that was clearly your intention."

I scrubbed at my jaw, acting casual. "Athletes are notoriously superstitious. We don't like change before games or matches."

"Rhys," she sighed. "You can't throw your bouts because you want me to sit next to you."

"I can," I uttered. "You're *supposed* to be beside me, Delilah. This is where you belong."

She rubbed her palms on her thighs, looking down at them. "Did you arrange for the boys to follow me around?"

She didn't sound angry, so I chose not to dance around the answer. "Yes."

Her head tipped up. "Why would you do that?"

"I told you already, you won't suffer for my screwup. The boys were more than happy to help out. They like you, although I forbade them from liking you too much. Or looking at you more than strictly necessary."

Her giggle was a breath of fresh air after being buried alive. "I doubt any of them will fall madly in love with me since they don't speak to me."

"I'm glad to know they're maintaining their directive."

She gasped, her gaze whipping to mine. "You directed them not to speak to me?"

"Why should they? They don't have anything interesting to say. I don't want them to waste your time."

"So, it's for *my* sake."

I lowered my chin, pinning her with an unflinching stare. "Always, princess. That's how I work now. I think of you first."

"And Owen."

Hearing his name from her pretty lips hit me hard. Some fundamental part of me vibrated like a banged gong. Strange but right.

"Owen is important, yes, but he has a pretty devoted mom. *I'm* devoted to you." I took her jaw in my hand, turning her to fully face me. "Listen to me. I learned to set aside my ego with you back in the beginning. I don't need it. It's just us here, and I'm telling you the truth. I will always tell you the truth."

She swallowed, and after a moment, she leaned into my hand. Her warm, soft skin on my palm was bliss. There was no other word for it.

"I forgive you, Rhys." Her lashes fluttered down to her cheeks. "I wish I could say I have set aside my pride, but I haven't. Your boys are protecting me now, but they can't forever. I hate that it's a consideration, but I can't stop thinking about how humiliating it would be to let you come back after *everyone* knows what happened."

My knee-jerk reaction is anger. How could she give a fuck what any of those idiots thought? If she had forgiven me, we should have been together. Everyone else could fuck right off.

But I took a deep breath and reminded myself I wasn't the one who had been flayed in front of a good majority of our school. That had been her. They all got to see her in an incredibly vulnerable state. Ruining Charles would only solve so much. There had to be more I could do.

"I understand."

Her eyes narrowed. "You do?"

"I do. I'll work on it."

"That frightens me."

"I'm not going to hurt you."

Her sigh grazed over my lips. "I am beginning to believe that." A faint line formed between her brows. "I've been listening to your chapters."

A weight in me lightened at hearing her admit it. "I thought you might be." I toyed with a lock of her hair. "What do you think of Fathaniel and his merry band of ruffians?"

"He's sort of a dick."

She surprised me so thoroughly a laugh burst out of me. "Don't hold back. Tell me what you really think of my favorite story ever."

Her grin was unguarded and true. "I didn't say I don't like the book. I really do. I've been tempted to read ahead of you."

"But you haven't because you're a good girl."

She rolled her eyes but didn't deny it. "I haven't because I like you revealing the story to me." Our gazes caught. Slowly, our smiles slipped, and we were left looking at each other. "It's only the first book. There is lots of room for character growth. I have faith in Fathaniel."

"It's heartening to know you believe someone can change and do better."

She ignored my comment, which had been a poor job on my part at fishing for some hope. "Is Fathaniel going to find his father?"

I tapped her nose. "You'll have to keep listening, princess." I leaned closer until we were breathing each other's air. "You have no idea how badly I want to kiss you."

"I have an idea." She rubbed her lips together. "You can't, though."

"Disappointing."

"For me as well," she murmured. "Why is Fathaniel able to walk under Glavspor's eighth moon when Binboa can't? Aren't they both Dorfits?"

My stomach did a roller-coaster swoop. As if my Delilah hadn't been perfect before, dear god. Not even Beckett had read *The Shadow of the Isle*. It was like the redheaded stepchild of *The Lord of the Rings*—which was probably why I loved it. Now, this gorgeous girl was asking me questions, eager to find the answers. I barely stopped myself from crashing my mouth into hers.

"God, I love you."

Well, there was that. I hadn't stopped that.

She blinked, her lips parting.

I laughed at her shock. "You heard me, just like you heard me when I passed out in your bed."

"You were out of it," she rasped.

"I knew what I was saying." I tugged on her hair, then let her go. "Do you have music for me to listen to?"

Her wide eyes roved over me. "Um, yes." She fished around in her bag for her phone and earbuds. "You aren't going to badger me anymore?"

"No, I'm not. You're where I want you for now. I'd like to enjoy it while I can." I held out my hand, and after a beat, she placed an earbud on my palm.

"What do you want to listen to?" she asked.

"I think we need some Florence."

"I think we do."

She pressed play on the song we had agreed was our favorite. I took it as a sign. A message. If she was playing me love songs, there was hope after all.

That was all a boy like me needed.

Delilah sank down in her seat and slowly let her head fall against my shoulder. I wasn't so slow about letting mine rest on top of hers.

The moment was fleeting. I knew this all too well. But the time she gave me during those miles rolling down the highway was everything good and right.

And that made me even more determined to have more of them. Indefinitely.

CHAPTER THIRTY-SIX
Delilah

THE DINING HALL WAS jam-packed this morning, as it normally was on Mondays. Our classmates took breakfast seriously on a sliding scale, giving Monday the most importance. By Friday, it would be a ghost town.

Bella, Ev, Luc, and I grabbed our food and searched out a spot to sit. By some miracle, there were four open seats at our usual table.

We sat down, and I turned to Luc. "Won't Beckett be disgruntled that he can't sit beside you?"

She grinned. "Probably, but he's cute when he's grumpy." She bumped me with her shoulder. "Don't worry about the boys. They'll find seats whenever they decide to show up."

Bella leaned into me on my other side. "I talked to some of the JV field hockey girls last night. At first, none of them wanted to say anything about Charles because, even though admitting it makes me want to vomit, he has power at this school. But I promised them nothing they said would get back to him and a couple broke ranks and gave me more names of fourteen-year-olds Charlie Boy has gone after."

I pressed my hand to my stomach. "What do we do with that information? If the girls won't talk..."

"I'm not sure yet." Bella tugged on a ringlet. "I looked up California laws, and the age of consent is eighteen. Charles would catch a charge if even one of them stepped forward."

Luc wobbled her fork in front of her. "I'll talk to them. A lot of them look up to me as captain, so they might listen."

I nodded. "We should try. Charles is vile. I hate to think of the next poor girl who will fall victim to his overinflated pecs and smooth lines."

I caught Ev's eye on the other side of Luc. "No offense, darling."

Her mouth twisted. "He does have very chiseled abs too."

We laughed and moved on from the topic, the very thought of him enough to sour anyone's stomach.

I was almost finished with my porridge when the vibrating bang of the doors being thrown open had a hush falling over the dining hall in a wave.

"Attention," someone yelled over the quickly quieting din of voices. "I will have your attention!"

"What the hell is that?" Bella stretched her neck to see over the people who'd stood to check out what was happening on the other side of the hall.

Luc and I exchanged glances, then the three of us hopped to our feet like everyone else. Ev stayed seated, quietly eating her breakfast, uninterested. I'd tell her later anyway.

We were all too short to see what was going on, so we pushed in front of a few tall guys, Bella leading the way like a tiny bulldozer.

She suddenly stopped. "Oh, dear god. What are they doing?"

I moved up beside her, disbelieving what I was seeing. "Is that Rhys?"

"And Beckett?" Luc chimed.

"Felix too," Bella growled.

A group of boys were holding court near the door, Rhys in the lead. They were all dressed in cloaks, some with elf ears, others with curly wigs. Rhys was the most ridiculous, his face painted sparkly, pointed ears, thick pelts of fur on his arms, a tall, wooden staff, and a billowing gray cloak.

He cleared his throat and patted his chest. "Fine friends of The Meadow, we leave for our mission to the Great Black Wall today. It is time we bid you farewell."

Felix slung his arm over Rhys's shoulder. "What's our mission about again?"

Rhys drew himself taller. "You fool. I've explained it to you many times. We must locate the Great Black Wall, for that is where the last dragons live."

Beckett sputtered. "There are no more dragons!"

Ryan elbowed Felix in his side. "Oh, silly Fathaniel. He's just like his father, running off on fool's errands. I won't be part of this!"

Rhys pointed his staff at Ryan. "You're the silly one, Sharthu. When I soar through The Meadow on the back of a fire-breathing beast, you shall eat your words."

Ryan rolled his eyes. "Yeah, okay."

"What is happening right now?" Bella asked.

"I have no idea," Luc whispered.

But I knew. Somehow, someway, Rhys had convinced all these guys to dress up as characters from *The Shadow of the Isle* and act out a scene in front of the majority of the student body.

What in the world was he up to?

The boys went on for a few more minutes, at one point breaking into a fight. All the guys pushed and shoved each other while Rhys stood in front of them, surveying every perplexed face in the dining hall. When he landed on me, the corners of his mouth hitched, and he winked.

My knees went weak. I didn't understand the point of any of this, but I got the sense he was doing it for me.

Beckett sidled up to Rhys and pointed at me. "There's Binboa, the one you never stop speaking of."

Rhys pushed Beckett's face to the side. "Don't look at her, Dalto. She isn't for the likes of you. She's much too precious for your unworthy eyes."

"Is this a Rhys Astor mating ritual?" Bella asked.

I shook my head. "I don't know." I was, however, fairly certain those lines were *not* part of the book.

Rhys stepped forward, separating from the group. "Thank you for your attention, everyone. The guys behind me fulfilled my 'make a wish.'" A collective gasp went over the crowd, and Rhys waved his staff around, quieting them. "No, no, I'm not dying. Well, dying inside, but they don't give you trips to Disney World for that."

Rhys paced back and forth as murmurs spread around the room like wildfire. When he was ready to speak again, he banged his staff on the hardwood floor.

"As I was saying, my wish has been to reveal my deep love of cosplaying *The Shadow of the Isle*." Raising his chin, he pressed his hand to his chest. "I, Rhys Astor, am a cosplaying, fantasy-book-reading, love-song-listening, massive fucking nerd. Say what you will. I don't give a flying fuck. This is my true self."

He did a dramatic bow, rolling his hand in front of him. When he straightened, he winked at me again then raised his staff high. "To the Great Black Wall!"

The boys yelled, "To the Great Black Wall," and marched out behind Rhys.

Thick silence fell over the dining hall. We all looked at each other as if wondering if that had all been a fever dream or if it had really happened. My chest had a tight band circling it. My heart was thrashing against it, trying to break free.

What had he done?

Bella crossed her arms. "Well, I can tell you one thing: I'm not forgivin' Felix just because he helped Rhys out with that."

Luc grinned, her cheeks flushed. "But they were all so cute."

Bella's eyes narrowed. "You mean Beckett was cute."

Her blush deepened. "Well, yes. But I bet the other guys were cute too. I just wasn't looking at them."

I swiveled around to face them both. "I have to go."

Bella bobbed her head. "Damn right you do."

Luc waved. "I'll let Ev know you left."

I didn't have any idea what I was going to do or say when I found Rhys, but I knew I *had* to find him.

CHAPTER THIRTY-SEVEN
Delilah

IT TURNED OUT FINDING Rhys hadn't been difficult at all. He was waiting for me outside my suite, clutching his staff, one foot kicked up on the wall.

He'd shed his cloak, arm pelts, and pointed ears, but he still sparkled.

I walked up to him, stopping when we were toe to toe. "You're crazy. Why did you do that?"

His eyes raked up and down my face, then he dragged his knuckles along my cheek.

"I've been private about all this"—he raised his staff slightly—"for a long time. I don't like just anyone knowing more than surface-level stuff unless I trust them implicitly. But I sucked it up because..." He shrugged.

I licked my suddenly dry lips. "You were trying to make it up to me?"

"It may not have looked like it, but that scene back there was viscerally uncomfortable. I embarrassed the hell out of myself. In no way do I think it makes up for what happened to you or even touch how you felt, but I had to try."

"Rhys..." I pressed my hand to his chest.

I didn't have words for what I felt. He'd been shamed by a man he should have been able to trust about the hobby he'd shared with his father. Rhys was outrageous on the surface, but everything below, he kept closely guarded.

For him to not only publicly embarrass himself but recruit his friends to make it an even bigger spectacle, he had to mean it.

He meant he was sorry. That he understood what that day in the dining hall had cost me, and he was willing to pay the same price.

My fingers curled around his tie. "I *never* want you to hurt yourself for me."

I let my hand drop to the doorknob and pushed the door open. We were terrible about locking it, but today, I was glad we hadn't. I was trembling too badly to attempt inserting a key into a lock.

Taking Rhys's hand in mine, I pulled him to my room. He kicked the door shut behind him and leaned against it, blocking me in like he liked to do.

I shook my head. "I'm not going anywhere."

One thud of my heartbeat, then two, and Rhys opened his arms. I walked straight into them, my head pressing against his chest, my arms banding around his waist. He held me tight, touching his lips to the top of my head again and again.

"I'm getting sparkles in your hair," he murmured, though he didn't seem sorry for it.

"I don't care." I tipped my face up, but he was still too far above me. "I want your sparkles everywhere."

He bent down, and I braced for a kiss, but this was Rhys. What I got was a long lick from my collarbone up the side of my face, then he rubbed his cheek against mine, making a sound that was almost a purr. Rough and content at the same time.

"You're back?" he asked.

I gripped the back of his shirt and shuffled my feet to move into his space a little more. "I'm here. I want to be with you."

That was all he needed to whirl me around and walk us to the bed. He sat and brought me down with him. I shifted to straddle his lap, and even though I was exactly where I wanted to be, a black curtain began to fall over the relief of being close to him again.

Rhys caught my waist as I started to slip to the side. "Where are you going?"

"I'm going right next to you. Not far."

He squeezed my sides, and a shudder ran through me. "No. I need you right here. Tell me why you want to leave. And if it has anything to do with you thinking I'm not strong enough to hold you, I'll be really fucking insulted, princess."

"It's not you," I whispered, leaning forward to hide my face against his neck. "I don't magically feel great about myself. I'm still trying to get that back."

His chest rumbled unhappily. Wrapping me up tight, he fell back with me plastered on top of him.

"You might not feel great about yourself, but if it's worth a single thing, you're the most beautiful girl I've ever seen in my life." He stroked my back, long and leisurely. "When I look at you, I feel like I've found a fairy-tale creature. Like Binboa in the flesh. I'm fucking shocked you'll even speak to me, much less get naked with me. And you, naked...I don't have words. There is nothing better, Delilah. Your tits, ass, thighs, every soft part of you keeps me awake at night. If I sleep, then I might wake up and find it wasn't real. That you don't exist."

I smiled against his neck as my stomach fluttered. It was impossible not to let his conviction settle in my heart. That was how he saw me.

"Binboa has silver hair," I said.

He picked up my hair, brought it to his nose, and inhaled. "So, some of the details are off. You're *my* Binboa. You walked out of the pages of my favorite book. That's what you feel like to me." He sniffed my hair again and let out a soft groan. "Did you hear the part about rewriting the stars for you? I will, princess. You're my girl, aren't you?"

I exhaled, hot and steady, onto his skin. Letting myself lay on him wasn't easy, but he was doing a good job of making me believe every word he said.

Rhys Astor didn't do things he didn't want to. He put me here, and he was keeping me here. That meant this was exactly where he wanted me.

My body, which I knew without asking, was far rounder than any of the girls he'd been with in the past. But I also didn't have to ask if he'd held any of them this way.

This was solely my spot.

He'd given it to me.

Who was I to tell him I didn't belong here?

"Yes, trouble. I'm your girl." I lifted my head and pushed myself up so we were nose to nose. "I'm in love with you, too, you know."

He took my face in both hands and glared at me like he was angry. "No. I did *not* know that. Are you sure?"

I grazed my fingertips over his frowning mouth. "Yes, of course I'm sure. I wouldn't have said it if I wasn't. I love you and all your madness."

"Fuck," he gritted, tugging me down to his chest again. Rolling us to the side, he curled his body around mine and hugged me so hard I was breathless. But then, I didn't need to breathe when I was being loved with such fierce intensity. "I need you to know I'm probably not going to ever be able to let you go. I've never…"

"It's okay," I whispered. "You don't have to let me go."

He dotted kisses all over my forehead and temple then hugged me tighter. "I can't remember a time I'd felt as right as I do now. Are you sure you love me?"

"Yes." I didn't laugh. I understood what it was like to doubt that someone could love me without any strings. Just me. All of me. "I'm completely sure, Rhys."

His exhale was ragged and hot. "I love you too, Delilah. You drive me mad, and I don't think I can live without that feeling."

"You don't have to. I'm here."

He drew my face to his and slanted his mouth over mine, coaxing my lips with his tongue. I parted for him, and he swept inside, giving me thorough lashes. He held my face and kissed me until I was dizzy. Then kissed me more and more.

"I need to feel you." He nipped my lips, top and bottom. "Can I?"

"Yes, please."

We sat up and watched each other undress. He was faster, his fingers a little more deft at unbuttoning his shirt than mine were, but my body was quaking. Nerves and desire, in equal measure, vibrated my limbs.

I pulled my shirt off my shoulders, then he was there, cupping my breast with one hand, unhooking the strap of my bra with the other. Once my bra was undone, he tossed it aside and tugged me against him. His mouth slid down my neck, licking along the path he'd created. Lips latched over my collarbone, sucking my flesh deep. I tossed my head back, giving him the space to work, and he did. He kissed and sucked my shoulder, then gently moved my head in the other direction so he could do the same to my other side.

"Rhys." My fingertips glided over the flexed muscles parallel to his spine. "Please."

We fell back on the bed, pausing only to lose the clothing on our bottom halves. Our legs tangled, lips clashed, and hands roved. It had been a week and a hundred years since we'd touched. Absence had made our hearts grow desperate and our appetites for one another explode.

Rhys rolled me to my back and moved over me. His soft brown eyes were on mine as he took my nipple into his mouth. I gasped and arched into him. He opened wide, taking as much of me as he could between his lips while he slipped his hand between my spread thighs, drawing a line down my slit.

He stroked me there while he laved my breasts. Swirling and sucking, back and forth he went. And while he touched me, his eyes kept coming back to mine. They were always soft, gentle, and his hands on me were as loving as they were needy.

My fingers carved lines through his hair and along his shoulders and back. Anywhere I could reach. He just felt so good. So right. And now that I was certain we were in love with each other, I wanted him more than I had ever wanted anything or anyone.

Dropping to his belly between my spread thighs, he pressed his lips to my clit in the softest kiss then peppered kisses on my swollen outer lips, then spread me with his thumbs to kiss my slick folds.

I was so worked up and had missed him so badly, my belly was already fluttering, and he had barely touched me.

"Rhys, I'm close." Closing my eyes, I cupped my breasts, rolling my nipples between my fingers.

"I have you, princess."

Warm lips closed over my clit. Pulsing suction pulled me taut all over. My hips bowed off the bed, and I let out a moan that came from the hollow part of me Rhys had begun to fill. This was mine. He'd learned to do this for me—to bring me pleasure and make me happy.

"I love you," I breathed as my climax carried me over.

Rhys kept licking me through it until I was stroking his face and urging him up my body. He pressed kisses to my clit and inner thighs before crawling over me and covering my mouth with his.

Slipping his hand under my head, he pulled me to my side so I was half sprawled over him. My fingertips glided down the square muscles in his abdomen to his thick cock, resting hard and hot on his lower belly. I wrapped my fingers around it, giving it slow pumps to the same rhythm his tongue worked inside my mouth.

He held me tight against his chest, kissing me like he was in no hurry to get off. Like this was what he wanted most in the world.

I pulled back enough to look at him. His mouth curved slowly, tipping into a happy grin that made me feel like I was on a roller coaster.

"I missed kissing you." His thumb pressed against my bottom lip. "Your mouth is the sweetest thing, Delilah."

"Then don't stop kissing me. Just get inside me at the same time."

With a grin, he planted one hard kiss on my lips, then reached to grab a condom from my bedside table. Once he was sheathed, he fell over me again, pushing my thighs up and out, and settled his hips between them. His forehead was pressed to mine as he sank into me in one smooth, slow motion.

At my end, he stilled, our breaths mingling, our eyes locked. He stroked my face and smiled again, beginning to move inside me.

We kissed and held on to each other. His shoulders were my mooring, and my thighs were his tether. Wrapped around one another, we rocked and slipped, never once looking away unless our mouths were molded together.

I'd once believed I'd known what "in love" sex felt like, but I'd been so very naive. What I'd had before couldn't touch what Rhys and I had now. The connection between us was powerful. While also being so delicate and wistful, I wanted to cup it in my hands and tend to it to keep it safe.

Being so connected to Rhys brought my pleasure to another level. He didn't need to do the moves I'd always thought were the only ones that worked on me. He touched me with reverence and passion, showing me how much he desired and loved me. That made it easy for me to let go of my preconceived notions and simply fall into my *feelings*.

And what I felt was his cock dragging along my sensitive walls. His pelvis hitting my swollen clit. Hands on my breasts and mouth on mine, drugging me with deep, licking kisses. Every sense was engaged. Every part of my mind was present in this moment, with Rhys over me, inside me, lovingly fucking me.

"Please," I whimpered, wanting this to go on forever, but so close to the edge I had to fall.

"Come for me, princess. Show me how pretty you are when you let go for me."

He ground against my clit, swiveling his hips to give me the friction I needed. My inner walls clamped down, and my neck bowed as I cried out. Rhys made short pumps, keeping pressure on my clit while I came. His grunting breaths heated my already warm skin, then he fell with me, gritting out my name as he spilled inside me.

We lay wrapped around each other for some time. Lazy kisses and languid strokes over sweat-misted skin.

A thought occurred to me, making me giggle. Rhys chucked my chin, tipping my face back so he could frown down at me.

"What's so funny?"

I grinned at him. "I was thinking all our friends will know exactly what we were doing when we didn't show up for class."

"Good. Let them be jealous." His lips landed on my forehead, followed by a sigh.

I laughed at that. "I didn't say anything about them being jealous, sir."

"But they will be." He squeezed me tight. "I fucking love you. You know that, right?"

"I do. I know that. And I love you too. You know that?"

His exhale was shaky, but he nodded once. "It's beginning to sink in."

We dressed, watching each other the same way we had when we'd shed our clothes. Rhys was so beautiful he took my breath away, and it was a shame to cover up his smooth, freckled skin, but he made his uniform look so dapper it was hard to be disappointed for long.

He led the way to the hall and waited for me to lock up—I remembered this time. When I turned to him, he took my hand in his, weaving our fingers together. He still held me a touch too tight, but I couldn't complain.

"I'm not screwing up this time," he said softly as we rode the elevator.

"I believe that." I wiggled my fingers between his. "I'm in this."

His gaze raked over me. "I didn't know how lonely I was until I had you, Delilah."

I sucked in a breath, then slowly released it. "Neither of us has to be lonely anymore."

There was so much to face outside these walls. So many wrongs.

This was the first step, getting things right with each other. Now that we had gone through this, there was a growing sense of confidence within me that we could get through everything we would face because we would be together.

Fathaniel and Binboa.

Rhys and Delilah.

Chapter Thirty-Eight
Rhys

OF THE TWO KASTANOS twins, I'd landed the patient one. Delilah had seen I was a hopeless case and took me under her wing—and between her thighs—anyway, teaching me everything she knew.

Evelyn did not share that trait with her sister. I could tell she was trying. Her face, though, gave her away. Every time I screwed up, her cheeks grew closer and closer to tomato red. They were hovering around watermelon currently.

"No, no, Rhys, that's not how I showed you to hold them," she admonished through clenched teeth.

"I'm sorry, Evelyn. I moved my hands, then I couldn't get them back to their original position. Show me again?"

With a sigh, which she didn't bother disguising, she held up her needles and yarn. "Put your right needle to the left side of the stitch."

I did.

She narrowed her eyes as if waiting for me to screw up. That was inevitable, so I didn't blame her, but goddamn, I could get one step right.

"Okay, now scoop it through the loop, along the back side of the needle, creating an *X*."

She demonstrated at full speed. I'd always considered myself smart and quick with my hands, but knitting was stumping me. That might have had a lot to do with the fact that Evelyn had been on the verge of tossing me out of her suite since I showed up.

I managed to do as she said, knitting a few stitches. She peered at me with tense shoulders for a long moment before going back to her own knitting.

The door to the suite opened, and I turned to find Delilah standing there, her mouth hanging open. She looked cute like that. We'd have to address that later. If I exited my knitting lesson to see what I could fill her pretty little mouth with, I sensed Evelyn might stab me with my own needles.

"Have I gone around the bend?" Delilah uttered.

"Nope. Evelyn's giving me knitting lessons." I held up my needles and yarn.

"I didn't offer," Ev added. "He showed up here, and I couldn't say no quickly enough, so now I'm giving him knitting lessons."

"She isn't a very good teacher," I mock whispered.

Ev released a beleaguered sigh. "You're an awful pupil."

I shook my yarn at her. "You know, this is your fault."

She rolled her eyes. "I told you I would finish the sweater if you brought it back."

"Nope. You first told me to knit it myself, so that's what I'm learning how to do."

Delilah rubbed her eyes. "You're taking knitting lessons from my sister?"

I nodded. "It's our first day."

"It isn't going well," Ev said dryly.

"I suppose I should have asked *why* are you taking knitting lessons from my sister?"

I smiled at her, which was easier now. She had done something to the muscles in my face that allowed them to slip upward almost without thought.

The last week since we'd made our way back to each other had been, unequivocally, the happiest of my life. That wasn't saying much since my life had served me a whole hell of a lot of lemons, but Delilah Kastanos was the juiciest, freshest glass of lemonade that had ever washed over my tongue.

"Over Christmas, she'd tossed a half-knitted sweater at me and told me to finish it myself."

Ev lifted her chin. "Rightly so."

"Sure, I deserved it." I put down my needles and hopped up. Striding the few feet to the door to take Delilah in my arms, I planted a loud kiss on her cheek. "I have a long way to go before I'm up to finishing the sweater, but I'm determined."

"I don't share that determination," Ev muttered behind me.

I grinned at Delilah. Her plump lips slowly slipped into an answering smile. I understood without her saying a word what was making her happy.

Me and Ev getting along like siblings. I would have made an effort with my girl's sister, no matter what, but I genuinely appreciated Evelyn now that I was getting to know her. She was reserved until she wasn't, revealing a filterless girl who said what was on her mind. A little bit caustic, but funny too, she was my kind of people.

"I like your sister," I murmured against her lips.

"She must like you too, or she wouldn't have allowed you through the door." Delilah hugged me tight, rubbing her cheek over my heart.

My breath got lodged in my throat. Only a week back with her, and I still wasn't used to receiving this kind of love. But I'd become so dependent on it if she took it away, I'd wither.

Before I could do something stupid, like propose marriage or knock her up so she'd be tied to me forever by our gorgeous and incredibly clever spawn, the door behind her was thrown open wide. I had to spin her away to keep her from being hit.

Luciana, Beckett, Bella, Ivan, and Freddie poured into the room.

"Brilliant, everyone's here," Freddie announced.

I scowled at him. "You nearly hit Delilah with the door."

Bella knocked me with her shoulder as she barged past. "Maybe you should find a better place to make out with your girl, Astor."

I held up my middle finger. She responded by curling her fingers into her palm, leaving the index finger straight to form a gun, and took aim, shooting my bird to the ground.

Fucking Texans. Cowboys, all of them.

Delilah pulled away from me, but not far. My arm stayed firmly banded around her waist. Her fingers were latched on to the back of my waistband.

"What's going on?" she asked.

The room quickly became crowded with bodies, egos, and voices. I noted Evelyn gathering her things and edging toward her bedroom. She didn't leave entirely but hovered in her doorway so she could escape at a moment's notice.

Smart. I started to tug Delilah toward her own door when Beckett's voice broke through the buzzing din.

"The girls have made a move against Charles."

Everything went still except Delilah, who pressed her tensed muscles into me.

I'd barely spent time in my suite since everyone had come back from break. The times I'd seen Charles in passing had been brief seconds wrought with violence. The only reason I didn't go after him was Delilah. I could not afford to risk being taken away from her. Staying here with her meant more to me than taking the pound of his flesh he owed my girl.

As for Charles, he must have sensed he was walking a razor's edge. When we had run into each other, he'd kept his arrogance in check. Otherwise, he'd made himself scarce, so our interactions had been few and far between.

"What have you done?" I asked carefully, slowly stroking a long path over the dips and hills of Delilah's side.

Luciana was the first to explain. "I brought Sera"—she shook her head—" I mean, Mrs. Umbra—with me to speak to three of the freshman girls from the field hockey team."

Beckett's sister-in-law, Sera Umbra, taught part-time at the academy. She was one of the few people in the world Beckett trusted. It made sense to go to her.

"What happened?" Delilah prompted.

Bella planted her hands firmly on her hips. "They spilled it all with very little nudging. Charles Bloomberg is disgusting. That's all you need to know." She shuddered, and from the look of her, I questioned why I'd held myself back from beating him until he couldn't stand.

Then, my reason clenched my shirt in her fist.

Never letting you go, princess.

"They're with the principal now," Luciana concluded.

Delilah straightened against me. "They are? They agreed to come forward?"

Bella nodded. "Once they heard each other, they got pissed. Mrs. Umbra helped guide them into wantin' to take action so Charles can't continue his campaign of deflowering and discarding freshman girls." She made a fake-retching sound. Or maybe it wasn't so fake. "He's so disgusting. I hope Daddy Bloomberg flies in to drag him away in disgrace so I never have to see his meaty, steroid-swollen head again."

I'd forgotten Ivan was in the room until he spoke from the spot where he'd leaned against the wall near Ev's doorway.

"Unfortunately, things like this always take time."

Bella groaned. "Thank you, Ivan, for your dose of reality."

But the truth of Ivan's statement settled over the excitement like a suffocating blanket. The girls might've been willing to talk now, but that didn't mean action would be immediate or happen at all. That wasn't how things worked for people with the last name Bloomberg. Hell, that wasn't how that worked for most of the students at SA. Our familial wealth made us untouchable, even to each other.

And once Charles caught wind of the action taken against him, he'd become even more insufferable, which was barely possible to believe.

Unless there was a smoking gun, Charles would undoubtedly carry on like the raging bull he was.

Talk went on for a few more minutes, most of it consisting of Bella and Freddie's gruesome fantasies of Charles's death. While I agreed with the sentiment, I had knitting to do and my girlfriend to make out with. Once their chatter grew repetitive, I suggested they take their leave.

You know, politely.

Eventually, they did.

After I was told by more than one person that I was a dick.

Not by Delilah, though, so I didn't give a damn.

· · · · ● · ● · · · ·

Ivan waylaid me on the way back to my room that evening. He kicked off the wall when I approached, standing at his full height, his arms crossed over his chest.

My eyes narrowed. "Are you waiting for me, comrade?"

His mouth twisted. "That is still offensive."

"I'm aware. You didn't answer the question."

He cocked his head toward the stairwell. Curiosity overtook my better judgment, and I followed him in there.

When he didn't immediately speak, I did. "Is this where you ask to suck my dick? Because as handsome as you are, I have to tell you, my dick already belongs to another."

His nostrils flared. "I am pleased to hear you are aware of who you belong to, though I'm not convinced you are good enough for her."

I chose to shake off how much his protectiveness of Delilah bothered me. First, because I had no doubt she was mine. And second, because there would never be too many people looking out for my girl.

"I am well aware. Do you want to tell me the reason you're so protective over her? As far as I know, you're only interested in her as a friend. Has that changed?" Okay, so I hadn't shaken it off.

A muscle in Ivan's cheek barely twitched. "Are you not protective over your friends?"

"Sure. But your white knighting is a bit extreme." I hadn't failed to notice his *naked pony* routine in class. While I'd appreciated the way he'd shoved the spotlight off Delilah, I questioned his motives.

"Maybe it is. Delilah is a very good friend, and I have messed up with her in certain ways. Perhaps this is how I make up for it. I don't want Delilah or Evelyn to be hurt more than they have been."

My brain buzzed at the mention of the other Kastanos sister. "Evelyn too, huh?"

His stare was direct. "Evelyn too."

Hmmm. Curiouser and curiouser. "I wasn't aware you and Evelyn had any kind of relationship."

"You don't know me well, Astor."

"True. I could say the same."

He hummed in acknowledgment, but he didn't seem to have anything else to say on the topic. It was time to get this show on the road.

"Now that we have that covered, is there a point to this clandestine meeting, Sokolov?"

"Yes." He tucked his hands in the pocket of his jeans. "There is a way to speed up the process of removing Charles."

My brows popped in surprise. I'd been expecting some kind of warning about treating Delilah right—as if I needed it from this classically handsome asshole—not something like this.

"Oh, really? Care to enlighten me?"

"Of course."

Ivan had a plan. It involved spilling blood—something I hadn't been afraid of since Preston first backhanded me and knocked a baby tooth from my mouth. Blood didn't bother me. Charles Bloomberg's continued existence did.

But if things went as planned tonight, Charles wouldn't be a concern of mine any longer.

CHAPTER THIRTY-NINE
Delilah

I WOKE WITH A certainty that I was not alone.

Evelyn never snuck into my bed. It was always the other way around. I knew it wasn't her depressing the mattress beside me. Besides, she wouldn't have been sneaking a hand under my blanket to feel me up.

I smiled without opening my eyes. "What are you doing, trouble?"

My semiconsciousness spurred him on. His hand slipped inside my shirt to squeeze my tit and flick my already pebbled nipple. I moaned, arching into his touch.

"Good morning, princess."

Something about the sound of his voice sent me on alert. My eyes fluttered open, taking a moment to bring Rhys's face into focus.

Gasping in shock, I jackknifed upright so fast I dislodged his hand from beneath my shirt.

"What happened to you?"

Oh, his face. His beautiful, lovely face. It was Christmas break all over again, bruised and bloody. I slipped my fingers in his hair, desperately searching for bumps like he'd had that night. He sighed, holding still, allowing me to check him over.

"I'm okay, princess." He caught my wrists, stilling my hands on the sides of his head. "It looks much worse than it is, and that is by design."

I blinked at him. My stomach dipped at the mottled bruises along his cheekbone and the crescent of black under his eye. The flaming red ring around his throat was what did me in, though. My tongue felt two sizes too big for my mouth, and my heart went mad.

"Did Preston do this?" I choked out.

"No." He shook his head. "Charles gifted me the shiner and busted lip."

"What do you mean?" My head was fuzzy. I couldn't quite grasp what he was saying.

He chuckled like this was somehow funny. "*Someone* informed Charlie Boy I was responsible for the girls going to the principal about him. He didn't take kindly to that and let me know with his fists while I was innocently sleeping in my bed."

My stomach bottomed out, and tears pricked my eyes. "Oh my god." I jerked at his hold on my wrists, frantic with the need to check his scalp for bumps. "Rhys, I need—"

"Shhh." He brought my hands to his chest, holding them against his steadily thumping heart. "I'm fine, Delilah. Look at me. This isn't like last time, I swear to you. He got two hits in before Ivan pulled him off me. That's all. Two measly hits aren't going to keep me down."

"Your throat." My eyes flicked from his to the redness crawling up the column of his neck.

I stared at him, unblinking as tears slipped down my cheeks. I couldn't stand seeing bruises on his face. All I could think of was Preston hurting him again and again over the years, wishing I could have stopped it. Protected him, even though I hadn't known he existed. And now, he had more bruises. More pain. And I couldn't understand why. Charles had hurt him? Ivan had stopped him?

"This doesn't make sense," I whispered. "Please explain it to me, Rhys."

As soon as he let go of my wrists so he could touch my cheek, my arms looped around his shoulders, and I pressed my face against his throat, gently kissing his inflamed skin. His arms encircled me, dragging me onto his lap. Then he was comforting *me*, which was all backward. He was the one who was injured. But I accepted it because being in Rhys's arms was the only right in this early morning of wrong.

"Don't you cry for me, Delilah. We're going to celebrate."

"If you don't want me to cry, then don't come to me looking like you've been pummeled." I heaved a sigh against his throat. "Tell me what happened."

"I can't take it when you cry." He palmed the back of my head and slowly stroked through my hair while rocking me in his arms. "Ivan had an idea of how to get rid of Charles. I see why you had a crush on him, princess. He's playing chess while the rest of us yokels are stuck playing checkers."

"Must you mention that right now?"

I felt his smile against my temple. "Your little kiddie crush is what got us started, so I don't mind thinking about it. I know whatever you felt for him pales in comparison to how much you love me."

He almost had me. I nearly laughed. "You won't distract me. Tell me what you and Ivan did."

His arms tightened. "Tell me I'm right first."

"Of course you're right."

"Yeah," he breathed. "I know."

I lifted my head, my watery eyes meeting his. "Please, Rhys."

"It's beautiful in its simplicity. Ivan let it slip to Charles that I ratted him out to the authorities. Charles, who doesn't have two brain cells to rub together, charged into my room while I was pretending to be peacefully sleeping and started wailing on my unconscious body. Ivan got it all recorded. Neither of us could have anticipated Charles attempting to strangle me, but your boyfriend yanked him off before he could cut off my air. He has the reflexes of a cat to go along with his big brain."

All I could do was stare at him. My mind and body were at war. Finish the job Charles had started or lock him in my room to keep him safe since he clearly had no regard for his own health.

Rhys cradled my head in his palm and dipped down to touch his nose to mine. "He left campus this morning and won't be back. In the middle of the night, while you and Evelyn were safe and sound in your beds, I agreed not to press charges so long as Charles was expelled permanently and his father took him back to New York. He should be on a plane, halfway there, as we speak. You'll never have to see him again. None of the girls will. And I know you're angry with me for putting myself in the line of fire—"

"Furious," I whispered without any heat.

"Furious." He touched his lips to mine. "I know you're furious, Delilah, but I had to do something. I couldn't allow him to continue breathing the same air as you and Evelyn. Now, he won't. He's out of your life."

I pulled back to meet his brown-eyed gaze. My stomach was in knots, but my heart had never beat with more purpose. "You've been hurt too much. I never want you to be hurt for me." I released a long breath. "Thank you. Not just for putting yourself on the line for me, but for my sister and the girls."

"Mainly for you."

I touched my finger to his lips. "I know why you did it, and I love you for it more than I can ever say. But if you *ever* go behind my back and do something that might get you taken away from me—"

He opened his mouth to argue, but I tapped his lips, and he shut it.

"He had his *hands* around your neck, Rhys, and he's a monster. He could have killed you, and I..." I bit down on the inside of my cheek. I couldn't bear to continue that line of thinking. Losing Rhys like that would be impossible to recover from. "Don't take chances with yourself. I won't be happy with you."

He shook his head. "I won't do anything that will take me from you, princess. This was something that had to happen. I'm sorry you're scared, but I wouldn't do anything differently."

I knew that. As badly as I wished he could have found another way, relief that Charles was gone for good was beginning to seep in. And my love for Rhys was blooming like it was the height of spring.

"I love you, trouble." I took his jaw in my hands and tipped his face toward me to plant kisses everywhere I could reach. "I love you for protecting me and Evelyn and the girls. I love you for caring for me. I love you very much, Rhys. You're very important to me. I'm going to take care of you like you take care of me."

"You already do," he rasped as his eyes slammed closed under my kisses.

He tried to stop me from sliding out of his lap, but when I reached for his waistband, he caught on to what I was doing and let me go.

On my knees between his spread legs, I kissed his thighs over his pants and murmured how much I loved him. He hadn't been hard moments before, but once I reached for him inside his sweats, he was like steel, hot and ready for me.

I kissed his rippling stomach, then I took his velvet head into my mouth and lovingly caressed him with my tongue. He combed his fingers through my hair and whispered encouragement.

The urge to love him, to make him feel good after putting himself through pain he didn't deserve, drove me to take all of him into my mouth. Lips wrapped around him, I slid up and down his length. My hands were on him, caressing his taut muscles and smooth, warm skin. Eyes open and on him, I traced my fingertips over the constellation of freckles on his flank I'd discovered and claimed as mine.

"My sweet princess, you are too fucking good to me," he uttered as he stared down at me. "Never letting you go. Do anything for you. *Anything.*"

I knew that to be true. I trusted him more than I'd believed I could trust anyone, especially after what we'd been through. We belonged to each other in a way that felt irreversible.

I took him to the end of my throat and held him there, curling my tongue around his pulsing length and moaning to add vibration. He grunted and pushed himself even deeper.

Then he grabbed my arms and pulled me up to the bed to straddle his lap. My shorts were shoved aside, legs parted, and he was inside me in one powerful thrust. He gripped my ass, slamming me down on him.

We kissed and bit each other's lips, moaning pleasure, grappling to hold tighter, get closer, prolong this fleeting, desperate *need* to feel alive and connected, express this thing between us that was more than love. What it was didn't require words but action. Contact of heated skin and the press of fluttering hearts.

I rode him with no concern of what I might look like or how he might have seen me. Rhys's love was mine. That, I would never question. Not after he'd proven to me what I was to him. I no longer doubted he wanted me as unequivocally as I wanted him. That my body was his destination. My face was what he saw when he closed his eyes, just as his was there when I closed mine.

"I love you."

"I love you."

We came within moments of each other, letting our shared pleasure move us until it was nothing but trickles and echoes.

Together, we fell to the mattress, watching each other with bright eyes. The day was new. Clouds had parted.

"You mean so much to me," I told him.

"And you're everything to me," he replied.

I believed him.

Just as I believed that Rhys Astor would spot any wrong in my world and make it right. That's how he had to love me, and he deserved nothing less from me. I wasn't quite the warrior he was, but if I could right his wrongs, I would do it for him.

CHAPTER FORTY
Delilah

IT WAS SILLY, REALLY. I doubted most of the student body of Savage Academy would be interested in fencing, even when their team had made it to regionals, but I couldn't stop myself. Rhys and his teammates deserved to have as much support at the last tournament of their season as they could, so I was determined to make it happen.

This was why I was in the office, making copies of flyers with the tournament information to hang up all over school.

A hundred should have done it.

The door to the copy room opened, and a woman stepped in. She moved to the machine next to mine. I glanced up, noting blonde hair and a baby-blue pantsuit.

"Excuse me. You're Delilah, aren't you?"

I turned to the woman, taking her in fully. Recognition struck me in the gut. Rhys's mother.

"Hello. Yes, that's me. It's nice to see you again, Amanda. How are you?"

She stepped toward me, looking as though she might reach for me, but stopped herself, clutching her hands in front of her.

"It's lovely seeing you too, Delilah." She patted her smooth hair. "I'm just here to help out. I like to stop in from time to time and lend a hand."

"That's nice." This was painfully awkward. What was this woman doing here? I knew it wasn't to see her son.

"How is Rhys? Are you still...?" She raised her brows as far as she could, given the amount of Botox she'd injected into her skin.

"Rhys is great, and yes, we're very much together." I patted my copy machine, which had to be almost finished. "I'm sure you know his final tournament is this weekend. Will I see you there?"

Her mouth instantly pressed into a thin, white line. "I wasn't aware..." She shook her head. "No, I have obligations that will prevent me from attending. But please tell him I wish him well. If he would take my calls, I would tell him myself, but he's rather angry at his stepfather and me after a blowup over Christmas break."

A blowup? That was what she called the damage that had been done to her son? If I were as violent as her husband, I would have smacked her.

"I know, Amanda." I locked eyes with her and didn't let go. "I saw him directly after the blowup."

Pink crawled up her skin as she averted her gaze, flitting her hands around as she started and stopped speaking.

Fortunately, she didn't offer any defense of her husband. What he had done to Rhys was indefensible, and we both knew it.

My copies were finished. I could have walked away but found myself compelled to say something to this woman who had done nothing to protect her son. This might have been my only chance, and I couldn't let it pass, whether that was wise or not.

"I wish you knew what kind of person Rhys is."

She went still, listening, but still turned away.

"Under the bristly exterior he's had to fashion to protect himself, he is incredibly sensitive and empathetic. His heart is capable of deep love that belies his age. Some of it is just who he is, and some, I think, he learned from his father."

Her hands pressed to her chest, but still, she refused to look at me.

"He's been reading *The Shadow of the Isle* to me. He still keeps the copy he read with his father next to his bed. He won me over with that book. And he's an incredible fencer. I've watched him all season in awe. This weekend, he'll have his last match in high school. I'm hoping to draw out a big crowd because his kind of talent and devotion to his sport deserves attention. I wish you could be the type of mother who would be able to set aside her grief or whatever it is that keeps you away from supporting your only son and show up for him. Just once, show up for him."

I paused, allowing her space to say something. Anything. She remained statue still and just as silent. My organs knotted in frustration. Would anything shake her out of the haze she lived in?

Probably not.

I grabbed my stack of flyers and brushed by her for the door, deciding I couldn't leave without throwing one last dagger.

"I didn't know Rhys's father, but from everything I've heard about him, I have a feeling he would be deeply ashamed of the kind of mother you've turned out to be."

* * * * * * * * * *

The gym wasn't packed to the rafters as I'd hoped, but the turnout was far bigger than it had ever been. Rhys and Beckett's friends had all shown up, and Luc and Bella had rounded up the field hockey girls.

Evelyn and I walked in together and found spots with our friends. I didn't want to sit too close to the front and distract Rhys. He knew I was there, cheering him on. We'd find each other afterward.

I was explaining the rules to Ev when I felt a small touch on my knee. I turned, finding a tiny boy with red hair and bright brown eyes smiling at me.

"Hi." He waved his hand, which was clutching a truck.

My heart lurched as I raked my gaze over his freckled cheeks and saucy little grin. I knew this face, that expression. "Hello."

"Owen, I told you to wait." A soft-spoken woman wrapped her arm around the boy's shoulders and sat on the bleacher beside him, bringing us to eye level. Her face was familiar too. I'd just seen an older version in the copy room earlier this week, but her smile held all the warmth her mother's had lacked.

"Catrin?" I asked, my spine straightening.

Nodding, her smile grew. She'd covered her blonde hair with a stylish newsboy cap and wore a Savage Academy hoodie, blending in with the crowd. A million thoughts were racing through my mind. Did Rhys know she was here? Was it safe?

Catrin didn't seem to be worried. "It was the Rhys clone that gave me away, wasn't it? I birthed him, yet he looks like he came straight from my brother." She pulled Owen onto her lap and squeezed him. "It's nice to meet you, Delilah."

Owen tipped his head to look at his mother then back at me. "Nice meet you, Didah!"

I had to laugh despite my shock at their appearance. "No one's ever called me that before. I love it." I turned to Evelyn, who'd been watching the encounter with wide eyes. "Ev, this is Rhys's sister and nephew, Catrin and Owen."

Catrin shook Evelyn's hand without hesitation. "My brother talks about you guys nonstop. It used to be me doing all the talking, but now he can't shut up. I love it."

Catrin wasn't what I had expected given what I knew about her. She was sunny and friendly, not the beaten down, single mother, former addict I'd envisaged in my head.

"Does Rhys know you are here?" I asked.

"Not really, no. I wasn't sure I'd have the guts to bring O-Go to this. My guy gets antsy. But we were having a good day, and he was dying to see Unca Rhys poke people with swords, so we're here."

Owen smirked at me, then crawled off his mom's lap to run his truck along my leg, vrooming as he went. I exchanged a look with Ev. She had a perplexed half smile on her face. I felt much the same. Owen melted my heart, and Catrin's friendliness struck me as authentic, but their sudden appearance had left me somewhat reeling.

"Is it...safe?" I asked Catrin.

Her mouth twisted to the side, then one shoulder popped up. "I don't know, but I want to support my brother after all he's done for me and O when I really didn't deserve it. I left him in that house with that m-o-n-s-t-e-r, and I was a s-h-i-t big sister."

I couldn't refute her claims. "He'll be happy to see you." At least, I hoped.

Catrin clutched my arm. "Oooh, they're coming out. There he is!"

The team emerged from the locker room, Rhys in the front. He carried his helmet under his arm, looking so sharp and sleek in his white suit he took my breath away.

Brown eyes sought me out. The corner of his mouth hitched, and I bit my lip. I'd never felt anything close to the headiness of Rhys Astor's full attention.

Catrin leaned into me, and Rhys's gaze flicked to her, flaring in recognition. She waved wildly at him, and he lifted his chin in response, his expression unreadable.

Then, he was crossing the gym, heading straight for us. When Owen noticed him coming, he screeched and held his arms up.

"Unca, Unca!"

Some of the fierce determination melted off Rhys like an ice cube in the summer sun. He climbed to where we were sitting and swooped Owen up in his arms. Owen slapped at Rhys's face and giggled, yammering about his truck and swords. The two of them were in their own world for a solid minute before Rhys directed his attention back to us.

"What are you doing here, Cat?" he rumbled.

She stood and patted his shoulder. "What do you think I'm doing here?"

He stared at her for a long beat, then me. "You met Delilah?"

She rolled her eyes. "Of course I did. I'm on my best behavior and everything."

Reaching up, I tugged on his hand. "Everything's fine, trouble. There's nothing for you to concern yourself with. Go concentrate on winning this thing."

He gave Owen to his sister and bent over me, cupping my cheeks. "Say the word and they're gone."

"Why would I want them gone?"

His eyes darted between mine. "I don't want you to feel uncomfortable."

"I don't. I really like them." Hooking a hand behind his neck, I drew him lower for a soft kiss. "I love you. Go do your best."

He released a shuddering breath. "My princess. Love you madly."

Another quick kiss to me, a ruffle of Owen's hair, and a promise from Catrin to watch what she said, and Rhys was back in serious fencing mode, striding to his place on the sidelines.

My stomach somersaulted. I couldn't wait to see him in action one more time.

· · · · ● · · ● · · · ·

At some point during the day, Owen had made friends with Evelyn and, to my great jealousy, crawled into her lap and fell asleep. His round little cheek was pressed against her chest, and he was utterly limp.

She had a blissed-out tilt to her mouth as she snuggled him and listened to music through her headphones.

As much as I wished Owen had chosen me, him being in Ev's arms left mine and Catrin's free to clap and cheer for Rhys, who was dominating the day.

No one focused like Rhys. His bouts were works of art, and the truth was, his skill level was so far above his opponents' it was almost unfair.

Catrin shook her head. "I should have come to more of these. I've missed so much."

"You can't change what's happened, but you can be here now."

"I will be. As much as he'll let me, I'll be here for him."

Her attention caught on something over my shoulder. The fresh pink color she'd gained while yelling her head off for her brother slowly drained from her cheeks, and alarm bells sounded in my ears.

"What is it?" I asked.

"They're not supposed to be here." Her fingertips dug into her knees. "They don't...why are they here? They can't be. I—"

Straightening, I peered in the same direction, my gaze sweeping over the crowd. When I saw the two people who'd changed her entire demeanor, my heart stuttered.

Preston homed in on me, and it fell like an atom bomb as recognition tightened his already pinched features.

"He saw me," I uttered.

"Me too. He saw me too." She patted her hat. "I don't think he knew who I was. I look different than the last time—and he wouldn't expect me to be here and—"

"Should you go?"

I peered at them again and nearly fell from my seat. Preston and Amanda were headed straight for us.

"They're coming, Catrin."

"We have to go. Owen…" Her eyes had gone glassy, and I could feel the panic bleeding from her.

Thinking fast, I snagged Evelyn's attention. She snapped out of her daydream and was up, following Catrin and me toward the exit doors with a still-sleeping Owen.

We just weren't quick enough. From behind, Amanda called my name, then Catrin's. There was no avoiding speaking to them, but the least we could do was keep them from seeing Owen.

Catrin and I positioned Evelyn and Owen behind us and waited as Amanda and Preston approached us. Dread curdled my gut. It was difficult to stand there, knowing what was coming wouldn't be pleasant or pretty. Fortunately, we were hidden from the rest of the crowd by the side of the bleachers, so at least this conversation would be private, and if luck was a thing, Rhys wouldn't notice.

"Delilah," Amanda said again, then took in her daughter standing beside me. "Catrin, oh my god. It's really you."

Catrin shrunk into my side. The sunshine, bubbly girl she'd been minutes before had disappeared, leaving behind a dim, shriveled, almost unrecognizable husk.

"Hi, Mom," she croaked.

Preston nudged his wife half behind his shoulder, and he wasn't gentle about it. His stance was combative, and he'd been raking his scornful gaze over Catrin like she was riddled with bubonic plague.

"Who invited you here?" Preston barked. "You are to have nothing to do with this family. Did I not make that clear?"

I put my hand on her arm, not as cowed by Preston as Catrin and Amanda were. Having seen the violence this man was capable of, I should have been, but my fury made me brave. "I invited her here. She is my guest and friend. I don't quite see how that's your concern, given we're all adults here and she has as much right to be here as you and Amanda."

Preston swung his barely concealed disgust toward me. "And who do you think you are? You're no adult, young lady. This is a family matter, so you'll see yourself away."

My fingers curled into my palms. "Was it a family matter when you slammed Rhys's head into the wall over Christmas break? How about all the other times you raised your fists to him? Or when you shamed him for his hobbies? What about when you tried to wipe away every trace of his father so you could live off his money?"

I'd gone too far. I knew this by the purple mottling of Preston's irate face and the aggressive steps he was taking toward me. Backing up, I tugged Catrin with me. The exit was behind us. So close.

But also, Evelyn and Owen were behind us. In my outrage, I'd forgotten how close they were. I collided into Ev's arms, jostling Owen.

"Mama?"

His voice was so small. Tiny. It shouldn't have been audible over the cheers and screaming coming from the tournament.

Yet it was.

It traveled past me and Catrin, straight to Preston and Amanda.

In seconds, they both reacted to that little voice that was a bomb dropping out of the clear sky.

"A baby?" Amanda rasped, her hands flying to her mouth.

Preston's calculating gaze landed on Owen's red hair and undeniable features. He swiveled to his stepdaughter, and the way he looked at her was nothing short of sickening.

"I always knew you were a whore."

CHAPTER FORTY-ONE
Rhys

Where the hell were they?

I tossed my helmet aside, ignoring Chevalier's objections, and prowled to the bleachers. My sister, nephew, and girlfriend were nowhere in sight. Ev wasn't there either.

That didn't feel right. They wouldn't have left in the middle of my match, especially not Delilah.

Movement at the side of the bleachers caught my eye. There and gone in a second. It could have been anything, but instinct told me to check it out, so I didn't waste any time doubting myself.

Dodging people on the sidelines, I sprinted around the bleachers. My feet stopped moving on their own when I came upon the scene unfolding there.

Preston had a hand on Catrin's shoulder. That single touch was enough to enrage me, but before I could get to him, he shoved Delilah so hard she stumbled backward and fell on her ass.

No hesitation. I went straight for Delilah, pulling her off the ground and into my arms. Her muscles were vibrating, but she didn't cling to me.

"Let go of her," she gritted out. "I'll scream if you don't."

Preston dropped his hold on Catrin, who immediately whirled around and took Owen out of Evelyn's arms. Murmuring to him, she stroked his back as she turned away from Preston and our mother, protecting him from this ugliness.

I would fucking die before Preston touched him, and I knew Catrin would too. That was the difference between us and our mother. I guess we took after our father.

"It's okay now," I told Delilah. "I'll take care of this."

My mother looked like she'd been through a war. Her eyes were haunted as mascara trailed in rivulets down her face.

"Did you know about this?" she asked.

"I'm not answering your questions." I shifted to block Catrin, Ev, and Owen. "You need to leave. Both of you."

"That's where you're wrong," Preston blustered. "You'll answer all the questions we have, including how you could have let that...filthy *addict* have a child in her custody. We should have been informed. We would have—"

Delilah tried to take a step toward him, but I yanked her back. She wasn't getting one inch closer to Preston. I didn't trust him not to act in a way that would make me lose my mind more than I already was.

There was nothing I could do to keep her quiet, though.

"You would have tried to ruin him too. Is that what you were planning to say? It's what you did to Catrin and Rhys, isn't it? Tried to beat them into your bland, boring, sniveling image? Thank god it didn't work."

My girl had lost it. If I was angry, she was flying on the steam of her righteous fury.

"Princess—"

She shook her head. "No, Rhys. This monster doesn't get to come here and ruin your day. He doesn't get to call your sister a whore, and—"

My anger had ratcheted right up to meet hers. "You did what?" I seethed. "You called Catrin what?"

Preston lifted his chin. He had never apologized for anything he'd said or done, and I didn't see him starting now.

I met his hard eyes, silently daring him to say his worst.

"I called her a whore because she is one." Preston carefully enunciated every syllable. "The evidence is in her arms. I don't want to even imagine what kind of deficiencies that poor child must have with all the chemicals Catrin pumped into her body. Your mother and I will be seeing a lawyer first thing tomorrow. There is no way we'll be leaving him in her care."

"Oh, really? And what makes you think you're a fit parent? Is it your easygoing temperament? You'd never lose it on a kid, would you, Pres?"

His eyes narrowed. "You have goaded me since the moment we met."

"I was a *child* when we met," I said as evenly as possible. My eyes never left him, but I was aware of my mother standing there, saying nothing through her quiet, racking sobs as she stared at Catrin and Owen.

Preston tugged on his cuffs. "An obnoxious child who needed discipline, which I *gave* you because I cared."

I scoffed bitterly at his assessment. "A grieving child who should have been able to trust you, but all I got was a backhand and sent to stand in the corner of the living room for an hour."

Delilah gasped. "You never told me that."

"Clearly, I went too easy on you. That, I regret," Preston said evenly, without emotion, talking about the abuse of a scrawny, defenseless kid. "You've turned into a nasty, entitled little fuck. Every time I laid a hand on you, I should have done it twice as hard. Maybe then I could have knocked some sense into your thick skull. And your whore sister should have been sterilized like I told your mother."

I peered down at him, letting all he said roll off my back. It didn't matter anymore. This was over.

I shrugged. "I guess I'm truly my father's son. You can't touch me, no matter how many times you hit me, Preston, because you'll never be even half the man he was. It must rankle you to live in his house, spend his money—"

He charged me before I could finish, but he never made it.

The thing Preston didn't realize was I wasn't alone anymore. I had Delilah now, but more than that, I had Beckett, Ryan, Felix, and even Ivan and Freddie. I had Luciana, Bella, the field hockey girls, the soccer boys. The fencing team, some of the football players. Then there was Mrs. Umbra and Mr. Chevalier. The principal and parents from SA and other schools. They had all crowded in behind Preston during our confrontation, but he hadn't noticed.

I had, though.

He'd admitted—no, fucking *bragged*—about his years of abuse in front of an audience, some of whom had been filming him. I had spurred him on, and when he came at me, more than one set of arms held him back.

He couldn't touch me. Those days were done.

· · · · ● · ● · · · ·

Through the chaos that followed, the questions, the attention, the explanations, Delilah stayed calm at my side, and I remained calm at hers because of that.

Once Preston and Amanda were escorted from campus, there was a pause in the tournament before it was resumed. Anyone would have understood if I'd bowed out, but I saw it through and won.

And that was good. Right. But even if it had gone the other way, I would have felt like I'd won.

Seeing the rows of people who had my back, even after they'd witnessed the darkest corners of my life, was the true victory for me, trite as that sounded.

There would be repercussions to handle after tonight. Beckett wasn't pleased I'd kept most of Preston's abuse from him. Catrin had scurried off with Owen, frightened all over again—though I was certain Preston and Amanda would *not* be contacting a custody lawyer. And I didn't pretend the rumor mill wouldn't have a field day with what had gone down here.

That was for another day.

I wove my fingers between Delilah's and held her hand like she'd taught me. I always had to stop myself from holding her too hard, and I suspected I still wasn't always successful based on the winces she couldn't fully hide, but I was getting there.

We were strolling around campus, stealing a minute of calm only for us. We hadn't had a chance to be alone since this morning, and a hell of a lot had happened.

"I love you."

She nodded. "I know you do. And I love you like mad. I'm proud of you too."

"For what?"

She brought our joined hands to her chest, cradling them over her heart. "You let that happen with Preston. You let everyone see something you'd wanted to keep hidden to protect Catrin and Owen."

"It wasn't all selfless, Dixie. I—"

Her groan vibrated her chest. "Oh no. Not this again. It's still not charming."

"No? Not even after my heroics? I'd think anything I do now is charming."

Her teeth dug into my knuckles as she tried to stifle a laugh. "I love you, trouble, but no."

"All right, Dolores. I won't do it again."

She stopped walking to slug my shoulder. It wasn't even gentle, which was rude, but I'd been asking for it. Because when it came to Delilah, I'd always be the kid tugging her ponytail to get her attention. I ate it up with a spoon. Even when I had it, I wanted more.

She flung her arms around my neck and pressed her soft body flush with mine. I wrapped myself around her, head on hers, arms circling her shoulders, as close as we could get on a path in the center of campus.

"I love you," she murmured into my chest.

"Love you too. Madly." I touched my lips to the top of her head. "I let that happen with Preston because it was my chance to be free of him. I never have to go back to that house. If I tried, Beckett would probably tie me down and lock me in a closet to stop me."

"I'd help," she told me with vehemence.

"I'm done," I said with just as much vehemence. "I was always afraid of the idea of cutting ties with the only home I've ever known, but I realized that house isn't my home anymore. When it's time, I'll find a permanent place to hang up my hat, but that's not going to be my home."

She pressed deeper into me. "What is?"

"Who is, you mean." I nuzzled her crown, my eyes closed as I slipped into the euphoric plane holding her like this always sent me to. "You're my home now, Delilah. Where you go, I do too."

I felt her nod. "I'll shelter you, love."

"I know you will. You were fierce today, standing up for Cat and me."

"I'll rewrite the stars for you too, you know." She rubbed her forehead back and forth over my heart. "I think your mother had good intentions today, but it all went so wrong."

"The road to hell is paved with good intentions. I don't give a damn why she came. She had chance after chance to do the right thing, and she didn't. I'm not waiting around for her to change. Not anymore."

"Okay," she whispered. "Can we go back to your room and read *The Shadow of the Isle*?"

Heart in my fucking throat, I stepped back, cupping her moonlit face. "Yes. We can absolutely do that."

The reality that Delilah Kastanos was as much mine as I was hers struck me like a gilded arrow from Narknanian.

The fact that she would understand that reference made that reality ten times sweeter.

This was my happy ending.

Delilah

Five Years Later

I smoothed the lace-trimmed veil, butterflies dancing in my stomach.

"You're beautiful. He won't know what hit him."

Catrin's smile was wobbly. Tears were threatening to spill from her lined-to-perfection eyes. "Are you sure?"

I took her hand in mine and gave it a shake. "If you cry, your makeup artist will murder me. Do you want that on your head? Your favorite sister-in-law slain on your wedding day?"

She choked out a laugh, but what she didn't do was cry. "No, I do *not* want you dead because we both know the second my brother found out I was responsible, it would be like *the red wedding* out there."

I grinned at her. "Rhys would appreciate your *Game of Thrones* reference."

She huffed, the corner of her painted mouth hitching. "I've only watched the show. I know my brother, and he would not be impressed by that."

"You are correct." I smoothed her veil again. "Now that your tears have been vanquished and no one is going to be killed, what say you go get married?"

Her smile wobbled again, but the tears stayed back. "I'd say that is the best idea you've ever had."

I rested my hand on my rounded belly. "I don't know. I've had a few other good ones."

The best one so far was falling in love with Rhys Astor. Although, I wouldn't call that an idea as much as a fever dream.

My husband was the love of my life. He gave me security, wild passion, and a home. We'd gotten married after our second year at Savage U. None of our friends had been surprised or tried to talk us out of it. We had been young, but it had been the right decision for us.

As was the swimming, kicking, wild little boy growing in my belly. He was due to grace us with his presence in two months, but if he was anything like our daughter, Maia, he'd hold out for as long as possible.

Catrin and I left her dressing room to stand at the closed doors of the chapel, waiting for our musical cue to enter. I was her only bridesmaid, and she had decided to walk herself down the aisle, so for the moment, it was just the two of us.

Since we'd met all those years ago, we'd become best friends. Not quite sisters since I could never be as close to another woman as I was to Evelyn. That was unbreakable, no matter where either of us lived. Thankfully, Ev loved Catrin too. Though, deep down, we all knew she was in it for Owen. Owen and Ev had been tight since day one.

Catrin sucked in a breath. "Marriage is good, right? All these nerves are worth it?"

"It's worth it, love. You're going to be so delirious."

Catrin had found a good man in Sam. He cared for her, and Owen and Rhys approved of him, though he'd most likely always give him the side-eye. Rhys was naturally suspicious, especially when it came to the safety of the people he loved. Add in the trauma his own stepfather had caused him, and we'd had many discussions about why it wouldn't be productive to hog-tie Sam, throw him in a trunk, and scare him into agreeing never to harm a hair on Catrin and Owen's heads.

Rhys was nearly convinced the hog-tying wasn't necessary.

· · · ● · ● · ● · · ·

The music played, and I began my slow walk down the aisle, holding flowers under my burgeoning belly.

The first person I focused on was Evelyn, who was seated by the aisle midway to the altar. I raised a brow at her empty arms. The last time I'd seen her, she'd been holding Maia, but now my daughter was nowhere in sight.

Ev tipped her head to the side and smiled.

I looked at my husband, who was standing beside Owen and Sam under an arch of wildflowers. My stomach dipped at the sight of Rhys in his tailored, navy-blue suit, the chain of his pocket watch dangling from his waistcoat pocket. He'd only become more beautiful over the years. His features had been honed and chiseled as the last vestiges of childhood fell away. Every time I looked at him, my body reacted.

When he held our daughter in his arms—like he was now—my knees often went weak. And when they smiled at me the way they were, mischievous and happy, I wondered if I was still in that fever dream.

When I reached the front, I paused. "You're not supposed to be holding her."

Rhys's grin widened. "She asked. How could I deny her?"

Maia waved her chubby little hand at me and kicked her feet with glee. She had her daddy's red hair, just a shade or two darker. She shared his brown eyes too, along with his wicked grin. Rhys's genes were strong, and I wasn't at all disappointed about it.

"You couldn't."

Owen leaned against Rhys, who slung his free arm around his nephew. "Is my mom coming?" he asked.

"She's coming very soon. Listen for the music to change and you'll see her," I told him before moving to my spot.

When the music played for Catrin, I looked at Rhys, watching his sister walk down the aisle. A tear trickled down his cheek, and I thought of how far he'd come since we'd met.

He was no longer the boy who didn't care.

Somewhere along the way, he'd cracked himself open and let himself feel. *My* Rhys, the man I would love until the end of all ends, didn't shy from his emotions. He was no longer afraid to care for those he was close to. We weren't a big group, but we were the luckiest to be loved by him.

After it was all said and done, the bride had been kissed, rings had been exchanged, and Rhys and Maia had escorted me down the aisle.

"Have I told you how beautiful you look?" he asked as I looped my arm through his.

"Not recently. Thank you."

"I adore you, princess."

I smiled at him. "Madly, right?"

"So madly." He managed to move his palm to my belly. "And my boy?"

"Wild as ever."

"Exactly as he should be."

"Yeah," I agreed.

With him, our girl, the life we were building, the love we shared, *everything* was exactly as it should be.

Epilogue
Rhys

Five Years Later

Delilah collapsed against her pillow, tears rolling down her temple into her hair. I bent over her, kissing her forehead and cheeks, stroking the warm, smooth back of the new life that had just been placed on her chest.

"Does she have red hair?" Delilah croaked.

"She does."

Her mouth tipped in a sleepy smile. "Good."

Everything was good. So fucking good, I could barely stand to be in my skin.

This baby girl—Cora—was our fourth. Our friends had begun to question our sanity, and sometimes, we questioned our own, but we liked our kids. Delilah and I had discovered together that being surrounded by our own little army was our ideal life.

So, we kept them coming.

First, there was Maia, then Nick. Two years later, we had Orion, and today, we welcomed Cora. All of them with hair a shade of red and freckles dotting their skin. Maia looked like me, while Nick and Orion took after Delilah. We'll see about Cora. If she looked like her mom, I'd be fucking thrilled.

··········

Once my girls were cleaned up, we were moved into another room so they could recuperate and rest. Cora was latched on to Delilah's breast while I fed my wife her own breakfast. She could have fed herself—she'd mastered doing most things one-handed years ago—but she'd just brought another one of my spawn into the world, and it hadn't been an easy job. My children tended to cling to her insides. She deserved to be served for all she'd done for me.

I read the messages on my phone. Maia had recently discovered how to text me from her iPad, and she took full advantage of her knowledge. I'd already sent her pictures of her new sister. She was the first to receive one. But Evelyn was with the kids, so she probably got to see the picture within seconds. Beckett and Luciana would have to wait until later.

"How is everything at home?" Delilah asked.

"Maia says Nick stood on Orion, so Orion headbutted him."

She nodded. "So, typical day, then?"

"You know it."

Orion was in his headbutting stage. Fortunately, his head was small, and Nick, who was taking the brunt of this stage and usually deserved it, had bones made of steel and a healthy padding of baby fat, so he mostly went uninjured.

She released an exhausted sigh, stroking Cora's fine baby hair. "Are we crazy, trouble?"

"Yes. Absolutely. Why do you ask?"

She gave me a crooked grin. "We keep having kids. You should be focusing on your career, and we're still so young..."

"I'm able to focus on my career and grow our family, princess. Never doubt my ability to multitask. And if I ever have trouble finding balance, the thing that would be dumped would be my career—perks of being independently wealthy."

Technically, I was a doctor. Not the deliver-a-baby kind, though that skill would have come in handy. I was the know-far-too-much-about-modern-literature kind. PhD from Savage U, I was now Dr. Rhys Astor, professor at my alma mater.

I taught bright-eyed coeds about *The Shadow of the Isle* on a daily basis. That wasn't the only thing I did, of course, but those were the days I loved going to work most.

Back when I was younger, I never saw my life going in this direction, but that was because I was too focused on surviving to think about the future.

Now, I was living. Big and full. Deep and meaningful.

I knew, without a doubt, my father would be proud of who I'd become.

Whether my mother was...I'd never know. Last I'd heard, she was still with Preston, which meant we had no relationship.

It sucked that our kids didn't have grandparents. Well, Delilah's parents made appearances in their lives once or twice a year, as did Michael, but they weren't exactly warm and fuzzy. They were rich with aunts and uncles and cousins, though—both by blood and our chosen family. They wanted for nothing and never would.

"You're not dumping your career," Delilah said as she lifted Cora off her boob.

"Give me my girl."

Delilah pressed a kiss to the top of her fuzzy head and handed the milk-drunk baby over to me. She curled up

on my chest like she'd been there before and remembered her spot.

"What about your career?" I asked. "Shouldn't you be
focused too?"

Her eyes raked over me with our daughter. My wife
really liked seeing me holding our babies. It was part of
the reason we kept winding up with more of them.

"I'm focused," she murmured. "Accounting really isn't
quite the same as teaching."

"Why are you trying to talk me out of all our children?"

She blinked once, then twice, pretty eyes shining. "I
think I'm getting emotional."

"Already? We haven't even left the hospital."

I climbed onto the bed beside her, cradling Cora
beneath my chin and wrapping my other arm around
Delilah. She still felt as good in my arms as the first
time. It was always a relief when she walked into them.
I didn't see that changing, not after four kids or ten.
She'd always belong right here.

"What do you need from me, princess?"

"Just you, Rhys."

"You have me, always."

"Tell me you love our life."

"I love our life, Delilah. God, more than I can even put
into words. Do you?"

"So, so much," she whispered. "You keep giving me
these beautiful children, this home, your unconditional
love...you rewrote the stars for me. I love you so much."

"I love you madly." I dragged my finger along her
velvet cheek. "And you're wrong, you know."

Her brows popped. "About what?"

I leaned down to kiss her lips and inhaled her rose
scent. I'd loved this woman for a decade, and I'd keep
loving her until they buried me in the cold, hard ground
beside her. She was my home. We'd gone from two

lonely people without a moor to building the kind of family we'd only read about in books. It was real because we'd made it that way. We'd turned all the wrongs committed against us into fuel to launch us, and now, we were powering it ourselves. Getting it right every single day.

"You're wrong about the stars, princess. We rewrote them together."

Acknowledgments

I love crazy, unhinged heroes who don't think they're capable of being loved until they meet their heroine. Honestly, just pour those stories into my veins.

Writing Rhys was so much fun. It felt like I was watching my own baby boy blossom. That being said, this book wouldn't be what it is without several key people.

My beta readers Jenny and Jen, you guys always have the best words of wisdom for her when you read my rough, raw, terribly unedited stories.

Alley Ciz, my author buddy, never fails to offer the most helpful suggestions, and pushes me when I get stuck.

To my editor Monica, and proofreader, Rosa: I'm sorry. One day I'll learn how to use a comma.

Thank you to my daughter and artist, Maya, for being (sort of) patient and giving me the redheaded hero of my dreams.

I have to give a massive thanks to my sensitivity reader, Hannah G. I wanted to get Evelyn's character just right, so that when it was time for her own story, she would feel fully fleshed out and authentic. Hannah G. confirmed my portrayal of Ev, offered future suggestions, and pointed out areas that could be better.

I must also thank my twin sons, P and J for letting me lift pieces of their personalities and relationship for Delilah and Ev. My guys fight like cats and dogs, but like the sisters, they are fierce friends and protect one another. One of my sons is neurodivergent, and his twin is always sensitive to his brother's needs, and will stand up for him just the way Delilah does for Ev. I couldn't have written such a rich relationship without having my guys as a firsthand example. They will probably never read this, since Mom's books are "gross", but they deserve to be acknowledged anyway!

THE SAVAGE UNIVERSE

THE SAVAGE CREW
Start a Fire
Through the Ashes
Burn it Down

· · • • · • · · ·

Savage U
Soft Like Thunder
Bright Like Midnight
Sweet Like Poison
Real Like Daydreams

· · • • · • • · · ·

Savage Academy
Save One Thing
These Two Wrongs
Jump on Three

About Julia

Julia Wolf is a bestselling contemporary romance author. She writes bad boys with big hearts and strong, independent heroines. Julia enjoys reading romance just as much as she loves writing it. Whether reading or writing, she likes the emotions to run high and the heat to be scorching.

Julia lives in Maryland with her three crazy, beautiful kids and her patient husband who she's slowly converting to a romance reader, one book at a time.

Visit my website:
http://www.juliawolfwrites.com